PUPPET MASTER

The dark shape towered over the girl. The mouth opened, revealing a set of very nasty teeth, but she did not seem intimidated. Instead, she looked up at the thing, right into its huge oval eyes. Slowly, jerkily, its right arm was coming up, gun still firmly in its hand. It began to turn the barrel inward toward its mouth.

"No!" Brazil yelled at her, trying to project as much emotion as he could. What he particularly didn't like was what he was getting back from her.

Nothing. A cold, empty nothing, devoid of humanity.

She felt his revulsion, though, and hesitated. The big creature turned, walked stiffly over to the rail, and dropped into the water, still holding the gun.

That she had this kind of mental power was scary enough, Brazil thought, but to do it so coldly was damned frightening. *What if they all can do this? What kind of game are the Glathrielians playing, and with how much of this world?*

By Jack L. Chalker
Published by Ballantine Books:

THE WEB OF THE CHOZEN

AND THE DEVIL WILL DRAG YOU UNDER

A JUNGLE OF STARS

DANCE BAND ON THE *TITANIC*

DANCERS IN THE AFTERGLOW

SHADOW OF THE WELL OF SOULS

A Well World Novel

Jack L. Chalker

A Del Rey® Book
BALLANTINE BOOKS • NEW YORK

A Del Rey® Book
Published by Ballantine Books
Copyright © 1994 by Jack L. Chalker

Library of Congress Catalog Card Number: 93-73660

ISBN 0-345-38846-1

Manufactured in the United States of America

First Trade Edition: February 1994
First Mass Market Edition: September 1994

10 9 8 7 6 5 4 3 2 1

For Fritz Leiber,
who enjoyed the original Well saga
but left us before this one was done, and
likewise for my old friend Reg Bretnor,
also gone too soon, my writing opposite of sorts,
who packed more laughs into fewer words than
any science-fiction author in history.
The worst thing about growing old
is the increasing number of missing,
and missed, friends.

Preface
"Oh, No! Not Another *Trilogy*!"

A FUNNY THING HAPPENED ON A JOURNEY BACK TO THE WELL World . . .

The Well of Souls series was the only five-volume trilogy I had ever written, and I felt it was basically symmetrical and right; I had no intention of going back to it after I finished *Twilight at the Well of Souls* in 1979. For one thing, I didn't want to be "typed" and wind up cheapening the concept or the original book(s) by ripping off Well World No. 386. I didn't get into the writing business to do that.

Still, when Del Rey came to me with the proverbial Offer I Couldn't Refuse, it had been ten years since I'd as much as *looked* at the series, and I had a number of other very successful books, multivolume big books, and one or two series as well. Footnote: Publishers call all multivolume works "series," but actually only a couple of mine are. A series is an open-ended set of tales having in common a setting, a premise, or a set of characters. Anthony's Xanth is a series; so are King's Gunslinger saga, Zelazny's Amber, and, for that matter, Mark Twain's Sawyer and Finn books.

The multivolume novel is what happens to writers who like to write novels the size of *War and Peace* in an age of computerized budgets and mass market-publishing. The writer simply outlines a single, stand-alone novel as he would any other but then is informed that there are "price points" and that he has to cut to fit the prescribed maximums or, frankly, production costs on the book will push it beyond its "price point" where there is more sales resistance than acceptance. So you split it in two, or three, or whatever.

Tolkien's Rings books are in fact both a series and a multivolume, or "serial," novel. *The Lord of the Rings* is a serial novel; its middle volume, in fact, ends on a classic cliff-hanger (worthy of Republic film serials of the thirties) with Sam shut out of the evil dungeon and in the land of the enemy, beating his fists futilely against the closed gates while the narration says, "Frodo was alive, but captured by the enemy." To be continued. Of course, since the concept began with *The Hobbit*, a totally independent novel, and has continued even after the author's death, the Rings is in fact a series which contains a serial novel.

Midnight at the Well of Souls was a single novel and remains today a single novel in one volume, a totally stand-alone work. Acceptance of it was so great that both I and the publisher couldn't resist so vast a canvas, so I outlined a second novel that, as it turned out ran about 250,000 words, or about twice the length of *Midnight*. Presto! It was a serial novel, a single book in two parts, that was also a sequel to an independent book.

I then found that even with this addition I couldn't finish the story I wanted to tell. Oh, I wrapped the novel up, but there was a ton of material I couldn't put in it and more that I wanted to do, particularly visiting the northern hemisphere. That brought forth another novel outline, which, again, ran very long and wound up as two books. Hence, a five-volume trilogy, a series containing three novels in five books.

This is a fourth novel in the series (and when you go beyond the trilogy that Tolkien seems to have defined as the cliche-length of a serial novel, you find that ad agencies say you're writing a "saga"), and it's longer than the preceding three. I really thought I could wrap it in two in the same way I was certain that I could do the second book in about the same amount of space that I'd used for *Midnight*. It didn't happen.

So, I could still have done it in two if I were willing to cut out much of this volume, which is the philosophic heart of this *über*-novel and begins to make some sense of what happened in *Echoes of the Well of Souls*. Never mind all the heady discussions between characters and all the mushy stuff, some would say—cut to where you start the massacres. Well, I don't work that way, either. A novel is as long as it takes to properly tell the story; it shouldn't be any longer than that or be cut any shorter than it absolutely needs.

Hopefully, if you aren't familiar with the original "Saga of the Well World," you'll pick it up—it is, or should be, available at finer booksellers everywhere—and start from there. If you have read the original series but missed *Echoes of the Well of Souls*, it's still out there and you should find it. In fact, all competently run bookstores should certainly have copies of it available when this book comes out. If they don't have it where you found this, go back and tell them what you think about that fact and how it reflects on them.

There will be one more volume of this long novel. It's already outlined, and it's got my usual very big finish. Some of it will be what you expect after reading this, but I think there will be a number of surprises. There are in fact several surprises in store in *this* book, if you wait for them. But you can see we're shaping up here for one cosmic cataclysm, and I do not plan to disappoint you. So if you already have *Echoes*, let's go. If you don't, go out and get it first and "see it from the beginning"! This is, after all, the middle of my 350,000-word novel!

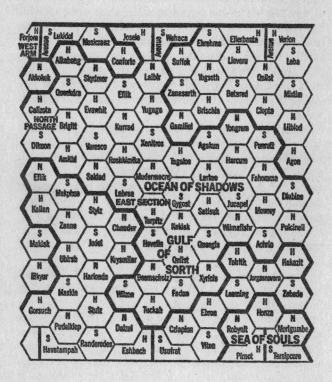

WORLD
Southern Hemisphere*

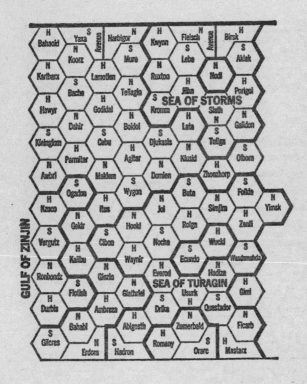

H—Highly Technological
S—Semitechnological
N—Nontechnological

*continued on overleaf

THE WELL WORLD
Section of Southern Hemisphere
(continued)

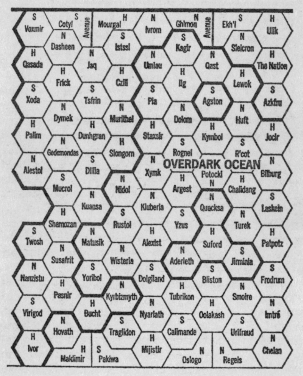

H—Highly Technological
S—Semitechnological
N—Nontechnological

Somewhere
Between Galactic Clusters

THE KRAANG HAD GOOD REASON TO BE COMPLACENT. AFTER so long, so *very* long, its plans were coming to a head, and with each passing day its link to and power within the Well Net grew. It could already send within the field and could receive and track and monitor as well. While none of the principals in the drama it had concocted were directly addressable—unless they were in a full Well field such as traveling through and between hex gates and Zones—and the Watchers were outside its direct monitoring abilities, the others whom it had identified as they were processed by the system were far easier to track.

When the Kraang's ship itself was not in the slingshot gateways, it was now possible to see through the eyes and hear through the ears of the others who had been processed, and that was more than sufficient to monitor the Watchers' track, while both Watchers and their monitors were unaware even of its very existence. And although unable to send to them under normal circumstances, it could do more than merely receive; it *knew* them. It knew their innermost thoughts, their loves, hates, fears, and nightmares. It knew that little band better than they knew themselves. That not only allowed the Kraang to filter out subjective impressions from the raw data, it also provided such deep individual knowledge of them that when more *was* possible, when they finally opened the gate that would bring it to them, they would be as soft clay, as easily remolded inside as they had been outside to serve the Kraang's purposes.

It had been nothing less than the remaking of the cosmos that had allowed the Kraang's liberation, although close to a billion years had passed until chance had ultimately given it access to the net once again, access the Ancient Ones believed had been denied it for eternity. The rest of the system had provided just a moment, mere nanoseconds, when the program that had bound it for billions of years could not control its destiny. That tiny moment had been sufficient for the Kraang to alter the system, however slightly, without detection by the net or the Watchman, so that when the program was reimposed, it was flawed. Afterward it had been a mere matter of waiting, suspended of activity, until eventually chance would place the Kraang and its prison within distance of possible direct contact with a Well Gate. The Well computer became aware of the flaw only when that contact came, and then it was too late: the Kraang had access to the net. And the Kraang could be disengaged from the net only by the Watchman, since the Well was powerless in and of itself to do harm to one of its creators. Only another Maker could do that.

So the Kraang had done what it had to do. The world upon which the Watchman lived was still primitive; there was no space travel of consequence, no way to create a situation by which the Watchman could be drawn to a gate. The gate, then, had to come to the Watchman by the crude but effective method of sending Well Gates down to the planet of the Watchman as meteors.

But there had been two Watchers instead of one at this juncture, the second created by the original Watchman when the cosmos was reset. Multiple gates were required because the two were separated. And so the gates had fallen, remaining open until the Watchers were collected, operating in their normal manner until the Well could safely close them. During that period it was almost inevitable that others, natives of the planet, would fall through, and it was amazing how few had actually done so.

Few, but enough.

The newspeople—Theresa Perez, the producer; Gus Olafsson, the cameraman; and Dr. Lori Ann Sutton, the university astronomer tapped as the expert for the newspeople—had been captured by a primitive Amazonian tribe deep in the jungles of Brazil. A tribe whose mysterious leader was the female Watcher, who had taken them through with her to the Well World, along with the Peruvian gangster and drug lord Juan Campos. And, before them, two of the always-inevitable investigators of the meteor, Colonel Jorge Lunderman, Brazilian Air Force regional commander, and Julian Beard, U.S. Air Force scientist-astronaut. *Those* two had been taken while posing for photos atop the "meteor," perhaps as an object lesson for all others to stay away.

The other, the original Watchman, had also been in Brazil, but on the civilized coast, taking a sort of holiday in the nation that shared his name. Only two natives had been taken in with him, both at his invitation: the blind former airline pilot Joao Antonio Guzman and his dying British wife, Anne Marie.

Eight natives who were processed by the Well, each becoming *something else*, another creature, another race, yet with their memories and essential selves, their souls as it might be colorfully put, intact, for good or evil. The Kraang had no influence over what they had become, but it ever after had been along for the ride.

During the processing, a link could be and was established.

Even communication with the Watchers was possible during that period, but it was dangerous to go too far. Surface thoughts and surface memories triggered by the experience had been available even though the Watchers themselves remained essentially out of the Kraang's control. One thought, however, one memory, one weakness, particularly on the part of the newer Watcher, was sufficient. Had *been* sufficient.

Now the game was commencing. Now one of them certainly would open the way. Now one of them, at least, would be the unwitting agent freeing the Kraang and summoning it home. Home to the Well.

Home to become God.

Hakazit

ALTHOUGH IN MANY WAYS THE WELL WORLD FELT FAMILIAR, even comfortable to him, in other ways, Nathan Brazil reflected, he always had a sense of wrongness when on it.

It wasn't the bizarre variety of creatures and cultures, the things that made new entrants so uneasy; rather, it was the common things. *Some* things might be expected to change when crossing a national boundary, but not the climate, and absolutely not the gravity, yet one could cross from the tropics to snow in a few footsteps or have gravitational fluctuation of up to twenty percent in the same distance if one were near one of those borders. And of course it should be cold at the poles and grow warmer toward the equator, even more so than on Earth, as the Well World had no appreciable axial tilt and thus no natural seasons. The days, and nights, a bit longer than back on Earth, were nonetheless always pretty close to equal.

But Glathriel, near the south polar region, was tropical; Hakazit, a thousand kilometers or so west of Glathriel yet only a bit north, was raw and cold, the winds off the Ocean of Shadows brisk and biting, carrying small droplets of ice and snow and swirling them around, not in the sense of a storm but rather as persistent irritants, felt but not really seen.

He pulled his fur-lined jacket tightly about him, hoping to ward off some of the wintry chill, his breath causing huge puffs of steam as it came from his warm interior and struck the frigid air with every exhalation. He looked over at the girl standing atop the rocky cliff looking out at the pounding surf. Although as Earth-human, in some ways *more* Earth-human, than he was, she was wearing not a stitch of clothing, and Brazil marveled again at her total insulation.

He would have liked to know how they had pulled it off. Some sort of internally generated energy field, certainly, a true cosmic aura fueled from within by some autonomic source he couldn't imagine. Certainly she didn't do it consciously; it was simply too perfect for that. But even if he granted the unlikely and heretofore unsuspected power to Type 41 humans to do this sort of thing, he couldn't imagine why it would evolve in a primitive and totally tropical hex where only "wet" and "dry" had much meaning. Nor did it account for the selectivity. She was standing there in temperatures well below freezing on rock that itself was cold enough to freeze any water it had, but the cold didn't affect her. She was warm to the touch even on the surface of her skin, and the icy droplets that were turning his own hair into a miniature ice field were hitting her as well, as warm and liquid as a summer drizzle. Yet her long black hair blew free in the wind, a wind that made the chill factor almost Arctic on bare skin but that, in that incredibly small fraction of a millimeter before it struck any part of her, was suddenly turned as warm as a tropical breeze.

Clearly the talent had not been evolved for situations like this; it merely served this function as well. What was it, then? What was this mysterious inner-produced energy field's primary function?

Clearly it required a lot of energy. The photo he'd received here of her in the Zone Gate corridor, taken off the monitor recording, had shown her very lean and somewhat muscular; now she was, well, *fat.* Not obese—nobody who could move like she did could be considered that—but the thighs were very large, the ass ample, the breasts enlarged to substantial proportions and resting on an ample tummy.

She ate a lot, yet it never seemed to slow her down, and he'd never seen her pant for breath once, even while running. That surplus wasn't there for the usual reasons; most of the Glathrielians he had seen were at the least chubby. It was there as fuel for whatever additional engine they had within themselves.

She was more than merely another of the Well World's many mysteries, though. The Well World left no one unchanged who entered through its Zone Gate save Mavra and himself, yet she was clearly not of Glathriel, the only Earth-human hex here. Her west African heritage showed clearly in her skin and lips, yet her naturally straight, lush, long black hair and general facial features betrayed an equally obvious Hispanic ancestry. She had been made by no Well computer; she had been born and had grown up like this. Whatever changes had been made, they had been inside, in the adaptation stage, in which the brain was slightly reprogrammed to accept a new situation.

But the Well World wouldn't have programmed in an evolutionary change made after the last reset. It would use the basic template.

Conclusion: She had not been changed inside by the Well at all, but by some other force, and that force could only be the Glathrielians themselves.

And *that* disturbed him most of all, because the last time Glathriel's template had been examined and revised, he had done it himself, and while he might well have expected some sort of tropical tribal primitive society or some other variation of it, he'd given them nothing with which to develop the society, if it could be called that, and the powers that they now possessed. A society that used no tools, built no structures, altered its environment not a whit, had no apparent spoken language or even the concept or need for one, consuming only what it found day by day, and not even using fire. Yet somehow they presented the sensation of a tightly knit and intelligent tribal society.

He had no idea who this girl was, or what she had been, or where other than Earth she'd come from. She'd almost snuck into Zone on her own and crept past the officious and preoccupied duty personnel there. The recordings of her from South Zone, discovered too late, showed a picture of a primitive savage, painted and dressed in little but bones, but she didn't look like any Amazonian Indian he'd ever heard of. The group she had followed in, Mavra's group, had entered similarly primitive-looking, yet had proved to be from a modern and articulate educated society. He'd like to know that story one of these days; it was probably a hell of a saga.

Was she from one of the primitive tribes of the Amazon, a native who had been caught in the hex gate, perhaps after seeing the others go through? Some orphan, perhaps, or a captive raised by them, which would explain her different look? She was tough and had guts; she'd taken on an Ecundo whose body was armored and whose tail meant death without a second thought—and with her bare hands. Yet even as she rejected all the fruits of technology as a Glathrielian would, she'd not been surprised or even curious about them. She seemed to know exactly what was dangerous to touch and what was safe, and she seemed to understand the setup of a developed society even if she did not join in on any of its activities.

Despite this, and for no logical reason he could determine, he found her attractive in ways he couldn't really explain. He hadn't remembered feeling this way about anybody, possibly ever, certainly not in countless thousands of years. It was oddly sexual, stirring in him feelings he'd believed dead so long that they'd ceased to be more than abstractions to him. He had of course felt closeness, friendship, even a sort of love for individuals over time, as much as he'd tried to repress such feelings, knowing the brief time they had compared to him, but not on this level. It was also clear that she sensed this and, in what ways she could, reciprocated. She was anything but naive and unsophisticated in the art of making love, and while nobody had longer experience than he in that sort of thing, she made him feel things, physical things, to a degree he knew he'd never reached before. It was as if she were some powerful and addictive drug, one that, once taken, he could never again be without. It was the first new experience he'd had since ... since ... since before he'd re-created the universe.

Of course, he suspected that it wasn't entirely natural. Glathriel's revenge, he thought with a trace of genuine irony. Take *us* out of our nice, comfortable high-tech little worldlet and stick us in a nontech swamp designed for a race of giant beavers, will you? Well, it took us a million years, but we finally figured out a way to get back at you! Then, through *her*, it is *we* who will control *you*!

He considered that a distinct possibility, although he wasn't certain how sophisticated the Glathrielians were along those lines. It did not, however, overly concern him. For one thing, she was at least partly Earth-human, no matter how changed she might be, and he'd had a very long time to learn to read beyond the surface of Earth people, to detect even slightly corrupt attitudes or motives as well as pure ones. He'd never sensed any deception in her. If it *was* something Glathrielian women did to snare men, it worked both ways, of that he was positive. If she was the only girl in his world—pretty well true at the moment, come to think of it—then he was her only boy. He was absolutely convinced that she would not, *could* not act against him. Whatever unsuspected potential lurked in the Type 41 brain, the link that bound the two of them together was empathic in nature, and that was the most revealing sense of all. Even telepaths learned how to cheat each other just to survive; an empath seldom could, since the very power dealt in emotions which no one could ever fully control.

Within their own subjective limits, he felt what she felt, and she felt what he felt. That was what made physical intimacy so intense, but it also left him convinced that she could not knowingly play false with him.

"Knowingly," of course, was an important distinction, but even if there was something sinister at work and he was deluding himself, he knew in the end that it didn't matter.

Once inside the Well, he was invulnerable to anything the universe could throw at him, even betrayal. And once inside, he would be able to find out what the hell was going on.

In the meantime something deep within his own psyche, his own deep chasm of loneliness, despair, and alienation from others, assuaged over long years only with tiny morsels of hope and self-delusion, had been, however temporarily, partially filled, and for the moment that was enough.

Still, it was *too* damned cold for him, even if not for her, and the kind of warmth she could give him was not the sort he now required. He went over to her and put his hand on her shoulder. She turned and smiled at him, and he made an exaggerated shiver and gestured back toward the town. She nodded and looked sympathetic; clearly she was also no stranger to a cold environment, even if she couldn't feel it herself.

All seaport towns had a certain basic similarity to them. Although the towns themselves and their urban layouts tended to vary in wild and bizarre ways, reflecting the very different races that lived in them, there was always a section by the docks generally known as the International Quarter, even though it was a far smaller piece of the town than that. Where ocean ships crewed by a polyglot of races made ports of call like spaceships docking in new tiny worlds, a level of comfort, convenience, and service was necessary to cater to alien needs. Some were far better than others at this, of course, but Hakazit was a high-tech hex with a huge automated port, and its facilities, were first-rate. The Hakazitians were a bit harder to take, if only because they resembled, to Brazil's mind at least, human-sized mosquitoes with a proboscis that looked like a giant version of one of those Happy New Year whistles that unrolled when blown. But the Hakazitians' "nose," when extended, proved to be not one but six sticky tendrils capable not only of feeding but also of doing almost any task hands could do and a few they could not. Their huge hivelike structures dominated the landscape as far back as anyone could see.

The girl—she'd never taken to or responded to any name

he'd tried, so she'd just become the girl—never liked being inside a structure. Glathrielians, it seemed, were a bit claustrophobic even in fairly large rooms. It was a measure of how attached they'd become that she was willing to enter most buildings, even sleep where he did, although she was always clearly uncomfortable and still preferred floors to beds, at least for sleeping. She almost seemed to get a charge, though, out of walking unconcerned and unafraid stark naked down bustling streets and in crowded hotel lobbies, something unthinkable on Earth. But since the only other one of her species was her companion and lover, it gave her a rush of liberation that was as unique to her as his feelings for her were to him.

Vagt Damstrl, which meant "the Hotel Grand" in Hakazit, or so they said, was an imposing structure that dominated the skyline in a way only the huge port cranes could match, and its management prided itself on being able to provide both accommodations and necessaries for any race of the Well World that might be a guest. As usual, considering the state of Glathriel and its people, it had nothing *precisely* the way he'd want it, but many races liked carpeting on the floors and many others liked soft beds and many bathed in pools or tublike creations, so that they were able to assemble a spacious room for him that not only was to his standards but went beyond them. Nor was food a problem; a fair number of races who traveled for various reasons ate things close to or even the same as Type 41's, and a short scan by a clever little device he'd never seen before resulted in room service deliveries of meals, even some sort of meat and fish, that were tasty and had no unusual side effects. Even silverware was provided to his specifications.

The girl ate no meat, nor would she use tableware. Still, she could and did pack away an enormous amount of fruits, grains, nuts, and starchy vegetables, all raw, all completely consumed, including rinds, skins, and seeds. She also ate whole sticks of whatever butter they provided and large squares of what appeared to be lard. It was fascinating to see the lengths she would go to to avoid using tools or utensils, though. Milk—he wasn't sure what kind and didn't want to know, but it had a distinct buttery taste and a kind of goatlike aroma—was fine, but not in a glass. Put it in a large bowl, and she would not touch the bowl but would put her face into it and drink or, if it was ample enough, cup it in her hands. But just about everything she could eat she *did* eat.

The aversion to using tools or mechanical devices wasn't absolute, but it was as absolute as she could make it. She would not take the elevator; she walked up and down the stairs or often ran. Neither would she open a door or even indicate that she wanted it open; she would simply stand there until it was open for her. Somehow, though, she always knew the right floor to stop at and wait for him.

Even dicier was when she had to go to the toilet. Although the one in the room wasn't built for Earth humans, it was close enough to be useful, but she would not sit on it or even touch it. She squatted, and that was that. But she had no aversion to the large oval-shaped sunken tub that filled and drained automatically. She had no problems adapting the tub to her bodily needs, which was okay, but it kept him from enjoying it. She, however, immersed herself in it with no compunctions. Overall, until he arranged with the management for an alternative shower, she smelled better than he did.

That night, feeling finally warm and comfortable, Nathan Brazil sat in the room and looked over some maps. The shortest route to the Well was over the Straight of Sagath to Agon, just three hexes away via the water route, then north through Lilblod, through Mixtim or Clopta, and across Quilst to the Avenue. It wasn't an area he knew from the past, being well off his normal track, but it was direct and didn't require too much travel in nontech hexes. Indeed, if he went via Clopta, Betared, up to Lieveru, and approached the Avenue from the west in Ellerbanta, although it would be a bit farther, he could limit the nontech part to Lilblod alone. That didn't ensure friendly receptions, of course, but high- and semitech hexes had means of transportation other than muscle power, and that meant speed. By getting on the ship the girl had shown that she would ride in such things even if she didn't like it, adjusting as best she could, as she was doing just being inside the hotel and the room.

The other alternative was to head northeast, but in addition to being longer, that route had the almost equal problem of being partly in areas well known to him. He wasn't at all certain he wanted to put himself under the authority of the Yaxa, whose high-tech devices might well contain some vestigial residue of suspicion or identification of one Nathan Brazil even after so very long a time. He didn't trust them much in any event.

Getting to Agon, however, was proving to be harder than he'd been led to believe. No matter what shipping company or booking agent he tried, nothing was going there. Coming *from* there, yes, but even when he found two ships on the schedule, he was informed that one had developed hull problems and would be in drydock for months and that the other was skipping the port because of scheduling problems and lack of business there. It almost seemed as if nothing was crossing the relatively short strait. Somehow some new natural law had been passed, or so evidence suggested, that ships traveled only east and west. It was almost making him paranoid.

If it wasn't so ridiculous, he thought, *I'd swear I was the victim of some massive conspiracy to keep me here.*

Well, he had to decide on something, however unsatisfactory, fairly quickly. At the rates charged by the Grand, they'd be on the street in two more weeks. In a way he envied the girl—that wouldn't bother her a bit, and he knew it. While she was mortal and he was not, the inseparable gulf between them that even empathic linkage couldn't get around, *he* felt the cold and hunger and was subject to many of the infirmities that she was somehow shielded against. He had no intention of being frozen stiff in some cliffside hideaway until somebody found him and thawed him out in years to come.

It was while coming out from yet another fruitless en-counter with a shipping agent that he met the colonel.

"Of all the sights I have seen in this beautiful but ac-cursed world, that has to be the most amazing," said a voice behind him, a voice that sounded both eerie and men-acing, the kind of voice that would give the same impres-sion if it just said "Good morning." It was Sydney Greenstreet, but on steroids and in a mild echo chamber.

Brazil and the girl both stopped dead at the sound and turned. Brazil felt her sudden reaction to the speaker and understood it. She never reacted to the outward appearance of anybody; he wasn't even sure she considered it relevant. But the inside, the important part of an individual, *that* she got immediately and with unerring accuracy. Not that he needed the loan of her talent for this case. The voice kind of *oozed* with a silky sliminess that would put anyone on guard. The fact that the figure who spoke matched the im-pression only reinforced the sense of menace.

"I beg your pardon," Brazil responded politely. "Were you speaking to me?"

The creature they faced was less a form than a mass; it seemed almost made of liquid, an unsettling, pulsating thing that had no clearly defined shape, its "skin," or outer membrane, a glistening obsidianlike shiny brown that re-flected and distorted all the light that struck it. He couldn't imagine how it spoke aloud at all.

"Pardon," it said, revealing a nearly invisible slitlike mouth in the midst of the mass. "I had not even the slight-est suspicion that there might be Earthlike humans on this planet, although God knows there is certainly every other nightmare creature."

Brazil frowned. "You know Earth?"

"Of course. I was born there and once looked much as you." The mass changed, writhed, and took on an increas-ingly humanoid shape, until, standing before them, it be-came what looked for all the world like a life-sized animated carving in obsidian or jade of an Earth-human man, middle-aged but ramrod straight. There was even a suggestion of a bushy mustache and the semblance of, yes, some sort of uniform. "Colonel Jorge Lunderman, late of the Air Force of the Republic of Brazil, rather abruptly retired but at your service."

"So *you're* one of the two officers that they told me about! I wondered who you were and how you wound up coming through. Oh—sorry. Captain Solomon is my name. David Solomon."

"Captain? In the service of what nation?"

"None, really. Merchant marine. Countless ships under the usual flags of convenience."

"You were in port, then, in Rio?"

"No, just on holiday there. I hadn't been in Brazil in—a *very* long time."

"I was commandant of the Northwestern Defense Sector— the area mostly of jungle and isolated settlements between Manaus and the western and northern national borders. A very large meteor struck, harmlessly, in the middle of the jungle, but a mostly American television news crew who went in to investigate and report on it vanished completely. There was quite a search using every resource at our command, but it was as if they had vanished into nothingness."

Brazil nodded. "I understand. Somehow they must all have fallen through to here."

"Well, some Peruvian revolutionaries had camps just along the border, and they were in alliance with some very powerful drug barons, one of whom had guaranteed the newspeople's safety. We had fears that the crew had been disposed of for some reason, but we found only cooperation from the Peruvians. It seems one of Don Campos's sons was among the group that vanished. We searched for weeks before giving up. Nothing. But this meteor, it was so strange that they were flying in scientists from all over to test and check and measure it. There seemed no harm there, though. They'd poked it and probed it and tried to drill into it, and nothing much had changed. The Americans sent a liaison, a NASA astronaut who was a geologist, to help coordinate. The two of us stupidly agreed to pose atop the meteor for the news media. It seemed harmless enough. The next thing we knew, we were here."

Brazil listened carefully to the account, musing over the implications he couldn't fully discuss with the colonel or anybody else. Why had a huge chunk of meteor with a fully operative Well Gate fallen so far inland? Hell, that was a thousand miles from Rio, where he was, and the Well computer hadn't had any trouble almost hitting him on the head with one. Had Mavra been in Brazil as well? Maneuvered there by the subtle shifts of probability the Well was capable of when it concerned a Watcher? That still didn't make sense. One didn't go to the upper Amazon for a casual trip, but he couldn't see her either in the drug trade or playing local revolutionary. Not unless she was leading the rebels, anyway. Or . . .

Just why *had* he decided to take his holiday in Brazil? Maybe it was *he* who'd been manipulated. The savage looks of the other party, the accounts of how primitive they and the girl had seemed . . . Mavra living with a tribe of Stone Age Indians deep in the jungle? That *had* to be the answer. How and why would have to remain a mystery, at least for now, but it explained a lot. But the colonel and the astronaut had come through *weeks*, maybe longer, before Mavra's group.

Maybe the colonel's initial search and, afterward, the colonel's and the astronaut's apparent on-camera disintegration would have made it hard as hell to reach the Gate. That *had* to be it. But then, who *did* come through with Mavra when she finally managed it? Others of her tribe? And if that was the case, where was that news crew?

"Captain? Are you all right?" the colonel asked.

"Oh, yes, sorry. I was just trying to fit events together. What brings you to Hakazit now, Colonel?"

"Why, I thought that would be obvious. You do. Both of you, in fact. I mean, it is still something of a shock to me to find myself here in this form and situation, but I accepted what had happened out of necessity. But I had not seen or heard of a race here that was like the one into which I was born, and suddenly there is news that at least two and perhaps more of what I still think of as 'humans' were around and apparently unchanged. I had to find out who you were and what you were doing and, of course, how the both of you manage to remain as you were. I *assume* she is as she looked before and is not some native human stock unknown to me. Your pardon, but the only surprise greater than seeing someone like you here is seeing her, standing there, stark naked, on a cold and windswept coast, apparently feeling no discomfort."

"You're right; both of us are from Earth. I suspect she came through the same gate you did. I came through in the hills behind Rio with two others I haven't located as yet. She's a mystery girl—arrived naked, painted up, bone jewelry and the like, and snuck right past everybody and entered the Well World without being noticed until too late. I have no idea why the computer they say controls things here decided to keep us both as we were, but I can hazard a guess as to why she's more changed in other ways, including the ones that are obvious, than I am. There *is* a human hex here, but the people don't quite look like any race or nationality we know and they're primitive, mysterious, and very un-Earthlike in their ways. They took a different path somehow. Seems that long ago their ancestors plotted to take over an adjoining nontech hex, Ambreza, and forgot that lack of machines doesn't equal lack of intelligence. The Ambrezians bred some kind of gas-producing plant that grew like weeds in the human hex and basically knocked their brains all to hell. Then they switched hexes, so now the humans are nontech and apparently have been ever since. It changed them. There was some sort of mutation. Had they remained high-tech, they'd have been fairly familiar, I think, but being nontech, they went to the ultimate nontech system. Because the computer still has them in their original hex, however, that's where both the girl and I came in. I stayed and made myself useful to the Ambrezians—they look like giant beavers—while she fled to the human hex and fell in with them. It was *they*, I'm sure, that made her this way, not the computer."

"Does she not speak?"

"I don't think she speaks or understands a word anybody says. Sometimes I'm not even sure she thinks the way most of us think. The Ambreza said that they did have a small number of sounds that were consistent, but not enough to be considered a language. I'm not so sure it's more than the equivalent of the sound codes used by many animal species. You know—warning the tribe of danger, warning enemies off, sounds that relate to fear, and things like that. A scream, a warning cry, a sigh, a purringlike hum—that's about the range of it. If they communicate more complex information, and I'm convinced that they do, it's by means other than what we think of as language. I hope she *was* one of the Stone Age Amazonians. I'd hate to think of the frustration I would have, let alone anyone from a more civilized and technological culture, under those limitations imposed on her."

"She is definitely not a native," the colonel noted. "However, she looks like many people in my old native land for all that. It is not unheard of for such tribes to find or adopt lost children of outsiders and raise them as their own. I pray that it is so, for then she is probably better off and will live longer by coming here. It would be terrible if, say, she was one of the missing television crew. I mean, I may look, even *be* very different but inside, in my mind, I am still Jorge Lunderman. But like *that*, not even as you say *thinking* as we were raised to think, how much of either of us would be truly left after a period of living that way? I am the same man that I was, living a different life in a very different place and as, frankly, something very different than what I was. Still, there is continuity, is there not? The mind and soul are my own. I would much prefer that to retaining my body and losing my mind, my memories, my very way of thinking. I would not be me anymore. I would be someone entirely different, but perhaps with just that lurking suspicion somewhere telling me that I was once someone else. Terrible, sir! Terrible!"

Brazil glanced at the girl, who was still looking at the creature with some disdain on her face but with no hint that she'd comprehended, or even *tried* to comprehend, any of the discussion.

"Well, she seems neither tortured nor unhappy," the captain noted, "so I will continue to just accept her as she is."

The colonel shifted a bit, the human statue distorting a bit eerily. "You must tell me what you are doing and why she is with you instead of remaining back there!" he said enthusiastically. "And about all the rest of what you know as well. It seems like *ages* since I was able to speak to anyone with a common frame of reference to my past! But sir, I apologize! While the cold is of some little discomfort to me and apparently none to her, you must be *freezing*! Forgive my manners. Have you a hotel?"

"Yes, I'm at the Grand. You?"

"I am currently living out of my cabin aboard the ship I used to get here. It will be in port here for three days, so there is little reason to consider my course of action beyond that until then. My cabin is, of course, at your service, but I'm afraid it would be neither spacious nor comfortable to one not of my new kind. Shall we go to your hotel, then?"

"Might as well," Brazil sighed. "It doesn't look as if I'm *ever* going to get out of here."

They begin walking, or, rather, Brazil began walking, as did the girl, a bit behind, while the colonel sort of oozed along next to him.

"That *is* a good question to begin with as we walk," the colonel noted. "Why *are* you in this inhospitable and out-of-the-way place?"

"Well, if you must know, I'm in a far worse position than either you or the girl there. I can't set up anything permanent in Glathriel—the human hex—unless I want to take on her ways and life style. The Ambreza could be strung along just so much, but they're still paranoid about humans, particularly the kind who can talk and know technology like me, and they've basically barred me from returning. I'm the man without a country. I am not, however, without a good deal of experience and skills that even the Ambreza found useful, which is how I have any cash at all. By the time you can command the kind of ships I did, you became something of an expert in almost everything practical and useful. Way up north around the equator there are two high-tech hexes separated by a narrow strait, neither of which has ever seen or heard of the likes of Glathriel, and both are highly dependent on shipping and import-export trade at this stage. They've both been looking for qualified ship's officers and as usual aren't particular about the race or nationality involved. They also serve as flags of convenience for hundreds of coastal hexes, particularly the nontech and semitech ones that have to get ships and crews from high-tech places. It's my best shot at a life here."

"Yes, I understand," the colonel said. "But you have been frustrated?"

"I can't get a ship north for love or money. It's driving me crazy—not to mention quickly broke before I've started."

The colonel thought a moment. "Tell me, Captain, do you think you could handle the sort of ship they must use here?"

The Well World *did* require rather bizarre ships, since there were water hexes as well as land ones and those water hexes had the same technological limitations as their dry counterparts. Thus, a large ship had to be able to move entirely by sail through nontech waters, switch to basic steam fed by manual labor or ingenious cog-drive mechanisms for the semitech, but could use an efficient fusion plant for the high-tech regions.

"I began in sail, if that's what you mean," Brazil told him. "And I've got—*had*—a master's license for steam as well. My latest ships were big diesels, but the power source of a modern plant isn't relevant if the power's fed to the engines in the amount the bridge demands. I'm a little out of shape to climb rigging myself, but I could handle most anything else."

"Then why do you not sail there yourself?"

"For the same reason you, as an air force colonel, didn't have your own personal supersonic transport. That would take an incredible amount of money, and I'm afraid I'm still a wee bit short."

The colonel chuckled, a very eerie sound. "Yes, I see. But there are much smaller craft making the runs. Private and government yachts, ferries that are built in one place and must be sailed to where they are needed, smaller fishing boats or their equivalents, that sort of thing. Like many other high-tech coastal hexes, Hakazit has a very competitive shipbuilding industry, you know, and they often have only skeleton crews to take those ships to their customers, as most experienced crew live on and have a share in their own ships. Forget shipping agencies, sir! Try the shipwrights! Why, I managed to finagle passage here because they needed someone familiar with government-type contracts to check on an overdue naval vessel my nation has on order. Permit me to ask around when I go down there tomorrow morning. Perhaps I can find something for you. One-way, of course, and probably not precisely to where you wish to go, but sufficient, I would expect."

"I have no papers for this world," Brazil reminded him, "so I never even thought of that route. But, if you can find somebody who'll take me north, I'll be glad to sign on."

"Done, sir!"

"You sound very confident," Brazil noted dryly.

"Why, sir, I am first and foremost a Brazilian! In my country you learn very quickly how to deal with mosquitoes, however large they are!"

In point of fact, Theresa "Terry" Perez *did* remember who she had been and where she had come from, but that only accentuated the change within her. What was different was that it no longer mattered to her, nor even did it disturb any part of her in the slightest that it no longer mattered to her. Nothing that mattered to virtually all the others in the hotel and in the city really mattered to her, except for a few basics. That was at the root of this new, nonlinear way of thinking that the Glathrielian group will imposed upon her, and not unwillingly on her part although she hadn't known at the time what it would mean and the old Terry might well have fled instead.

In point of fact, the Glathrielians had not imposed a great deal; rather, they had in effect rewired her brain so that it processed information in a way more alien to Earth standards than most of the cultures of the wildly varying races of the Well World. It created a new Terry, one who automatically saw the world in a new and very different way.

The Glathrielian imperative was essentially quite simple: At all times, consider only all the things that are relevant to you, and miss not a one of those. Anything irrelevant or unnecessary was a distraction; distraction was the way to destruction, so anything unimportant must be literally factored out of the mind and not even allowed to register. It would take years of self-training to master it completely, but Terry, helped by the experience and self-training of the Glathrielian elders, had achieved an amazingly high level of mastery in so short a time.

If she could filter out all distractions, all things not directly relevant to her existence and what was of true importance to her, and automatically observe only what she needed, the amount of information that simply *came* to her was enormous, far beyond the sort of knowledge others might possess. Thoughts, actions, and processes that did not require decisions should be automated so that they, too, ceased to exist as a factor. The energy field that her brain could generate and her body could use for so many things was one such process she had already relegated to that status. Although she didn't know or care exactly what it was doing, or how, it protected her from the elements that might cause distraction—extremes of heat and cold, for example, or even adjusting gravitation or filtering out any impurities from an atmosphere so that if the chemicals needed to breathe were present in any mixture, it would extract only those and allow them into her lungs.

Of course, it was also useful both as a defense and as an offense, if needed, and those functions, too, were automated.

Without even realizing she had done so, she had reordered much of her digestive system and metabolism for maximum efficiency and maximum reserves of power.

What she ate, so long as it was not poisonous to her system and was not of flesh, was irrelevant to her, and even much that might have made her ill or killed her was now separated out and isolated and passed through without harm. The body maintained its own vitamin, mineral, fat, and sugar requirements as best it could with whatever was at hand; it basically controlled what and how much she ate. She didn't even think of it.

All the knowledge of her past and the person she'd been was not gone, but it had been reordered and placed in an out-of-the-way, protected area of the brain. The sight of an object or an assemblage of objects brought forth an instant reaction based on that knowledge but only what was needed to deal with it. Thus, the sight of electrical cables or sockets might evoke a warning of danger rather than a definition or a picture of what they were. By simply obeying those impulses automatically, she did not have to deal with them, either. The standard senses—sight, smell, sound, taste, and touch—were processed on a wholly subconscious level, almost as if she had a second parallel mind with access to all the same data whose sole function was to evaluate each and every "frame" of information, sixty or more per second, calculate if an action was necessary, and send the irresistible order to her consciousness.

This alone gave her enormous abilities of which she was as yet not completely aware that when used would not be thought about or reflected upon but merely accepted.

She was totally unaware that she was in a city, let alone a strange city on another planet peopled almost entirely by creatures alien to her. Yet her senses and her past knowledge of cities allowed her to cross busy streets at peak hours safely and, quite literally, without thinking about it. That was knowledge the Glathrielians themselves would have lacked, and they would have been easy targets for the first speeding truck. That was why she was unique even for Glathriel. She could survive in wildly unfamiliar places because her previous knowledge base gave her sufficient information for her to do so.

She felt uncomfortable inside because walls and barriers blocked not only the irrelevant but the important as well. Enclosures distracted and had to be dealt with. Still, the knowledge base informed her that the object: Mate was subject to environmental weaknesses that no longer plagued her, and it was unthinkable that she would keep him in discomfort when it was possible to do otherwise. The concept of separating from him any more than necessary was simply not allowable. She and he were linked in biophysical and biochemical ways that neither understood but that she realized and accepted. That she had in fact induced the linkage to ensure that he took her with him she no longer even remembered; it was irrelevant. *Is* mattered; *was* did not matter and was thus dismissed from the mind unless *was* was absolutely required for a current action.

And all of *is* was composed of objects. *Mate* is. *Interactor with Mate* is. At that moment those two objects were the only things in her mind. All else was filtered out as irrelevant. She understood nothing that was said; indeed, those very sounds were filtered out as irrelevant. But she *felt* what Mate felt; every little nuance of feeling was input, to a level he could not have comprehended. These were assimilated and appended to the Mate object's *is*, which in turn formed a complete and constantly changing whole object picture in her mind.

The Glathrielian way saw life as a series of assembled objects leading to clearly pictured objectives, the latter simplified to the most basic form. Situation: hunger. Objective: find, consume sufficient food. Her one larger objective since turning Glathrielian had been to accompany nowmate. Having achieved that objective, she'd had no need for another. She understood, however, that Mate had his own objective. Because she lacked any data that the objective affected her in any way she would consider important and lacked any overall further objective of her own, Mate's objective was in control and she would support him as he required. Just what Mate's objective was she neither knew nor cared, nor would she care until and unless it affected what she considered important.

Her conscious mind saw no irrelevant external details; it saw other life as a seemingly infinite variety of colors and color mixes and patterns. She saw what was *inside* rather than what was *outside* in this circumstance.

Mate's *is* was warmth, comfort, interaction with Other; interaction produced in him a range of sensations, none of which were unpleasurable and which included some hope and optimism, which meant that Mate was interacting with Other in pursuit of Mate's objective. The Other, however, was radiating a very different *is* that Mate seemed oblivious to. *Deceit, dishonesty, coldness, cruelty—danger!* These impressions all came to her as they could only when her mind was freed of distractions. She could not interact with the Other, but she could with Mate, both empathically and physically. She knew that Mate was getting the information in the same manner as she was sending it, but while he did not reject it, it seemed only to reinforce his own instinct about the Other; neither did Mate act upon it as she would have.

If she still could think in the old ways, she would have thought to herself, *He knows the colonel is a lying, two-faced bastard with ulterior motives, but for now he's stringing the creature along.*

She was uneasy about this only because she lacked any knowledge of what the creature was and how it might be dealt with. With the creatures she'd taken on in the past, she'd been able to absorb sufficient data from Mate to formulate a course of action; in this case, however, Mate didn't seem to know anything about the damned creature, either, meaning that the only course open if the thing turned dangerous was to run like hell.

For his part, Nathan Brazil was getting a little irritated by the waves of warning coming from the girl. He fervently wished there was some way to tell her, *"I know, the guy's a slimy, dangerous son of a bitch, but I need to know what he's up to."* Still, she seemed to actually be making an important point. If this creature were to try anything now, he hadn't the slightest idea how to hurt it or just what it could do to him. He was suddenly so astonished that she had actually managed relevant and intelligent communication with him that he almost fumbled acting on it. Repressing his excitement, at least for the moment, he got control and asked, "By the way, Colonel, I don't want to sound insulting, but just what the devil *are* you, anyway? Your race and nationality, I mean. You're a new species to me."

That wasn't quite true, but it must have been eons ago when he'd last encountered such a creature as this, and he just didn't have anything to go on.

"The nation is called Leeming, sir," the colonel told him. "At least, that is the way the translators spit it out, and that's acceptable. And our kind are called Leems, not Leemingites or whatever, which is very close to the actual sound."

The name, pronounced a bit differently but still close enough, did indeed ring a distant bell. They had no skeletal structure, and the brain case was a rock-hard ball that could move to any part of the fluid body. The outer membrane was thick enough to stop most projectiles, and yet they could control their skin and fluid interior almost down to the cellular level. What they needed, they could quickly create the internal musculature to make. Arm, hand, tentacles, functional eyes, functional mouths and voice mechanisms, ears, even the semblance of a former Brazilian Air Force colonel. They could maintain simple shapes or appendages almost forever but were unable to sustain complex forms for very long, especially when under stress. The Leem were asexual, but two were required to reproduce, each consuming a massive quantity of food and growing to almost one and a half times its normal size, then splitting off that new half, which then joined with a half from the other to produce a whole new being. They ate by secreting an acidic poison that could dissolve virtually any organic life to a puddle of warm goo, which was then absorbed directly through the skin.

Now where the hell did all that *come from?* Brazil wondered. From the Well data bank was the obvious answer, but it still startled him. The Well had never been so generous or so obvious or so detailed with him before.

The data flowed into Terry from him and were added to her own internal knowledge base. This in turn changed the conscious picture of the Other dramatically, and it startled her. Mate had not known; then, suddenly, there had been a tiny burst of energy and a data stream had come from no specific point into his mind and then secondarily from his mind to hers.

She felt his surprise and initial puzzlement at it, then his comfort of recognition and his surprised pleasure rather than continued bafflement. It was something unexpected, new data that could not now be correlated.

Like her, Mate had a knowledge base that gave important data, but unlike her, the source was *external.* And while he knew the source, he had not expected the data to be given. There was something very important about that fact beyond its obvious comforting factors and its convenience to Mate, but as yet she could relate it to no objective of hers. But if it was not important to his objective beyond the obvious, and not relevant to hers, but was relevant and important beyond a doubt, then to whose objective did it relate? The priorities were clear: SELF < FAMILY < TRIBE. Mate + external knowledge base = great power. Family + external knowledge base = great power^2. Tribe + external knowledge base = ? ∞?

Such speculation was fruitless and irrelevant to her now and was immediately wiped from her conscious mind as if it had never been considered. What remained was the relevant part: that she had a tribal objective that overruled all other actions, and that was for her and Mate to reach Mate's objective. Until that was attained, reaching Mate's objective was the sole motivator of all subsequent actions. And any actions on her part to further that objective were justified.

Without exception.

Cibon,
Off the Itus Coast

IT HAD NOT BEEN A PLEASANT VOYAGE FOR THE FORMER JULIAN
Beard, although at the time she didn't realize how unusual
the experience was.

The monks of Erdom, pledged to maintain a stable society, had been faced with a pair of Erdomites, one male, one
female, from another world, another culture, another race,
now in Erdomite bodies but with their old minds and memories. Lori Sutton, once a human female and an astronomy
professor as well, was now an Erdomite male through the
oddities and occasional sick humor of the Well, two meters
tall, strong, fast, an equine humanoid with a horn on his
head and a pair of legs that could propel him at up to
twenty miles an hour in deep sand. Julian Beard, once a
handsome human man, an engineer and a shuttle astronaut,
was now a pastel yellow Erdomite female, small, with little
upper body strength, with a mane of hair and a matching
tail, coping with not one but two pairs of breasts, and with
hands that were little more than mittenlike split soft hooves.
Both were trapped in a Well World nation where only mechanical energy was allowed, a medieval desert society
where females had neither status nor rights, and where education and knowledge were tightly held and controlled by
a pervasive church run by Erdomese eunuchs. To the
monks these two were the very definition of a pair who just
would not culturally fit.

The original plan had been simple: to use one of the monks' great herbal potions to essentially hypnotize them into being good Erdomites, with a posthypnotic command that each should take the drug every night and then reinforce the hypnotic commands on the other. Only the monks' failure to command them to forget their pasts and past knowledge and a fortuitous plea for help from Mavra Chang had taken them out of the monks' clutches before the conditioning could be completed.

Julian had found herself totally submissive, without any sort of aggression or defenses, in a mental state where her whole reason for living was to please her husband and anticipate his wishes. Lori had become the strutting cavalier male, accepting Julian and *all* Erdomese females as incapable of more than pleasing men, doing household work, and having babies. He associated with other males and treated his wife as some kind of chattel slave without regard for her feelings.

Three days out of Erdom on the voyage north to Itus, they had taken the last of the drug without remembering it. The fourth day out, they went to take it and there was none left; they both went through the commanded ritual anyway, but without the potion they were aware of it and could understand what had been done to them. The effect was even worse because the old dosages had not worn off. When they said them, the statements sounded somewhat reasonable. It was only well after, when they awoke the next morning, that the full significance of it hit them.

The first realization was that they had been badly had by the monks of Erdom. The second was more than a little guilt and shame at having fallen for it.

That morning, in the cabin, they did not speak to one another for quite some time. Finally it was Julian, uncharacteristically, who broke the silence.

"I think for sanity's sake we should speak to each other in private *only* in English from now on. I think we both need the mental equivalent of a cold shower, and that's it. Not to mention the vocabulary."

"That's fine with me," Lori replied softly, not looking directly at Julian. "It seems to me that we're in enough trouble with those monks that it hardly makes a difference if we break our other promises now."

"Were you a feminist back in your previous life?" Julian asked. It seemed an odd question for the situation.

"Of a sort, yes. The word had come into disrepute because it was co-opted by radicals with a different agenda from most women, but on the basic issues I was. Something of an activist, in fact." *Although*, Lori admitted, *I compromised my ideals more than once to get or keep a position.*

"Well, now you're going to find out the truth of one thing they told you and one other thing they didn't. First, men *do* control and set the rules in society—at least in the two I know, Earth's and Erdom's. Maybe a lot of other places. That's true. And now you're a man and have to know the second thing."

"Huh? What are you talking about?"

"The men who rule? You're not one of them. You're stuck with those stupid rules the same as every woman, and you can't change them much, either."

"Thanks a lot. After the way I treated you the last four days . . ."

"Think of it as an education, or the start of one," Julian sighed. "We were trapped. Both of us. But we couldn't escape because it was built into the society. If we hadn't agreed on the temple visit, I would have been stuck with that tentmaker and gotten the treatment later, when the local monk got the drugs he needed. If you agreed but then didn't show up, they'd have sent people looking for us, and in that society it's pretty hard to hide for very long. And *then* we'd have been *kept* in the temple, but instead of just being drugged and hypnotized, we'd have been the subjects for their chemical inquisition. We'd have come out of there with our brains scrubbed so clean that not a trace of Julian Beard or Lori Sutton would have remained."

Lori shook his head in wonder and sighed. "I wonder

what would have happened if they hadn't passed me that letter. Or if they'd told me to simply forget I was ever anything but an Erdomite and *then* handed me a letter I couldn't read."

"I suspect that this friend of yours paid a handsome bribe to ensure that we'd get the letter. As to the other, remember, they'd never had two people like us before. They couldn't think of everything that quickly. But we'd have continued to drug and hypnotize each other, and over weeks, months, a year, we'd have had reinforcing visits to the temple so they could correct any problems. Eventually we'd be so steeped in our roles and behavior and so indoctrinated into the religion and culture, nothing else would have been needed. I shouldn't wonder that my next prescription might have included some mind-dulling chemicals, slowing down my mental processes until I couldn't keep two thoughts in my head at once or have much long-term memory. I'd just be another of those stupid bubbleheads."

"You think they're smart enough to have stuff like that?"

"I think it's about time we stop thinking of them as ignorant and stupid just because they live in a feudal, primitive society. They are a very old culture. Ancient by Earth standards. I think they know an awful lot about everything that is possible to use in a nontechnical society and even more about keeping things the way they are and under complete control."

"But—we're Erdomese! You said it yourself a week ago. We're Erdomese whether we like it or not. Sooner or later—"

She nodded. "Sooner or later we'll be back there and even more suspect because we've traveled abroad. I hope by then we'll have figured out some way to beat them."

"If we survive this, and if this woman's telling the truth or anything close to it, we might have a crack. The promised reward is 'anything we want.' Maybe even out of here, if we wanted it. I take it that you're not so enamored of being female after the last few days."

"Not treated like *that*, I'm not! I don't mind being the junior partner along for the ride, but I treated my *dog* better than I got treated by you! And the dog didn't have to work, either."

"I—I know. You think I'm *proud* of that?"

Julian grinned. "I think it's a lot tougher holding to principle when you're on the top of the heap instead of on the bottom. But for your information, it's not the gender I'm upset with, it's the bottom position and its permanence. Being a culturally correct Erdomese female is the pits, I'll tell you. If I were forced to go back to *that*, I'd *cheerfully* take their stupid pills. Like *this* I can manage, I think, although there's still some residual effect from that stuff. Alone in the cabin with just you, I find I can fight it, but out there, among others, particularly other Erdomese on the ship, I'm not so sure I won't have a relapse."

"Until we're well away from Erdomese it might not be so bad to keep to the fiction, anyway," Lori noted. "I wouldn't be at all surprised if some of these businessmen traders here didn't also report back to the temple on just about everything they see and hear. I doubt if they could do anything this far from home, but we are citizens of Erdom, and we can't hide that fact. They do all their diplomacy in the polar Zone, but it's as if they have a voice in every one of these hex-shaped countries. We left pretty suddenly. If they decided to trump up some charges against us, we could easily wind up being arrested and sent back through one of those gates right back to Erdom, with the monks waiting for us at the other end. I think it's best not to relax too much until we have some protection from others who know this place better than we do."

It was a sobering thought. "Thanks. Just what I needed— more reasons to jump at shadows. Actually, the residue of these past few days is different from what you think I meant. I mean, I *know* how to play the sniveling little bimbo if I have to. I hate it, but it's kind of a survival skill. No, it's not that—it's the fear."

"Huh? Fear of what?"

"Of anything. You see, up until we got the treatment, I was playacting. To a certain extent the lifetime and instincts of good old Julian Beard were still there. Spending these days as a 'pure' Erdomese woman, though, I didn't have those old senses to call upon. For the first time I faced the added burden of being a female in a male-dominated society that places women somewhere just above the herd animals or even below them. Without you around as a protector, I was absolutely *defenseless*. I had to take all the feelies from those merchants, all the guff, and all of a sudden every single one of them looked like a threat. My body was entirely at their mercy, and I needed, *required* you to stand in their way. I didn't want to be out of your sight, and if you went off, I got back to this cabin in a hurry and locked myself in, scared to death all the way here. Until now I hadn't understood why I felt the need to be locked up to be safe. I put it down to the drugs or the body or the changes in me. *This* brought it home. The old me, the *male* me, would have explored this ship from stem to stern and never had a second thought. Now, suddenly, I was in the midst of strangers, and I didn't know friend from foe. I was scared to leave and scared to stay."

Lori felt a sudden sympathy for Julian. "I think I know what you mean," he responded. "It explains a lot about how *I'm* reacting to all this, too. I've had a cavalier, adventurous attitude since becoming male and a kind of charge-straight-ahead-and-damn-the-consequences feeling. Until now I was only aware that some sort of burden had been lifted off me but not what it was. It was just that the sort of feeling I had growing up female back home was gone. When I was seventeen, I was raped by my prom date. At the time I felt disgusted, but I never said anything because there was always this feeling somewhere deep down that I'd encouraged him somehow, *let* him do it—I don't know. I *do* know I changed after that. Cut my hair real short, started to be a slob, got fat and stayed that way, just about never used makeup—made myself unattractive in general. I stopped dating for a long time, until after I'd gotten my

Ph.D., really, hung out in women's studies centers and even socialized with a lesbian group, although I never really wanted to go to bed with them. I *did* go to bed with men—a lot of them—but they were always men I picked out, and they were mostly nerds who were desperate for any female interest. They were going to love me for *me*, no frills or compromises, or to hell with them. Don't get me wrong—I knew I was reacting—but I had a justification for everything. And, surrounded by lots of women I knew and trusted, or by men of my choosing, I managed to keep the fear down. I guess that's why I took to the all-women tribe so easily. No men to threaten, and women who were not only self-sufficient but actually dangerous."

"And now we both realize that, just like in physics, nothing is really lost, it's just transferred," Julian said with a sigh. "Now I've got the burden and yours is gone. About the only thing I can cling to as a real advantage is that this body sure delivers *dynamite* sex."

"I guessed as much, considering your responses. And that's the downside of my change. I can turn on like a light switch, but everything's concentrated in just one spot. It explains a lot about my previous lovers. I feel a lot less guilt now."

They had a laugh at that and then went on to more immediate worries.

"What do you know about this Chang woman, anyway?" Julian asked.

"Not a lot. As far as I was concerned, she was the leader and demigoddess of a tribe of primitive rain forest Amazons—literally. Though, mean, and ruthless; that was her reputation among the tribe. Then, suddenly, all *this* comes about and suddenly she's claiming to be some immortal from this world. I would have sworn she'd have barely recognized anything beyond Stone Age technology as anything but magic and that she had no experience beyond the jungles, yet here she is, suddenly a different sort of person, comfortable with technology well in advance of our own and writing notes to me in ancient Greek!"

"Yeah, how'd she know you knew Greek?"

"I don't even know how she'd know I knew German, let alone Greek. Our only common language was that of a Stone Age tribe. I don't count it because I can't speak it, and I was surprised that I could read the note at all. She made it pretty basic, though, and it all came back to me. She certainly knows no English, and if she did, it would probably sound more like Shakespeare's or even Chaucer's. She'd been in that jungle an awfully long time. It was almost like she was hiding out from the world."

"From that other fellow with the appropriate name, perhaps. Brazil."

"Maybe. But I get the feeling it's not that simple. She's not just a small woman, she's *tiny*. Under five feet, skinny, wiry, but moves like a cat. She also has a confident, brassy voice and manner, but I wonder if that's just a mask for what we were talking about."

"Huh?"

"The fear factor."

"But—she's immortal, or she says she is. And according to you, the tribe at least believed that any injuries to her, no matter how severe, would heal without scars and that she could even regrow limbs."

"Yes, she's beyond some of our most common fears—if it's all true, anyway. But she still can be badly hurt, and she feels the same pain. I wonder if she also feels the same kind of psychological pain. She's strong for her size but no match for an average man. Suppose she is immortal and started life on Earth thousands of years ago? The way the Erdomese look at women and women's rights is about standard for most cultures in human history until fairly recently. I wonder . . . After a few thousand years of being a victim with no end in sight, *I* might run off to a rain forest and surround myself with cast-off and runaway tribal women, too. I sort of ran away socially for years from just one incident. And this Brazil person—I *assume* they started out together and they got separated centuries or longer ago. I wonder if that's not part of the problem."

"What? That she lost her protection?"

"That she needed his protection in the first place. Her ego is pretty damned strong. There would be only so much protection she could stand before cracking."

"You think he was abusing her or something?"

"No, I don't think so. Even in Zone she described him as basically a good person. She would have cast him as the epitome of evil if he'd done anything to her. No, I think it's more basic than that. Thousands of years in a series of what must have seemed *very* primitive societies to her, always with that fear factor . . . Suppose he simply never noticed? Suppose he, the immortal *male*, just couldn't comprehend it?"

It was something to think about but not something that could be proved one way or the other, not until they actually met this mysterious Brazil—if, indeed, they ever did. This and their mental hangover and associated guilt produced a minute or two of silence.

Finally Julian spoke. "I really don't understand a lot of this at all. If what we're being told is correct, much of what I learned about creation, evolution, the birth and death of the universe—it's all wrong. Yet everything, all the laws of science, seem to be more or less holding in spite of all that, and it doesn't make any sense. We've gone from a solid foundation down through the rabbit hole to Wonderland."

"Not exactly," Lori responded. "We don't know enough to draw any conclusions about the universe at large. There were a lot of theorists in physics who postulated bizarre theories that were at least mathematically possible. White holes, parallel universes, and much more. Even in the Einsteinian sense we casually accepted gravity bending time itself. This doesn't show that what we knew was wrong, only that we knew far less than we thought we did. You know the old saw—I believe it was Arthur C. Clarke—that says that a civilization separated by countless years of development from our own would discover and know so much more that its technology would seem like magic to us. I think that's what's bugging you—all that work, all that knowledge, and we're as ignorant of this sort of stuff as the most primitive tribes of Earth are ignorant of our science."

"It's that," Julian admitted, "but it's more than that, too. We're not talking here about centuries ahead, or even thousands of years, but *millions* of years—maybe even more than that. All that time, and look at what they've come up with! Stagnant fundamentalism, ignorance, sexism, racism, violence—all the things *we* were trying to beat. All that knowledge, all that experience—and look at it! It's not the science that they know, it's what they *don't* have, or don't use!"

Lori sighed. "I know. Still, I keep telling myself that this *isn't* the future, it's an experimental slide. This is an artificial place, maintained by a computer. The civilizations here aren't futuristic, they're by definition stagnant, limited, leftovers after the experiment's done, left over and forgotten. Their populations are fixed, their capabilities are fixed, they can't grow, they can't progress, and they can't leave. Long ago—*very* long ago—they adapted to the situation. Some of them went mad, I suspect; some developed religious justifications for all that they had. Others went savage; still others just settled into a static condition where there's no future beyond the individual's. A few may have wound up like the People in the Amazon or some of the tribes of Papua New Guinea, where they repudiated all that had been learned, rejected all progress in the same way that we were told that the makers of this world rejected and turned their back on near godhood, equating progress with evil. In many ways this is less a romantic world than a tragic one."

"Maybe," Julian said thoughtfully. "But that brings up a nasty little thought for the immediate future. This Mavra Chang is from another age, another time, no matter what her name and appearance. I think we can take that much for granted."

"She sure knows her way around. And if she's been here before, and the only way out is through this Well, this control room, then we can assume she has even more knowledge."

"But knowledge isn't wisdom," Julian pointed out. "That's exactly what we were talking about. If she's been here before, she's very, very old. Maybe 'ancient' isn't even a good enough term for her. Never changing, never able to have a decent relationship with other human beings—they age and die in what for her would be a very short time—she's pretty much an individual example of what these hexes have gone through."

"Huh? What do you mean?"

"Well, if these hexes, trapped as they are, turned into the kind of things we're seeing, what must the effect be on an individual isolated from all around her? Maybe there's another explanation for why she might have shut herself off from the world, from all progress, in a never-ending primitive tribal group in the middle of nowhere for all those centuries. She *created* her own hex, a stagnant, never-changing one, just to cope. That doesn't make her sound very sane, either, does it?"

Lori didn't like the logic of that. "And if *she's* insane, in some sense, anyway, then what does that make this much more ancient Nathan Brazil? Thanks a lot. What you're saying is that we're on our way to help an ancient, probably insane demigoddess do battle with an even older and probably madder demigod. Now, *that* is a way to cheer me up!"

Julian shrugged. "At least it makes the whole problem of Erdom and the monks seem rather trivial, doesn't it?"

Itus was, if anything, as hot as Erdom but additionally was as humid as Erdom was dry. The air seemed a solid thing, a thick woolen blanket that enveloped one and made one slow, groggy, and exhausted from fighting against it. The gravitation, too, seemed greater; they felt heavy, leaden, and it took effort just to walk. Julian, particularly with the added dead weight of the four breasts, found it next to impossible to walk without support on just her thin equine legs, and dropped to walking on all fours, something that didn't seem at all unnatural. Lori almost envied her after walking a couple of blocks. Julian did not seem as pleased, but the alternative was next to impossible. And frankly, even standing on all fours, bringing her height down to about a meter plus, she was still on a reasonable level for the natives of this place.

The Ituns were insectoids, large, low, caterpillarlike creatures with dozens of spindly legs emerging from thick hairy coats and faces that seemed to be two huge, bulging oval eyes, and a nasty-looking mouth flanked by intimidating, curved tusks. They seemed to be able to bend and then lock themselves into just about any position they required and, supported by the hind rows of legs, use their many forelegs as individual hands, fingers, or tentacles. Far worse for the newcomers than the eternally nasty faces and fixed vicious expressions, though, was the sight of all that thick hair in the constant heat and humidity. It made them feel even hotter just watching.

The Itun behind the front desk of the transients' hotel seemed a bit larger and older and perhaps a bit more shopworn than the average denizen of the hex but was accustomed to dealing with alien types on a daily basis. Unable to form the kind of sounds that Common Speech required, it relied on one of the benefits of a high-tech hex: a small transmitter attached to the top of its head right above and between the eyes.

"Lori of Alkhaz," he told the desk clerk. "Party of two Erdomese. I was told that we would be expected."

Lower feet were already tapping something into an Itun terminal. The head cocked and looked down and read something on a screen.

"Yes," the clerk responded in a toneless electronic-sounding voice. "An Erdomese suite was prepaid for you. Do you have much baggage?"

"Very little," Lori responded. All that they owned was in one small pack.

"Very well," the clerk said, and pushed a small plastic card over to him.

"Um—are there any messages for me?"

"No, nothing. It would have shown on the console."

That was disappointing. "Uh, then—how do I find the room?"

"Follow the key, of course," replied the clerk, and turned to take care of someone else.

Lori picked up the plastic card, which seemed a plain ivory white in color, turned it over, and shrugged. There was nothing imprinted on it at all, not even an arrow or a magnetic stripe.

He was about to ask how the thing worked when he noticed that a tiny spot was pulsing a brighter white along one of the edges of the card. As he turned to face the lobby, holding the card out, the spot moved. He turned the card in his hand, but the spot moved to always keep the same relative position.

"Come on, Julian. I think I have this thing figured out," he said, and moved toward the rear corridor in the direction of the blinking light.

"Moo!" Julian snorted. "I feel like a damned *cow* like this!"

You are *a cow*, Lori thought, but checked himself before he said it. Damn it! It was *tough* not to reflexively say something that sounded patronizing or offensive! And the truth was, Erdomese, for all their resemblance to equine forms, really were biologically closer to the bovine family with perhaps a bit of camel. Even their sexual temperament was more bovine, with the male overly dominant, competitive, territorial, and violent, the female by nature passive. Even the native language was divided and reinforced the differing natures; there were strict masculine and feminine forms of every part of speech, without exception. They were in a sense speaking two complementary but different languages in which every word form had two variants. In this dual track of Erdomese, the male spoke Erdomo, which was what *he* thought in, and the female Erdoma, which was what Julian naturally used.

It was why they tried so hard to converse in English; to even *think* in Erdomese was to impose and reinforce the expected roles of attitude and behavior. It was, however, tough to get around without constant effort because the Well acclimation process imposed the native language as the primary one, since language defined a culture and the system was designed to ease the transition, not to fight it. Both of them lapsed into it more often than not; they thought in it, even dreamed in it, and it gave a heavy accent to and put a cast upon even their translations into their former native tongue.

Living in a high-tech cosmopolitan hex, however, the Ituns were well aware of the burdens their comfortable home placed on most other races and did what they could. Corridors back into the hotel were wide moving walkways, and there were very large elevators at regular intervals. The key, however, kept telling them to go straight back, until they were at the back of the building itself. It then indicated a turn to the right, and they walked slowly down a long, wide corridor until the key suddenly stopped blinking and became a bright white in front of an extratall, extrawide door. Lori saw the slot and inserted the key, and the door slid open.

"Air-conditioning!" Julian gasped in English, there being no term for it in Erdomese, but she quickly lapsed into the normal tongue, too tired to think straight. "I beg you please to shut the door, my husband, so that its coolness might not flee." She plopped down on the cushions, still wearing the pack, obviously exhausted.

Lori knew how she felt. Both had their tongues hanging out, panting, their forms, so suited to the desert need for retaining moisture, unable to sweat in the humidity.

It probably wasn't all that cool in the room; they were accustomed to greater heat than even Itus provided. But the air conditioner also dehumidified, and that created a level of comfort that was unbelievable.

"I am never going to leave this room again. Ever," Julian gasped. "I am going to live and die here."

He unhooked and pulled off the small pack on her back and tossed it into a corner, then slipped off the leather codpiece he wore that felt like it was cutting him in two and tossed that over with the pack. The thing was more for propriety than for protection, and he wondered if he really needed it so long as he wasn't going to pay a call on the Erdomese consul. While a number of races wore bright and ornate clothing, many others wore little or none, even some of the most developed, unless it was needed as protection against the elements. Here—well, he probably would, since there were enough Erdomese passing through Itus on various business that he might well be noticed. If and when they got farther away, though, so that he and Julian were more curiosities than familiar forms, he might just chuck it until needed.

Clothes had been a mania with him once, as an Earth female; now, as an Erdomese male, they seemed totally uninteresting except for utilitarian value.

He looked over at Julian and saw that she was asleep. She looked so tiny and nearly helpless without him, he thought. And so damned sexy ... A whole rush of stereotypical Erdomese male attitudes, thoughts, and feelings came into his mind. The lingering aftereffects of the monks' treatments, he wondered, without really fighting them, or was it the onrush of male hormones shaping him into somebody he didn't know, somebody he should think of with disgust? Damn it, there was something new in his nature, something that made it a virtual turn-on that she was here and dependent on him. In a sense, that terrible feeling was beginning to define him. She was at least as smart as he was, perhaps smarter. Oddly, he valued that, too, so much that it was a real fear that she might *not* need him at some point, that she was essential to him while he'd been more an escape route for her. Away from that suffocating culture and away from any who might even know it, she might well eventually find him superfluous. The thought raised his insecurity to almost the fear level.

And the old conflicts surfaced as well. Damn it, he *liked* having someone dependent on *him* for a change, even though it made him feel guilty as hell.

What was at the heart of the conflict, though, was not that he could continue to suppress or fight that kind of feeling, but now, as things were, did he *need* it so badly that he might not put up the fight?

Considering how mild her own reaction had been when the drug supply was exhausted and they became aware of the conditioning, he couldn't convince himself deep down that despite her protestations, she hadn't liked it in that role, too. No, *no*! That was a damned rationalization, no better than "Well, dressing like that, she asked for it."

Had she liked it? No, of course not, he told himself. Had *he* liked it, even to the far lesser degree that he'd experienced it growing up an Earth female? But the argument somehow failed to totally convince the dual nature within him.

Maybe it was simpler but more insidious than that. In the end it hadn't been a matter of liking it or not liking it. It had simply been easier, more comfortable not to be in a constant battle against one's own language and culture, particularly when every personal moral victory was no more than that. That culture, that society, wasn't about to change, ever. And neither were they from who and what they were now.

He felt confused and depressed, as if his whole life's attitudes had somehow now been proved bogus, a self-delusional sham. People on the bottom of systems always said they wanted equality, but did they, really? Or did they, deep down, yearn more to have the situation reversed? Did the oppressed really believe the ideals they espoused, or was that just rhetoric? Did they in fact *really* want to instead become the oppressors?

It was his most disturbing fear, a fear that it might well go deep down in the "human" psyche as the sort of flaw people did not want to admit, even to themselves. But how many times had sincere reformers run for office against entrenched corrupt politicians and won, only to slowly turn into exactly what they'd run against? How many idealistic Third World revolutionaries had overthrown the horrors of dictatorship and been at best no better and often something worse? What kind of revolution had the feminist movement been when it had been limited to rich Western nations, while the women who made up ninety percent of the rest of the world's female population remained mired in the muck?

"The first thing the freed slaves from America did after founding Liberia was to build plantations and enslave the African native population . . ." He remembered that from a history lecture long ago.

He wondered if that was why Terry and the news crew had been so cynical. They'd covered the Third World—Terry's parents had been from the Third World—and they had more perspective than the closed, ivory-tower lives of the American and west European crusaders. Maybe that was why so much of the press in general was so cynical.

How much easier it would have been for her if the Well hadn't played its cruel joke on the two of them. If Julian had emerged as the male and Lori as the female, both could have retained far more of their core beliefs. Neither was really comfortable staring their alternate selves in the face, each playing the other's role.

And there was still Mavra Chang, an enigma from a previous *universe* for God's sake, who'd chosen for her own reasons to live as the leader of a band of Stone Age women deep in the Amazon jungles. Instead of trying to dominate men or help create a new equal society, she'd rejected men and all that they'd built.

And that brought up another point. It was only because of Chang's call that they were in Itus, but what the hell did he owe Mavra Chang? It was Mavra Chang whose abduction of the whole crew had destroyed his life and led inevitably to Erdom and what he was now. Indirectly, even Julian was here because of her, since without her jungle adventures he'd have been nowhere near that damned meteor.

True, Julian Beard and Lori Anne Sutton had both been at low points in their "real" lives when all this had happened, but he doubted that either of them had wanted *this*.

But the question remained: Now that they were here, what did they owe that mysterious crazy woman?

Well, of course, it was a job of sorts, something definite to do, and it got the both of them out of Erdom and might allow them to see some of this strange world. Although if there were many more of these "hexes" as miserable as Itus, he wasn't sure his curiosity and enthusiasm could stand it. But that was exactly what it was and would remain. A job. A job that could be quit. A job in which he would feel no outstanding loyalties or long-standing obligations to the employer.

Most of all, maybe it would be a chance to sort out, removed from cultural and church pressures, who and what they now were and what options there might be for the future.

Fine words, but the dual nature persisted. The intellectual half wanted to make this a totally new start, to prove that things didn't have to be the way they were back home no matter who was on top. But the other half, that dark, primal part of the psyche, wanted to bury Lori Anne Sutton, her ivory-tower ideals and her guilt trips, and become the new Erdomese man that the monks wanted. Even her logical side couldn't work out a point to fighting it, considering how much everything was stacked against change. Without even a hope of change, how could clinging to the old ideas result in anything more than a life of frustration and misery?

"Some men do run the world," Julian had said. *"The bad news is that you are not one of them."*

Damn it all! It was a hell of a lot harder to fight this nature when a person was the one on top!

He finally did begin to nod off when suddenly there was a series of steady beeps from a small room between the main one and the bath. He went in, anxious mostly to silence it lest Julian awaken, and discovered that while the small room was of a very odd look and design, it had all the earmarks of a telephone booth. There was a red bar that was beeping on the far wall, and above it a small speaker that could be detached if need be, and above it a small screen. Thinking fast, he did what seemed logical and pushed the bar.

The screen popped on, and he was looking at the face of Mavra Chang.

"Wait a minute," he said, hoping he didn't have to pick up or push anything to be heard. "I'm going to close the door."

He peered out, but Julian seemed to have just shifted position and gone back to sleep. He pulled the sliding door closed and turned again to the screen.

"Holy shit!" Mavra Chang said, shaking her head. "Is that really *you*, Lori?"

Chang's whole appearance had changed. She seemed younger, her skin smoother, her hair expertly cut very short, wearing some kind of black pullover outfit. Cleaned up and made over, she looked very Chinese indeed. Only her big, dark eyes were the same, those ancient, weary, yet penetrating eyes.

"Yes, it's me. You knew how I wound up, surely. You were there."

"Yeah, I know, but it takes *seeing* for it to sink in, I think. I don't know what my mental picture of you was really, but it wasn't *that*. Don't get me wrong, but it's just not the Lori I knew."

"I—I'm not," he admitted. "I'm just not sure exactly who I am now, that's all."

"Yeah, well, it's a shame you had to undergo all this before we could talk normally, but we'll need brawn as well as brains on this trip, so it might just work out. I gather everything went okay. God knows the bribes I had to spread around—with accompanying curses and threats of curses—to make sure you got at least one of my messages. I decided to take a gamble on Greek; my Greek's rusty as all hell, but it seemed a better bet than Latin or Portuguese."

"You picked one of the few I could handle," he assured her. "Who would have guessed that we had something of a common language all along? We could have spoken back in the Amazon, at least by writing in the dirt."

"No, no. I was pretty far gone back there; it took the shock of coming through the Well Gate to bring some useful things back to me. I'd been in that jungle, by my best guess, maybe three hundred years or even longer. I think I was right on the edge of losing all memory of anything but the jungle. But that's a long story for another time. Things are different now, and in many ways I'm as different a person as you are from the life back then."

Different, yes, but not in the same ways at all, he thought.

He noticed that her words, although they sounded like they were coming in her voice with normal intonation and expression, weren't really matching what her lips were forming. He had seen this on the ship as well. In fact, it had been very strange to walk into a room filled with a number of races, and understand some plainly while others made just weird-sounding noises or spouted gibberish. "You have a translator now," he said a bit enviously.

"Yeah, well, the one I had originally gave out long ago, and they're only useful here, anyway. It was one of the first things I had done once I had the method and the means. It's very quick, and there's no more pain than the prick of a sharp needle. The trouble is, they're not available at just any shop and they're incredibly expensive. I've got quickly dwindling fortunes here and a very long way to go. And I assume that you have your wife with you—Jeez! That sounds funny to say!—and that she was some kind of soldier or pilot or something who came through ahead of us."

"Yes. *She*, in fact, was once a *he*. An American, like me and the news crew, only sent down by the government to help with the investigation of the meteor. He was in fact a space shuttle pilot. An astrogeologist, I think. Got sucked in long before we entered while posing for a picture on top of the thing."

"Huh! Think of that! And you thought *you* had a shock! Believe me, it's not at all unheard of for the Well to switch sexes when it switches forms, but it's very rare to have two from so small a sample wind up the same race, let alone *both* switching sexes. In fact, I know of only one other case, and at least I think I understand why that one happened."

"I was thinking of that myself. She was so despondent in that culture that she was on the verge of suicide when I found her. Our marriage, I think, was the only thing that saved her life. It seems like amazing luck."

"Yeah, well, there's luck and then there's the Well. I can tell you about luck. The Well doesn't have any means of reversing its first random decision once you're processed and incorporated into this strange big family, but it monitors everything that goes on. I can't help but wonder if it somehow sensed your Julian was in danger of death by its actions and used you to correct that when it had the chance. Now, though, you're both on your own. Don't count on the Well to save you anymore, either of you."

"Well, it might explain what happened, but I haven't counted on the Well to save either of us from anything, anyway. In fact, *you* saved us from becoming good little loyal feudal types." Quickly, he told her what had happened in the temple.

"Wow! Nick of time, sounds like! Well, look, as comfortable as this high-tech hex might be, I don't want to be here or any other spot too long. I'm already sure I'm being watched, bugged, and monitored, and I'm not even sure by who."

"You won't get any argument from us," he assured her. "This added gravity and tremendous humidity are doing me in slowly, and Julian is having even worse trouble with it."

"Oh, yeah. I've been here awhile and I've gotten somewhat used to the slightly higher G, and the climate's no worse than the Amazon, but I keep forgetting that you're a different species of creature now, designed more for a desert climate and sandy soil. You guys must be *miserable*! Well, at least in a high-tech hex you don't have to walk unless you want to. It might not be the soul of comfort, designed as they are for giant caterpillars, but there is a kind of train going to almost any point we need in this hex. But it's a long, nasty way to where we're going, and I've seen worse than this place. Look, I'll tell you what. I'll figure out how to float the two translators somehow, but I want to get the implant done fast, and then we're out of here. Could we do it this afternoon?"

"I suppose I could. Julian's asleep. But look," he found himself saying, almost without thinking, "if it's too much of an expense, then we could do without the translators. Besides, in Julian's case, an Erdomese female with a translator would in the best case be exiled from any contact with foreigners once we returned. It might do her more harm than good."

Mavra considered that. "Hmmm . . . I forgot about that damned culture down there. Woulda made me puke if I hadn't seen and been forced to live in so many similar cultures back on Earth. In China some families actually drowned girl babies because they had no value or status! And they were still having enough babies to one day overrun the planet!" She sighed. "Well, it would be a savings I could use, and she will be able to understand anybody else with one. Still, I'd like more than one of us to have one. Okay, I'm going to give you a name and address. The front desk will be able to tell you how to get there. It's not far. Just be warned—that loud crackling and buzzing you hear all over when you go out will sound like a huge mob of people all talking at once when you come back. You'll understand it, but don't expect to make full sense out of it. The Ituns don't exactly have the same frame of reference as we do."

Lori got the address and repeated it back several times until Mavra was satisfied. Fortunately, the city was on a grid system, and the streets were basically numbers and Itun alphabetical characters so that he could use an Erdomese equivalent and the concierge's translator would understand.

"Okay, then. Get it done, come back, have dinner—make

sure you order room service; you won't even want to *see* Ituns eat—and get as much rest as you can. We'll finish up what we need to do today as well and meet you tomorrow at the hotel. Since I'm being so thoroughly and obviously shadowed, there's not much point to cloak-and-dagger stuff—yet."

"We?"

"Yes, there will be more of us."

"You mean you found Gus?" He hesitated a moment. "Not—*Campos*! Please, not *him*!"

"No, neither one, really. Your Gus wound up a Dahir, or so I'm told, and that's a fair distance from here, although we might be able to contact him somehow along the way. I didn't really know him, remember. We kept him and the other guy kind of out of it."

"Yeah, well, Campos is a psycho. Rapist, drug dealer, gangster—you name it. The lowest common denominator of all the worst things in humans. Now, *there's* somebody who should have been an Erdomese female! *That* would have been justice! Gus was a nice guy, very gentle, a photographer in fact."

"Well, I got no word on Campos, but I know the type. I doubt if he's anywhere near Erdom or even Itus, but the Well's been known to have a sense of humor about some people. I don't pretend to understand it, but I was led to believe that the Well actually takes your personality, both conscious and subconscious, your dreams and ambitions, even your fantasies and your fears, into consideration, but on a kind of loopy basis I doubt if anybody but another giant machine could fully understand."

"Then—the colonel Julian spoke of, perhaps?"

"Nope. Don't know where or what he is, either. No, you don't know them. They came in with Nathan in about the same way that you wound up coming through with me. I needed a source of information on him, and we hit it off. It's a kind of sweet story, as unique, I suspect, in the very long history of the Well World as your own story and Julian's, and as oddly perverse as well. You'll have to see and hear the story for yourself. Let's leave it until tomorrow, when we'll all have to discuss our options. Besides, it's getting past midday, and I want your translator in today."

He sighed. "All right, then, until tomorrow."

The connection was broken.

Lori went out as silently as possible and saw that Julian was still asleep. He got his codpiece and put it on, then went silently to the door, feeling a pang of guilt at sneaking out for this without her. Why had he done that? Denied her a translator? The devices were unlikely to process Earth languages, so she'd have to speak Erdomese to be understood by them, and as with Mavra just now, the speech she'd hear from the translator would be in Erdomese to her as well. Erdomese didn't possess a lot of technical terms, the feminine form even less so. Anyone who didn't have a translator—rare and expensive, Mavra said, so uncommon—or speak Erdomese—highly unlikely, particularly as they went farther from Erdom—would be unable to communicate with her or she with them except through someone like him. And even then some very basic technical terms wouldn't translate at all—they'd be gibberish. She'd had to use English just to say "air-conditioning."

Outside the door he felt like a heel. As he was on the moving walkway, though, he began to rationalize. Mavra *had* been groping for him to give her an excuse not to spend the extra funds and had readily accepted his explanation. And he wasn't kidding, either. Back in Erdom, where they would surely eventually wind up, for a female to even *speak* in the male "voice" was considered a sin, and in Erdom sin equaled crime. Suppose, when she spoke to a male back there, the translator changed things to the male form of the language? Even if that didn't happen, he had every intention of living in the capital and not out in the middle of nowhere when this was all over with, and she was too smart to consistently fake ignorance of a foreign tongue if it said something interesting or relevant.

Lori knew he was groping for good reasons to get rid of

the guilt, but by the time he had gotten his directions and left the hotel, he had decided that what was done was now done, and besides, if he was really wrong about this, he'd make sure she got a translator at some point along the way. By the time he reached the Interspecies Clinic near the docks, he had almost fully accepted that version.

The procedure to implant the translator really wasn't all that much. The medical personnel at the clinic, supervised by Ituns but of several races from hexes along the main coastal route here, put him through an imager, ran a three-dimensional scan of him through their medical computer, and determined exactly where and how to insert the translator—a tiny little gem that apparently was grown or cultured by one of the undersea races. They showed him how to activate it, then they put him under a light anesthetic with a simple and painless injection, and the totally computerized surgery began. In less than twenty minutes he was coming out of it with a headache from the anesthesia and a sore spot on the back of his neck.

An Itun and another creature entered and did a visual examination. The creature looked like nothing imaginable but was as close to a living version of an Earth child's toy—a long-necked little bird that hung on the side of a glass and dipped its bill into the water, then sprang back up, only to repeat the motion until the water ran out. Lori had the distinct feeling that the birdlike thing with the incredibly long, thin, straight neck could see right inside and through him, but he couldn't explain that feeling.

"How are you feeling?" asked the Itun, and Lori started to put his hand up to his neck and then hesitated.

"Uh—all right to touch the area?"

"Oh, yes. It is completely sealed. The soreness is internal bruising, but it will pass very quickly. You should feel nothing by tomorrow."

"And—it's in?"

"Oh yes. I wear no speaker to allow someone to hear me in their native language, you will notice. You are hearing me directly in Erdomese, although I speak only Itun, a tongue you are as physically incapable of uttering as I am yours, and I am hearing you quite clearly in Itun at the same time that my colleague here is hearing you in what passes for a voice in Wukl."

"You be not born as form utilized," the strange, comic birdlike Wukl put it, the voice sounding like nothing Lori had ever heard or imagined. It was a kind of chilling sound, yet without any emotion or inflection whatsoever, and it seemed only partly said aloud and partly formed inside his own brain. It *was*, of course, male-voice Erdomese, but apparently the way the creature thought wasn't exactly compatible with the Erdomese language. There were limits on these things.

Still, he was amazed and impressed almost beyond words. "Incredible! Uh—no, I wasn't born Erdomese, if that's what you mean. I entered through the Well. But how do you know?"

"Conflict is," the Wukl attempted to explain, "clear to sense. Know not base not knowable. If unpleased could mediate self."

"Don't try and follow it too closely," the Itun warned. "You will just turn your thoughts to boiling. We, too, think differently than you do, but I have had much training in dealing with others. The Wukl—well, they see things so differently from most races that we know it is difficult for them to understand others, but they are very skilled surgeons and they have good souls and desire to help. Their help, however, can be as convoluted and as unwanted as the initial problem. If given its own way, what would result would be what we might euphemistically call a surgical compromise that would be at best unique and not at all an improvement, as the injured and shipwrecked of a number of races have discovered when washed up on their shores. Nor should you take it too literally. The Wukl see everyone of us as horribly flawed, you see. We're not Wukls."

The headache was passing, leaving only the slight stinging. "Yes, I see."

"No want Wukl betterment?" the Wukl asked.

"Um, no, not at this time, thank you. But—as of now I'll be able to understand all the other races, whether they themselves have translators or not? And they will understand me?"

"Within limits, yes," the Itun responded. "You will find those limits can be daunting indeed, as the Wukl here demonstrates in one area, and there are some races simply too different in their thought patterns to allow any meaningful communication. But for the most part you will find that it will take more practice editing out the sounds than understanding what you wish. It will take a little getting used to, but for a traveler to foreign hexes it is the one thing to not be without."

"Can I go now? I think I'm all right," Lori told them.

"Yes, the Wukl is a superb diagnostician within limits, and if it hasn't noted a problem by this point in the procedure, then there is none. We have received payment in advance from your benefactor by messenger, so you are free to go as soon as you feel able."

He *was* still a little groggy, and the humidity and heavy gravity made him not totally steady, but he decided he should get back to the hotel.

He soon experienced the strangeness of hearing those alien speakers all about him, and the initial disorientation, since while the *words* were understandable, the meaning was in most cases more obscure than the Wukl. His respect for the Ituns like the doctor and the hotel people went up enormously; Ituns definitely did *not* think along the lines of humans or Erdomese.

Julian was awake and apparently had been for some time. Although Erdomese did not take baths on the whole—a complete immersion for any length of time would remove naturally protective oils and could lead to an ugly and sometimes painful itchy skin condition akin to mange—spraying their faces and upper torsos with a showerlike wand could have a cooling and freshening effect. Clearly she'd spent some time in the bath area and had made some use of cosmetics and oils both from their meager case and from what the hotel provided. To him, at least, she looked refreshed and smelled quite sweet.

"Hello, my husband," she said in Erdomese. "You have been gone a long time. I was beginning to worry for your safety."

"Chang called and made arrangements for me to get a translator put inside my head. It was no worse than going to a dentist, but it was not pleasant. You were still asleep, and I decided you needed rest more than news at the time, and almost the last words you spoke were that you didn't want to leave this room again!"

She accepted it. "This thing in your head—it means you can speak to and understand all not-Erdomese speech?"

He nodded. "Pretty much. It was a simple task, but it is very expensive. I am sorry that Chang did not have the money for both of us to have one. Perhaps someday."

Julian had no reason to doubt him, but she was disappointed. "Yes, probably someday," she repeated, knowing how unlikely that "someday" might be. It did, however, increase her sense of isolation.

"This Madam Chang speaks not English?"

"No. I don't think so. She mentioned Greek, Latin, and Portuguese but not English. But it won't matter in that case. Since *she* has one of these things in her head, too, you will be able to understand her and she will be able to understand you—in Erdomese."

She sighed. "In Erdorma, you mean. Oh, well, it is better than silence." She paused a moment, then asked, "Is there no other news?"

"Oh, yes. She's coming by tomorrow, with others—I'm not sure how many. People from Earth who came in with the other fellow, her counterpart. I don't know what race. She wants to leave pretty quickly—don't worry! She says we're going to *ride* out of here. Hopefully all the way out, and quickly."

He thought that would make her happy, but she just let it go by. She seemed off, depressed, and he went over and stood behind her and massaged her back and neck. She *did* react as always to that, and she seemed to relax a little.

"We should eat and rest," she said at last. "After tonight we may not be able to do it when we need to."

He nodded. "I'll order something from the hotel. I'm starving, anyway; I didn't eat because of the surgery."

Nor did I, because you forgot, Julian thought, but said nothing. She couldn't quite explain her feelings even to herself, but she was generally irritated by him today, leaving without a word or a message, more like the drugged and hypnotized Lori than the one from before or even the one of this morning. She'd deliberately kept using Erdoma, which made her sound like some sort of Arabian Nights wimp by its very nature, maybe to test him and see if he'd switch to English. He hadn't. When that was coupled with sneaking out for so long, the apparent start of a new pattern depressed her. Well, maybe it wasn't a trend. Maybe he was just too tired to realize the way he was acting, she hoped. Maybe it was just this extra gravity that made her feel like a hippopotamus. Maybe she was just getting her period, and *that* was a wonderful thought to look forward to when they were starting off on a hard trip.

Most of all, she needed somebody else to talk to.

Mavra Chang arrived early the next morning, as promised. The door buzzed irritatingly, telling them that someone was there, and Julian, still feeling heavy and bloated but somewhat better than the day before, went to the door and pushed the opener so that it slid back. She'd hardly remembered that there would be more than one, but she had been curious almost since hearing Lori's story to see this mysterious, ancient immortal human female.

She was not prepared for someone so incredibly tiny. Julian, although petite compared to Lori, was nonetheless pretty much the same five foot ten she'd been as a human male; if Mavra Chang was over five feet tall, it was because of her high-heeled black leather boots, and it would be amazing if the woman weighed a hundred pounds. She had a nearly perfect waist but almost no breasts at all, and big almond-shaped eyes looked up at Julian from a classically pretty Han Chinese face.

The ancient, imposing immortal of Julian's mental image shattered in front of somebody who looked thirteen years old.

Chang's tiny form was set off even more by the two figures behind her. Both stood almost as tall as Lori and stared at Julian through big green eyes with the longest lashes Julian had ever seen. From the waist up, where it curved inward in the expected way, they seemed quite human-looking except for the pointed equine ears that emerged from a thick gusher of strawberry blond hair. They were, in fact, stunningly beautiful young women of perhaps sixteen or so—from the waist up.

From the waist down they were most like palomino ponies.

They were female centaurs—centauresses, Julian thought, amazed.

And they were absolutely identical twins down to the smallest detail.

Mavra Chang smiled. "Hello. You must be Julian," she said pleasantly in a deep female voice that nonetheless sounded hard-edged and tough in spite of its speaking Erdoma. "I'm Mavra Chang. And the girls—well, you two think *you* have problems! Don't worry, though. You won't have any trouble telling *this* pair apart. Meet Tony and Anne Marie, the only other case of two entries to the same species. You see, before they went through, they were a married couple . . ."

Hakazit

FOR A COUPLE OF DAYS NOW NATHAN BRAZIL HAD HAD THE oddest feeling based on long experience that he was being followed. He'd learned to trust those instincts, but over the countless years he'd also become nearly infallible in eventually tripping up any shadow that might try it, particularly over an extended period of time. This time he'd failed, even though more than once he'd become *certain* that he'd nailed the bugger. He'd walked down to the docks, gone down a very long deserted pier to the end, then used a little secret he'd discovered for ducking down below the pier and making his way back along a safety catwalk below. He'd *known* that the shadow had followed him onto the pier; he also knew that he could not possibly have been seen going below the pier and coming back, even with the girl inevitably in tow, and he'd heard the creak of timbers and the sound of a few heavy footsteps above, going out toward the end of the pier, yet, when he'd emerged and staked out the pier from the only exit, nobody had come.

The girl was another thing. She was absolutely uncanny at spotting any potential threats or irritants, and they'd been together long enough that he could read her reactions when somebody was around who was taking an inordinate interest in them. Several times she'd had brief flashes of this wariness when he'd sensed the tail, yet after a moment, she would frown as if puzzled, then seemingly dismiss it. She could sense the colonel coming three blocks away, but she barely reacted, and then only for this brief check, when he felt a shadow so close that he could almost smell its bad breath.

He had tried without success to convince himself that it was nerves. Certainly he was antsy and frustrated as hell at being stuck in this desolate place for so long, and his money was virtually gone while his prospects for earning any more were negligible unless he moved quickly. In this one sense he envied the girl; she appeared to need absolutely nothing except his companionship.

Still, he knew that someone was around, lurking, always near. At this stage in his life such feelings and instincts were almost never wrong. But what could it want?

He was as certain of the shadow's reality as he was that there was only one, and the same one, too. Like at the pier whenever he'd temporarily shaken the tail, he'd heard it, and it wasn't a tiny creature like the pixieish Lata, who could fly and hide in any number of small places, or any of the other obvious possibilities. The thing was *big*, bigger than he was, and certainly heavier by far.

In his hotel, away from close prying eyes, he'd gone through his reference books on the Well World. The standardized written trading language had definitely changed a lot, but the basics were still there and there wasn't a language with a fundamental multicultural linguistic base that he hadn't been able to master in the amount of time he'd wasted here. Not that his reading ability was perfect, but at least he was at the point where it was mostly nouns that stymied him, and those one could look up in a dictionary.

Fifteen hundred sixty separate species of sentient beings ... That was a lot, but one could eliminate a couple of hundred off the bat: those who were not mobile, unable to function in the south, or too insular to leave their hexes, etc. That still left more than half, though.

Which could it be? And why?

The books, which were of course simplified and intended for businesspeople, diplomats, even tourists, were of little help in his attempts to solve the mystery, but they did give him a different sort of shock.

How they had *changed*! How much almost *all* of them had changed. Some socially and culturally—although few as radically as the Glathrielians—and physically as well. Up until now, the only familiar species he'd encountered were the Ambreza, who, while becoming even more xenophobic as the reasons for it had faded into half-remembered legend, weren't all *that* much different from what they had been the last time.

Dillians, though . . . He'd always loved the centaurs. The last time they'd been basically the stuff of ancient Greek legend, large and gruff and looking very much like ordinary Earth-human types welded to sturdy working-horse bodies.

If the two photos in the book could be believed, though, they looked quite a bit different now. Sleeker, smaller, almost streamlined. Of course, Dillia wasn't about to pose anything but its best-looking for an international publication, but the changes were too radical in the male and female shown to just be a matter of centaur public relations. They just, well, no longer looked like the hybrids they'd always seemed, but perfectly and logically designed as a whole. If those two were typical, he almost felt as if he were half a Dillian rather than a Dillian being half man, half horse.

And if they'd been the only ones, he still might have passed it off as a slick photograph, but they weren't. Quite a number of old familiar races looked at least as different. None were unrecognizable; none had undergone *that* radical a transformation. But the Uliks looked more streamlined, a bit less of the serpent, and the lower pair of arms seemed to be quite different, almost as if they were changing into clawlike feet. The Yaxa body had become fuller, a bit more humanoid, the head and chest enlarged as well . . . It went on and on. Nothing so glaring as to shout at a person, but noticeable in picture after picture.

Something was definitely going on here, something totally unexpected.

There was no shot of a Gedemondan, of course. He hadn't expected one, and for one to have been there would have been as radical a change in their culture as had happened in Glathriel. The book indicated that one could now climb their mountains if it were just for sport or passage and that Dillians had an actual trail network through there all the way to Palim and the Sea of Storms and through Alestol to the Sea of Turigen, giving them access to much of the Well World in spite of their less than hospitable neighbors. But, the book also warned, do not expect to see a Gedemondan at any point, and those who damaged their land or strayed off the prescribed trails or took anything with them had a tendency to suffer mental torments of one sort or another or, in cases of gross transgression, to simply disappear.

Well, it was nice to know that at least the Gedemondans hadn't changed much.

He wondered idly if the shadow might be a Gedemondan. It was certainly large and heavy enough. The Gedemondans could also play tricks with one's mind and had other strange powers and abilities, but overall, he doubted it. Their religion, their culture, the focus of their entire race required isolation. Sending one out into the world would be as radical a change for them as, well, the Glathrielians.

Maybe it *was* a Gedemondan, after all. It fit, and he hadn't really found much evidence of more mobile cultures who could perform the kind of vanishing act this one could. Several could blend in, chameleonlike, with their surroundings, but that wouldn't explain the speed and variety of places this tail had been or the wide-open spaces where he'd *felt* the thing nearby and yet could see nothing out of the ordinary.

Well, there was no way to get around the tail, particularly when he was stuck here. This invisible follower had also scotched his idea to just take a hike west, maybe to Jorgasnovara, a nontech hex that might well be a place to shake anyone. What difference would it make, though, if the shadow just followed at a discreet distance and remained invisible?

Better to get out by sea if possible. Such creatures as this had to eat and sleep; either they'd miss the boat or they would become more obvious, and more manageable, out in the middle of the ocean. He was pretty sure that a Gedemondan would have a tough time if forced to swim, although, damn it, the big bastards could probably walk on water by now.

He slammed the book shut. Damn it, he just couldn't stay around here! He didn't want to live in a damned tent out in this perennially lousy weather, and that was what would happen within another week. It was time to move, to do *something*, no matter whether it made a major difference or not. The colonel had been delaying and hemming and hawing about sailing opportunities but had yet to come up with anything concrete. Tomorrow he'd give the old bastard an ultimatum. Come up with something *now* or it was farewell. Damn it, if Jorgasnovara was any sort of option, he'd take it. If not, he'd use the Zone Gate and go back into Ambreza and get the hell out of there somehow via Glathriel to the Sea of Turigen. He could certainly work that out with the Ambrezan Zone ambassador, and *that* would shake up any tails and meddlers! If nothing else, this damned shadow would have to follow him through the Gate, where he'd be perfectly satisfied to sit and wait awhile for it, or give it up.

At least it would be doing *something. God knows where Mavra is by this time*, he thought sourly. *Probably doing better than I am, anyway.*

The shadow was there in the hotel lobby. He could *feel* it, even though, as usual, he could put neither face nor form to it. It was another reason why he felt he had to bolt. He'd shaken it once and was certain he could do it again. The watcher depended too much on its invisibility or whatever it was using; it hadn't been subtle in any other way, and that would be its undoing.

The colonel was his usual oozy self, and that didn't apply *just* to his external appearance, Brazil thought. In this case at least, the Well's oddball sense of humor—some sort of reflection, probably, of an early puckish programmer—had simply made the outside match what was already there inside.

"I can't wait any longer, Colonel," he told the Leeming. "I believe that this is farewell for us. I will be leaving very soon."

The colonel was visibly upset, as shown by his sudden involuntary imitation of a gelatin mold. "But—but just give me a few more days, Captain! The ship is almost completed. These things take *time*, you know, and one cannot *will* a complex ship into seaworthiness!"

"It doesn't matter. Either I'm on a ship within the next day or I'm out of here," Brazil said flatly. "And since, as you say, you can't materialize a working ship going anywhere near where I want to go, I'll be making other arrangements."

"Indeed? What other arrangements, if I might be so bold? I mean, there is considerable ocean between this continent and anywhere else."

"I have other possibilities. They're just more work, that's all. I've been getting too soft and lazy here, and too broke. No, Colonel, it won't do. I'm gone."

The colonel, still quivering, was also thinking furiously. "Well, give me until tomorrow morning at least. One more night. That is not asking too much, I think. If I do not come up with anything useful, you can still leave."

Brazil frowned. "And what makes you think you can come up with something in so short a time when you haven't been able to come up with anything for weeks?" he asked suspiciously.

"Oh, well, ah, we have been waiting for the ship to be completed to go where you wished to go, have we not? And if you leave on your own, you will have to make a very circuitous route, is that not so? While it is true that I might not be able to get you near your destination, I can certainly get you on the same *continent*. Let me look at what ships are in. What I find might not be very comfortable, but at least it will get you somewhere closer. Agreed?"

A half smile crept over Nathan Brazil's face. "I believe I understand things perfectly now, Colonel. In fact, I feel somewhat chagrined that it took me this long. Tell you what—you go and see what you can come up with and then contact me back here. If I'm still here, we'll talk some more. If you find that I've checked out, forget me. That is the best I can do."

"I—I think you are being very unreasonable, but I will try and find something with all speed, I promise you. Wait for my call. Until tonight at least."

"We will see, Colonel. We will see."

He watched the creature slither off and knew that he didn't have much of a window of opportunity. Within minutes the colonel would be calling in, reporting to whoever had sent him here, telling them to find him some kind of passage in a hurry, but something slow and sure to wind up going in the wrong direction. Others would be dispatched to put a close watch on him in case he did try to leave.

Of course, there was also the shadow, but somehow he didn't think that whatever it was worked for the same people who obviously employed the colonel. He wasn't sure why he felt that way, but as usual, he knew to trust his instincts.

The girl seemed surprised when he went back toward the room, but she followed. He'd gotten into the habit of using the stairs with her most of the time, not because it was easier for her but because he'd felt he was getting soft and needed the exercise. Well, he'd get his exercise now, that was for sure.

The shadow rarely followed them to the room either because it had trouble with the stairs or because it didn't feel it needed to cover him from that point.

He'd been settling his bill on a day-to-day basis, so he didn't need to clear anything with the desk. If they wanted to complain that he hadn't formally checked out and owed another day, well, let them find him to collect.

It was easy to pack, particularly now. He wanted to travel light and had almost everything he needed in a backpack. He already wore the warm clothing required, and while he might get a little gamy after a while from the lack of too many changes of clothes, he'd coped with that and worse before.

The thermal windows were not designed to open, not only to insulate the room but also to contain any climatic adjustments that inhabitants from other hexes might require, but he'd long ago figured out how they were fastened on and how they were removed for servicing and replacement. It took him about twenty minutes to undo the window he'd picked long ago and to scoop out the puttylike sealant. The window was stubborn, and while working it he almost caused it to fall outward and crash down below, but he managed at the last minute to catch it and carefully manipulate it into the room. Another bill they'd have to send him.

The girl watched, both puzzled and fascinated, as the cold, damp wind blew into the room. She watched, too, as he took out a thin rope of some very strong synthetic material, looped it and buckled one end to a grate just inside the window, then let the rest drop almost five stories to the extended lobby roof below. Satisfied that he had a good solid hold, he put on the backpack and his hat, hoping he wouldn't lose it in the wind, and went over to the open window. He looked down a bit nervously, then nodded to himself and turned back to her. There was no way around this, and he felt he knew her well enough that she'd figure a way to follow. Her refusal to use things was more a belief pattern than anything imposed, and as with most religious tenants, followers could and did compromise when they had to.

"Well, you either come out this way or you stay here," he told her. "I am going, and I am not coming back. At least I *hope* I'm not."

She stared at him, not comprehending the words, but she

got the idea as he climbed up onto the sill and grabbed on to the rope. She knew that he was leaving, sneaking away so that he wouldn't be seen or followed, and it was no contest in her mind between using the rope and remaining until somebody opened the door. She ran to the window as he was making his way down the side of the building and looked down. When he was clearly close enough to the roof level to jump, she reached out, grasped the rope, and began to descend.

Brazil watched her come down, admiring her seeming effortlessness at the pretty daunting descent. When she reached his side, he took the rope and twirled and twisted one end; the other came free and fell at their feet. He quickly coiled it back up and went to the left side of the roof area.

They had been clever in making certain he had a front-facing room, although he doubted that they had expected anything like this. The roof ran the length of the building's front but had only a small turn on either side, tapering quickly down to nothing. It was constructed of some metallic-looking synthetic, smooth as glass and unlikely to take anything driven into it with any power he could muster. The drop itself was five, maybe closer to six meters—makable, but he preferred not to unless it was forced on him since it would be onto a stone-hard surface. Nor was there anything he felt was secure enough to attach the rope to. He wished he had plungers or a basic chemistry kit, either of which would allow him to create some kind of suction cup, but while such things were readily available, their purpose would be easily divined by anyone watching him, and he *knew* they were watching him. Maybe more than one group.

He took a deep breath. Well, there was nothing for it but to jump and risk a break or sprain. He'd jumped worse and made it. He was just getting up the nerve when he felt her hand on his shoulder. He turned, puzzled, and she pointed to the rope. Curious, and relieved at least for the moment from thinking about the jump, he handed it to her. She took it and twisted a fair amount of it around her waist, then handed the rest back. He understood immediately what she was offering to do, but he was unsure about the wisdom of it. She wasn't, after all, any taller than he was, and while she undoubtedly weighed more, it still would be quite a load with no handholds. Still, he could hardly argue with her, and if she managed to hold long enough for him to get halfway, he could easily drop the rest of the distance. He assumed that she would then jump; she was extremely athletic for one of her hefty build.

It was starting to rain, one of the icy rains that passed for a warm front in beautiful Hakazit, but in this case he didn't mind since it had pretty well cleared the streets of general traffic. Not that there weren't various denizens of the hex and people of various stripes from the hotel bustling about, but they were hurried and busy. Still, it would have to be fast.

"Okay," he told her with a sigh. "Here goes." With that he dropped the rope over the side, took it, and climbed quickly down hand over hand. It wasn't until he dropped the last little bit to the sidewalk that he realized that the rope had been rock steady.

She did not wait to uncoil the rope but jumped the instant he was down, hitting on her bare feet, flexing the knees, then standing up straight. For all it had seemed, it might have been a one-meter jump. She slipped the rope off and handed it to him. He did not wait to coil it but took off for the rear of the building, the girl quickly following behind.

Walking the long distance out would have been absurd; both Brazil and the girl stuck out like lighthouses in this hex. The watchers would have the transport terminals covered, of course, and even if they didn't, they could trace them easily. That was why Brazil had decided not to leave in those ways but rather in his own.

As the rain came harder, mixed now with ice and creating a frigid slush, he made his way by the alleys and service lanes down toward the docks.

He didn't care if the Hakazit workers saw them; they were doing nothing illegal or improper using the back ways, and so they would be nothing more than idle curiosities in a boring routine. He was in his element once they reached the docks, where he'd even managed to give the slip to the mysterious shadow.

The lousy weather, even for Hakazit, was something of a blessing to him. He brushed wet snow from his beard and walked along an alley about a block from the docks, heading west toward the commercial fleet and the shipbuilding area.

Just beyond was Pulcinell, a water hex whose dominant race, he gathered, was a bottom-living species that somewhat resembled lobsters with tentacles and that tended vast undersea farms and built vast, strange cities out of coral, sand, and shell. The higher, lighter layers were inhabited by various kinds of the usual sort of sea life, including a kind of jet-propelled swimming clam called a *zur* that was considered a delicacy by many land races and by a species of water-dwelling mammals called *kata*, who, in carefully rationed numbers, were used for fur, leather, and meat. A delicacy and quite limited in the allowable catch, the creature was a high-profit item. The Pulcinell had been known to somehow punch large holes in the bottoms of poachers' boats. A nontech hex, they had some needs that required trading, and they wanted their share of the carefully managed harvest.

A *kata* boat was a bit too large for him to manage alone, but a small *zur* troller was generally a two-person craft and could, with its single mast, be handled by one man. It would be no picnic to cross an ocean in it, even at a narrow point, but he'd sailed halfway around the world alone in something not much better, and if he could move down the coast or use some of the small islands to get water and provisions, it might not be a dangerous trip.

Still, he fervently wished that he could somehow communicate with the girl and teach her how to set a sail and otherwise handle a boat. It would make life a lot simpler.

There were a *lot* of the small craft in. Small wonder, considering that the weather visible just beyond the hex barrier didn't look all that much better than the weather here. He didn't care. There were no conditions he could imagine that he hadn't already faced at one time or another in almost any type of craft.

Of course, he'd sunk quite a few times, too, but he preferred not to think about that.

And there they were, down the small street through the dock buildings, bobbing in the water between two long warehouses, "parked" in diagonal slots on both sides of three long piers.

Although the design of the small boats differed markedly, as would be expected considering the number of races that built and sailed them, there were certain basic similarities to all of them, and none looked so bizarre as to be unmanageable. The physics of floating objects didn't change all that much, either. At least, if it *did*, then more was wrong here than he suspected.

The trick was to steal the one owned or operated by a race that ate what he could eat and would be likely to have palatable supplies aboard.

He walked down the alley, crossed the main street, and walked out onto the center pier, where a large number of the boats were tied, the girl following. He was not worried about being spotted; for one thing, the sleet was turning to steady, fine snow and starting to lie on the street, piers, and boats, and the dock area was nearly deserted.

Experience had also taught him that one of the best ways to be barely noticed was to go where one wanted and act like one belonged there. With so many different races in at this ocean port, it was unlikely anybody would even figure out his species—or care.

A number of the small boats could be rejected out of hand. For one thing, about twenty percent of them had people aboard, and that disqualified them. He had no stomach for a fight if it could be avoided, particularly not against creatures that might have nasty natural defenses or firearms, and he was never big enough to win even a fair fight with his own kind.

Of the rest, about half could be dismissed as being too alien either to run efficiently or to have a chance of containing useful supplies. A winch was a winch, it was true, and a wheel was a wheel, but the designs were very different if one was using tentacles or suckers or something other than hands.

He was getting cold, wet, and somewhat snow-covered himself by the time he found what he was looking for. It was an attractive little sloop, sleekly built and designed to take heavy weather at a good clip under sail. The creatures who had sailed it here definitely had hands, and the design was in many ways quite conventional for Earth circa, perhaps, the early 1800s. There was no sign of a stack, so either it was built from the ground up as a no-frills sailing craft or it came from a nontech hex and did much of its business in similar places. That suited him, since the passage between Hakazit and Agon was either nontech or semitech and the useful high-tech navigational aids would be of no use anyway in those waters. He would in fact have little problem staying out of high-tech hexes entirely if he made a direct crossing and then proceeded along the coast.

Something inside him just told him that whatever these people were, they ate what he could eat. More of his "intuition," he supposed, drawn from the Well's own catalog.

Looking around and seeing no one obvious, he climbed down onto the trim little craft, and the girl followed, eyes darting around, ears alert for any signs of danger.

There were no tides to speak of on the Well World, but there were many currents, and ports in general were designed to take advantage of them. The diagonal bloat slips were the first step; each was basically a small canallike lock which filled when the ship was docked and raised it a few meters above the surrounding sea. If he triggered the lock mechanism, it would open, and, casting off at the precise moment, the ship would float out into the harbor on the outflowing water. Then he could turn, raise a single sail by that winch over there, and make his way out and into Pulcinell. The wind wasn't entirely favorable in the storm, and it would mean moving quickly, but he thought it was possible.

Not for the first time did he wish he could at least tell the girl how to do something. It would be very useful if she could take the wheel, trigger the sail winch, or even push the damned lock button. He sighed. Well, he was on his own, and that was that. He checked the mechanical winch on the small sail he would need, figured out the safety and the release, and decided it would work. Then he walked over to the outside wheel aft of the mast and removed the blocks and wheel lock, testing it to ensure that it was free.

Gesturing for her to stay aboard, he then climbed back on the dock, found a small metal pole with a rectangular box on it, opened it at the hinge, and found two large buttons there, one depressed. He pushed the other one, cursed as it rang a *very* loud bell that seemed to echo over the entire harbor area, then ran back and jumped onto the deck from the pier, slipping and falling in the snow as he did so. The lock was opening pretty fast—a lot faster than he'd figured—and he let go of the bowline and rushed back, let go of the stern line, and almost slipped again as the small sailing vessel lurched free and then began to move with more speed than he wanted backward into the channel. He climbed up and grabbed the wheel, feeling out of breath, then worried that the damned lock wouldn't be completely out of the way by the time he passed the wall. It almost wasn't; he felt a bump, and the ship lurched and groaned, but it continued out into the channel.

There were several yells, curses, and threats from behind him as the bell and the launch had made it clear to some of those still aboard other boats that this one was leaving in the storm and probably not with its owners, but he didn't care. He spun the wheel for all it was worth, turning the little craft so its bow faced the inner marker buoys, then locked it with the latch and ran forward to trigger the sail. He barely noticed that the girl was watching him, fascinated, and it was probably a good thing. He would have been furious had he seen her just sitting there on a hatch cover when he was so frantic.

The winch jammed when he pushed the release; he cursed, then started hitting it and banging on it for all it was worth. The damned thing was frozen! He looked up and saw that the ship was turning slightly on its own and was beginning to drift sideways out of the docking area and back toward the other boats, many of which now had very nasty-looking creatures on them just waiting for him to drift near.

The girl sensed the danger and saw what he was trying to do. She got up, came over to him, and put her hand on the stuck lever. There was a sudden electrical crackle, and steam actually rose from the winch mechanism. The lever moved back, releasing the sail.

He was far too busy and too worried even now to consider what he'd seen. Two ropes came down from either side of the sail, and they had to be grabbed and tied to the pulley mechanism on either side of the boat. He grabbed one and tied it off as she watched, then the girl went over and caught the other and handed it to him when he reached her. It was a big help; he wouldn't have expected most people to know how to tie into the remote mechanism.

By this point they had drifted very close to the pier. At least a half dozen angry shapes were atop the various lock gates just waiting for him, and he wasn't at all sure he could get out of there in time to keep from bumping into one of the gates and giving whatever was there an open invitation to board.

He ran forward again, expertly engaging the intricate system of levers, pulleys, and gears that allowed a single pilot to handle the steering and sail adjustments, and brought the craft under some control. Momentum, however, wasn't that great, and he felt a mild bump as the ship's side struck the closest lock door. Something screamed and cursed at him, and a large black shape jumped aboard and fell to the deck.

By this time he had things under control and was working the ship back out into the docking area and toward the inner markers. That, however, had allowed the unwanted newcomer to regain its footing, and it now stood there, almost in front of and just below him, glowering menacingly.

It was two meters tall and covered in thick black fur, and its huge eyes glowed yellow; when it opened its mouth, it showed more teeth than a shark, all very large and very pointy. Although something of a shapeless mass with no clear waist, it had huge, thick, fur-covered arms ending in clawed hands. On its feet was the only clothing it apparently wore or needed—an outlandish pair of what could only be galoshes, size twenty, extra wide. It did, however, have one other thing that was even more intimidating. In its right hand it held what looked very much like some kind of humongous pistol.

"Turn this ship around!" it thundered menacingly. "This is a Chandur ship, and you're no Chandur, thief!"

"And neither are you!" he shouted back, thinking fast and still steering for the markers. "I know very well whose ship this is! I was hired to repossess it for failing to make payments for much of this past season!"

"Repo—! That's *worse* than a damned thief!" the creature roared. "I *ate* the last repo agent who tried it on *my* ship! We watermen stick together!" It looked around and saw that they were still headed out. "I said turn this boat around! *Now!*"

"If you ate the last repo agent, then I've nothing to lose, do I?" he responded, trying to sound as cool as possible. "If I'm going to die, I guess I might as well take you with me. That barge over there looks solid enough to crack us up and put us under."

The creature raised the pistol. "Get away from that wheel or I'll blast you where you stand! Move away, I say! Down here! I'll take her in! Don't think I won't shoot, either. It'll blow your wheel, but I can use the other one in the wheel shack amidships!"

Nathan Brazil sighed and stepped back from the wheel

and over to the right as directed. *Well, I almost got away with it*, he thought glumly.

Suddenly a dark shape moved from the center deck behind the creature forward to where it could sense something moving. It whirled and immediately faced the girl.

It towered over her, and the mouth opened, revealing the very nasty teeth, but she did not seem intimidated. Instead, she looked up at the thing and right into its huge oval eyes.

"You! You get over with your friend—" it began in the same deep, threatening tone it had used on him, but suddenly it stopped. The big eyes seemed to squint, and the huge mouth took on a look of undeniable surprise and confusion. "You—you get—I—uh . . ." it tried, then stopped, seemingly frozen to the spot, unable to move.

Brazil didn't wait to find out what was going on. With the gun no longer aimed at him, he went back to the wheel and began adjusting the course. Still, one eye was on where they were heading and the other was on the drama unfolding just below.

Slowly, jerkily, as if fighting something that was making the creature move against its will as if it were some sort of giant marionette, the right arm was coming up to the face, the gun still firmly in its hand, and when it was at mouth level, the wrist trembled and began to turn the barrel inward, toward that mouth.

"No!" Brazil yelled at her, trying to project as much emotion as he could that she should not go through with what she was obviously doing. What he particularly didn't like was what he was getting back from her.

Nothing.

A cold, empty nothing, devoid of pity, hesitation, question.

Devoid of humanity.

She felt his revulsion, though, and hesitated, as if waiting for instructions.

They weren't very far from the barges. The water was icy cold, but with that kind of insulation the creature shouldn't have any trouble making it to them before he froze to death. Frantic to try to communicate with her and upset by this terrible, almost machinelike coldness he felt inside her, he tried mental pictures of the thing jumping overboard and said aloud, *"Splash! Swish!"*

For a moment nothing happened, then she seemed to get the idea. The big creature turned, walked stiffly to the side of the boat, bent over the rail, then dropped into the water, still holding the gun.

He spun the wheel back toward the center channel and then shouted, "Let go of it! *Let. Go. Of. It!"*

She again seemed to get the message, and from perhaps ten meters behind he heard the creature break to the surface and roar with fury. When the curses and threats came, Brazil relaxed. The big thing would be okay.

The girl seemed to be back to normal now. The feelings he got were the basic ones, of satisfaction at dealing with a threat, of a job properly done. That deep, abiding coldness he'd felt was now once again hidden, but he would not forget it.

That would-be hero was too much like himself, a fellow sailor doing what honor required him to do. He would kill such a man in a fair fight if he had the chance and no other choice, but always out of necessity, never coldly and never without profound regret.

She either didn't understand that or had discounted it. It was almost as if she'd observed the situation, done a cold, mathematical calculation, and taken the easiest route. No regrets, no second thoughts, no recrimination, nothing. The fact that she had a kind of mental power that could do this at all was scary enough, but to do it so damned coldly was . . . scary.

He had never been this frightened of something. Not in a very, very long time. If she could do that to the sailor, then she could do that to him and might well do so. He tried very hard to suppress the fear, but it was there, niggling, and that was the worst of it; he knew she could feel it inside him as surely as if it were inside her. The only thing that gave him some comfort was that she had acted only for his protection, and she had listened to him when he had insisted that the sailor should live.

The truth was, he could sense in her no danger to himself, but that wasn't what scared him so much.

What if they can all do this? What kind of game is the population of Glathriel playing, and with how much of this world?

He was out into the full channel now and approaching the hex barrier, and he turned to a more practical concern. At least the weather had prevented the other sailors from pursuing them; now *he* had to prove he was enough of a sailor to get through it himself. The snowstorm wasn't a big deal, but the dark, swirling clouds in Pulcinell right ahead didn't promise anything better.

He passed through the barrier, feeling the very slight tingle that was all anybody felt when going through one of the energy walls, and he was suddenly in tropical heat and a roaring wind. For several minutes he was again frantically working for control of the boat in ankle-deep snow on the deck while sweating from the heavy clothing he wore.

He estimated the winds at gale force, no worse, but it meant trimming sail to the minimum, heading upwind, and battling the sea with a wheel that had a mind of its own. He only hoped that the girl didn't suffer from seasickness; this was going to be one rough time.

No rest for the weary, he thought glumly, but if he could hold out, it would be very much to his advantage. He didn't care how far he went or if he went very far at all; if the storm grew no worse and if he maintained his current heading, it would put a lot of water between him and any pursuers. He fully expected to use this wind once it slackened off enough to trust.

For now, though, it was a matter of keeping the damned boat afloat. He watched wave after wave crash into the bow and engulf it and then felt that bizarre sensation only those who had sailed into a large storm knew, that of the deck shifting suddenly both horizontally and vertically at once as the bow came up and broke free to await another wave.

There was a lashing post, and he considered tying himself to the wheel station, but he'd sailed worse-handling craft than this in even rougher weather over thousands of years and countless endless seas. Once he got his sea legs and the rhythm of the ship, he would feel fairly comfortable with it. Still, it would be nice to sit down, strapped to a fixed chair rather than having to stand through the storm for who knew how long. Still, he dared to lock the wheel long enough to slip off the heavy coat he was wearing and noted for the first time that he'd lost his hat somewhere along the way.

Finding himself pretty well soaked anyway, he slipped off his shirt and was just deciding if he could go any farther when the small boat gave a sudden, violent lurch to one side, throwing him to the deck.

"What the—?" he asked himself, getting up and looking around. It was still pretty rough, but it wasn't *that* rough. *Must have hit a reef or something*, he decided, shaking his head and turning back to the wheel.

He suddenly froze, a cold chill going through him to the bone even though it was as hot as ever. He looked around for the girl but found her sitting just behind the mainmast, cross-legged, looking forward at the huge swells exactly as she'd been when he'd locked the wheel. And, yet, and yet . . .

Wet and crumpled, his hat now sat atop the topmost spoke of the ship's wheel.

Itus

"I UNDERSTAND THAT WE HAVE SOMETHING IN COMMON," ONE of the twin centauresses said to Julian in heavily accented English as they entered the hotel room.

"Yes?" was all Julian could manage, still startled both by the unexpectedly diminutive appearance of Mavra Chang and by the startling if imposing twins who seemed to have stepped out of *Fantasia*.

"You were a human male, were you not? And so was I. Not so Anne Marie, who was my wife."

"I'm afraid Tony is having a very difficult time with this," Anne Marie put in, her voice absolutely identical to the other's but with a definitely softer and gentler, almost "sweet" tone, while Tony seemed much firmer, almost aristocratic. There were clearly two different personalities inside those mirror-image heads, not to mention the fact that Anne Marie's accent was very British.

"I will survive the shock," Tony commented, as if reassuring herself as well as Anne Marie. Tony was in fact looking at the very feminine, pastel-colored, and four-breasted Julian and already seeing how much worse things might have been.

Mavra walked over to Lori and stood looking at him. While she had always projected the feeling of someone much larger, in fact she now barely came up to the middle of his chest, heeled boots and all. She gave a low whistle.

"Man! The Well outdid itself on this batch! The two guys become girls, one of the girls becomes a guy, and the other girl becomes the exact identical twin of her husband. Boy! Talk about screwing around with people's psyches!"

Lori was as stunned by the twin centauresses as Julian had been. "I thought you said two entries to the same species was just about unheard of," he said to Mavra. He left unsaid that he was startled to be "hearing" the centauresses in Erdomese in spite of the fact that since Julian could understand them, they were most likely speaking English. Was that, he worried, a price of the translator? That it translated even languages one *knew*? He wondered for a moment why he hadn't noticed this with Julian, then realized that they had uncharacteristically spoken only Erdomese to one another since his return the previous afternoon.

Mavra nodded at Lori's comment about same-species conversions being uncommon. "They are. Sex changes—no, they happen all the time. The reason generally is to maintain the balance in the hex, since you can't add territory. Dillians—that's what this pair is—tend to mate only a couple of times a year and have long gestation periods. I know the race well myself. The result is that they often have periods when there are fewer births than normal, so they're a natural to add to during one of those times, and newcomers are almost always females there because with that long gestation, they're not necessarily going to increase the population before the Well can balance things out. It would also be most common to be female if you got put in Erdom, as Julian was, since they have a lot more females than males. Lori, I think you were the exception for reasons we discussed. On the other hand, if *you* had come through first, you'd undoubtedly have been female, and Julian wouldn't even have wound up Erdomese. Hard to say. For my selfish purposes, anyway, I'm glad it worked out the way it did. Happy to have you both aboard."

The twins, as it were, were stunning creatures on both the "human" and nonhuman halves. Both stood about 215 centimeters tall, with thick, billowing strawberry blond hair that cascaded from their heads and went down the back like a mane, out of which stuck two very equine ears that seemed to be able to pivot independently of one another, and big green eyes set in an exotically beautiful face that contained elements of classical European but had other influences from many races. The complexion was a golden brown, although it was difficult to determine if it was tanned or naturally that way. The breasts were rather large and seemed designed more to hang down when the torso leaned forward, suggesting that centaur young nursed standing on all fours; otherwise, the figure was close to perfect, going down to a very small waist at the point where the humanoid torso merged into the equine half just about where a horse's neck would begin, so that the entire humanoid torso seemed to be slightly forward of the main body.

The lower half was not quite horse, either, but rather an equine extension of the torso, clearly having a single, supple backbone that ran from the humanoid shoulders all the way to the tail. The ponylike body tapered in just forward of the rear thighs and was covered with short golden hair, ending in a large, bushy tail of the same strawberry blond as the hair on their heads. They were for all that almost supernaturally supple; the backbone had to be able to flex effortlessly in almost any direction. They could bend the humanlike torso down so that they were able to actually touch the ground without bending at the knees, turning it almost backward, while swiveling the rear hips around to reach their own tails. It was in form a masterpiece of beauty and functional design.

They were the sexiest-looking creatures Julian had ever seen or imagined, all the more so because, while bipedal, she shared some of the equine look herself. She found herself thinking, *Now, that's the way it should be done!*

Lori had much the same reaction and was somewhat amazed and embarrassed to discover that he was becoming turned on just looking at them. He decided he'd better sit down.

The room, which had seemed large, was pretty cramped

with the two centaurs inside, but they made do as best they could. "We ordered some coffees and teas," Julian told them. "It was all we could think of since we did not know the nature or needs of your companions."

"Tea is fine with me," Mavra told her. "Tony, being a native Brazilian, will probably complain about the coffee, but he won't drink much else. Anne Marie, being British, is self-explanatory."

"I feel like I should help you, dear," Anne Marie said apologetically, "but I'm afraid I haven't gotten used to all this excess baggage on my rear end in rooms like this yet. Both of us have already made some *frightful* messes knocking over things."

"No, no. You are our guests," Julian told her, and went into the corridor to the bath and prepared the drinks, then brought them back out. The sight of the two centauresses standing there holding cups and saucers was almost funny.

Anne Marie looked at Julian as if studying a sculpture. "You know, I always fantasized about becoming what I am now, but I do believe that had I known of or imagined your form, I should have preferred it. You are so pretty and combine much of the best of both human and animal form."

"I think you got the best of it," Julian told her. "The status of females in Erdomese society is that of objects. It would be unthinkable for one or two females to travel alone even there, let alone to other lands."

"Oh, yes, I'm afraid Mavra has told us about that. What a *shame* for you, poor dear! At least you are fortunate to be married to someone from your own culture. I will say that Dillian society is quite comfortable and relaxed. Oh, the men like to show off their strength and do a lot of man things like drinking heavily and boasting and competing in all sorts of games and silly contests, but women are equal on the councils and in education. The people are all quite civil, so there's not the fear and pressure there is back home. I can—and did—walk the trails alone at night with no more worry than that of tripping over a log. There's quite a lot of stock taken in family. Not much privacy, but you can't have *everything*, after all. It's quite pleasant, really. More than I hoped for and much less than I feared."

Julian looked over at Tony, who seemed in general a bit less happy about the situation, but she decided it was a matter for later, more discreet discussion.

"I'll get right to the point," Mavra told them, her sharp, penetrating voice more than compensating for her tiny size. "We've got passage on a cross-country train this afternoon that will take us directly to the Ogadon border. Ogadon's a water hex, so that means taking another ship." She unfurled a map on the cushions, and they all looked at it.

"There are some places here I'd rather not revisit if I can avoid it," she continued. "Makiem is definitely one of them; dealing with an absolute monarchy of giant toads with little love for their own kind, let alone others, is not something I want to do. Parmiter is a whole nation of professional thieves and scoundrels, I'm told. I have a fondness for Awbri, but it's not much for trade and few ships stop there, and since they're fliers, there are no roads or even trails to speak of. Agon is the most likely jumping-off spot and about as far as I think I can afford. Trouble is, once we're ashore, we're in totally foreign territory for me. I'm much more familiar with the regions north and particularly east of here."

"Then why not go north through that one, there?" Lori asked her, pointing to Wygon and wishing she could read the scratches that served for writing on Mavra's map. "Or even hop a ship east? There are lots of those."

"Well, several reasons," Mavra told them. "For one thing, while the Wygon are good folks, we'd be heading up to this point here, the Yaxa-Harbigor border. I don't know how the Yaxa are now, but I doubt if they're any nicer or dumber than they were, and they were not people easily tangled with. That route is also mostly overland; we've got no flying races in our group and will be walking or riding blind. In fact, this is the first time I ever had this big a party with me and only two races represented! As for water, it damn near broke me getting Anne Marie and Tony here from Dillia, which is *not* an easy hex to get out of, not to mention the bribes I had to spread around Aqomb to reach the two of you. If all I could get us back to was Zhonzhorp, we'd be as far from any possible goal as we are now and dead broke. I think I can get us a deal to Agon. Not fancy, maybe, but it's only four days' sail. We'll also need supplies before we take off into unknown country. You can't assume anything about climate, edible food, or much else when you go overland, and in a lot of places you can't use money even if you have it. I'm not going to go over our exact route now; I'll wait until we're well away from here and in a place where I'm not certain I'm being recorded and examined. Any questions I *can* answer right now?"

"Yeah, one," Lori said, staring at the map. "What do you need *us* for, anyway?" Mavra had said more words in one gulp since entering the room than she'd spoken altogether in all that time in the Amazon. Her whole manner was as domineering and pushy as ever, but now it was accompanied by nonstop talking, as if she were making up for all those years of near silence.

"Basically, because it's between difficult and impossible to get any distance here by traveling only overland," Mavra responded. "You really have no idea yet. And also because somebody—either hired by Nathan or on their own or a combination of both—definitely doesn't want me to get up there, or at least not to get there first. If Nathan gets in before I do, the first thing he'll do is take me out of the Well master system. That'll mean I'll be processed just as you were, forced to go through a Well Gate and come out as something else. I'll also become just another mortal. I know that's my problem, but it means you guys will be stuck far from even your new homes with nothing to show for it. If, on the other hand, *I* get in first, I can pretty well call my own tune, and yours as well. You can't believe what power I can have inside there, and more important, if what I think is true really *is* true, I may well be able to take some of that power out with me. You can get whatever you want—the race and sex of your choice, riches, power, or, if it turns out that what I suspect is true, you can come with me and travel the whole damned universe."

"That sounds exciting," Anne Marie said with typical understatement. "But is it really as dangerous as you make it out to be?"

"There are things worse than death here," Mavra Chang warned. "Once I was captured and transformed halfway into a donkey. Human torso, donkey legs, ears, and tail. No hands, just legs, and unable to raise my head. Then, getting away like that, I fell into the land of the Wukl, who decided to 'perfect' my design. I spent many long years as a fat pig-like creature, always looking down at the ground. And that wasn't the *only* experience I had. No, you never know what's going to get you here, and with every evidence that somebody somewhere *is* trying to get me, there's more safety in numbers. Besides, I like the company."

There were passenger trains across Itus, but the kind of passengers they were designed to carry were built quite differently from the party of travelers. The result was that they had the choice of riding in the Itun equivalent of a boxcar—which looked as if it would easily heat up enough to fry eggs no matter how many hatches were open—or the same equivalent of a flatcar, with some thin but strong metal fencing, a meter or so high, placed around the edges. They chose the latter.

After watching the increasingly boring countryside go by, Lori decided to try to nap; Anne Marie—at least Julian *thought* it was Anne Marie—went over and spoke to Mavra, and that left Tony down on the other side of the flatcar staring off into space. Hesitantly, Julian made her way over to where the centauress who had said that they had much in common but had otherwise said little was standing. Julian wasn't really sure how to approach either of them or even if she should, but it was worth a try. Still, she stood there, waiting to be noticed.

For a few moments the centauress continued to stare vacantly to the side, but then she said in that same accented

English, "I think you are even more unhappy than I, are you not?"

"I—I'm not sure. You are—Tony? Is that right?"

"Yes. And you are—Julian? Is that right?"

"Julian Beard. Or so I was. Lori-Julian now. I can understand how it can be tough on you, winding up the identical twin of your wife, but I still envy you. I would trade places in a moment, except I couldn't do that to *anybody*."

"Yours is one of those medieval cultures where women are chattel, I gather."

"Pretty much, yes. Sort of like some of those Middle Eastern societies back on Earth, only worse. This culture is built into the genes. The fight, the aggression just sort of drains out of you. Not all at once, but little by little. I was a hell-raising bitch like they'd never seen when I first woke up there, but over time it began to dribble away. The body chemistry, brain chemistry, whatever, just takes over. It's not that you like it—even the ones born this way mostly don't like it—but you just can't help yourself. I was able to keep a little of my old self, enough for my self-respect, so long as Lori was remembering his own former self and giving me some room, but lately he's been acting, well, as badly as I think *I* used to act when I was a teenager. I was a handsome guy—triple-letter athlete, honor student, you name it. The girls used to fall all over themselves trying to get my attention, and I was so macho and so full of myself, I pretty well treated them like toys. I admit it. Even after I got married, I cheated. Hotshot air force officer, poster boy, often away from my family."

"You were married?"

"Divorced."

Tony paused. "I see. But this Lori, she was on the other end of such behavior, was she not? Growing up, I mean. And now the tables are turned. Are you Catholic?"

"No. Not much of anything, really, although my parents were Methodists."

"I was just curious. I have many differences from you and your life, but in one way I find a certain sameness. I feel as if I am in purgatory, that I was not that bad a man, but the angels have found the one way to show me my sins and crumple my pride. Perhaps that is what this is. *Purgatorio.* Not as Dante imagined it but the same in the essentials. For Anne Marie it is different, because she never even had much chance to sin. For her this is a wondrous fantasy, and she is amused but not overly upset by my own state. One would think it would be more difficult to deal with having four legs and the bottom half of a horse than with changing to a woman, but I am a Latin and I was raised in a culture where this is simply unthinkable. I believe that if it were not for my love of and duty to Anne Marie, I would have killed myself." He hesitated. "No, that is not true. The nuns did too good a job on me for me to take my life. But I would have left alone and wandered this world until I died, a hermit to my own kind. This now I cannot do, so I must learn to deal with it. In a Latin culture, *macho* means more than merely what you Americans would call being a 'male chauvinist pig.' In fact, it should not even mean that at all. It is a code of behavior, a set of duties and responsibilities for men, a way of thinking and approaching life. Not that there are not millions of womanizers, but I was brought up too well to be one of those. I *respected* women and loved them, but as a man. Even though we could never have sex, I was never unfaithful to Anne Marie."

"You could never have *sex*?"

"She was badly crippled when we met. I was a pilot for Varig, and I was blinded in an accident. At one stroke my passion and livelihood were taken from me forever. It was while recovering in an English hospital that I met Anne Marie. She was so much more battered and broken than I, yet she was not there as a patient but as a giver of care and love. Other than her mind and soul, which shone through anything, even my darkness, the only other thing that worked perfectly on her was her eyes. So, together we became one person. She provided my eyes and my soul, and I provided the body and strength she never had. It was a love beyond anything you might imagine, and sex had virtually nothing to do with it."

Julian was absolutely amazed at hearing this. "I think that's an amazing story! My God! And you came through together and wound up the same species and still together, too."

"I fully admit to never quite believing the whole story until we went through that gateway in the fallen rock," Tony admitted. "Even then I did not believe that we were truly in another place, on another world. I was not sure that we had not died, except that I was still blind and my knee hurt from falling on that hard floor. Anne Marie almost *did* die; her wheelchair did not arrive with us, and the shock of being flung onto the floor was almost too much for her. Captain Solomon, as we knew him, led me as I carried her to the place where they gave us comfort and what is, I suppose, the standard briefing. Still I did not quite believe. I thought that it must be some sort of dream or trick, or a hallucination, that we had begun our suicide pact or perhaps that I had gone mad. *Still* I clung to her, afraid to let go, and they decided we should go through without delay because of her failing state. I thought she was at least unconscious, but just before we leapt, she whispered, 'Centaurs. There are *centaurs* here, Tony. I saw one! Hold me tight and leap and think of me and centaurs!' And I was so desperate that it was all I *did* think of, down to my core. At that moment, and only at that moment, I found myself believing it, believing all of it, and the thing that I was horribly afraid of was that we would be separated, that we would be separated forever by distance and perhaps by species itself. That we would become monstrous to one another. With all of that in my head, I went forward . . . And I awoke in a forest glade as you see me now."

The first thing, the very first thing he did, was open his eyes and see. See normally, see perfectly, see as well as he had when he had taken his first pilot's examination. There were

*colors and shapes and textures that had been but somewhat
blurred and idealized memories.*

He could see!

*And then he had seen her, stirring, trying to get up, and
he'd known instantly who she was although he'd never
seen her picture or allowed anyone to describe her. He'd
known her hair was blond and her eyes were green, and
that had been enough.*

*He'd thought, wonderingly, that she made the most beau-
tiful centauress in all creation.*

*He also felt the weight and the difficulty in breathing and
orientation and hauled himself up to standing at almost the
same moment that she did. Standing on all fours, facing
her, looking at her, knowing that his prayers had been answered. They were together and of the same kind!*

*And then she had stared at him, first in awe, then in
wonder, and said, "Tony? That can't be you, dear, can it?"
And she had continued to stare, an expression that was half
shock and half bemusement on her pretty face.*

*"Then—it is true!" he'd responded, his voice sounding
very strange to his ears. "Then we are still together! And
whole!" He did not care what form they were, human, centaur, crocodile, or swamp rat, only that they were no longer
blind or infirm but healthy and still together. Still, he sensed
that something was wrong. "What is it, Anne Marie?"*

*"I'm afraid that we're a bit more together than either of
us thought," she'd responded hesitantly. "I wish we had a
mirror, but, well, look at as much of your new self as you
can and be prepared for a bit of a shock."*

"It was the one thing that I, that *neither* of us, had ever
thought about, even *considered*," Tony continued. "It is still
very hard for me. Not for Anne Marie, I don't believe. Not
really. As before, she sees more inside a person than the
surface. But for me, and the culture in which I was raised,
it is much, much harder. I think it gives the old term 'soul
mates' a whole new meaning, does it not?"

Julian could think of a lot worse fates, but needing sympathy, she decided not to deny it to another. Still, she really thought he was lacking a lot of perspective. "It could have been much worse. Both of you as females of *my* race, for example. Or the ultimate fear you mentioned—that you would be of two species monstrous to one another. I of all people understand your shock, but I would trade with you in a moment."

"Oh, I do not doubt that!" Tony responded. "And I sympathize. Still, hormones can only account for so much of anyone's behavior, true? Otherwise, why do both of you have minds and wills? Both you and Lori must learn to control your new selves. The real problem is that you see yourself in your husband because you grew up a man, and you see yourself as the equivalent of how you perceived those young girls who threw themselves at you in your youth. Neither of us grew up female. Neither of us has the grounding of experience in the differences that brings, so we do not know how to cope. You yield because you do not know how to defend as *she* would. I fight when I should yield because my subjective universe was far more rigidly divided sexually than yours by my culture and upbringing. You are in despair because you cannot be *her*, and you cannot be your old self, and you do not have the experience or tools to be someone new. I—I can accept this. I was, after all, prepared to die with her, and I find some old prejudices crumbling now, the most basic of which is that it really does not feel that much different to be a woman. The problem is not with the body but with the mind, with needing a whole new frame of reference—not just accepting it and living with it myself but accepting the way others now perceive me and react and interact with me."

"You mean the way men treat you."

"No, I mean the way all others treat me. The way men look at me even when they are being nice, the very words and approach they take when speaking to me, the way certain conversations are closed to me now. And it is not just the men. The women react differently as well. As I am certain you know, a conversation strictly among women is quite different from one between men or between men and women."

"You can say that again," Julian agreed.

"So it is a matter of learning the rules, as it were. But I can no longer be Tony, the old Tony. Not like this. Not even to her. And I do not know how to be anything else, particularly with her. And *that* is something that I understand and she, not having been male, cannot yet grasp. I can be her—sister, her best friend, but I can no longer be her husband."

"Maybe. Maybe you're right. We've all got a lot to learn." She decided that this was enough mutual wallowing for now. What Tony had said was true, but it was damned hard to feel sorry for the centauress when *she* would sell her soul to be either one of them. "On the other hand, this Mavra Chang is something else, isn't she? She reminds me of a couple of women astronauts I trained with. Tough, knowledgeable, able to handle almost anything or anyone no matter what her size and sex, but still undeniably feminine."

"She is indeed someone quite unusual," Tony agreed. "I can only hope that toughness rubs off on the rest of us."

"Um, I'm curious," Julian said cautiously. "Is this what Anne Marie says she looked like? I mean, are you now a clone of her?"

"Clone is a good term," Tony replied. "We *are* clones of a sort—they were so amazed at us that they sent us off to a hospital and took samples, which, I believe, were sent out to one of the high-tech lands. I believe the interest was in the fact that we even had the same fingerprints. Even identical twins do not quite have that. We are genetically absolutely identical. Only the personalities and experiences are different, and that makes quite a difference indeed."

That was fascinating but not the answer to the question. "No, I mean, do you look like she used to? I know you said you didn't want to have her described, I assume so you could hold a mental picture, but surely she's said something now."

"Oh, I see. No, we do not look like she used to. In fact,

I can see something of my mother and one of my own sisters in us. I think that somehow, we were designed out of the genetic patterns of her mother and my maternal chromosome. Or so it was theorized. We are a combination of the pattern and look of the best of both of us. As for the horse part, well, I have never seen a horse built quite like this, with such style and grace, as it were, looking at her and thus myself from my old male vantage point, but I am certain that wherever it comes from, it is not in either of our ancestries."

Julian chuckled, then suddenly realized that it was the first time she had laughed at all on the Well World. Tony had at least a sense of humor about things, and that was what would certainly pull her through to some solution to her own inner conflict. The Erdomese could use something to laugh about, but there had been little to do up to now.

Anne Marie came over to them. "Oh, I'd hoped you two would get along!" she gushed. "Tony has been too much in a shell since all this, haven't you, dear? I, on the other hand, have been quite excited by it all. I've done more and seen more in the past few months than I had ever *dreamed* to do in a lifetime! I find everything here so *frightfully* fascinating!"

Julian wondered if that sense of adventure would last if they got into a really bad situation. She couldn't imagine that Anne Marie could kill a fly willfully and with malice aforethought.

The train ran silently along on a magnetic track, levitating just above the surface. There was no engineer, no crew; the entire process was automated, and each car could be switched in and out at will or become part of a new train at almost every junction. They'd gone through a large number of such junctions, when everything slowed to a crawl and pieces of train were diverted, some were added, some were taken away on spurs or alternate tracks, and a new train was put together. It was a marvel of efficiency and served the hex well.

Now they slowed for one more switching yard and in a

matter of minutes watched the long train divide into five separate sections and go off in all directions. There was a slight bump as their own car was joined to other sections old and new, and then everything speeded up once more.

It was a few minutes after this that Mavra Chang had the odd feeling that something wasn't right. At first she couldn't put her finger on it, and she began to inventory her surroundings to see what it was that was setting off warnings in the danger-sensing area of her brain. The car was the same; the other cars were innocuous enough, and the surroundings looked little different from what they had looked like before. What was the problem?

She was almost ready to dismiss her feeling as being too jumpy when suddenly she had it. The sun!

They had been going generally due west. Now, suddenly, the sun was not behind them as it should have been in late afternoon with the Well World's west-east rotation, but on their left. They were still going west, but it was now south-southwest. Clearly the car was no longer heading for the port at all. Something, or someone, had ordered them diverted.

"Everybody! Listen up!" she shouted. "Lori, wake up! We've got trouble!"

Lori stirred and shook his head to clear it. "Huh? What?"

"They've switched us south onto another line," she told them as they gathered around the tiny woman.

" 'They'?" Lori asked. "Who's 'they'?"

"If I knew *that* for sure, I could deal with them!" Mavra snapped. "Never mind that now. Somebody with influence who definitely doesn't want me to get up to the Well first, that's for sure. Anybody here a good judge of land speed? About what speed do you think this car is making now?"

It was Julian who spoke up. "At its maximum, no more than two hundred kilometers an hour," she stated with a certainty that surprised them. "At average, about one hundred forty."

"That's a fair enough estimate," Mavra responded, impressed.

"You were never in astronaut training."

"That's *right*! I'd forgotten you were a spacer! Okay, and according to this cheap watch I bought months ago, we've been going for three and a half hours. That would mean we're about two-thirds of the way, or were when we were switched. At the angle we're now traveling, if it stays fairly constant, we'll still reach the coast, but way, way south of where we want to be. There's only one decent harbor on the west coast, or so I'm told; the coastal waters are otherwise too shallow. Mostly small towns along there dependent on rail. I'd say that they're aiming to bring us in down there at one of the small towns on the southwest border, maybe the southernmost one, at or after dusk."

"But *why*? That's the question," Lori said, frowning.

"That's easy enough. We miss our ship, we've got a long, slow walk up, since we can't trust the trains anymore, and we're in the kind of area where we always will stick out like sore thumbs."

"But we can't *walk*, not in this humidity and gravity!" Julian protested. "At least *I* can't!"

"This is not as much of a problem for us," Tony pointed out. "If need be, I could carry you and Mavra, too, and I am certain that Anne Marie could carry Lori."

"Of course," the other centauress replied. "It is a *bit* more difficult for us, and we have to go slower because of the burden on these thin legs, but you would hardly add to the burden."

Mavra shook her head. "Uh uh. We might do that for a short distance but not a long one. Not only do I want out of here, I want to get lost. At least to whoever's behind this. And the *last* thing I want to do is make a grand march under these conditions to a place where somehow I know they won't have a ship for us."

"But what is the alternative?" Tony asked her.

"If we keep going this way, we'll come in to the southwesternmost yard in a small town almost at the Gekir border. Gekir's a nontech hex and I've never been there, but my experience has been that if you want to get lost, get into a nontech hex. No mass transportation, but no mass

communications, either. Nontechs are also the most dangerous for a lot of reasons, but while I don't remember much
about them, what was said indicates that the Gekir are not
a mean or hostile people, and there's some trade between
there and Itus. As to what kind of creatures they are, I
haven't a clue, even though we might or might not have
seen them among the races back in the capital. If we're
lucky, there might be some kind of sailing vessels that call
along the coast. It's worth a try."

"But if whoever is chasing you is influential enough to
divert our railcar, they will have people watching out for us
at the town, won't they?" Julian asked worriedly.

"Yes, so we'll have to get off before that point and avoid
the town. It shouldn't be too hard to do. They're bound to
have a decoupling yard just before the town to route the
various cars to loading areas. When the train slows, we get
off, fast. It'll still be moving, so watch yourselves, but it
should be moving at a crawl, at least up to the switch.
Tony, I assume you and Anne Marie could jump off."

"I don't think that would be a problem, but we'll have to
time it right," Tony replied. "I don't think either of us
should risk a broken ankle at this point, and the heavier
gravity is a major threat. Wait a moment! Anne Marie,
come give me a hand here."

The two centauresses went over to the left side and studied the short staked fence. "They look just placed in," Anne
Marie said, and with both hands tried to pry one up. She
tried as hard as she could, but it wouldn't budge. "No go,
I'm afraid, dear."

Tony got close beside her. "Both of us together, then."

They tried, but it was as if the panel were welded on.

Julian came over and looked at the panel as well, bending down to see what might be holding it in. "I think it's
more magnets," she said at last. "This train runs on the
basis of magnetic polarity. There are two strong electromagnets underneath, one the track and the other on the undercarriage. When power is applied, they repel, we float
essentially friction-free, and by moving one set, speed can

be quickly achieved or slowed, even stopped on a dime. But the stakes, I bet, are matched to the polarity of the undercarriage. When it's powered, they're pulled tight." She thought a moment. "I wonder if there are any dead spots."

"Dead spots?" one of them asked.

"Yes. Have you ever ridden on a subway—underground, metro, or whatever—or an electric-powered train? There's often points where the track is either not powered because of some repair or connector or the power source changes. The lights might flicker or even go off, but it's brief and the train's forward momentum keeps it rolling until it gets to the next powered section. I thought I felt a slight loosening at one point while I was leaning on it here, and there were the vibrations rattling the stakes briefly, but then it was tight again. If there's another, then in that brief moment this panel should be able to be pulled. *If* it's really held by the electromagnets, that is."

"There is only one way to find out," Tony said. "I will just stand here and pull on it and see."

Although it was a rather simple explanation of the principle, Lori found himself momentarily taken aback by Julian's sophisticated knowledge, even though he knew her background. He hadn't been used to her being very assertive of late, and it gave him oddly mixed feelings he neither liked nor wanted to deal with. Julian had come up almost effortlessly with the solution to a problem of the sort that only seemed obvious when it was explained. The rattling had happened every few minutes off and on since they boarded, yet only Julian had put it together. Although he was quite proud of her, the two warring halves of his nature could not have been more divided on interpretation. The Lori Sutton part was cheering; the Lori of Alkhaz part was furious that she'd just given it to them all rather than tell him in private so that he could bring it up to the group.

Several minutes passed, and a bored Tony, feeling circulation going in her arms, was just about to give it up when suddenly the panel came up and she staggered back a bit, barely keeping balance. It didn't come all the way out but was now held only by two flat pins, no longer flush with the flatcar floor.

"If need be, I could probably kick it down at this point," Tony commented, "but I think that Lori might do better pushing up from beneath. Just be sure you don't fall off the train when it comes up!"

Lori looked at it dubiously. "Yeah, right," he said, but lay down, got his body in as close as he could with his legs well beyond the almost-free panel, and pushed against the very solid-feeling section.

When the moment came, tense as he was, the panel almost did take him with it; it flew up and away, and he suddenly felt himself going forward into the opening. Only Anne Marie's strong hands grabbing his legs and bringing him back in saved him, and, being hauled back on his stomach, he was suddenly *very* thankful he'd kept wearing the hardened codpiece.

"Wow! Can she *bend*!" Julian gasped. "She didn't even have to *kneel*!" But she rushed to Lori.

Mavra nodded and said to herself, "Things aren't quite as static as they seem on the Well World. Dillian evolution has sure done a neat job on them!"

Julian bent down next to Lori, concerned. "Are you all right, my husband?" She asked in Erdomese.

He nodded. "Just bumped around a bit. I will be all right in a minute or two." He turned on his side and looked back and up at the centauress who'd grabbed him. "Thanks a lot, Tony."

"Think nothing of it, dear," responded Anne Marie, not taking any offense at all at being confused with her twin.

Mavra came over and inspected the opening. "Okay. That means Lori, Julian, and I can sit on the edge and then jump off rather than having to contend with a meter-high hurdle, and you two have a straight jump."

"How much longer will it be, do you think?" Julian asked her.

Mavra looked at her watch and then at the sun. "Maybe fifteen minutes. Okay, you've all seen these switching points; you know what they look like. Get as far away to the south—the direction that you'll jump—as you can as fast as you can and stay out of sight of anybody in the yard area. Assemble behind the first building that gives us cover and wait until we're all there. Understood? They may not be expecting us to jump, but they're sure to have somebody at the station to keep a tail on us, and it'll most likely be an Itun hired for the job. From this point we avoid Ituns until we're across the border."

They waited as the shadows grew and the light began to fade around them. Darkness came quickly to the Well World, and within a few minutes it would be pitch black. That actually bothered the two Erdomese the least, since they could simply lift their natural eye filters and see the full spectrum. Mavra and the two Dillians, however, had no more night vision than ordinary Earth humans, a thought that occurred to Julian.

"We should jump off last," she said to Lori, "because we can see."

He shook his head. "No, I think we go first for that very reason. We can find *them* a lot easier than they can find *us*, and I think it would be better to be on the ground just in case one of them has a problem with the jump."

"All right, then. You go and I'll follow. Night is almost completely upon us, and there are many lights not far ahead. I can already feel us slowing just a bit."

Lori turned to Mavra, who had noticed the lights as well, and she nodded. "Any time you feel right after we're slow enough. Just don't take it too fast. We'll get out."

The Erdomese moved to the opening in the flatcar stakes. Lori sat, legs over the side of the car, uncomfortable sitting on his behind because of the tail and tailbone. It was not a normal position for Erdomese, and he decided to jump as soon as he felt it was safe.

"Remember the heavier gravity," Julian warned him. "You will hit very hard, my husband."

"You take care, too."

The train was definitely slowing now, going perhaps thirty

kilometers per hour, and it continued to slow. Lori's tailbone was hurting badly enough that when it was down to about twenty, he took a deep breath and launched himself into the night. He hit as hard as Julian had warned, pitched forward, and found himself rolling down a small embankment into a fetid, muddy drainage ditch. Covered with stinking mud, he almost panicked, got control, and clawed himself out of it and up onto dryer land. He lay there, breathing hard, for a minute or so, then picked himself up. He not only stank, he was sore, and his left ankle and right wrist stung when he moved them. For a moment he was afraid that he'd broken something, but he quickly realized that they were probably only sprains and not that serious. By force of will he made his way in the darkness just below the tracks toward the lighted area about half a kilometer farther on.

Julian came to meet him, walking on all fours. "Are you all right?" she asked, concerned, then twitched her nose. "You sure don't *smell* all right!"

"Rolled all the way down into the drainage canal. Didn't pay enough attention to the slope. I've got some twists, but I can handle it. You?"

"A little bruised but not bad. It was slower, and I had a more level area. About the only problem I'll have is getting grass stains out of my fur."

He managed a chuckle at that. "The others?"

"Mavra was right behind me. She just jumped out, rolled once, and landed on her feet almost beside me! Like an acrobat or something. She told me to find you and she was going to check on the Blondie Twins."

"Let's join up," he told her, gesturing forward.

"You are limping! Come! Put your hand on my shoulder, and I will help you," she invited, standing erect.

"I—I can make it on my own," Lori insisted, then grimaced and almost fell forward. She caught him and helped brace him, and this took just enough weight off that he was able to manage it.

"I thought you couldn't even move, let alone stand in this place," he noted.

"I grow strong when I am needed," she responded, quoting a female Erdomese proverb.

Both Dillians had jumped without a hitch and now waited with Mavra for Lori and Julian to join them in a dark area behind the first automated switching tower. Mavra, seeing them in the very dim glow of the tower lights, motioned for the much larger centaurs to remain where they were and ran toward the two Erdomese. "What happened?" she asked. "Are you hurt bad?"

"I'm not sure," Lori answered honestly. "I *thought* the ankle was just twisted a little, but now I'm not so sure. It doesn't feel broken, but I think it's a hell of a sprain."

"Well, a very ancient man who knows the Well World far better than I do once said to never travel without a Dillian if you can manage it. We can repack all the stuff on one of them and put you on the other. Don't argue! Whoever's watching us has probably already discovered that we're not there. The sooner we get away from here, the better!"

When they reached the Dillians, one of them was already repacking the saddlebags on the other. Then the one who carried all the equipment helped Lori onto the other's back.

"Ride forward," the centauress suggested. "That should take the pressure off your tail as well. And watch that horn on your head! I don't want to get stabbed if I have to make a sudden stop!" Left unsaid was the rather noticeable stink of swamp and mud permeating his hair.

He felt awkward and helpless and, even worse, stupid. It was almost like a horse riding a horse. He was just never designed to ride on the back of a soft animal, but there was little choice at the moment.

Mavra turned to Julian and said, "Well, you're leading the way because you can see and we can't. Can you handle it? I know how hard this high G is on you."

"I'll be all right," she assured the woman in black. "You said south, right? How far do you wish to go tonight?"

"Well, we're going to be moving a lot slower and more cautiously than I planned, but we ought to go on until at least one of us has to stop. It shouldn't be more than a dozen kilometers or so to the border if we head due south. That's a haul on foot in the dark under these conditions, but we haven't done much more than rest on our duffs all day. Can you make it?"

"Yes." No equivocation, no hesitancy. Mavra liked that.

"I think you're gonna do just fine, Julian. You sure you know which way's south? We had a bend just before we came in."

"I know. It is something in the Erdomese brain. Once we have a fix on the sun at any point, we always know direction, even when the sun is gone." She looked around, thinking. "The first thing is to find a road or trail of some kind going in our direction and parallel it. I do not think we should risk Tony or Anne Marie tripping over jungle vines or fallen logs. Just keep close and I will get you through."

"You sound like you've done this sort of thing before."

"Air force survival training. This is no worse than the jungles of Panama or Honduras."

"That's *right*! Lori said you were once captain of a spaceship."

"No, captain was my rank in the air force. A military service. I was a mission specialist on the space shuttle, not a pilot or commander, although I had a jet pilot's license."

"Too much of this is new to me," Mavra admitted, her translated voice coming to Julian's ears as an odd but understandable mixture of Erdomese and English, depending on the terms used. "I was in the jungle, cut off, for so long that it wasn't until a few years ago that I even realized that Earth had progressed to power tools, let alone flying machines and spacecraft, and by that time I saw them only as evil magic. Until I spoke with Tony and Anne Marie here, I had no idea Brazil wasn't still a Portuguese colony, let alone that your own country even existed. It was all very ironic. All I was doing was holding out in the wilderness until technology advanced to where I could get off that planet, and I managed to fall into a trap where I rejected all technology. Even now I'm sweating like a stuck pig. I still haven't gotten used to clothing, and these boots feel bizarre."

"What's stopping you from taking them off? The nearest Earth-human type is probably a thousand miles from here, if even that close."

"Practicality, mostly. Certainly not modesty. I was *born* without that word having much meaning. Back in the Amazon, that was *my* jungle. I loved it and still do, but I knew everything about it. Everything. This isn't my jungle. I don't know the effects of anything I step on here, and any protection is better than none when you've only got bare skin in an unknown land." She dropped her voice low. "Hell, I remember when female Dillians wore bras, and they weren't nearly as hung as those two."

Julian also lowered her voice to a high whisper. "Is it just me, or is it really difficult to tell which is which unless they speak? I mean, I've had the eeriest feeling that the same one I spoke to who was Tony, definitely Tony, was later talking like Anne Marie."

"I know what you mean," Mavra whispered back. "Actually, I'm sort of relieved that somebody else feels it, too. Maybe it's just how absolutely identical they look, but it's spooked me more times in the past few weeks than I can tell you."

"That is what I mean. Is there something else about them I do not know but should?"

"Could be, but if so, I don't know it, either. If it *is* more than mental confusion on our part, I'm absolutely positive that they aren't aware of it themselves. I just don't know. Every time I say that absolutely nothing can surprise me anymore, something does. How the two of them were processed is unprecedented; you and Lori make a different but equally unprecedented case. I don't know *what's* going on here, but until I get to the Well, I can't find out for sure myself. Even the Well World seems odd. I always thought of it as static, too tightly managed to change radically, but there are many differences. Differences you wouldn't notice from one time here, but it's *different*. Some of the cultures are changed, a few radically so. There are differences in alliances, attitudes, you name it. Even the races are different. Not a lot in some cases, a great deal in one or two that I've seen, but there are changes from radical to subtle in all the ones I knew. It may be a normal thing, as with all worlds, but this is not a normal world, nor was it ever intended to be. I can't help wondering if it feels the same way to Nathan, wherever he is."

That brought up a point Julian was even more interested in. "This Nathan. Tell me about him."

"He is—well, he cannot be described. Oh, I can tell you what he looks like, more or less, and from what Tony and Anne Marie have told me he's changed very little. You'd like him. Most people do. There's a kindness and gentleness in him that comes through, and he's the loneliest creature in all the cosmos."

"You were not just—associates. Or even teacher and pupil."

"No."

"You still speak of him with affection, yet this kind, wise, gentle man you describe is out to get you and maybe worse."

Mavra sighed. "I think so. At least the evidence points that way, and it almost *feels* like his handiwork. You can be seduced by him in many ways, and at the time he means it, but deep down, where the soul resides, he's also something else. Something almost—monstrous. It's hidden most of the time, I think even from himself, but it's always there, and in the end it's always in control. You won't see it much when he's human, but inside the Well it's much clearer. It is nothing less than the collective will of the ancient creatures that built this place and remade the universe as they pleased. *He* doesn't even like it. Last time he fought like hell against it and wound up almost forced to do its will, kicking and screaming all the way. It is there, and I find it most significant that this time he didn't even try to fight it. He's surrendered to it, I think, and that alone makes him the most dangerous creature since the universe was born."

"And yet—he gave *you* immortality and the key to this Well, this God-computer," Julian noted.

"Yes. I've come up with many theories as to why, some more flattering to my ego than others, but it wasn't until I came here once again that I found out the truth. He is two creatures—the kind, gentle, but tough and resourceful man I knew and described and this—*thing*. He's been the man so long, it is more his true self than that hidden within him, but he knows he's in a trap, an eternal trap. By taking me in there, by making *me* reset things last time, he dodged his own conflict while still doing what he was compelled to do. Now I think it was more than that. I don't have this thing inside me. I was born to this form and grew up as you see me. I think his human half wants to be stopped. In the end, I think that was the idea all along. The next time, *this* time, I'd be there, too. Something inside him wants me to beat him and seize control. To stop his compulsive pattern. Maybe it's because he became too much like us; maybe it's simple logic. The stress of last time and its responsibilities brought it home to him that there was a flaw in the plans of those who created this place. They wanted a new, even greater race of true gods to evolve, but even they couldn't foresee all the things that could happen in so vast a universe over so much time. So they left him as their guardian, to keep it on track, but they blew it. They didn't just set it going, they made it a controlled experiment instead, all the variables taken into account."

Julian saw where she was going, or thought she did, as much as this whole place made any sense. "You are saying that they overcontrolled. That by insisting on things developing as they designed, they gave it no opportunity to develop differently."

"Well, they sure weren't as godlike as they thought they were, that was for sure," Mavra agreed. "They couldn't conceive that being a race of true gods *would* become boring as hell after some great length of time. Their whole racial history was motivated by a belief that true and absolute perfection was possible. They could not face the fact that it wasn't, and so they built this world, and the races that were successful here were sent out into the universe to see if *they* could attain that perfection. If anything loused up the experiment beyond repair, though, they had a mechanism for resetting things to start so absolute that everything would develop *exactly* the same, except that whatever caused the collapse would be factored out. Even you were probably there in the past creation, the one that I, many relative centuries in the future, wiped out and re-created. The same nations, the same races, the same *people*, being born, living, progressing, dying, over and over."

"My God! You mean I've done *this* before? Or someone exactly like me?"

"No. I have no doubt there was a Julian Beard who lived your life and did all the same things—up to the point where you were sent to investigate the meteor. And a Lori who remained the first female full professor of astronomy at wherever she taught, and a Tony and Anne Marie who probably died in a suicide pact, and the others as well. Your coming here changed that for you and for the others. I believe Nathan has at one point or another changed a number of individuals' lives. It is difficult to say this, but most individual lives, if removed or altered, won't change the fabric very much so long as the number of them is kept very small. It is said that the Well Gates react to people's wills and that no one who *would* mess up the master plan is ever transported here. I don't know. But I *do* know it can't continue. Reset after reset, the same people, the same races, the same lives over and over . . . In the end, if *that* keeps happening, then *nobody* really matters. Nobody at all. And if I fail this time, that's what is going to *keep* going on again and again. A continuous wheel, a perpetual replaying of the same damned recording over and over until the universe dies. That's what this is all about. That's why you're all here."

"Sweet Jesus!" Julian gasped, thinking of the implications of what she was saying.

"What are you two girls whispering about?" Lori called to them.

Mavra Chang gave a crooked smile. "Us *women* are talking *woman talk*," she replied aloud.

It was a long way yet in the dark to the border.

Pulcinell

THE SIGHT OF NATHAN BRAZIL'S BROAD-BRIMMED HAT, SOGGY and crumpled though it was, atop the top spoke of the ship's wheel made everything else, from the escape to the weather to the girl's extraordinary powers, seem distant and pale. More, his empathic link with the girl told him that not only had she not done it, she was unaware of anyone else around to do it, either.

Either I'm losing my mind or there's somebody else here, he told himself.

The girl, riding out the storm just behind the mainmast, instantly sensed his feelings of danger and confusion and turned to look back at him, all her vast array of senses and powers deployed against a threat.

There was nothing. No threat at all. She frowned. No threat, but there was something else, something *different* here. Something that had not been there before, not until that odd lurch the ship had taken. Whatever it was, it was no enemy, but why couldn't she see it or find it? There was only something vague, and that something, like a fuzzy, friendly ghostlike presence, was back there with Nathan Brazil.

Brazil had no choice but to retake the wheel, removing the hat first and throwing it forward. The wind caught it, but it was too soggy to blow away; it skidded across the deck and stuck against the side. He unlocked the wheel and began to try to think of ways to use this wind rather than fight it. It was no use, though. Somebody—or *something*—had put that hat on the wheel. Something that was there with him now. Something that even the girl could only dimly perceive.

"What are you? Who are you?" he yelled against the howling gale. "Stop playing children's games and show yourself! Where the hell are you?"

"Right here at your side, Captain Brazil," responded a low, deep, resonant voice that nonetheless was not formed by humanlike lips.

Nathan Brazil almost jumped out of his skin. He whirled around, letting go of the wheel.

"Right here," said the voice, and when it spoke, he could suddenly see it, if only vaguely.

It *was* big, big enough to tower the better part of a meter over him, and broad and strong of body. It had a head much like a snake's or a giant lizard's, long and flattened with two big, yellow catlike eyes that popped up from its surface, and a large, thick serpentine body that was balanced on two thick legs that ended in clawed, webbed feet but started too far down the torso to be a main support for the rest of it. It balanced now on those two feet and on the remainder of that body, which ended in a broad, almost shovellike tail. Extruding from either side of the torso, a bit below where the shoulders ought to have been, were two very thin, frail-looking arms terminating in four clawed, long webbed fingers and an opposable thumb. Like the legs, they extended out from the torso, more like a reptile than a mammal. The whole thing was covered in silvery scales that seemed to give off a rainbow of colors as the swirling clouds varied the available light and which were probably spectacular in direct sunlight.

"Don't you think you'd better tend to the wheel first?" the creature asked him in a calm, pleasant voice. "I just had the very *devil* of a swim just to catch up with you. I'd rather not go back in the water again for a while."

"Uh, yeah, sure," Brazil commented, turning back to the

wheel and, with some difficulty, wrestling it back under control. It was a miracle that the lone sail, even deployed as little as it was, hadn't been torn to shreds. Whoever had built this boat had *really* known how to build.

"Uh, if you don't mind," Brazil said, trying not to look around or away but keep his eyes on steering, "just who the hell are you and why did you go to all the trouble of swimming after us in the first place? And why couldn't we see you?"

"Survival trait, they tell me. The arms, as you might have noticed, are very limber, but they ain't real big or real muscular, and the legs, while strong, don't let you move real fast. That would've made us sittin' ducks in our own land, let alone from outside threats. Dahir's a nontech hex, you know."

"So you're a Dahir!" *Another one I don't quite remember looking like this, let alone with this trick,* he thought. "A *very* long way from home, aren't you? And a damned good swimmer for an inland race."

"It was another thing that just came naturally, sort of. Dahir's inland, true, but it's real swampy. Lowlands, wetter than the Everglades. The routine's to swim along pretty much like a snake and stand up to feed or do whatever else you feel like doin'. Of course, we walk around the houses and lodges and the like, but for any kind of travel, well, it's kinda like takin' the car even though the grocery store's only two blocks away. You know you *should* walk, but it's so much easier to ride. Even though this is ocean, to tell you the truth I never even *thought* about not bein' able to swim in it. I gotta admit, though, I almost lost it when it got so rough all of a sudden. I'd actually missed you and was gettin' dragged away to the side and then forward a little when one of them waves just picked me up and dropped me *kerplang* on the deck."

"So *that's* what shook the ship! You're another one of the people who came in through the gate from Earth, I gather. You're a long way from the Everglades and corner grocer's here."

"Yeah, but I didn't have a lot of choice in the matter, neither. I was dropped, drugged, dragged around a jungle for I don't know *how* long, then carried through to here and more or less thrown in. I really don't remember a lot of it, except that I knew I was dyin'.'"

"You're from Mavra's group, then."

"I guess. I know who she is, but only by hearin' about it. I understand she was the leader of that group of nutty Amazons who grabbed us. As I said, I was drugged and sick most of the time, and it's all a daze. Not nearly as much of a shock as wakin' up like *this*, I gotta say, but the in between's a little fuzzy. For the record, I'm Gus Olafsson. Everybody just calls me Gus, even in Dahir."

"A Swede?"

"Minnesota. United States. To tell the truth, though, the area's kind of Scandinavia west, with the Swedes there, the Norwegians, and even the Finns up in the Iron Mountain district. You know the place?"

"No, sorry. I've actually spent very little time in the States, and I don't know much about the interior at all. I heard much of it was flat, dull, and cold."

"Well, not all of it, but that describes where I come from pretty well. Pretty area, though, up around the lake district. It was a nice place to grow up but not a great place to make a livin' in if you didn't want to do the same old things. I didn't. Instead, I picked a way to see the world, all right. More than one, as it's turned out. In fact, the things you can do as a Dahir woulda been real handy for my profession, except, of course, when somebody would have to see me, which would cause a right good monster movie–style panic, I'd say. Shame, though. It'd be a real advantage not to be seen in most cases. I coulda done great investigative work right in plain sight."

"You were some sort of reporter?"

"News photographer. Television, actually. Started at small stations, worked my way up until I got some really good footage, then went freelance, gettin' work from the networks and local stations. Finally impressed folks enough, I guess, that I got an offer from the news network, and I've been doin' that, well, until them Amazons more or less killed me and I wound up here like this."

"You're the one who's been following us for the last week or so, then."

"Yeah, pretty much. You only gave me the slip once, out on the dock that one time. Pretty slick, but I figured it out. I also figured when I heard you talkin' to that bastard blob of Jell-O that you wouldn't't've been so straight with him if you hadn'ta finally figured you'd been had and was already fixin' to light out. I got to admit you picked a lousy day in particular to do it, but I just had this feelin' you would."

"Yeah, but how'd you track us from the hotel? We climbed down a sheer wall on a rope."

"Hey! I was a news photographer, right? I mean, the only way to get the picture nobody else gets is to think like the guy you're shadowin'. The rubes and the lazy ones, they'd stake out the lobby just like the colonel's boys and wait for you to come through, figuring you would try to shake 'em. Me, I decided you was smarter than that, even if you did take a long time to catch on to the colonel's game, and then it was just figurin' how I would do it if I was you."

"I was able to at least sense your presence most of the time," he noted. "How come I didn't sense you back there?"

"Because a good stakeout depends on not bein' made, right? I mean, if you hadn't given me the slip back on that dock last week, I would never have guessed you'd figured I was there at all, but since you did, I thought you or maybe Terry might be feelin' me, and I hung back. I mean, you made tracks all through the snow, right? The only thing was, hangin' back and not knowin' how they launched these things, I couldn't get close enough to jump on the boat. When you had your problems, I wasn't in the right spot, so I couldn't jump on like that other fella, but I figured I was close enough to swim out to you. Almost caught up when you got over near the barges, but then that guy came overboard almost into my face, and by the time I got my bearin's back, you was headin' through the hex boundary. I hadta swim like the very devil to get even close after that."

Brazil frowned. "But, if you're not part of the colonel's crowd, then what are you doing here in the first place?"

"Lookin' for you, and Terry. She and I go back a long way. I was the only cameraman she worked with if she could manage it."

"Terry?"

"Her," responded Gus, and a small finger pointed out at the girl on deck.

Brazil was suddenly excited. "You *know* her? Know who she is?"

"Sure. Theresa Perez. Hotshot producer for the news channel. It was her I was workin' for when we come down to Brazil for the meteor coverage. Had an exclusive, too. Pretty good pictures, if I do say so myself. Hope they got 'em okay."

Theresa Perez. *Terry* . . . At last, at least, she had a name and a past.

"But—she can't see you, either? Even now?"

"I guess she could. She should if I was talkin' to her or tried to make her, I guess. It ain't somethin' I can turn on and off, you know. I don't even know how it's done. All I know is that we're like just about invisible to anybody except another Dahir. Works on every race I ever saw or met. Kinda handy, really, when you're off on your own with nothin' like I was. Just walk on any handy ship. They don't even notice you. Need some food? Just take it. Gets to be kinda fun after a while. The Dahir, they got somethin' of a religion about how not to abuse the power, but I didn't stay for the lectures. Hell, I wasn't a good Lutheran; why should I be a good and loyal follower of a religion I wasn't even born to?"

Nathan Brazil laughed at that. "You'll do fine around here, Gus. That's just the attitude to survive."

"Yeah, well, maybe. I dunno. It ain't foolproof. I found

that out a couple of times. You can't fool a camera, or an electric eye, or any number of security devices. Recorders record your sounds even if the folks around don't notice them when they're made. I almost got picked up more than once back there in Hakazit, and I knew they'd just send me back home by the Zone Express, and with the kind of stuff I was charged with, that damned system woulda throwed the book at me. I guess I'm kinda on the lam myself now."

"Well, I won't turn you in, and I'm going to try as hard as I can to keep away from any more high-tech hexes for a while myself. The way you talk, though, everybody everywhere already knows who I am."

"Well, not everybody *believes* it, or at least all the stories and legends, but it's kinda the talk of government and official types, anyway. That's how I heard about it. They had me in the capital, in what you might call a school on how to be a good Dahir and love it. They was also tryin' to pump me for what I knew about the others, which wasn't all that much. I doubt if most folks in the country, most places, have heard of you, but the big shots all have. They're kinda in a whole set of arguments with each other, too. Some don't believe you're the guy in their legends; some believe you are, and it scares hell out of 'em. Some of the believers want to nab you; others want to just make sure you don't *do* whatever they're scared of you doin' without first makin' deals with them. Those who don't believe you're anybody special want to knock you off just to show the true believers they're right, and so on. No matter how you look at it, though, Cap, you're as made as me and twice as wanted."

Nathan Brazil sighed. "So that's the way it is. I'd kind of hoped nobody would spot me and I could be kindly Captain Solomon. So even the colonel knew all the time."

"Oh, he knew, all right. Kept givin' them regular reports on you. I stood there and listened to him give 'em. For now he was just gettin' orders to stall, stall, stall, so I guess they still ain't made up their minds. The guy was a perfect toady, I bet, back home, and he might have changed race, form, and loyalties, but he's right at home doin' just the same here. Uh—just out of curiosity, *are* you the guy they're scared of?"

Brazil shrugged. "I suppose it wouldn't hurt to admit what most of the leadership already half believes. Yeah, I'm the same guy. And yes, they have some reason to be scared of me, too. More reason now than before, if they get me too pissed off."

"They say you're some kind of like, well, god or something. That you're really one of them guys who built this nutty place."

"Well, that's a bit exaggerated. Right now I've only got one important power they don't, pretty much like your one big power. The Well—the master computer that keeps things running here—won't let them or anything else kill me."

"Huh! I'll trade you!"

"Don't tempt me! But still, it's not as big a deal when you think of it. I can be hurt, hurt bad. If it's *really* bad, I can take a very long time to heal. I can be kept prisoner, drugged, you name it. In other words, they might not be able to kill me but they can sure *stop* me, and if everybody and their sister knows about me, then I've got real trouble. I had this kind of situation once before, but then I had a number of friends and allies. Now—I don't know. And Mavra Chang's just like me, Gus. She's heading where I'm heading, too. If she gets there before I do, all bets are off, including on me. She doesn't really know how complicated this business is, but she can get me out of the loop, anyway. She could even . . ." He paused a moment, as if the very concept were hitting him for the first time. "She could even *kill* me."

"Yeah? Would she do that?"

"She might. I don't know, Gus. I haven't seen her in . . . well, a *very* long time. We're strangers, really, at this point. And you say she was leading a band of Amazons in the Brazilian jungle?"

"Yep. The Stone Age type, too. Naked and painted and

little poison darts and all that. I wouldn't worry as much about her as you are, though."

"No? Why not?"

"Well, they like got the same idea about her as about you. She's not in their legends and stuff, but the ones that believe the stories about you also believe she's another one like you. They're doin' the exact same thing to her. You can bet on it."

That made him feel a little better, but not much. "So they have us both running on treadmills, pushing hard and hardly moving."

"You're movin' now," Gus pointed out.

"Yeah, I guess. But sooner or later I have to land this thing. Hell, maybe sooner than later. I haven't exactly had a chance to check below and see if we have any usable provisions. If not, we're all gonna get very hungry and very thirsty very fast."

"Well, that's a point. Is there anything I can do?"

Brazil thought a moment. "Yeah. I don't want to try you at the wheel in this weather, not unless you have some experience with these kind of ships."

"Canoes are my speed. Canoes and speedboats."

"I thought so. But you know what we need and you know what you need. You could look below and give me an inventory."

"No problem."

"Gus? Also look for charts. I know you probably can't read the stuff here, but you know what I mean by nautical charts. They have to have them somewhere. We're going to have to get our bearings when we get out of this blow and then decide where we have to go."

"Will do. I'll be back as soon as I can."

"Uh—Gus?"

"Yeah, Cap?"

"One more thing. You never answered my question as to why you didn't contact me before."

"Well, I started to, but then I saw Terry, and I didn't know what to do. I mean, you didn't know her before, Cap.

She was bright and educated, spoke a half dozen languages, damned brave and good at her job, and real pretty, too. But more important, she was a talker, a real extrovert. I wasn't so sure I'd seen her lookin' anything like she did before, considerin' what happened to me and the colonel and all, but I didn't figure she'd be any more changed, you know, *inside*, than I was. Then I see her, and she don't notice me—it's not invisibility, Cap, it's just that folks don't *notice* me unless I wanta get noticed. And then she's stark naked, which is weird under most conditions but particularly weird in a climate like that one, she don't say a word, and she's got this weird blankness about her, even in her eyes. I mean, it didn't take no Einstein to know that somethin' far worse than what happened to me happened to her. Thing was, Cap, I didn't know how or why it happened, see? I mean, for all I knew, particularly with what they was sayin' about you, I mean, *you* coulda done it to her. I couldn't do nothin', see, until I was sure which side I wanted to be on."

Brazil didn't immediately look around, dealing as he was with keeping the ship righted, but finally he said, "Okay, fair enough. Let me know what you find!"

There was no response, and he looked around and saw nothing at all. For a moment he wasn't sure he'd seen the creature at all, but then he spotted the open hatch to the main cabin below and realized that the Dahir hadn't waited but had gone on down after their last words. Gone on down, and he hadn't seen him!

In a way, though, it was reassuring. The girl—Terry—hadn't seen him, either. Hadn't in fact seen him *yet*. There were limits on her as there were on him, after all.

He wondered just what the trick was about something that big being so invisible to others. Gus said it didn't work with cameras, so that meant it wasn't some kind of blending in, no chameleonlike attribute that somehow masked even so large a creature against a background. Sounds, too, seemed to be masked somewhat, maybe totally. He'd heard the creak of the timbers in that warehouse, and that had brought a sensation of footsteps, but had he really heard them? He certainly hadn't seen a damned thing when Gus hadn't wanted to be seen.

He also wasn't sure what Dahirs ate, but he certainly had sympathy for any of their menu items.

His thoughts drifted back to the girl. It was impossible to even imagine her as a worldly, vibrant mistress of technology and show business, a producer of highly visible news who'd probably been in a hundred danger spots all on her own and managed to survive and even thrive on that kind of thing. He had no reason to feel that Gus was putting him on; both he and the girl had, after all, been completely at the Dahir's mercy over the long haul, and Gus's own explanation of his actions rang true. But squaring the Terry that Gus had known, worked with, perhaps even loved, considering his devotion to finding her, with the eerie wordless mystic with the icy heart and strange and terrible powers who was back sitting behind the mast was next to impossible.

How much of that old Terry was still somewhere inside her? Had her essence simply walled off, or had she been reprogrammed beyond any hope of recall? Or was Terry the newswoman somehow still all there and along for the ride? Was her old personality erased or suppressed? Were her old memories gone or modified or merely filed under "old business" somewhere?

There *was* a real human being in there somewhere, he was sure of that. The girl who'd made love to him and fought alongside him and who had sent him signals on all those others with whom he'd come into contact was certainly no monster, and even if she had rejected or hadn't been able to use the sophistication of Ambreza or Hakazit, she'd understood it and coped with it. A savage would have been awed, amazed, confused by high-tech life; a savage would have had to be protected from being run over at the first busy street. She was neither ignorant nor stupid. What she did and what she would not do were conscious decisions to accept or reject, not the products of either upbringing or lack of understanding.

She manipulated that sailor as coldly as if he were a puppet ... And with a coldness he'd never felt inside her before, not really. It was almost as if ... as if she were two creatures, both Terry the human and *something else*. That something else, the coldness, had the power and made the rules, but in exchange it protected her against everything from the elements to sailors with guns, and so long as she followed its rules, then *it* was the passenger, emerging only as needed. Its control over her was not absolute; she, Terry, had overruled it and opted for his plea for mercy for the man over the other's computerlike direct and deadly course.

Not parasitism, then, but symbiosis of some sort. Terry had not been infected; rather, she had made a bargain and now had to live with the consequences.

If what he'd been told was true, if her news crew had been kidnapped out in the middle of the jungle by some Stone Age tribe of women, then the way Gus said he was treated made one kind of sense. But how did they treat the women they also took? From the pictures and data he'd gotten from Zone, they *all* looked like they'd walked in out of some cave in the distant past.

As with most primitive tribes who captured people, the prisoners were given a choice: join, assimilate, or die. All things considered, he'd have signed up if they'd have let him under those circumstances.

So they had been lost, taken captive, forced to live a Stone Age existence in a hostile jungle they didn't quite know and thus had become dependent on the tribe for survival—and then they had been translated here.

Terry hadn't come with the initial group, and that was a story only she could know. But she'd come before the gate had closed, alone, sneaking in past the monitors, seeing bizarre places and even more bizarre creatures. She'd followed to the Zone Gate and gone through, probably trying to catch her friends, and had wound up in Ambreza stark naked, defenseless, and scared to death. Why she went to Glathriel was another unknowable, but it was not hard to figure. Maybe she just saw some recognizable humans working for the Ambreza and followed them. It would be the natural, cautious choice of a survivor in a horrendous situation ignorant of where she was or what the hell was going on. So she'd gone in, made contact . . . and then what?

A bargain. Under the circumstances and considering what she'd just been through, who wouldn't take such a bargain? As in the jungle, what was the alternative?

It explained everything—and nothing. A bargain with whom? Or, more properly, *what*? There weren't any creatures like that on the Well World. At least no creatures designed and created here. The Well protected them from external influences, anything that would be a contaminant. It *couldn't* be an external force; even if it somehow got by the Well, such a thing would have caused the system to summon him long before it got this firmly established. Whatever it was, whatever had happened to the Glathrielians that had made them what they were, was homegrown, of *that* he was certain.

"There's what looks and smells like several kegs of beer, some fresh water, and those charts you wanted," Gus's voice suddenly said next to him.

Brazil jumped and lost the wheel again for a second. Wrestling it back, he yelled, "Now cut that out! You do that one time too often and we *are* going to capsize!"

"Hey, sorry! I *told* you I couldn't exactly turn it on or off."

"Well, make some noise, then! Yell at me as you're coming up! *Something!* At least when we're not in dangerous territory."

"Hey, I'll try, but it's always turned on. I practically have to shout in your face for you to consciously notice me."

And that, of course, was it. Somehow, something inside the Dahir broadcast something that could be received on some mental level by just about every other organic race. Something that made other beings simply not notice them. That was why he'd almost always been able to tell that somebody was there, following him. He *could* see Gus, would even give way for him, maybe with a "Beg your pardon." So could the girl; so could everybody else.

But some signal in the mind said, "Pay no attention to him. Don't notice him at all. He's not interesting or important."

Gus, he decided, for all his worldly experience and ambitions, was a bit too much the product of his roots to see the real possibilities here. Why, with a little technical help, Brazil thought, the Dahir could become the greatest bank robber in history.

Still, for all the problems a being he never noticed until it yelled for his attention presented to his nerves and his longstanding paranoia, he was glad to have the big creature along. In one being Gus gave his team physical strength, unparalleled scouting, and spying potential, and most of all, Gus gave him somebody to talk to.

"How long can you keep this up?" Gus asked him worriedly, watching the small man fighting the wheel and seemingly doing three things at once all the time.

"Oh, a good while. I've had a lot of rest these past several weeks, and I've seen worse than this. If I can get us around the storm to where we can use it, you might spell me. Until then you'll probably have to find me something to serve as a chamber pot before long. Until then, could you get me a tankard or mug or whatever they use of that beer?"

"Sure. You want some of the bread, too? It's hard as nails, but it looks edible. At least, I'd have eaten it if I were hungry enough and still my old self."

"Yeah, thanks. You didn't mention the bread. That will help. But make sure those charts don't blow off anywhere! We're gonna need them bad as soon as I can get a look at them."

"I'll be sure. I'll leave them below until you want them. Beats me, though, how they'll do you much good here. I mean, how the hell do you know where you are now? We could be going in circles for all we know."

"No, I'm a better sailor than that. You're right, though,

in the sense that we'll need to see the sun or stars to get a bearing and figure out exactly where we are. You see that little dome atop the wheel housing?"

"Uh, yeah, now that you mention it."

"Well, that's the equivalent of a compass here. That bubble is always at true north in this hemisphere. That's how I know we're not going in circles. We *have* been going farther west than I'd planned, but I couldn't guess at our speed or how far we've come, but against this wind it hasn't been all that much. That's why I'm trying to get the western edge of the storm. If I can catch it and keep steering forward with the wind at our back, we can hoist some real sail and make good time. Now, how about that beer and bread or whatever it is? And if you can, find me something to sit on!"

The wind was brisk but behind them, and under nearly full sail they were making excellent time in a north-northwesterly direction. Although he was more than a little hesitant, Gus took the wheel after some basic coaching by Brazil and found that it wasn't that hard, provided that little changed in the weather conditions and the seas remained fairly steady. Gus still didn't really want to do it, but he knew that Brazil had been at the wheel and fighting the storm for the better part of a day and into the night; he had to be totally exhausted.

Still, the little man hadn't gone down for a rest yet. He had taken the opportunity to inspect the ship from bow to stern and to inventory the supplies below, but he insisted on remaining near the wheel in case Gus should run into problems and need him in a hurry. Protesting that he was literally "too tired to sleep," he now used an oil lamp and sat there going over the charts and navigational books about the region.

Although they were out of the rain, the sky was still completely overcast, and in the darkness the stars could give him no guidance. He knew the bearing they were now on and had a fair estimate of their speed, but the hours of battling the storm itself gave him no clue as to just where on the charts he'd started from. He particularly worried that they might have gone far enough west to cross the Mowry border, though he thought he would have felt the passage through the hex boundary. While that wasn't in itself a problem, Mowry was a high-tech hex with all the sophisticated technology for locating almost anything on, above, or below its surface, and it was dotted with thousands of small volcanic islands, some of which were submerged and could easily wreck a ship.

Dlubine suited him far more. While he probably couldn't outrun a sleek steamer without a wind at least this good if not better, both mass communications and navigation were far more basic. Before he could be caught, they would have to know that it was he and immediately engage the chase.

Dlubine, too, had a number of islands, both volcanic and coral, but they would be more handy than a threat, or so he hoped. He wasn't at all sure what the Dlubine looked like, but the chart showed small harbors on some of the islands, indicating that they did a direct trade with surface ships. He was willing to take the risk.

If Gus could continue to bury his moral qualms, there should be little problem picking up what they needed on one of those. He hoped the natives were at least initially friendly, but that was a secondary concern. First, of course, he had to find them.

Finally, in spite of everything, he drifted off into a deep, deep sleep.

When he awoke groggily, feeling as if someone had beaten the hell out of him and he'd just recovered consciousness, he grew suddenly aware that the wind was down and there was direct sunlight hitting his skin. He opened his eyes, and for a moment sheer panic went through him as he saw no one at the wheel.

"Gus!" he called.

"Oh, you're awake," the gravel-voiced Dahir responded, and in the blink of an eye the huge, colorful snakelike form was there, less steering the ship than kind of leaning lazily on the wheel. "I was thinking of waking you up, considering I haven't had much rest myself."

Nathan Brazil nodded and got painfully to his feet. "God! I need an intravenous coffee transfusion," he groaned.

"Sorry. Fresh out. Never touch the stuff myself. You're stuck with water or beer for breakfast. I used to have a 'Beer—Breakfast of Champions' shirt once. Wouldn't fit now, though, I suppose, and I don't have much of a taste for beer anymore, either."

"Well, let me get some water on my face and see if I can wake up," the captain moaned. "Then, if you can hold on for another couple of minutes, I want to take some sightings of the sun and get a rough position." He went over to the small jug that was just where he'd left it in the night and splashed some of the water on his face and neck. It felt warm, but it was better than nothing. "How long was I out?"

"Can't say, not having a watch, but the sun's been up quite a while."

Nathan Brazil looked up and took a sight reading. "Um, yeah. *Way* up. Sun's not quite over the yardarm, though, so I'll pass on the beer. Uh, don't take this personally, but just exactly what the hell do you eat, anyway?"

"Most anything that won't eat me, really. Preferably live when I get it, but anything that's reasonably fresh is okay. Strictly carnivore. These small vampire teeth inject a nasty venom into whatever I want that kind of kills it and then softens it up so it goes down. Not much in the taste business, but if the critter's big enough, I don't have to eat or even drink much for days. Don't worry—I'd eaten just the night before we all scrammed out of Hakazit."

Brazil wasn't all that worried, but he decided for now not to ask what, in high-tech Hakazit, the Dahir had eaten.

"Have you ever heard of Dlubine?" Nathan Brazil asked the Dahir, changing the subject.

"No. Sounds like the noise you make when you throw up, sort of. Hell, I'm new here. *You're* supposed to be the expert, right? The god of the Well World, or am I being too limited?"

Brazil chuckled. "No, that's the reputation but hardly the truth. I'm the genuine handpicked successor to the equally genuine handpicked successor of the creatures that helped build this whole thing. We used to call them Markovians in the old days, a term without meaning now, but if I use it, you should know that's who I mean. The highest race in all creation, at least as far as there's any evidence. Got to the point where matter-to-energy and energy-to-matter conversions were old hat. Roamed the whole universe using interdimensional pathways; never needed to take a lot with them because they could have anything they needed by just willing it. They could *become* anything, too—so close, nobody could tell the difference. Just rearrange the atoms. They *knew* they were gods, too. And that's what drove 'em nuts."

"Huh?"

"Well, you ever consider the real problem of being a god? No surprises, nothing more to learn, nothing new to discover, everything you ever wanted or needed there at your whim. Not even time has any real meaning to a god, not in the sense that it does to most folks. After a billion years or so things are absolutely the same, nothing to look forward to, just an endless present. Of course, they built this world as the center—the center of the universe, more or less. All their roads led to here, and from here. A whole damned planet-sized master computer that coordinated all the zillions of lesser ones and was the true source of their power. It's still here, still working, maybe thirty, thirty-five kilometers beneath us now. The whole damned ball except this surface shell is self-repairing, self-maintaining, just going on and on long after there was anybody around who could use its power."

Gus was appalled. "You mean they died of *boredom*?"

"More or less, I guess. I wasn't there, but I've kind of felt an affinity for them over time. But with me it's strictly one-way, from the Well to me, not me to the Well. To get in real communication with it and have access to any of its power, I have to be inside, at the controls, in the form of one of the founding race. No other form I know can handle it. A big lump of rubbery brain case with six huge but remarkably sensitive tentacles. You don't even need eyes or a nose or a mouth or any of that. You're kind of beyond all that. You don't just see an object in three dimensions, you see it in *all* dimensions, and you see it from all angles at once. Things you couldn't even keep all in your head become so simple and obvious, they don't even require thought. And what you don't know, the Well does, and it's all there and available to you. The powers of God almighty, almost."

"I'm surprised that you change back," the Dahir commented. "Seems to me it'd be kinda hard to give that up, at least until you had your own billion years or so to get bored in."

"No, it's not that simple. Maybe if I *was* one of them it would be, but I'm not. I have strict limitations on what I can and can't do. I've got the form and the power while I'm in there, yeah, but not the independence. I'm not there to tell the Well what to do, I'm there because the Well needs me to do something it can't do itself. And when I do it, it wants me out of there, pronto. Back in the tool chest, as it were, until the next time."

"But it's true you can't be killed?"

"It's true. Something, no matter how ridiculous the odds, always comes along to save my ass. Not that I can't get hurt or have all the other problems that anybody else might have, including all the weaknesses, but no matter what, I'll survive. The Well manipulates probability so I'm available if needed. You know, I once stood in front of a firing squad, and every damned rifle was defective. I've survived massacres, even a crucifixion or so. Even so, I guess I've been shot, stabbed, speared, strangled, drowned, you name it, many a time. No matter what, something happens to save me. I will tell you, though, that it's no fun at all."

"Yeah, I can believe that. Still, I'd think you'd be a mass of stumps and scars by now."

Nathan Brazil shook his head. "Nope. Every part of me constantly regenerates. Cut off an arm and it'll hurt like hell, but eventually I'll grow a new one. Even my brain regenerates, which causes trouble over time. There's not enough room in there to store or copy all the information you get from living so long. Eventually, things you don't need or haven't thought about in a long time just get spooled off, stored by the Well, outside of your head. I don't know how much I've forgotten, but it must be an enormous amount. There were times, I know, when I had no memory of who or what I was at all, until I got manipulated and wound up spending time here. The funny thing is, while I don't remember those periods all that much, I think of them as the happiest of times. After you live as long as I have, you discover that ignorance really is bliss."

"You sound like you'd almost like to join those Ancient Ones," Gus noted.

"Sometimes, maybe a lot of times, I think about that. The last time—the details are hazy, but I know I'd just gotten so damned sick of it, I was ready to at least start the process. See, I'm the safety valve, the one left around just in case there was something those Ancient Ones hadn't thought of. Like my predecessor, I can't quit until somebody else is groomed to take my place and has proved acceptable and competent to the Well."

"This Mavra Chang. She was supposed to be your replacement?"

He nodded. "In a way, anyway. At least it was a start. I took her in, changed her so that she was part of the Well's system, and made her do all the work. I remember that much. Then we had to go through a whole new cycle to see if she could and would be able to handle the burden. I really thought she could, but now I'm not so sure."

"You were—together? For a long time?"

"Yeah, a long time. Oh, we split up on occasion, but we always arranged to meet at some place, some time. Then, one time, she just said she was going down to the bazaar for a few things, walked out of the place where we were staying, and I never saw or heard from her again. We had our fights, but we weren't fighting then. There wasn't anything I ever could put a finger on. She just vanished. I searched for her, of course, not just then but for many long years after. Occasionally I'd hear stories or tales or ninth-hand legends that sounded like her, but they never panned out. After a while I just stopped looking. I figured that if she really wanted to find me, my habits and preferences were an open book to her and she'd eventually at least get word to me. She never did."

"Huh! How long ago was it when she split?"

He shrugged. "I've lost count. But the house was just inside the Ishtar Gate in Babylon during the reign of Nebuchadnezzar the Great. What would that be in current Earth terms? A few hundred B.C., I guess."

"Jesus! That's like twenty-five *hundred* years or so!"

Brazil shrugged again. "I said it had been a long time. You ever notice that the older you get, the faster time seems to run?"

"Yeah. It's a cruel joke. I guess it's because each day you live becomes a smaller fraction of your total life, or so I've been told."

"That's about it. Well, you can see how even that kind of time span might not seem so ancient to me. Funny, though. Some of that ancient stuff I can see like it was yesterday, while other stuff, maybe only a few months or years ago, I can't remember at all. I guess we remember the highlights and the lowlights, and the rest gets caught in the cracks."

Gus thought about it, but such a life over so much time made his head spin. "Sure would've liked to have had a camera and tape along back there, though. Man, I bet it was *somethin'*!"

"Yeah, well, it was. But it was also before any real medicine, before mass communication, before a lot of creature comforts. People died young, and they lived lives harder than you can imagine, most of them. Even the rich didn't live all that great by modern standards. Smelled like a garbage dump, too. Folks just tossed it anywhere at all, and almost nobody took baths because the water had so many parasites in it, you could die slowly from a refreshing dip. No, on the whole I prefer things as high-tech as you can get, except, of course, on this particular trip."

Gus wasn't thinking of Brazil's colorful past, though, but of what he'd said before. "This Mavra Chang—this Well computer or whatever it is considers her the same as you?"

"Pretty much, yes. Oh, I see what you're driving at. You're asking if she could do the kinds of things that are supposed to be my job if she got inside."

"Right. Could she?"

"Yes, I'm pretty sure she could."

"She's nuts, Cap. You know that. I mean, livin' as one of those naked savages in the middle of the jungle, all them women—she sure don't have much liking for men. Maybe she did once, but not now. I remember enough of it to say that for sure. Maybe she just couldn't handle it, Cap. Maybe all them years, what you got as memories she's got as hurts. Some guy, or a lot of 'em, put her 'round the bend but good. I hate to point this out, Cap, but you're the only equal she's got, and you're a man. You said she was groomed to take over. If she gets in there first, she could unplug you same as you plugged her in, couldn't she?"

Nathan Brazil felt a numbing chill deep inside him in spite of the tropical warmth as he saw just what Gus was trying to point out. It was the one thought he had not wanted to think or dared consider, yet there it was.

"Yes, Gus," he admitted. "Yes, I suppose she could."

It was something he had long thought about and even occasionally desired, but always before it had been an abstract problem, something safe to think about because it was impossible.

It wasn't impossible. Not this time. Gus was absolutely right.

I might actually die this time . . .

Gekir

EVEN IN THE NEARLY TOTAL DARKNESS IT WAS EASY TO KNOW when they had crossed the border from Itus into Gekir.

The dense jungle ended abruptly, as if cut off, and in its place was a wide, flat expanse of grasslands punctuated with groves of trees. The nearly omnipresent clouds were gone as well; the sky blazed brightly from the dense stars in the Well World's spectacular sky.

Walking through the hex barrier instantly lowered the humidity to a small percentage of what it had been, and instead of feeling heavy, tired, and dragged down by the earth underfoot, all of them felt a sudden sense of relief as if a very heavy pack had been lifted from each of their backs.

"Now, is this gravity back to normal, or is this place actually *below* normal as the last one was above it?" Julian asked quizzically, as much of herself as of the others.

"Impossible to say," a weary Mavra replied. "It would make sense to have a fairly large disparity, though, simply because it would keep Ituns from being interested in spreading out over here and probably the other way around, too. To tell you the truth, it hadn't been so dramatic in the places I was last time, at least so I could notice."

"Now what?" one of the centauresses—Tony, from the accent—asked. "Is anybody around here we should worry about?"

"You worry about *everything* on this world," Mavra

127

warned. "Even the friendly places. There's not much chance of diseases—all but a very few don't even travel well between species on Earth, and they're all much closer than the ones here—but meat eaters will eat the meat of carbon-based forms and many plants and animals are potentially poisonous. Even potentially friendly tribes tend sometimes to shoot first and ask questions later. Julian?"

The Erdomese shifted to the infrared spectrum and scanned the relatively flat grasslands. "There are whole herds of creatures out there, most bunched close together and showing little signs of activity. Asleep, probably."

"You think they're natives?" Anne Marie asked, suddenly feeling a little bit refreshed by the lowered gravity and humidity but still feeling sore from the burdens of Itus.

"Who can say? But I tend to doubt it. I've seen the same sort of patterns with cows out on the western ranges and such, and you'd figure that a race would have some kind of night watch and probably fires or the remains of fires that I could easily see. If Earth is any example, and it seems to be to at least *some* extent, then this is a savanna, much like east Africa. That means lots of herd-type animals, which is what the patterns here suggest. Like the antelope. There are probably a lot of other creatures who are also grass eaters here."

Lori had slept for a while and had finally awakened just before the crossing when he'd shifted a bit and his horn had jabbed Tony in the back.

"Where there's a lot of herbivores," he noted, "there are also carnivores. Probably not all intelligent, either. You've got a finite space here, no matter how large a hex is, so something, usually a combination of things, has to keep the population managed. The gravity barrier and maybe incompatible vegetation would keep the animals on this side of the line, but what keeps them in balance?"

Mavra nodded. "We've got to make a camp. Tromping through this meter-high grass for any length of time at night, we're likely to start a stampede, and that's the *last* thing we want. Who knows what this stuff could conceal, too?"

"There is a large stand of trees just about two kilometers

in," Julian noted. "It would afford some shelter and protection."

Mavra was dubious. "That's your Erdomese instincts talking. In the desert you head for the trees and the oasis. Think more like the Africa you talked about. I remember a part of it much like this, going on almost forever. It was *huge*, with vast herds of game and great cities and civilizations, until the coastal folks chopped down all the trees and the rains were able to erode and undermine the soft rock and good soil and the whole thing turned into a desert. The last time I was there, it was desert wasteland from almost the Mediterranean shore as far in as I knew. When I saw what had happened and what greatness had been lost, I cried, and I don't do that much."

She paused a moment, remembering the devastation, the eternity of baking hot sand, then regained control.

"Well," she continued, "the point is that when you had thick areas of trees like the ones you describe, it meant a water hole, maybe a spring at the surface, just as in the desert, but it also was where all the nastiest predators went and spent the night. Wouldn't you? They sure don't sleep out here in the grass. Otherwise the herds of prey would be somewhere else. You don't see any signs of some kind of camp, some kind of civilization in that grove, do you?"

Both Julian and Lori looked hard, using magnification as well. "No," Lori answered after a bit. "But you're right; there are some pretty large creatures in those trees."

Julian pointed to their left a bit. "The grass seems to get lower over there. It is possible that there is some surface rock. I do not see anything much right in that area, either. Lori?"

"No, I don't, either. It's a good bet, although it won't give us a lot of cover."

"Better than nothing," Mavra said at last. "We're not exactly inconspicuous anywhere in these parts, you know."

"Or anywhere else, as a group," Lori agreed.

"Well, I for one think we all look just *splendid*!" Anne Marie announced, missing the point.

The area *was* a rocky outcropping that wind and rain had worn clean of soil. It was a large tabular rock, cracked in a few places, that ran about twelve meters by nine. There were some raised sections of what looked like the same material along two sides, although nothing that would really conceal them from an interested onlooker. It was, however, barren of grass and didn't seem to have been staked out by anything else alive, and that was good enough.

"It's basically a form of sandstone," Julian noted, "not unlike on Earth. It's a common pattern. The stuff will eventually erode back to sand—and you can see some of that along the back side there—and probably underlies the whole plain. Basically, this isn't much different than Erdom, except that this region gets an adequate rainfall that allows the grass to grow and stabilize the rock."

Mavra nodded. "That's right. You were a geologist, weren't you? Okay, let's get the bedrolls down for us three bipeds. Anne Marie, do you still have the firestarter? I want to check on something."

"Yes, yes. I believe ... Half a moment!" With that the centauress turned on her forward hips almost all the way around and fumbled in one of the large packs, then said, "Aha!" She pulled out a long, thin metallic rod and handed it to Mavra.

As the supplies were taken off and the three bedrolls were spread out in the middle of the slab, Mavra went over, picked a strand of the grass, and brought it back to the center of the rock, well away from anything else. She pressed a button on the end of the stick, and from the other end came a tiny jet of flame, which she applied to the grass.

It caught fire but went out as soon as she removed the source of the flame. She tried it two or three times, and each time the result was the same. Satisfied, she tossed the remains of the grass stalk away and put the lighter back in the pack.

"If you don't mind, what was *that* about?" Tony asked her.

"Testing fire hazard. Either it's not long after the rainy

season or this soil really holds water well. Maybe both," Mavra explained. "It also means that the grass is probably just grass. Plus, it shows that the reason for not seeing any sort of fires or fire remains isn't because it's too dangerous to build one. And *that* probably means there aren't any Gekirs around at the moment, whatever they are."

"Either that or they just don't use fire," Lori noted.

Mavra gave her a look she hoped the Erdomese could see in the darkness. "Don't kill my optimism too quickly! I was *enjoying* this," she said grumpily.

Lori looked around with his night vision from atop the centaur's back. "I wonder what would be the most logical life-form for a place like this?"

"Either carnivores or omnivores," Tony guessed. "Probably carnivores. They would have the most stake in managing such a place, and it would explain the lack of any sort of groves or cultivation in such a desirable spot. I would wager that they eat a lot of meat, anyway."

Lori frowned. "Um, I hate to bring this up, but you Dillians are herbivores, aren't you? And Erdomese are basically herbivores, too." He decided not to mention that another staple of the Erdomese diet was almost any form of insect. He realized that that might well put the others off.

"*That*, I think, was the point," Mavra commented dryly, deciding not to remind them that she was the only true omnivore there. She looked around. "We *could* risk a fire, though, either to ward off our theoretical predators or even to cook something. I'm not going hunting out there, though."

"Get me down first," Lori asked. "I'm feeling a little better. Julian—help support me and I'll see how the ankle is doing."

She came over as Anne Marie lifted Lori off Tony's back and gently to the ground, where Julian braced him.

He tried a few steps, and although he continued to put a hand on her shoulder, it was more as a stabilizer than as a full support. "Not too bad," he said. "It's still sore, but it feels a *lot* better. At least I know now that it's not broken." He took his hand away from Julian and tried an uncertain step, then reached out with his right hand and pushed on Tony's side. "*Ow!* Damn! I think the *leg's* going to be fine, but my wrist feels *terrible*! Shit! And I'm right-handed!"

Julian looked first at his leg, then at his wrist. "There is very slight swelling in the leg, my husband, but as you say, it does not look like much. Perhaps one more day of riding and then you should be able to walk. The wrist, though, looks very bad. It should be in a splint and bandaged."

Mavra came over to them. "Trouble?"

"His wrist," Julian told her. "It is bad, and I do not know how bad."

"Can't you feel along it for a break?"

"No, she can't," Lori told her. "Because our females carry children to term on all fours, they need forelegs, and the way that's done makes their hand basically a hard, fixed surface and a thick separate segment for grasping. But no fingers as such."

It disturbed Mavra that she'd barely noticed. "Let me see. Give me your hand, Julian." She took it and felt it. It was hard and resembled a hoof, but unlike a true hoof, the hand was segmented in two parts, one tapered and rounded and a bit softer inside so that it could be used as a giant thumb against the other, slightly flexible part. When closed, it made a nearly perfect hoof. "That's *awful*!" she exclaimed, then immediately felt terrible because she'd said it.

"Oh, it's not bad once you get used to it," Julian replied sympathetically, remembering how *she* had felt when she'd first awakened and seen those strange hands. "You would be surprised what I can do with them. Not as much as true hands, but about as much as, say, mittens would allow. No, the *real* problem is, since I can use them as forelegs, I have no feeling in them. Having no sense of touch in my hands, I have to be looking at them whenever I am using them. That's all right for many things, but there is no way I can feel Lori's wrists."

"You'd be surprised how much she *can* do with them," Lori assured Mavra. "But not this."

"Well, then, big man, grit those teeth, because *I* sure

can," the tiny woman replied. She took his right hand, noting how squared off and hard his hands were, even with three distinct and bendable fingers and a fairly prehensile thumb, then felt back to the wrist.

"Augh!" Lori grunted in obvious pain.

Mavra let go and shook her head. "I think you might well have some kind of a fracture there. I didn't feel any protrusions, though, so it's not a clean break we can set. Probably some hairline thing or chip. That swelling *is* pretty bad, though. It's hard to say how it would heal—I don't know enough about Erdomese, obviously, to make a guess—but Julian's right. We're gonna have to bind it in some kind of splint so it's immobile and then bandage it. Bandages we got in the pack, and tape, so if we can find something to use as a splint, we'll be okay. I don't know what I can give you to treat the inflammation, though. The stuff that would help me might kill you or burn a hole through your stomach."

"Believe it or not, aspirin," Lori told her. "It seems aspirin is the number one miracle drug of Erdom. We don't make it, but I ran into a drug trader on the ship to Itus. One of our biggest imports."

Mavra sighed. "Well, I have a small tube of aspirin tablets in the pack for my own use. I wish I'd known—or thought to ask. It sure explains why I was able to buy it in the dockside shops! I doubt if there's more than sixty tablets, though, and you, with your large size and particularly with that break, will need all of it and more. Lie down on the bedroll and I'll get them."

With Julian's help, he managed to get over to the bedroll and sink down on top of it. Mavra came back with the small vial of aspirin and a canteen. "I'd take four of them now if I were you. Damn it! We should have started this as soon as we started out!"

They pried apart the plastic box Mavra had used as a medical kit and were able to form, with the aid of a large knife, a pretty rigid set of splints that were tightly taped to the wrist, lower arm, and hand, then wrapped with a green-colored plastic bandage. When it was done, Lori could not move the wrist at all, and after an initial, intense period of pain, it subsided and he felt some relief. Then it was a matter of waiting for the aspirin to kick in.

Anne Marie came over to them. "I do so hope that does it," she said, concerned. "I know how it feels."

Mavra nodded. "What do you want to do about something to eat?"

"Well, the grass *smelled* all right, so we tried some and it will do. We have to eat an awful *lot*, you know. While I'd much rather have it processed, baked in breads and cakes and pastries, or steamed with veggies and spices, that seems a *teeny* bit impractical here. We'll just graze nearby until we've had our fill. As basic as it is, it is ever so much better than those *horrid* jungle leaves!"

"Okay, but don't stray too far from camp," Mavra warned. "You don't know what's out there."

"We'll be careful. We drank our fill in that stream back in Itus, so water is not a problem. Back as soon as we can. Ta!"

"Are they *safe* out there alone and unarmed?" Julian asked worriedly.

"Dillians are tougher than they seem, or at least they used to be," Mavra assured her. "Those hooves can give a hell of a nasty kick, and while their arm strength isn't close to a male Dillian's, they're pretty damned strong compared to us or most others, and I have a feeling that they can twist and move those bodies in ways we can only imagine. And they're not unarmed, really. They both have the big knives we used on the jungle vines."

"You have other weapons, I assume?" Lori asked.

"Some. The absolute best weapons for the Well World are knives for close in and crossbows for long shots."

"Crossbows?"

"Sure. They're accurate and powerful, and they work anywhere: nontech, semitech, or high-tech. I have some other items, too, but they're for various special circumstances."

"I have a saber and scabbard in my pack," Lori told her. "I was pretty good with it, too, but I'm not sure how well I'd do left-handed."

"Well, we won't have to fight a duel with it—I hope. So long as you can stab something with it, I think it's better than nothing. You sure aren't gonna be winning any fist-fights any time soon!" She paused a moment. "What about food for you two? I have a small kerosene-type cooker that'll work here, or there are loaves in the emergency rations that supposedly give any of us what we need. They taste lousy, but they're better than raw grass."

"I could prepare something from the supplies," Julian suggested, but Lori shook his head.

"No, not tonight. Tonight's for resting and taking it easy. If Mavra can stand one of those loaves, so can I. I might like it a lot more than she does."

"Or less. Still, very well, if that is your wish. I could try that grass, but I do not want to leave you alone here."

"No! Eat one of the loaves, too. We're heading for the coast, which shouldn't be that far, right, Mavra?"

"Shouldn't be. Certainly not a day's walk."

"When we are hard up, we will eat grass. Until then we will do what is easiest and most convenient," he pronounced.

"As you say," Julian responded, and went to get the rations.

Mavra was a little irritated. Julian had talked about the confusion over Tony and Anne Marie, but at least there were two of them. She began to wonder if there weren't two Julians as well—the one that led them through a dark jungle safely, reconnoitered the area, and located and approved the campsite and the other one that she now was, subservient, obedient . . . somewhat sickening.

On the other hand, if she had four big tits, hands like claws, arms useless for much lifting and better designed as legs, and if the only hope she had of not being cast adrift as some kind of chattel slave was to keep the one husband who understood her happy enough to keep her around, then maybe she'd be two people, too, no matter how difficult it might be.

She had, after all, been in situations not any better than Julian's. Ancient Earth wasn't kind to most women. The way Tony, Anne Marie, and Julian had talked, that was true even now on much of the planet. Chinese peasant women still toiled in the rice paddies; the women in theocracies like the Islamic fundamentalist cultures were kept without rights, voices, or free movement. It was little better in much of sub-Saharan Africa, India, or even a lot of Latin America. In what they called the Third World, eighty percent or more of humankind was largely forgotten or ignored by the feminist crusaders in the industrialized West, most of whom also forgot or never knew that revolutions were often followed by reactions that could leave them worse off than ever. She had seen it happen.

She had *lived* it.

Time after time the great civilizations, the great ideas, the progress of whole masses of humanity were stopped dead and thrown back, often for longer than generations. Sometimes the darkness lasted many long centuries. Two steps forward and then one back was the norm, or so it seemed, but the darkness could rise and force one back even farther. If, as she'd been told, the status of women in some parts of Earth, let alone so much of it, was different from that in Erdom only by degrees, then the darkness still loomed, waiting to engulf the rest. And that darkness, the darkness of ignorance and slavery that was the dark side of humanity, would be replayed again and again if Nathan Brazil triumphed, even though he himself would have been appalled at that interpretation.

It didn't have to happen. It certainly didn't have to happen the same way and to the same people again. The Markovians—she still thought of the Ancient Ones by that name although Jared Markov, after whom they were named, had not yet been born this time around—were wrong in believing that there was a level of perfection attainable by races fighting their way up the evolutionary ladder. They were right to try to understand and fight the flaws, but the result was that the flaws were simply perpetuated.

That, at least, she could change. She *might* change. But if, and only if, she got into the Well first.

"I'll take the first watch," Lori said, breaking Mavra's reverie. "I slept most of the way here, and I'm fine now."

Mavra nodded. "All right. Julian and I will try to get some sleep. If the Dillians don't come back in an hour or so, wake me. If they do, then give me at least four hours. I've functioned on that little for days at a time." She thought a moment. "I don't want to give you a loaded crossbow with that pair still out there if you're not experienced in using one. I'll get your saber so at least you can hit something over the head if it jumps on you, but what I really want is a loud yell. I'll give you my watch. It's a windup type, so it works anywhere, too."

He grinned. "Don't worry so much. I can see in the dark, remember? I've even been keeping track of the centaurs. I'll be okay."

"In fact, I should take the next watch, not you, for the same reason," Julian pointed out. "The nights are long on this world, and it is best that the night guard be those to whom the dark is no barrier."

"I won't argue, but are you sure you're up to it on so little sleep?" Mavra asked her.

"Yes. I do not need a lot of sleep, either. I make it up when I can."

"Okay, it makes sense to me. If all else fails, we can let you sleep and ride as well." Mavra yawned. "Me, I'm gonna take advantage of your kind offer."

"You get to sleep, too," Lori told Julian. "I'll be all right."

"Yes, my husband," she responded, and lay down on the unoccupied bedroll.

Tony and Anne Marie came back a half hour later. By that time Mavra and Julian were both asleep, and the Dillians tried to make as little noise as possible. They didn't need bedrolls or much else; like horses, they lay down only when crippled or very ill. Instead, they simply stood, their legs locked and the humanoid torsos bent back somewhat, and went to sleep.

Except for the occasional heavy breathing of the centauresses, it was soon deadly still.

Lori, too, wondered about Julian's dual nature. He himself felt pretty well adjusted to the Erdomese form and now even to being male. Maybe *too* adjusted, he had to admit, considering some of his behavior of late, but he felt that he was being pragmatic about things. By Erdomese standards, he thought, he would always be a liberal, always remembering that the females had minds and thoughts and feelings and capabilities most of that society rejected and, hopefully, treating them better than most men there did. On the other hand, in *that* society any outspoken advocacy was a sure route to losing everything and to punishments including cutting out his tongue, castration, and beheading. For Julian it would mean instant death. With the church and its omnipresent spies and true believers programmed from childhood to believe in it and with the enforced insularity of most of the population from real knowledge of much of the rest of this world, nothing could or would change in Erdom's society until and unless there was violent mass revolution.

It might well come eventually, but considering how things there were now, it most assuredly would not be in his or Julian's lifetime. It wasn't until experiencing a real totalitarian theocracy that he had realized just how hard a revolution could be, battling not only minds but genuine power. Technology, discovery, enlightenment, the scientific revolution—*that* had started things on Earth, or restarted them. But what kind of science could one develop when a battery would not hold a charge and tended to dissipate in even short transmission? When technology was rigidly and forever limited to water, and wind, and animal and human power? Without mass communication how could anything be organized? When even writing was limited primarily to the church and the hideously complex ideographic language was so complex that even priests were middle-aged before they fully mastered it, how could knowledge be disseminated?"

"Some men do in fact run the world—and you're not one of them."

And the price for having a crack at being one of those men who *did* run Erdom was just too damned high.

Still, he had to admit, it *was* different being a man in a male-dominated society. The fact was, he was beginning to *like* this form, even if he didn't like the culture and chafed at the hex's technological restrictions. This form was beginning to—no, it *did* feel natural, normal, comfortable. He never even *thought* about it anymore. Funny. He'd been born and raised an Earth-human female and had spent almost forty years as one; he'd been an Erdomese male for a matter of a few months, no more. Yet Mavra Chang seemed an ugly, colorless, unattractive ... *alien* to him, while Julian was beautiful, desirable. Lori Ann had never been sexually attracted to women no matter how much she fought the male system. Lori the Erdomese couldn't remember what turned Lori Ann on in a man or see the least attraction there.

Each day it was getting harder and harder to remember what it had been like to be an Earth-human woman. Not the past, not the events of a life, or the people, or the learning and accomplishments, the struggles, losses, and gains, but remembering being the one who had lived it. That person seemed more and more to be someone else, like a character from a movie she'd watched, a movie spanning forty years of a woman's life.

Was that how it worked? First one got the new body, along with sufficient programming on the brain's subconscious level to use it without serious trouble, and a bit of suggestion so that one was not frightened or revolted by what one saw or what one might need to eat, but it was still the original person, superimposed on an alien form.

But that form's brain had to be different from an Earth human's, if only in subtle but important details. Neural pathways would be wired differently; thoughts would need to be rerouted so that action produced the desired results. If there were subtle differences in the wiring of the hemispheres in male and female human brains, how much more dramatic would that wiring difference be in a totally different species? Add hormones and other chemical differences that would eventually influence development as the mind "settled in," and one's old self, one's memories, one's very soul, would be reshaped day by day so slowly and subtly that a person might not even notice. But one day that person would be wholly of the other species, as if born to it.

Lori Ann had been *playing* at being a man, enjoying fooling with the very concept as if it were some kind of masquerade gender-switch game. He wasn't playing anymore, and he wasn't even sure when he had stopped. He *was* a male now. It was one of the basic things that defined him. What flowed from that sense of identity defined his actions and reactions to a host of things both internal and external.

If it had happened to him like this, it almost certainly had happened to Julian. She'd come in months earlier than he had, but her own situation had been so radical a cultural loss that she'd fought like hell against it, while overall, he had to admit to himself that he'd not really fought it in himself at all. Still, by the time he'd met her, she already admitted that she had accepted being female, that it was something that no longer disturbed her. She'd fought not that but the concept that she was property, that she was to be consigned to a base role as if in a medieval harem. It was something Lori Ann would have fought just as hard against.

Maybe those drugs and hypnotic sessions had accelerated the process for both of them; maybe not. But if Julian now felt as normal and natural as an Erdomese female as he did as an Erdomese male, she might also, away from Erdom but still with him, have stopped fighting the rest.

It made sense. He thought of the two Dillians, who seemed so alike outside and so different inside, and knew that they really weren't. Anne Marie really hadn't been required to adjust much, but to Tony it must have been as much of a shock to be a female as it had been for Julian initially—although Julian also had the restrictive Erdomese culture to deal with. They'd been here the longest of any of this party. They'd come through the night the meteors fell.

Tony still thought he hadn't changed inside, partly, Lori suspected, because Anne Marie still saw the old Tony inside the new body because she wanted to see him there. But he *had* changed. He *was* different. They had talked for a bit, being so, well, *close*, during the walk, and since he had the translator Tony could speak Dillian, which was easier. And when she spoke Dillian rather than English, there were only slight differences between her and Anne Marie's speech patterns. In her normal speech, in her manner, her movements, even many of the things she spoke about, Tony was as feminine as Lori Ann Sutton had ever been. Tony admitted that she'd stopped fighting when she had realized that Anne Marie never noticed any difference. In any event, Tony knew she couldn't stave it off forever and would have to let go sooner or later. Now she was just playacting being the old Tony; he was as past tense as the old Lori Ann was.

"I feel real pity for your Julian," Tony had told him. "I would not accept that life. But in Dillia it is different; the practical day-to-day differences in the lives of men and women there are not radical enough to cause alarm, and in the few areas where they are, the benefits of being male are balanced against the benefits of being female. It is not at all like my old culture, nor, perhaps, your old one, either. It would have been nicer, perhaps, and more romantic to have been Anne Marie's husband rather than her twin sister, but we can no more change that now than we could change ourselves before. This is second best, and we will take it."

In truth, the old Tony still existed only when she was required to speak English. Other than that, Tony and Anne Marie had each drawn from the other what they had found most valuable and had become, in Dillian terms, very much alike indeed. It was as if they had been born twin sisters, with the exception that Tony would never be able to grow proper roses or be half the cook Anne Marie could be, and Anne Marie would never be able to pilot a jet aircraft and would never be that good at repairing even simple mechanical things. That difference was enough to allow each of them to retain a sense of individuality and a connection with their pasts, and it really was enough.

Lori had asked Tony why, if things were working out so well for them, they'd agreed to undertake a very long and difficult journey over land and sea to meet a strange and mysterious woman they didn't know.

"Curiosity most of all," Tony had replied. "A way to see more of this strange and mysterious world than we could any other way. Our passage had, after all, been prepaid, and we verified that every hex had a Zone Gate and from Zone we could be instantly back in Dillia no matter how far in the world we roamed, so return tickets were not a worry, either. And, I admit, timing played some part in our motivation."

"Timing?"

"Yes. You see, Dillian women ovulate only twice a year, for about a three-week period each time. It is not that they do not do things recreationally, as it were, but it only *counts* during each of those three-week periods. While we have more control than an animal would, we were told that during that time women of childbearing age get 'turned on,' one might say, and *stay* that way for the duration. I can now tell you that it is indeed true and that it is a whole-body experience, and further that *much* willpower is required to function even close to normally at that time. Dillians grow up with it and learn to cope with their parents' help. In Dillia it is the females who almost always seduce the males. We, neither of us, were quite ready for that as yet, I fear, and if we had done it and even one of us had gotten pregnant—no sure thing, because the Well governs population—we would have wound up *never* traveling."

Lori could well understand. "Um—do you get periods, too?"

"Twice a year as well, and about ten days long. They are *most* unpleasant, but we can function feeling awful a lot better than we can function during the arousal stage, I can tell you."

"I know," Lori sighed. That was the experience that defined growing up female more than any other, and the lack of it now was one of the best things about being male. He looked back at Anne Marie, the twin of the creature he was riding, and commented, "Too bad you and Julian will both miss shopping for shoes, though."

Now, as he sat there in the darkness, he tried putting a little weight on the ankle and was pleased to notice that the pain was very mild now. In an emergency he would have no compunctions about getting up and running on it, even if he might still pay for that later. The hand, though, was another story. If anything, he was more right-handed than Lori Ann had ever been; his left hand was useful mostly for support of whatever the right hand was doing. The aspirin had helped; he never remembered it doing this good a job on a human headache and suspected that there was a different biochemistry at work here, for once in his favor.

Not enough, though. It still hurt, and the fingers felt numb, a lot more than could be explained by the splint and bandages. The automated clinic back on the east coast of Itus was a long way away now. He had no idea how far away the next high-tech hex they might reach was or whether they would know how to repair a broken Erdomese there. What if the hand had to come off? There weren't many prospects for one-handed men in Erdom. He began to feel panic at the thought, and that just made the awareness of the pain worse. He fought it, tried to push it back down, and finally got some self-control back, but he was feeling dizzy and nauseous. Scared, he reached over and shook Julian, who stirred, shook herself awake, then frowned and immediately was up and at his side.

"You have a fever," she told him in a concerned whisper.

"A very bad one. You are glowing like a camp fire. How long did you let me sleep?" She reached over and picked up the watch. "Five hours." The remains of the medical kit were on a blanket near them, and she went over and picked up the small vial of aspirin. "Here. *Curse these hands!*" She managed to get the top off but couldn't get the pills out. "Give me your hand and I will try and shake them into it."

Lori nodded, shaking now, and put out his left hand. She shook out a half dozen pills, then scooped up two with the lip of the vial and got him a canteen. He got the pills down, but it would take some time for them to have any effect.

"Lie here beside me, husband," she told him, "and try to sleep if you can. I will be here and keep watch upon both the camp and you."

He moaned and shook and thrashed around for the better part of an hour before finally passing into sleep. Julian wasn't all that certain if he was just sleeping or if the fever had finally put him out, but there was nothing more that could be done.

Julian's thoughts were mixed but all bad. For one thing, she felt almost helpless in the situation. She could comfort him and check on him and see that he got aspirin until that was gone, and she could cover him, but she could do little more. The biggest frustration was that she knew nothing of Erdomese infections or even whether this kind of fever reaction was normal or terminal. She *did* assume that if it didn't break within a day, it was very bad indeed, but *then* what? Should he be kept cool or, as she'd automatically done, warm under a blanket?

She assumed that growing up Erdomese tended to give one at least a rough idea of these things just as Earth people had a rough idea of human reactions and illnesses simply by growing up human. Maybe they shouldn't have bandaged the hand. Maybe that cut off air flow or something, although there was no open wound and the bandages were mostly to keep the splint on.

I'm not even a good First Wife here, she thought miserably. *A first wife should know what to do.*

Of course, if they were back in Erdom, help could have been called. Not here. *All that education, that sophisticated background, and what's it worth?* she asked herself.

Nothing. Nothing at all. The revelation struck to the core of her ego and identity. All that Julian Beard had been, all that he'd learned, every scrap of sophisticated knowledge and the numerous skills he'd mastered, were not merely useless now, they were useless period. Sure, in training he'd learned probably the ultimate in first aid, but how much of that applied to Erdomese biology and what good was most of it without the proper instruments and medications on hand? What could she do if she had a decent kit, anyway? Even if she could put a thermometer in his mouth, for how long should it be in and what would be the correct reading? Useless, all useless. Julian Beard was someone trained for other conditions, another time, another world, another life.

Julian of Erdom was furious at Julian Beard for being worse than useless. *Incompetent, irrelevant, and immaterial.* She had clung to him desperately for so long, even decided at one point to die for him, and he was worthless. She rejected him in her fury. She understood now: this was totally new, a start from scratch, from *less* than scratch. All the feelings, impulses, inclinations that she'd pushed back for the sake of that precious ego had been not a personal victory but a brick wall. Her past was the wall, a useless thing that had kept her unhappily tied to a world and life and viewpoint no longer relevant. But the old Julian Beard wasn't there anymore. He was a ghost, an evil spirit that had led her only to this helpless situation.

It was probably too late, but she hated him now, rejected him, cast him out. She felt him go, like something solid and tangible that had been inside her head and heart and now was removed. It felt good, but—what was left?

Erdomese women served their husbands and families and extended families. She had a husband, but neither he nor she had anyone else, even in Erdom. He was all she had, and she felt that she had failed him. She looked down at him as he slept fitfully, and for the first time she looked at him entirely as an Erdomese female. She looked at his cute horn, the gentle strength of his face, and a flood of emotions and self-realizations swept through her, this time unchecked, unfiltered, without thought or inhibition.

She bent down to his face and whispered in his ear, "I love you, Lori. I love you and I need you."

He didn't come fully awake, but he seemed to hear, and there was a gentle smile on his face all of a sudden, as if he had banished nightmares for a more pleasant dream.

Julian was not really thinking, just letting her Erdomese body and brain act as they willed, performing actions that she neither knew nor cared made any sense or not. She bent over, raised his head gently, and offered him her lower right breast, one of the water carriers in a nonpregnant female's anatomy. He took it and began to drink. At first it was a little, as in foreplay, but after a bit he began really sucking and taking it in, even as she was licking his face with her long, thick tongue.

She had no idea how long she kept it up, but it was probably an hour or two before she noticed a dramatic change in him. The fierce glow was gone; there was only a slight residual shimmer, the natural aftereffect of the dangerous condition he'd had.

Lori's fever had broken.

Julian pulled back, exhausted, dehydrated, but also very, very happy to see and sense the change in him. He was going to be all right!

"We might light a small torch and take at look at that dressing," said a deep woman's voice behind her.

She started, turned, and saw Mavra Chang standing there.

"How—how long . . . ?" Julian managed, her voice raspy and dry.

"Pretty much since you started. *Somebody* had to guard the camp."

Julian felt suddenly ashamed, as if she'd done something *else* wrong. "I—I'm sorry. But—he was burning up with fever. I felt his life burning up inside him. I *had* to do *something*." She paused. "I just wish I knew what I did."

"Don't apologize. I heard him crying out and thrashing around and knew he had to have something nasty—I don't think I've actually slept soundly since I was aboard a ship in space, and you can't *believe* how long ago that was, nor can I. At first I couldn't figure out what you were doing, though," she admitted. In fact, although she didn't say it, what she had first made out in the bright starlight and then watched for a bit seemed pretty damned sick, a kind of prenecrophilia in which one made love to the dying. It took her experience with many alien species and her analytic mind to finally see a method in the apparent madness.

Julian still couldn't. "Uh—what *was* I doing?" she asked hesitantly. She felt really rotten herself at the moment.

Mavra smiled. "A long time ago—it seems like I use that term a lot these days—when I was just pushing puberty, I pondered the Universal Sexual Design Question like most everybody else I knew. If most every mother had one baby at a time and multiple births were rare, why did girls get two tits? The answer, of course, is *redundancy*. Then I saw that Erdomese women had quads, yet Erdomese births are not all that much different in number than Earth-human births. So why *four* breasts? Wasn't that taking redundancy to an extreme? Then I was told that the bottom two were water jugs when the system allowed it, and, probably like you, I accepted it as some sort of desert survival thing. I mean, you only need one guy to knock up a lot of females, but a lot of guys can't produce any more babies with one female than one guy. Made sense. You probably thought the same thing. Probably most Erdomese think that way."

"Yes? So?"

"I don't think so anymore. Oh, maybe that's *one* reason, but it's not the main one. I have nothing but the evidence of my own eyes here and the results, but I'll bet you what you did is done whenever a male is seriously ill. The face licking cools down the head in the only area of the body where your race can perspire to exchange heat. But that

water—I don't think that's water at all. It's at body temperature, and the cooling effect is minimal, so what purpose
does it serve? Then I remembered the female Uliks from a
long time ago. Big, ugly suckers, cross between walruses
and giant snakes, with six arms and three pair of breasts.
That was bad enough, except that they laid eggs and the
young were born with developed stomachs and teeth and
were fed dead meat. Which of course brought up the question of why they had *any* tits, let alone six, when they
didn't nurse their young.'"

"Yes? And?" Julian was exhausted, but she really wanted
to know the point of this.

Mavra handed her a canteen. "Drink all of it. I *know*
there's water over there, and we'll get some in a few hours.
We have several more canteens, anyway."

Julian took it gratefully and found herself draining the
whole canteen in almost a continuous series of gulps. When
she was done, Mavra continued.

"See, the only thing you and a Ulik woman have in common is desert. I didn't think about it, but these ancient farts
playing God here long ago weren't *all* creative geniuses.
They stole a lot from one another. That's why there are so
many humanlike life-forms, and why most races here seem
to be themes and variations on other races, plants, animals,
birds, bugs—you name it. It's obvious to me now that the
ones working on desert races would peek at each other's
work, steal from each other, even critique one another's
work."

"The Ulik . . . ?" Julian prompted.

"The Ulik female takes in enough water to float a ship.
Once inside her, the amount she doesn't use, and that's
most of it, is stored in a series of sacs that have what look
like breasts as outlets. But each 'breast' produces different
stuff. There's a salt and mineral solution in a form that can
be handled by the body to replenish what's lost. Another
takes vitamins from food and creates a vitamin solution of
sorts. But the bottom pair have a solution that contains universal antibodies of some kind of supercharged type. Vi-

ruses, germs, inflammation, you name it. They attack, destroy, then work to help heal what was damaged. The Ulik males are big; the females are *enormous*, and they don't travel much, but I tell you the males really treat them right and bring them whatever they want. I thought it wasn't a bad system, myself."

Julian gasped. "You mean—my lower set—they're like those super illness fighters?"

Mavra nodded. "I think so now. No way to be sure, of course. I sure wouldn't bet my life on it being fact, but I'd bet a good amount of money it was the answer. I think you shot him up with the equivalent of megavitamins, minerals, body salts, antibiotics, you name it. He can't make that amount on his own, like the male Uliks. In fact, I'll bet the whole harem thing grew out of that. You're basically mammals. When you're pregnant, the body devotes itself entirely to one thing and one thing only, and all this good stuff gets shot into the nursing baby just like Earth-human breast milk transfers antibodies and nutrients well beyond mere food. Tell me—you ever cut yourself? Or had a bad bruise?"

"Yes. When I was being imprisoned, I was chafed and bruised by the chains, and I cut myself once trying to get away."

"Uh huh. And how long did it take you to recover?"

"I—I hadn't thought about it. Once I was freed and out of there, I never noticed."

"Lori injures a lot more easily and heals more slowly. He had some minor cuts and abrasions on him that were scabbed over. You have none, yet you've been here longer than he has and have been treated more roughly. Ever know a sick Erdomese female? Or see one scarred and bruised?"

Julian thought a moment. "No, now that I think of it. Oh, some of the old ones showed the wear and tear of their age, but among the younger ones, no. The men, however, all had some kind of cut or bruise, and a lot of them had dueling scars." The evidence of Mavra's suppositions was sinking in. "Many of the older women were fat and frumpy and didn't take great care of themselves, but I don't remember even one with *stretch marks*!"

Mavra nodded. "So you see, if this secret really got out and was understood, if they weren't kept so ignorant that they didn't even know what caused diseases and infections, the women of Erdom would have a hell of a lot of power over their men. If he tells you he needs you, he means it. I wouldn't push it too far—I doubt if you'll grow back a hand if it's chopped off—but for most basic illnesses and injuries, you women are immune. The men are patsies without your defenses."

"I—I want to believe that it's true. But—*how did I know*?"

Mavra shrugged. "When the Well processes somebody, it has to deal with him as an adult. An adult used to being something else. By definition, you can't have the same lifetime of accumulated experience as somebody who grew up in the new race, so the Well compensates. Biochemically, attitudinally, you name it. The most important parts of what Mama Erdoma teaches her girls, you receive as one-time knowledge, available when needed, like instinct. It was needed. It came out."

Julian shook her head a little from side to side. "I think you may be right—to a point. That, however, was not all that was needed to bring it forward. Somebody I once was and clung to fiercely and needlessly got in the way, too, and he proved useless. Looking at Lori, I knew that. At that moment, feeling so helpless, something snapped inside me. That old self died completely. Died or was killed. It is strange. I know it was there, was the driving force of my life for so long, but I cannot remember much about it. Tomorrow, when my husband awakens, I will ask him to give me a new name. It is all that is left of my past, and I do not want even the reminder."

Mavra had seen this before. Going native was the old term for it, one means by which the mind coped with what to many was an impossible situation.

"If I get into the Well first, you aren't necessarily stuck

in that body and role," Mavra pointed out. "You can be anything, any race, any sex you want, here or on a world out there."

"No, no," Julian responded, shaking her head. She knew what Mavra was saying and why, but she did not, *could* not, understand. "I am an Erdomese woman, I am Lori's First Wife, and I wish nothing else. If you can do what you say, and have the opportunity, then his decision will tell me my own. Until then there is no decision. Not until Lori decides."

Mavra shrugged. "Fair enough." She halted suddenly and looked out beyond Julian to the west. "Dawn is coming. At least we'll be able to see what we're dealing with. It may sound crazy, but I've had the damnedest feeling that some pretty big and possibly dangerous creatures are out there. They have moved in the dark here, both on the ground and in the air, although they haven't come near us. That may be caution or fear, or we might just smell awful. I wouldn't take it at all personally if that last is true. In any event, so far there hasn't been anything that kills first and sniffs later. In daylight, who knows?"

They let Lori sleep, and Julian was out pretty quickly, too, but the centauresses were up quickly, bright and alert.

Mavra had some coffee brewing atop a small oil-lit stove. Although she still hadn't reacquired a taste for it after so long, she had decided that caffeine, particularly at the start of a day, was a safety measure.

"Sorry about the lack of tea, but there's only one pot and the amount of rations was limited," she told Anne Marie.

"Oh, no bother, dear. When you live with a Brazilian for several years, you really start getting into the habit. A pity we have no milk, though."

"This is *not* exactly roughing it," Mavra warned her. "Not yet." She looked across at the other centauress. "Where's Tony going?"

"Where I've *been*, dear. I mean, after all, we *did* eat rather a lot last night, bland though it was."

"Oh. Never mind."

With a mug of coffee in hand and some of the pasty loaf

inside her, Mavra got out the field glasses and began to take a look around.

"Well, I'll be damned!" she said at last. "Those are the *weirdest* things I've seen in a life of seeing weird things. Whoever dreamed up this place wasn't all that original, but he, she, or it was certainly creative." She handed the binoculars to Tony. "Take a look."

Tony *did* look and had much the same reaction. The fields seemed covered with dense herds of a creature that looked like . . . well, *everything*.

"These Ancient Ones. I think they drank," Tony remarked, and handed the glasses to Anne Marie.

What they all saw was a creature about 120 centimeters tall with a head not unlike a giant beaver or great hare. Its ears, however, were two almost circular extensions that stuck out on both sides of the head like flapping plates. From the forehead, two pronglike horns extended either a mere fifteen or twenty centimeters or, on some of the larger ones, a good forty to fifty centimeters.

"Ten to one the short horns are females and the long horns males," Tony remarked. "Notice how there are far fewer long horns and that they're rather well spaced in the fields. Each oldster watching out for his wives, most likely, with the shorter ones inside probably sons. Oh, my! Look at them *jump!*"

Mavra took the glasses and saw immediately what she meant. They did not run, not exactly; they *leapt*, the larger ones springing free of the tall grass cover. The bodies seemed to be covered in a light, short beige fur, and for a moment they looked like yellowish kangaroos, but in addition to short, tiny arms they had two rather small hoofed front feet and two *enormous* rear feet that powered the leap and seemed all out of proportion to the rest of the creature. They had short, stubby fanlike tails that, unlike a kangaroo or wallaby, could not support them standing on the rear legs alone, so when still, they were on all fours with the long neck craning their heads up.

"Six limbs," Annie Marie noted. "Like us!"

Something panicked a gathering not far from the shimmering border wall—some large reptilian birdlike thing swooping overhead, it looked like. In any event, it almost started a stampede of the creatures, who leapt out of the grass as if one and then came down again, apparently on their front hooves, then launched using their gigantic rear legs once more. The movement of one group startled some of the others, but Tony noted that the larger long-horned ones he'd thought of as males turned and looked up at the threat above them and seemed to act almost in a coordinated fashion to track and if need be fight the predator.

The attacker, an ugly dark-looking thing with an impossibly long snakelike neck and a head that seemed to be all eyes and mouth, swooped down and found itself confronted by a series of male defenders who would leap, horns out, in an attempt to gore or at least scare the creature when it came too close.

It was quite an impressive bit of teamwork and was quite effective; every time the attacker would come down for some wee one in the still-fleeing herd, it would meet one or more of the males. Still, the herd was too large to guard against air attack. Eventually the thing outmaneuvered the defenders, swooped into the madly fleeing and scattering herd, and came up with something small and wiggling. Then the thing flew off toward the nearby grove of trees with its prize.

"Disgusting," Anne Marie snorted.

"Nature, that is all, my dear," Tony responded pragmatically. "One overpopulates; the other manages it. It is the same way on Earth."

"Not in England!" she responded, as if it made sense.

Tony turned to Mavra. "You know, I have been thinking. Do you suppose those herds are the Gekir? They have hands of a sort, or so it appears, and they have some sort of logical defense organizations."

"I doubt it," Mavra replied. "Too basic. After all this time they'd be about as sophisticated here as a nontech civilization can get, I'd say. No, you were right. That's instinct and nature. No tools and no weapons that are built with tools. I can't say I'm too thrilled by that thing that attacked them, though. I wish it had gone anywhere but in that grove."

"We can bypass it."

"Yeah, but how many more will we have to bypass if we do? And Julian needs a real long drink or we'll have to let her empty all our canteens." Briefly, and skipping the details, she explained what had taken place in the night.

"Poor dear! But she should *ride* today! I'm certain that either of us could take both of them," Anne Marie responded.

"Yes, particularly if she's the one against my back this time," Tony added, rubbing a bruise where Lori's horn had stuck her. "How far do you think it is to the coast?"

"Not far. Half a day at the most," Mavra told them. "An hour or less if it was just the two of us."

"Perhaps we can repack this differently," Tony suggested. "I think I could take both Julian and you and half the supplies, and Anne Marie could take Lori and the remaining supplies. He's the only one that weighs much of anything among the three of you."

"How sweet," Anne Marie remarked. "You want to ensure that we have matching bruises, too." She sighed. "Very well. Then we can avoid that horrid creature over there altogether."

"I'll go that far with you, about riding, that is," Mavra told them, "but I don't think we can skip water. No, if we run every time there's a predator around, we'll be running all the time. We'll give that pair another hour or two while we re-sort out this stuff. If that thing hasn't decided to leave and find somebody new to play with, we'll see if it cares if we show up or not. It might be too full to care."

Dlubine

THINGS HAD BEEN GOING WELL IN THE SAILING DEPARTMENT. The oceans had remained generally clear of other ships, although one or two had been sighted either as distant wisps on the horizon or as sets of far-off running lights in the night, but no one had come near, no one had challenged.

They had also managed to steer a northerly course with a good wind at their backs, and thanks to clear skies both day and night, Nathan Brazil now had a relatively decent idea of where they were.

The shortest distance to the north coast would have been straight through Mowry, but the hue and cry for him had to be all over the Well World by now and certainly would have reached a nearby high-tech water hex via Zone long before they got there. He had no desire to face all the locating devices, let alone the speed and weaponry, of a fast, well-armed naval corvette such as the one the colonel had allegedly been waiting to pick up.

They would also probably have come from Mowry to Dlubine with the news, including a halfway decent description of the stolen vessel and her rather distinctive crew, and they would certainly be waiting for him at all the island harbors.

Still, in order to give Mowry a wide berth and make the long crossing to nontech Fahomma—where they'd have a chance of either slipping ashore on the coast of Lilblod or perhaps skirting the coast all the way up to Betared—they would need supplies, and those tiny islands were the best sources. Any searchers would be looking for the ship and for two Glathrielians, male and female, in a hex limited to kinetic forms of energy. They could generate power here, but they could not store it.

Most important to their needs, though, was that those looking for the ship probably did not know about Gus.

Gus had accepted the relative technology levels at face value, as products of the culture. It wasn't until talking with Nathan Brazil that he had realized that the limits were *imposed* by the Well, hex by hex.

"The idea," Brazil explained, "was to approximate as closely as possible what the mother world of the race would provide. Of course, these are only rough limits, approximations, but the general idea holds. The world of the Dahir, for example, is probably mineral-poor, with all the heavy stuff too far down to use and not much surface volcanism—not a lot with which to develop a sophisticated technologically based culture. You're probably more limited here than the Dahir are on their own world, but I wouldn't expect television or trains or a lot of other stuff even after a very long period of development. They'd develop a different way. When resources are there but much harder to get at, and the land and water areas are conducive to some technological development but not on the scale of advanced electronics like computers and satellites, the Well imposes the semitech limit approximation here, too. Planets like Earth, with creatures like the ones we grew up as and with all those resources and conditions, get the high-tech treatment. No limits."

"Yeah? You mean there's an actual Dahir planet someplace? With Dahirs the boss civilization like humans are on Earth? Ain't that a kick in the pants!"

"There definitely is, and don't think that because you're nontech here that they haven't somehow developed a lot more than your people could. It would just be a lot harder than it was for us, and you know how long it took *us*. Who knows how it turned out? Or is still turning out, more likely. Your group here was just the prototype, to see if they could survive and prosper under conditions stricter than they would find out there. There's a huge number of races out there, far more than the 1,560 here. These are just the leftovers. The last batch, as it were. Why they stayed, or were stuck here more likely, I couldn't guess. At any rate, they've been here ever since."

"Huh! Talk about not havin' no future! Jeez ... Just *here*, huh? Kinda depressing, really."

"Huh? What do you mean?"

"Well, jeez, I mean, all these people—and all of 'em *are* people, no matter what they look like—bein' born and livin' and dyin' and it just goes on and on. No population explosions, no Tom Edisons or Philo T. Farnsworths or nothin' in most of 'em, at least none that can actually invent things and change everybody's lives, and the high-techs either gettin' fat and lazy or turnin' into ant colonies with traffic jams, seems like. I mean, you talk about havin' nothin' to look forward to! No big changes or revolutions or nothin'. The most you can hope is that your kids grow up to have just what you have. Now, *that's* depressing—to *me*, anyway."

Brazil thought about it. "I guess my viewpoint's different. To me, this is a place where maybe folks can find out what's really important."

"Well, that's 'cause you're the *audience*, not an actor in the play. Even so, I notice you went back and lived through all the shit in Earth history. You didn't stick around here watchin' folks contemplate their navels."

The captain sighed. "I don't know, Gus. Maybe you're right. Your whole life was trying to be where the action was, and I guess mine is, too. Don't exempt yourself, though, from that audience. We're both a couple of ambulance chasers, rushing off to see where the siren's going. Maybe that's the trouble with us. You didn't rush to rescue the child from the burning building or catch the robber or put your life on the line for a cause. You went there to *film* it. I didn't really have any cause, either. I might have tackled the robber or tried to save the kid, but it was just because it was something to do. Now it's *us* who are the story. This time we're the reason for everything that's going on. I doubt if either of us is comfortable in that role."

"Maybe. Maybe I just would rather have been one of them high-tech types here to tape all this for the eleven o'clock news. Maybe that's my problem. Or maybe it's just that this is the only game in town right now, and when it's over, it's gonna be boring as hell."

"Maybe, maybe not. Things *do* happen here, although on a smaller scale. There were some wars here once and might be again sometime, and revolutions *do* happen, cultures *do* get turned. Look at the ancestral home of Earth. Conquered by a nontech hex that forced it to switch places."

Gus looked out over the wheel at Terry, who still relaxed on the deck, seemingly oblivious to everything. "Yeah, and look at what we did with it. What the hell *did* they do to her, anyway? You can't *know* what a difference there is. You can't imagine it."

"I don't know, Gus," Nathan Brazil admitted, shaking his head slowly from side to side. "I don't know what happened at all. They weren't like that the last time I was here, and that was long after the switch. She—they—are the best example that things do change on the Well World. There are other things, too. I don't remember the Dahir being as sleek and streamlined as you are, and I sure don't remember ever hearing about this vanishing trick you do. I've seen some other races, too, races I knew, and they're different as well. A *lot* has changed here, for all the look of it. An awful lot. I haven't figured it out yet, and I doubt if I can get a real handle on any of it until I'm inside the Well, in that incredible form, able to digest all this and figure it out." He sighed. "And that is the only real priority."

And if I fail, I could die here . . .

Brazil was still having trouble with that, still fighting against the idea, but it wouldn't get out of his mind. It scared him, and he hadn't expected that, but there was also a bit more zest to this race because it was there.

For the first time his very existence was at stake. The sense of risk was both uncomfortable and oddly exhilarating. It was something totally new to him, and anything totally new was attractive, even in so perverse a fashion as this.

But then again, the girl was something new and unexpected as well, and for all Nathan Brazil felt for her, he still wasn't at all certain if she represented a true asset or yet another threat.

Why had she joined him in the first place, and stuck with him, considering the vast gulf between them? Why was she so intent on using her powers to help him clear obstacles from his path? Did she want to be put back, become Terry once again? He could do it, inside the Well, but how could she *know* that or anything else about his true nature? Was she perhaps fleeing from whatever had made her the way she was, or had that hidden intellect directed her to join him?

Gus went over to her as she ate some of the hard bread and tried to make her see him. He just couldn't believe that somehow, somewhere, deep inside her, he couldn't make her understand who he was.

She *did* see him when he put his huge reptilian face in front of her and stared into her eyes and began to talk. For a moment she was visibly startled to see this huge creature apparently materialize so close, but then she just frowned a bit and went back to the bread.

He had no way of knowing that at that moment she had looked beyond his surface appearance, looked deep inside him, and sensed only friendliness and a total absence of threat either to her or to Brazil. That had placed him in the category of factors not to worry about, and there seemed little point to anything more until and unless some concerted action was required.

He didn't accept that. "Terry! It's Gus! *Gus!* Do you understand me? It's Gus, at your side like always! You've just *gotta* be in there *somewhere*, damn it! We went through too much together!"

But Gus's words registered only as random sounds, and she could read or infer nothing at all from his features or form. She was aware that it was almost frantically trying to communicate with her, but she saw no possible point to the communication even if there had been a way. It seemed to feel some actual affection for her, which seemed odd, but that, too, wasn't relevant to her, nor was it a problem worth pursuing at this time.

She would, of course, have recognized Gus if he had looked as she had known him; those memories were still there, still accessible when needed. But she had not had the briefing for new entries in Zone. She had gone through the Zone Gate and emerged still human. All her experience told her that the Zone Gate was nothing more than another variation of the gate that had brought her to the Well World; she had no information at all on its transformation and adaptation abilities and functions. There was therefore no way for her to know that her companions of the past now looked remarkably different.

She did consider the problem of why she hadn't been able to see the creature until now. She *had* sensed it, even back on land, and knew it was the same one, but because it radiated only friendship and no sense of danger, it had been ignored.

She heard its heavy steps on the wooden deck going away from her, back toward the Mate, and looked up and was again startled to see nothing. That should not be. She could feel it, sense it, but only in general terms, enough to know it was there.

But where? It was so *big*, so colorful . . . She tried shifting through all the bands, but nothing showed up. *Now*, suddenly, Gus interested her a great deal. It was an unacceptable situation not to be able to see other creatures.

She sat statuelike, virtually all her mental resources suddenly fixed on this one problem, scanning every single energy band, mental and physical, one by one, examining and going through all sorts of tests on each, trying to find one that somehow wasn't right.

Busy with running the ship and with making plans, the two men hardly noticed that she sat there hour after hour, not moving, hardly breathing, all resources concentrated on this one problem.

And eventually she found it. One tiny, thin wave of medium power. She tried to block it off but found that impossible to do without also blocking off needed brain processing power. It was so perfectly located on the mental spectrum that it couldn't be jammed, couldn't be neutralized, without causing more harm than good. The best she could do finally was to narrow it down, localize it, pinpoint its source, then file it away.

She still couldn't see Gus unless he wanted to be seen, but from that point on she knew exactly where he was, which was more than sufficient. It was, however, an interesting capability for all that. The band was a common one, and the broadcast was strictly one-note, designed to do just one specific thing and to do that very well indeed. Given sufficient energy, it might be possible to duplicate the effect from the human brain. Almost casually, without even thinking about, let alone grasping, how she did it, she just *did* it.

Gus immediately popped into full visibility up there next to the Mate. One single narrow frequency; two broadcasts canceled out the effect on sender and receiver. Obvious and simple. Otherwise the creatures could never see one another, either. Once satisfied that she could turn it on or off at will, she filed the information away and finally turned her attention again to the now very old bread.

While all this was going on, late enough in the day to be nearing dusk and only a few minutes later than Brazil had predicted, they reached the hex barrier with Dlubine.

"Looks pretty peaceful," Gus noted. "Big fluffy clouds but not much else. Even the whitecaps don't seem real big."

Brazil nodded. "I'd hoped we'd reach it while we still had some light. I think we're pretty much dead on where I thought we were from the charts, too. I just hope it isn't freezing cold or something over there, although I doubt it. There'd be something of a permanent storm front at the barrier if it was, and while the sky looks a bit different, it's not enough to worry me. Still ... I gather you're warm-blooded, Gus, or you wouldn't have done so well back in that snowstorm. What's your range of comfort?"

"Can't say for sure," the Dahir responded. "I guess I'm pretty well insulated, since I haven't really felt uncomfortable in any extreme weather. Oh, I knew it was cold back in Hakazit, but it felt like I was wearin' a full set of winter clothes, if you know what I mean. Dahir's kinda high up, sort of a rain forest swamp like you find in northwest Washington, where it rains half the time and can get kinda chilly but not freezin'. I *hope* I don't need no clothes for any of this! I mean, jeez! Where would I get somethin' to fit *me*?"

"Well, we'll soon know. Here we go."

Pulcinell had been warm and comfortable for Brazil, with both water and air temperatures somewhere in the high twenties Celsius, very much like Rio had been in its spring. He felt the tingle as they passed through the barrier and was suddenly aware that the problem in Dlubine would not be freezing.

It was *hot*. It was a steambath of major proportions, and the sun was almost on the horizon! It had to be close to forty degrees Celsius. Even Gus wasn't unaffected.

"Wow! Feels like somebody just threw a hot blanket over me!"

"Me, too," Brazil responded. "This one's a hotbox, that's for sure. With heat like this near dusk, I'm not sure what midday might bring and I don't like to think about it. No wonder they had major storm warnings on the chart all over this hex! With this kind of heat and humidity you can get a hurricane between dusk and midnight! Evaporation here has got to be nuts!"

"Yeah, and when it's clear, it'll be Sunstroke City, definitely for you, maybe for me. I dunno. Maybe we oughta figure on riggin' up some kind of roof or sunshade or somethin' for tomorrow, though."

Brazil nodded. "At least it's calm right now, and we're in very deep water here with no shoals or reefs. I can pretty well lock the wheel down and the both of us can look for something to use. Otherwise we'll have to just drift through the day or find some shallows and anchor. Might not be a bad idea to do that, anyway. I can use some decent rest, and I get the bad feeling that there isn't a night in this land that isn't filled with thunder and lightning."

Gus looked out at the darkening horizon. "I'm not too thrilled to look forward to that experience, considerin' the storm we started with, but I'm just as worried at what I see out there." A tiny finger gestured to the northeast, and Brazil's gaze followed it.

"Well," the captain said with a sigh, "we couldn't exactly expect to travel even an ocean without company." He fumbled and came up with the binoculars from his pack and examined the horizon more closely. "Looks like all commercial traffic, anyway, just from the look of the sails. All heading pretty much the same way, too."

He made an estimate of the common heading of the three sets of sails still far off on the northeastern horizon and looked at the charts. "There," he said finally, pointing to a dot on the map with his finger. "Five will get you ten that they're all making for that island." He looked up at the sail. "Not much of a wind, but they should make it in, oh, two hours, I'd say. Maybe less if the wind picks up like I expect once things start to cool—and I say that in a relative sense. They cut it close, but they should be in the harbor there before any big blow comes up."

"What about us?" Gus asked him. "Shouldn't we put in someplace, too?"

"Well, the island, which is called Mahguul on the chart, is the only thing within *our* reach, too. Pretty small—only a few kilometers across by the look of it here, but with some elevation. I'd rather not risk getting bottled up in there if the word's out on us. It would only take somebody from Mowry to come over and post the gory details. A consortium could post a decent reward, but if they just posted that we'd stolen a fellow sailor's ship, it wouldn't take much of a reward." He thought for a moment. "Still, I don't want to battle storms all night even if I'm gonna fry tomorrow. I'm gonna head for it even in the dark. If we can just find some shelter off it, we might be able to get what we need."

"Sounds about as dangerous as takin' on the storms," Gus noted worriedly. "Still, you know the business."

"Yeah." *I hope.*

The night brought a stunning surprise. The ocean was alive with light; greens and blues and reds and yellows and all sorts of in-between shades were all over the place, forming patterns just beneath the surface and giving the whole sea an almost fairy-tale glow.

"Damn! Will you look at *that*!" Gus exclaimed at the unending parade of lights. "What do you suppose causes it? Could it be the lights of the people who live under the water here?"

"Unlikely," Brazil responded, fascinated himself by the beauty of it. "If it was coming from intelligent creatures, we'd see more movement in the patterns, and this is a semitech hex, so there wouldn't be any real power source. The water here is fairly deep, too, so it's not something pasted on or painted on bottom structures. That range of colors means they're not too deep. My guess would be some kind of marine life that forms large colonies that float or swim a few meters below the surface, but around here you can never take anything at face value."

"Terry seems to like it. It's the first really human reaction I've seen her have."

"She's probably analyzing its atomic structure or something equally absurd," Brazil responded grumpily. "Where is she, anyway? I can't see much in the dark, even with the glow lighting things up."

"Right there by the side rail, on the left. Easy to spot her with this light show. You've *got* to be able to see her. No-body who can grow a new eyeball can have vision *that* bad."

"No, I— Oh, wait a minute! Hold on! Damn it! Son of a bitch!"

"What?"

"She's solved your damned trick! Now I can't see *either* of you!"

"You're kiddin'! 'Course, how would *I* be able to tell? So I can see her and she can see me, but you can't see nei-ther of us unless we're talkin' to you or in your face! Ain't *that* a kick in the head!"

"Yeah, for me," Brazil sighed. "And I'm the one that could use it best right about now! More than either of you, since I'm the target."

"Yeah, well, I can't do much about that, but at least you don't exactly fit the wanted poster no more. I mean, they're bound to have the both of you on it, right? They won't ex-pect you alone, particularly when she was clearly aboard when you stole this skiff."

"Yeah, but that won't mean much. She's just an identi-fier, like me having a beard or black hair. You can lose peo-ple all sorts of ways, but my description's pretty well fixed. Still, I wish I could really get through to her, make her un-derstand what we need and persuade her to go get it. You can carry more, but she can climb and get in and out of a lot of places that you can't."

"Tried just about every which way, huh?"

"Just about. The only thing I didn't try, and I'm not sure it would do anything or not, was to try and connect on her level, body to body, mind to mind."

"Jeez! You can *do* that?"

"Of course not. But I have a suspicion that *she* could, if the will to do it was within me and if I could put myself into a trancelike state where I would not resist."

"I don't think *I* could do that."

"Yeah, well, I had some practice with such things while I was in the Orient. In a way, the state she's in and the power she has are very reminiscent of the goals of various schools of Eastern mysticism. Thing is, what I've seen ordinary Earth humans do with their minds once they were in a mental state totally removed from the material world awed and scared even me. I think, maybe, deep down it's everybody's inheritance from the folks who built all this. The potential is there, anyway, to some degree."

"Well, why didn't you try that, then?"

He gave a wry smile. "For the same reason I stopped short in the lamasery. Because I'm not so sure if I entered that mental realm that I could get back any more than she can. What if whatever force that has this metaphysical, mental, symbiotic relationship with her were to get that same degree of control inside me? With that kind of power and lack of dependence on most things physical, I could make it to the Well easily. The question is, what sort of mind would I be bringing into it? Could I shake it off when I had to, or would I be bringing a force I don't understand into direct contact and connection with the Well and all its powers?"

"You think this thing is evil, then?"

"Not in the absolute sense, no. It would be evil to some, good to others, I think. But it, itself, is, I think, beyond that sort of definition in the same way that the Markovians, the founding race, were beyond it. I don't know, Gus, but I would have to be in a very desperate situation before I could open myself up to that kind of threat."

"I think I might take the chance at some point if I thought I might be able to become one of them good guys myself. I could stand a billion years before gettin' bored."

"Well, I don't know. I don't know if I would want that or not. God knows I've thought about it enough. And it might not be the kind of godhood anybody would want, anyway." He chuckled. "Besides, I've spent half an eternity as a crook, con man, scoundrel, rogue, and pirate. To be able to do anything you wanted or have anything you wanted by wishing for it would take all the fun out of life. And you've got to ask yourself, What would the Glathrielians want to do? And what would a race of mystics that has sworn off all material desires want, anyway?"

"Um, yeah. I see your point."

They were silent for a while as the wind picked up and they began making some speed again. Off to the west the sky began a dramatic display of lightning, but it was still far enough away that they couldn't hear the thunder.

"Gus?"

"Yeah, Cap? I'm still here, watchin' the fireworks."

"Don't worry about that. It's not heading toward us. I've been looking at the lights, though, and I think maybe I was wrong. I think those *are* some kind of intelligent lighting system. The patterns ... Well, don't they remind you of something? A bit more color, but don't they kind of look like what a great city might look like when you're passing over it two kilometers high in an aircraft?"

"Yeah! Now that you say it, I do see that. I'll be damned! I *thought* there was somethin' familiar about 'em. But I thought you said this was deep water."

"It is. The first impression, I think, is an optical illusion based partly on the knowledge that this is a semitech hex and they can't have an elaborate electrical grid, even water-insulated somehow."

"Yeah, so?"

"It's the fact that they live so very deep that gives us this overall impression and view. They *do* have some kind of light source, probably organic, arising from chemical means. They've lit their city, their civilization, their little world with it. And to them, we're doing exactly what the vista suggests—we're 'flying,' as it were, on the very top of their atmosphere, looking down. Now *that*, to me, is impressive."

"Yeah." Gus breathed deeply and continued to look at the vast rippling field of lights. He wondered what the people were like down there and whether this was a city asleep or a city alive at night, bustling with traffic and commerce and all the things a great city might offer.

There was lightning all around after a while, and some

distant claps of thunder could be heard rolling hollowly over the waves. Slowly, too, the vast undersea city, if that indeed was what it was, began to trail off, the lights becoming fewer, and great dark patches began appearing. Still, a few lines of light continued on almost beneath their ship, as if they were lonely highways stretching out from the metropolis to others far distant.

Suddenly Gus realized that this was exactly what they were or at least what Brazil thought they were, and in fact their ship was following the broadest twin line of lights just as an airline pilot might follow a great road.

"It's going where we're going," Brazil assured him. "It's too bad it's so damned hot here that we get all these night storms. Otherwise this would be a dream stretch of ocean to navigate by eye alone. All you'd need would be a general destination or maybe a road map."

The captain had finally shed the last of his personal dignity in reaction to the steam bath heat. His clothes were designed for a cold climate, and Dlubine was anything but that. He was a little, bony sort of guy, Gus noted, although quite hairy, and it was easy to see why he'd be a hit with the women even though the rest of him was small.

Brazil himself would have preferred at least a pair of briefs, even though he was the only Earth-human male in a vast stretch of the world and the only Earth-human female around had seen him like this many times and indeed seemed to prefer him this way. It was just part of his nature. He had not, however, ever found any nonhuman on the Well World who could get the crotch right.

Yet, it felt better, even if he *was* still sweating like a pig.

"Lights ahead. On—maybe above—the surface," Gus warned suddenly.

Brazil nodded. "I see them. That looks to be a lighthouse to the left, and the lanterns just right of dead ahead—see? Two on the right side, one on the left—they're channel markers. Being northbound, I've got to lay just inside the double lights to remain both in the channel and in the lane."

"Must be coming in to that island, then. Can't see nothin', though."

"You can interpolate it, Gus. Look at the underground highway. The main drag continues right along the markers, but another goes off in a Y to the left, toward the light. I'll probably swing wide before it gets there, though, since the lighthouse is almost certainly marking reefs or shoals."

"You gonna take a chance on the harbor?"

"I don't know. I'm going to follow the markers around to it, that's for sure, and we'll take a look at it. If it's wide and deep enough, we might just slip in, do what we have to do, and slip out before morning. If it's small, active, and threatening, I might just do a go-round and see if we can find some kind of temporary anchorage well away from it. I'm going to get in, since the only thing I would like less than climbing over volcanic rocks in pitch darkness is climbing over them when they're hot enough to fry eggs."

The mountain itself, the top of which was the island, could not be seen in the darkness, only inferred, but the channel markers above and the glowing road below made it a simple matter to avoid any nastiness and move slowly around the mass toward the harbor area. Brazil couldn't help thinking, but didn't say, that it would also be simple defense by the Dlubinians to shift that road, extinguish a marker lantern or two, and pile everybody up nicely on the rocks he could hear the water slapping against all around the boat.

Damn it, though, he wished he had a cigar to calm his nerves.

"There it is!" Gus shouted. "Pretty damned small-looking, if you ask me."

"Well, the locals don't breathe air, so they've got little use for the place except as a trading center, and anybody hired to run the place would prefer it nice and compact and manageable, I'd think," the captain replied. "It's probably run by some international outfit. There's bound to be several offering services like this. Hard to say who or what might be running it, let alone what's in there."

"I make seven . . . no, eight ships, all pretty much like ours," Gus noted. "And one medium-sized thing with a smokestack parked off by itself over there."

Brazil nodded. "That's the one to worry about. Those are the cops, Gus. I'm giving the entrance a pass."

"Cops? Here? Whose?"

"Just like the trading companies and maintenance companies. All the hexes that have some concern with the sea or coastal security get together and maintain a multinational force run by a professional, multiracial naval authority. They didn't have anything like that the last time I was here, but I got an earful about them back in Hakazit. They've got a mean reputation. Discipline's about as ugly as a navy gets, but each crew gets a percentage of any seized contraband or reward money. You can get rich at it if you're good, and since it's an all-or-nothing share for the whole crew, if you're not good, you're history, anyway. We can't totally avoid them, but I'd just as soon not tangle with them or answer any nasty questions. You *can* challenge them if they're wrong, but we're a long way from a Zone court here—not that I would particularly want to see what a Zone court was, either, right about now."

Gus nodded, watching as they passed the harbor entrance and continued on past the island. "I see. But you said they only had volunteers from coastal hexes and those doing trade with the water hexes."

"So I was told."

"Then there ain't likely to be no Dahirs among 'em, and in *this* hex there's also not likely to be any automatic surveillance cameras or electric eyes, right?"

"I see what you mean. No, I'd expect you'd be invisible to them, since they wouldn't have much call to counter crooked Dahirs around here. Don't take them or the locals for stupid or ignorant types, though. You can trip a wire or any one of a thousand other traps that don't require any high-tech stuff and be just as caught. I'm also not so sure you're going to do any better over this terrain in the dark than I would."

"I wasn't thinkin' of that. I was thinkin' it wouldn't be much of a problem to swim *this* distance. Even if you anchor on the other side of the island, it's only gonna be a mile or so back, right? I figure I could manage a fair-sized sack and a keg or two for that distance, and I know what you two can eat and drink, havin' had some experience along them lines myself. As for findin' my way, hell, even I can follow these lights."

"You sure you're up to this?" Brazil pressed. "I have to tell you I'd rather not go in there at all if I don't have to, but it could be tricky."

"Jeez! This is a piece of cake! I mean, I got along in Hakazit for *weeks*, and they got all that electronic shit. Of course, I'm pretty fair with that kind of stuff myself, but I never saw cameras like they had or as tiny as they used, and I still never got tripped up. Man, I remember one time we was in the Congo when this riot broke out and turned into a kinda little revolution. They were shootin' anything that moved and had all the exits blocked. Me and Terry, we—"

He stopped a moment, suddenly struck once again by what Terry had become, and Brazil, realizing it, didn't press.

Finally Gus continued, but his tone was more distant, almost sad. "We ... well, we not only got out of there, we got out with the *pictures*. She told me we had to get the story out and sent me back with it. She insisted on staying to report the end of it. I spent four days in that muddy, crocodile-infested river in a cross between a too-old rowboat and a raft, dodgin' crocs and patrols. But I made it. *She* wasn't so lucky that time."

Brazil was curious now both for the story's own sake and for his own information about the girl and what she'd been like. "What happened, Gus?"

"She never said for sure, but she was a mess. I think they caught her and raped the shit out of her, the bastards. I'm not even sure they knew she wasn't just one of the locals or cared. And yet she *still* managed to get out, somehow, in a few days. Spent ten weeks in and out of hospitals and all. You know what was really weird about what happened?"

"No, Gus."

"When she come back, she still volunteered for the same nasty jobs, and she *meant* it. It didn't even slow her down. It was almost like, well, she'd survived the worst that could happen, and if anything, she seemed to have less fear than she had had before, which wasn't much. That Campos guy I mentioned, the gangster who come to the meteor site with us? *He* tried to get in her, too. I ain't ever been sure, but I think your old girlfriend did him a favor. He'da got away with it then, more or less, but some way or another she'da killed him—*after* we had the story and after the rest of the crew was safe. If Campos turns up somewhere here, no matter if he's a poisonous spider twenty feet tall, if she realizes that it's him and there's any of her old self left inside there, I wouldn't give a plugged nickel for his survival."

Brazil didn't say anything for a moment but finally managed, "Okay, Gus. You've convinced me. You see that set of markers there? That's an inlet, a sheltered cove. It's marked so a ship that might not be able to make it into the harbor can get some protection in bad weather. Ten to one it's surrounded by sheer cliffs, but we don't need to walk if you can get there by sea. I don't see any lights in there, and I didn't expect any with the weather okay—no reason not to make the harbor—so I'm going to lower sail and anchor inside there. *Then* you can go for a swim."

"Suits me."

The craft followed the small oil lanterns into the cove, and they were suddenly aware of high rock walls not just ahead but on both sides of the ship. It was a narrow channel, and it ended in a marked area that was all red-colored little lights.

"Who lights these and turns 'em off?" Gus asked worriedly, pointing to all the small marker lanterns around them.

Brazil was grunting and busily maneuvering several ways at once, hitting levers and turning small deck winches, but when he at last let go of the anchor and felt the ship lurch, then drift a bit to one side and stop, he relaxed.

"To answer your question," he said at last, "if you look closely, you'll see that they aren't oil lamps but gas. Semi-tech. With the volcano, they probably have some tap on a flammable gas supply, either natural or in a tank. They'll check them in some kind of routine, but only for mainte-nance. I wouldn't worry about anybody showing up at dawn to put them out, if that's what you mean."

"Yeah, that was what I was thinkin'." Gus sighed, a sound that was more like a soft, hollow roar. "Okay, I guess I'm ready. Anything waterproof that's likely to float that maybe I can use as a stash?"

"Yeah, here in the boat locker. This thing's got a pretty large emergency kit inside it, but if we take it out, it should give you plenty of room for what we need, and it's de-signed to be both floatable and waterproof at these seals. I won't worry about the beer supply, but we need food. Trust to the grains and veggies. They're pretty well universal among warm-blooded mammals, while meats are, well, questionable at best. Besides, she won't eat meat. She'll starve first."

"Okeydokey. Look, you may as well get some sleep while I'm gone. If anybody else comes in here, you're a sittin' duck before you can weigh anchor, turn around, and get out that narrow passage anyway, and if they take you, they'll probably bring you by the harbor, so I'll have a chance to spring you. Besides, no matter what else she is these days, I get the idea that Terry's one hell of a guard dog."

"You got that right," Brazil agreed. "Good luck!"

"Yeah, I'll do my best, like always," Gus responded, and tossed the emergency case into the water, then slid over-board himself.

Nathan Brazil sighed and sat down on the makeshift bed of spare sailcloth he'd set up for himself. He was too tired, too tense, and too worried to sleep even though he knew he was exhausted.

One of the storms was growing near, and while it didn't

bother him in this sheltered area and was still distant in any event, the lightning lit up the sky and played against the rock walls, revealing the shelter in intermittent bursts of reflected light.

It was an eerie landscape, as all volcanic areas tended to be, with no discernible vegetation. The outer rock wall, the eroded remnants of some great eruption, was at least ten meters high, almost sheer on this side but terminating in a series of jagged spires almost like the teeth of some gigantic beast.

He was actually comforted by the wall. It was taller than the mainmast, and thus it meant that he was virtually invisible to any ship passing via the channel outside as well as extremely well protected against any violent blow.

The rest of the area was much like a bowl, perhaps a hundred meters across, ending in sheer dark brown or black rock cliffs that seemed to go up forever. Here and there all along the sheer rock walls, though, were cracks and holes from which spewed steam and other gases, showing that this was still a very active place.

When it was dark between the lightning flashes, only the sky straight overhead showed, revealing the whole upper part of the fog- and mist-shrouded mountain. It helped reflect the lightning better, but it gave the distinct impression that one was in a room with a roof on it.

He felt a little better about the trip now that he had Gus, even if he couldn't see him half the time. At least, finally, there was somebody to *talk* to! Somebody who could speak with a frame of reference comfortable for both of them.

But, too, it was somebody else, somebody extra on the team, and in other ways he felt the Dahir a burden despite all that he was doing tonight. Maybe it was the girl, he thought. From knowing very little about her, he now knew quite a bit, perhaps more than she would have told him had she been able to do so. As much as he'd wanted, *needed* to know all that, he wasn't at all sure he liked knowing it. It was nothing about her; all the information Gus had provided had shown her to be more of a strong, gutsy woman than he'd have thought. It was rather that she was becoming, well, distinct in his mind. Now that he knew about her past, she seemed even more a tragic figure, a real person, not a cipher, and in a crazy way ciphers were often more comfortable to live with.

He wondered if he wasn't also a little jealous of Gus. That was funny in a way—having a two-and-a-half-meter-long snakelike creature as a rival. But Gus had earned her respect and devotion, as she had earned his. Even if they weren't lovers, there was definitely a kind of relationship there that he could not have even now and never could have, or *dared* have, with anyone else. That was what he envied.

And suddenly she was with him, kneeling down, then lying beside him, stroking him gently, as if she knew and understood what he was feeling.

Maybe she did, at least on that empathic level. Maybe more. *That* much he wished he knew.

Gently, he returned her affection and then embraced her and held her to him, as if trying to capture this one brief moment—just the two of them, with no other problems and no other questions, reaching together for the one thing which he wanted most and which had always been denied him because life was so short for everybody else, everybody but him.

The emotions then were real, not induced, not manufactured or manipulated, and not just on his part but on hers as well. The energy field inside her grew bright and enveloped them both, probing deep inside him and through every part of his being. He did not resist.

And when it hit his core, his soul, his true self, a center so strange, so alien that there were no terms of reference for it anywhere, it recoiled, unable to deal with it, powerless to go that last bit and totally absorb him.

Finally Nathan Brazil slept, a deep, intensely pleasurable sleep, the kind of sleep he needed most and rarely if ever could afford.

Gekir

THE CHANGES IN JULIAN WERE BOTH SUBTLE AND DRAMATIC, but Lori, whose high fever had been the precipitator of those changes, wasn't at all certain he liked it. One thing was clear: while she was as smart and capable as she ever had been, Julian seemed to have lost much of her past life, even though she knew that it had existed. It would probably take about ten seconds for an Earth psychiatrist to come up with a term to cover it, but to Lori it just didn't seem *normal*. Not for Julian, anyway. It was as if something was missing from her, some fire or intellect that wasn't really noticed and certainly not appreciated until it was no longer there.

Lori was feeling a great deal better. The inflammation in the wrist was down, although for a while it meant that the damned thing hurt *more* as it was no longer quite so rigidly bound, but his leg seemed completely normal. He tested it out, even ran on it for a short distance, and aside from a little stiffness it was fine. At least *one* thing was going his way, he decided.

Julian was in far worse shape. She was wan, worn out, and badly dehydrated. They put her, only half-awake, on Tony's back, tied her with the strap that had held Lori, packed up the rest of the camp, and started off toward the thick grove of tall trees about one and a half kilometers away.

There was no sign of the flying monster that had carried off the young "jackalope," as Lori had dubbed them, after a whimsical creature of the American Southwest. But it might well have a nest or den in the grove or be still feeding there, so Mavra broke out the crossbows, handing one to Tony and keeping one for herself. Anne Marie quickly but expertly assembled an obviously handmade, customized bow of great size and exotic design and removed a quiver of professionally manufactured but oversized steel-tipped arrows.

"Archery was one of the few varieties of sport a weak little woman could manage just for fun from a wheelchair," she explained, "and of course the classical favorite of centaurs from time immemorial. It *is*, too, even though the authorities have guns for serious sorts of things. *This* is the hunter's weapon of choice, though, even in Dillia. I'm afraid I'm still not very good at it, though. I have the eye and hold just fine, but I just can't get used to having this much *strength*."

Tony examined the crossbow. "Rather odd design, although I'm no expert on these things."

"You aim it just like a rifle," Mavra told him. "Align the rear notch with the front sight."

"No, no. The use is obvious. I meant this chamber in the rear behind the bolt. I'd almost swear it was for bullets."

Mavra chuckled. "Not bullets. Small compressed-gas canisters. When you pull the trigger, it works in the normal way, but if you have one of these little things in there, it gives a tremendous extra shove to the bolt, and a bit of a twist, at virtually no cost in weight or balance. Use it normally for defense; use the canister if you want to be sure you kill whatever you're firing at. It'll drill a hole through a tree thicker than your middle."

"Not very sporting."

"No, but it's damned effective even against somebody who thinks crossbows are no real threat."

Tony looked down at her. "I see that you are inserting one, but I have none."

"Double insurance. You make the first shot. If need be, I'll make the last one."

"Fair enough," the centauress agreed. "Still, it is almost disappointing somehow that even the crossbow should be turned into something so devastating."

Anne Marie nodded. "Doesn't seem *sporting* somehow," she agreed.

"When it's a sport, you're playing a game," Mavra responded. "On this sort of expedition I don't play games." She turned to Lori. "Can you scan that grove in the infrared?"

He nodded. "I've been doing it. Lots of little stuff, nothing major. It looks normal to me. I smell water, though. Possibly a *big* watering hole. If it is, that means we can expect most anything and everything around it."

Mavra nodded back. "I know. I haven't lost three hundred years of knowledge and experience in wild terrains," she reminded him.

"Yeah." The fact was, however, that the woman beside him was so different in so many ways from even the image of the savage jungle goddess of the Amazon that he had to remind himself that it was the same person. The conversation and the sophistication were large differences, of course, but it was also other factors not so easily nailed down. She had been so dominating, so commanding back on Earth, she'd seemed far larger than her size; now she was such a very tiny creature, he had to crane his neck just to see her. Even her form no longer seemed normal and familiar somehow but rather, well, *alien*. More alien than the Dillians, whose equine parts were more like the Erdomese and whose rears seemed, well, *sexy*.

Sexier than their torsos, in fact.

He began to wonder if what had changed in Julian was changing in him, too. Wouldn't *that* please the priests! But he had no desire to forget his former life and hoped that he could remember some of the lessons from it, as distant as they now seemed to him. Still, it was *Julian* who looked normal and pretty and sexy to him, as did his own reflection. Maybe it was crazy, but he realized that somehow, at some point, his own definition of "human" had flipped. He and Julian were "human"; the twins were, well, not human but kind of distant relatives. Mavra was not human. She was something else.

The grove was large and not at all like an Erdomese oasis, no matter what its geologic and ecological similarities. The foliage was far denser than it had looked from afar and heavy with life. There were hordes of brightly colored and cleverly camouflaged insects and insectlike creatures here, more, it seemed, than in the Itun jungle. Small animals were in the trees as well, some screeching or chattering at them and others just staring, often with huge eyes. There were things like birds, too, in that they had wings and flew, but they were more reptilian than avian, with often brightly colored but leathery skin and beaklike snouts. Even the small, pretty ones looked mean.

The group intersected a wide, well-worn trail that came in from the south, one that was adequate not just for the creatures they'd seen on the plains but for the two Dillians to walk side by side if they wanted to.

"Someone cut this wider," Tony noted, pointing a long finger at a lopped-off tree branch and to other obviously cut limbs and bushes elsewhere.

"Yeah, but why this wide?" Lori wondered. "I've got too many weird scents here to decide what might be odd, but I've sure not seen anything *this* big so far."

"Well, whatever it is, it's *very* large indeed," Anne Marie noted, gesturing toward the ground. "Those are not the droppings of a chipmunk, dog, horse, or anything else so tiny."

"Holy shit!" Mavra exclaimed, not realizing she'd made something of a joke. "I haven't seen turds that size since . . ."

Since where?

Lori stared at the droppings. "Since perhaps some sort of zoo or preserve? Or maybe a circus? Those look like elephant turds to me."

Mavra nodded. "That's it! But not a zoo or preserve or a circus, no. I saw them with soldiers on top of them in both military parades and in fierce battles."

"They're not that fresh—thank goodness," Anne Marie commented.

"And the cuttings aren't recent. Maybe a week or so old, maybe more," Tony added.

Lori looked over and down at Mavra. "Could the locals here be elephantlike? I mean, like Dillians are horselike and so on?"

"There are a couple that I know of who might qualify in that area," Mavra replied, "but none who'd mess up their own trail like that. You have to remember that we're talking intelligent races here. Out in the wild, thinking beings crap off their roads, not all over them. On the other hand, intelligent races ride elephants and use them as work animals as well. And if you ride in on something like that, there's *nothing* in this grove that's gonna argue with you, is there?"

"*We're* not atop elephants," Tony reminded them. "And there is the watering hole. The watering hole and something very much more."

It was indeed. The "hole" was a large pool or basin perhaps fifty meters across. It seemed natural, and the continuous rippling on the surface suggested that it was fed by an underground stream. Someone, however, had taken the natural pool and carved and shaped it until it was an egg-shaped oval with a two-meter-thick lip of mortared stones around it on all but its back side. That ended in a curved wall, with stairs of stone that went up on both sides to a flat stone platform above the pool. In back of it was a cone-shaped structure that seemed twisted, creating a spiral to its point.

The building, stairs, wall, and pool itself were partly overgrown with vines and creepers. A number of creatures from both the jungle grove and the vast plains were moving about the whole area. Still, it didn't seem like a ruin but rather like a place that was only seldom used but was still carefully kept intact.

"Temple?" Tony guessed.

"Maybe. Who knows?" Mavra replied. "Considering that there's something that looks a lot like a boa constrictor covered with peacock feathers and with a mouth showing more teeth than a shark snoozing on that platform, though, I don't think I'm curious enough to find out."

"I thought you were immortal," Lori noted a bit sarcastically.

"I wouldn't die, but I'd hate to waste months growing a new pair of legs."

The current rulers of the pool were two dozen small creatures whose appearance was unsettling. The largest male was only a meter high, and they all looked to be a sort of tailless ape, with thinly spread, soft, downlike hair covering their bodies except the chests, rear ends, and parts of the faces. They walked stooped over but were definitely bipeds, and for all their smallness and crudeness they looked very, very much like humans, even to the long hair on the heads. But there was just enough of the ape in their features to make them seem slightly more of an anthropological speculator's exhibit than small humans.

When the apes spotted the travelers, they didn't immediately run. Instead, the females let out loud, humanlike screams that panicked all the flying things and many of the smaller land creatures as well; the males stared at them, bared their teeth, and growled menacingly.

"Good heavens! They're Lucy's cousins!" Anne Marie exclaimed.

"Lucy?" Mavra asked.

"Doctor Leakey's fossils from Kenya. The spitting image! Claimed they were some sort of ancestor of Earth humans or some such rot."

Lori, in spite of his feelings of alienation from the race of his birth, nonetheless had that primal feeling inside and didn't much like it. "My lord! You don't suppose ... ?"

"Prototypes or more idea stealing by the makers," Mavra reassured him, although she didn't like how familiar they looked, either. "Odd, though. The mammals we've seen are

all six-limbed. They're bipeds. They don't seem to fit in
here at all."

"Well, I don't care about mysteries, but some of those
creatures best left sleeping are awake now. Whatever these
things are, they don't want to move away for us."

"Oh, *pooh*!" Anne Marie said, and with barely a glance,
both she and Tony reared up on hind legs, then kicked off
and charged right toward the little apelike creatures.

They could see the panic in the creatures' eyes. A couple
of the males gave hysterical gasps, then they all ran back
into the jungle and vanished as if they'd never been there.

The centaurs pulled up, turned, and looked back at the
other three.

"Poor little things!" Anne Marie commented. "I do hope
we didn't scare them all *that* badly." There was a trace of
a smile on her lips, though, and she added, "That was
rather fun, though, I do admit."

They moved in, Lori and Mavra well aware that the
feathered snake with the hundreds of teeth was now awake
and looking at them from the top of the balcony platform,
although it showed no intention of moving from its spot.

Even Julian was awake, looking weak and pale. Tony
had forgotten that she was strapped down on her back when
they'd reared and charged. Now the centauress's look
changed from playful triumph to embarrassment, and Anne
Marie quickly rushed over and untied the Erdomese.

"Oh, my dear! We're *so* sorry! Are you all right?" Anne
Marie asked in English.

Julian stared back blankly, and Lori ran over to her. "Are
you all right? *Julian!* Can you hear me?"

"Yes, my husband," she answered rather weakly and a
bit uncertainly. "I—I think so. But I am so thirsty and
weak . . ."

She seemed as good as she'd been, anyway. "Come,
we'll get you down. When you didn't answer Anne Marie,
I got very worried."

"I am gladdened that you were concerned, but I did not
answer because I did not understand the speech."

Tony frowned and looked up at Anne Marie. "You *did* ask in English, didn't you? With the translator it's hard to tell."

"Oh, of course. I'd never expect any of you to speak *Dillian*."

Lori steadied Julian and asked. "Do you understand her now?"

Julian looked blank. "I know nothing but Erdoma. Why should I understand the speech of an alien?"

Mavra looked up at Lori. "You better get her a fill-up. I think you bled her dry last night."

The water in the pool seemed remarkably clear and appeared safe. Mavra risked a left little finger and decided that it felt just like lukewarm water. Still, she got out a small test tube device from the pack, added some powder, then stooped and carefully let the tube fill with water. After she brought it up and looked at it, all the powder stayed on the bottom and the water remained clear.

"Unless I miss my guess, it's plain fresh water," she told them. "Actually, it's cleaner than it should be, all things considered. I don't think anybody should get in it, but we'll fill the canteens and Julian can drink all she wants."

"Fair enough," replied Lori, still concerned about Julian's dazed mental state. They began filling canteens and handing them to the Erdomese woman, who drank them down as if she'd been in the desert for months without a drop. The amount of water she finally consumed, particularly considering her size, was nothing short of astonishing. Each canteen held a little over a liter, and she easily and quickly downed a dozen or more canteens full of water before pausing, and she wasn't through. Even with the Dillians guarding, Mavra kept checking the surroundings for anything dangerous and soon lost count of just how much water Julian finally took in.

When she was finally, truly done, she looked quite different. The color was slowly coming back into her, and as the sacs in front of and just below her rib cage filled, they actually stretched the skin, pushing out the breasts and making them appear inflated and giving her the appearance of being slightly overweight. She was, too, Mavra thought. At the very least, she'd taken in fifteen to twenty liters of water, enough to add quite a bit of weight. Idly, the lone Earth human wondered if the Erdomese would slosh when she walked.

"I am much better, husband. Now you, too, should drink, for what you drew from me was not used in ordinary ways and the fever must have drained you."

Lori had passed a lot of particularly smelly and discolored urine already, but he knew what she meant. While by no means in the kind of shape Julian had been, he *did* feel a real thirst. On the other hand, he couldn't down more than five canteens full, and that was about as much as he'd ever taken in or needed.

While the others took turns, Julian asked him to sit so that she could clean off some of the muck still on him from falling in the muddy ditch when jumping from the train days earlier. Using her hands opened as fully as they could get, she began methodically rubbing and then brushing away the dried mud as if it were something she did all the time.

Since she seemed so much better, Lori asked her, "Julian, can you understand any of what the Dillians say? Have you remembered English?"

"I cannot understand their speech, my husband, if that is what you mean. I know only Erdoma. I do not know what the last word you spoke means, so I cannot answer that."

He lay down so she could work on his side and front, and this allowed him to see her face. "Have you lost all memory of the past?" *This is crazy,* he thought. *If anything, it's me who should be having memory problems after a fever like that.*

She shook her head. "I remember only that I was possessed of an evil spirit and that now that spirit has fled with your sickness. It would please me if you would give me another name, one of your choosing."

"But I *like* your name. I'm used to it."

"It is the name of the spirit, not me. It makes me feel bad, and I cannot even pronounce it as you do. *Please*, I beg you to use the name chosen at our wedding or any other that pleases you."

He didn't like this change one bit. Not any of it. Even if, damn it, it was the fantasy he'd had since they'd left Aqomb. Now that he had it, he didn't like it at all. She was too much like she'd been when they'd both been under the influence of that hypnotic drug. Too much like, well, all the other young Erdomese women. Still, it wasn't something he could do much about right now.

It was true that the "ju" sound was not in the Erdomese language, or anything else that might in English be pronounced with the "J" sound. Her Erdomese name, Alowi, had been given by the priest at the wedding at least partly for that reason, but they'd never used it except during the post-therapy sessions while under the drug. Ironically, although it wasn't a traditional Erdomese name, "Lori" had been just fine with the priests.

"Very well. For now I will use Alowi," he told her, and she seemed very pleased.

Cleaned and combed, he did feel better and certainly looked better. By this time they were packing up, and he told Julian—*Alowi*—to help but got Mavra aside for a moment.

"You know anything about this change in her?" he asked.

"A little," Mavra replied. "It's not something *I* can understand, and I never thought somebody with her background would succumb, but you can't tell about people sometimes. Basically, Julian Beard's been fighting with the Erdomese body, feelings, customs, and conditioning, and the old personality has been more or less dominant, even when the Erdomese self occasionally peeked through. Last night, in a place alien to both sides, the only person she cared about and really needed in this world was dying, and Julian Beard couldn't save him with all the accumulated knowledge and skill of a lifetime. Beard had to face not only helplessness but repressed feelings and emotions toward you that the Alowi part, the native part supplied by the Well and conditioned by her new body and situation, wanted so much to express. Beard needed you for any chance of survival or reasonable happiness in this life, but only Alowi had both the knowledge and the additional motivation that could save you. Unlike Tony or you, who surrendered on your own terms, Beard could not. It just wasn't in him not to fight. When the crisis came and he wasn't able to deal with it, something gave, and that was Julian Beard."

"But that's *crazy*! They're one and the same! Just as I am. It's true that I'm different; I've changed radically since being here, sometimes in directions I don't like, and I'm still trying for a balance, but it's nothing I can't handle."

"As a woman, did you ever find another woman sexually attractive? Did you ever fantasize about what it would be like to be a man?"

"Well, yeah, sure, but . . ."

"I will bet you that Julian never found another man sexually attractive, at least not consciously, and his fantasies were *about* women, not about being a woman. He could take tremendous stress, great pressure, and still accomplish anything he set out to do. But those same traits created an enormous ego, I think, that had a single and absolutist view of itself. What the Well did to him was, to him, so extreme that finding himself a female, she had to be locked up and drugged just to keep her from suicide. You said as much. When you came along, he tried to compromise with his female self, but all that did was shift her from one extreme to the other. On this trip the male side felt in charge again, but last night the crisis was just too much. To help you, she had to put everything out of her mind that was from her male half, both attitudes and experience, and let Alowi completely take over. When that happened, all that repressed emotion just gushed out, suddenly no longer under restraint. Alowi then saved you by doing something Julian could never do—by *not thinking*. By just letting that

Erdomese instinct take control and never doubting if it was right or wrong. She didn't work so fanatically because she needed you, not in the sense Julian had. She did it because she loves you, and being in love with a man wasn't something that Julian Beard could handle. When you push something that can't bend with a lot of force, it breaks."

"You sound like a pop psychologist," Lori noted, but wondered if she wasn't pretty well on the mark.

"I don't know exactly what a 'pop' psychologist is, but I think I understand your meaning. Yes, it's guesswork based on very long experience rather than on being a professional specialist in the mind, and it may not be stated in proper scientific terms, but I've had to read and guess right on all types of people to get anywhere at all. And you will have to trust me that I know what rigid egos can do to people."

"But—what do I do? Is Julian gone for good?"

"You live with it, that's all. All that knowledge and experience is still there someplace; it's just been sealed off in the same way the person she is now was pretty well sealed off. It might not come back at all, it might partly come back if absolutely needed, or it might creep back and merge with the current personality. Only time will tell. In the meantime it's causing some trouble for all of us."

"Huh? How is it a problem for *you*?"

"Since she doesn't remember English, she can't speak to or understand the Dillians. That could be a real pain in a tight situation. Damn! I *knew* I should have sprung for the translator!"

Lori felt a double pang of guilt at the comment but said, "Well, she can still get one somewhere, can't she?"

"I think she'd fight having one now. It doesn't fit with the new personality she's trying to build and lock in."

"I think she'd do it for me," Lori told her.

"She might," Mavra agreed, "but the knowledge of English is still in her mind somewhere, too. These mental things are tricky. A translator is a neat little device that's tuned to a part of the Well and translates speech, then feeds it back to the brain. Since the Well is everywhere, it seems instantaneous to us. But if her mental state won't allow her to accept the translation, won't transfer language except in Erdomese, the gadget is as useless as a computer would be to a Stone Age hunter. Data have to be processed, and if the mind refuses, well, it doesn't matter whether you get the data or not."

"Thanks a lot. One more thing to worry about."

Mavra turned sharply toward the wide road leading to the pool and picked up her crossbow. "We have something more pressing to worry about all of a sudden."

They could all hear it and even feel it. Something large—no, *huge*—was coming up that road with enough weight to shake the ground and once again panic all the surrounding wildlife.

"We could retreat into the jungle!" Tony called.

"All right! Move back and take cover if you can!" Mavra shouted, but Lori shook his head and said rather softly, "Too late."

Into the area strode a monstrous creature, in many ways the largest elephant any of them had ever seen, yet not an elephant, either. For one thing, it was covered in thick reddish brown fur from its small tail to its massive head, hanging down like some impossible fur coat. It moved very slowly on six tree-trunk-sized feet; the creature was probably unable to run or move at all quickly, but something that huge was an irresistible force that never needed to move quickly. Even its trunk was hairy, and on either side of the mouth, which was small only in relative terms, grew two very large, cream white, and dangerous-looking ivory tusks.

And riding just behind the massive head was a large orange and black catlike creature with a large, fierce head sporting protruding fangs, and a lower jaw and a mouth that was remarkably expressive, almost humanlike. The cat creature, too, was six-limbed, but the forward pair of arms, while fur-covered like the legs, clearly ended in some sort of hands, one of which held an ornate batonlike object.

It also wore a sash that was equally ornate, from which

hung a scabbard with an ornately carved ivory hilt that obviously led to a very large sword.

The cat creature tapped gently on its mount's head, and the beast trumpeted loudly enough to wake the dead. It was clear that the pair was leading at least a small procession, and the sight of the strangers at the pool had signaled a halt.

"Who be ye and why d' ye bear arms against the Gekir in the shadow of Basquah?" the cat challenged, the translation faithfully reproducing the archaic speech pattern. The voice was deep and seemed to have an underlying menacing growl, but it was also unmistakably female.

"Don't do anything!" Mavra cautioned Lori and particularly the Dillians, who were hearing only very threatening animal noises and had their arms at the ready. "She's just asking who the hell we are and why we're here!" It was, after all, a proper question.

They had finally encountered the Gekir.

Mavra lowered her crossbow but kept the bolt ready to go. With the gas propellant loaded, she was certain it would drill even through the mammoth, although whether that would do more than annoy it was impossible to know.

"The bipeds are called Lori of Alkhaz and his wife, Lori-Alowi, of far-off Erdom," she announced. "The other two are from even more distant Dillia and are the sisters called Tony and Anne Marie Guzman. I am Mavra Chang of Glathriel. We mean neither harm nor disrespect and have not entered your building. We are travelers forced by circumstance, not plan, into your nation, and we are here only to replenish our water supplies and move on."

The Gekir, whose feline face was so expressive and rubbery, frowned and cocked her head, looking them all over. "I be Shestah Quom Daahd, elected chief of the Quobok Knights. Put thy weapons away and stand ye all by the far side of yon pool that we may enter."

It wasn't a request; it was an order. Mavra turned and told the others to move where instructed. Right now it was better to try to make friends with these people than to start a fight.

As soon as they were away from the main area, the chief of the Quobok Knights moved her huge mount in and was quickly joined by four others, filling the area rather handily.

The leader's mount carried only the chief and an elaborate chest secured with straps. The next three, however, carried perhaps four or five Gekirs each, riding on top and in two basketlike carriers hanging down on either side of the animals. Another lone occupant sat atop the last beast, along with an enormous hutlike container that clearly carried all their supplies.

"Why does she sound like Long John Silver in drag?" Lori muttered.

Mavra frowned. "Who? Oh, you mean the archaic speech. You can get that and much worse when you're translating a language that's very different from yours. When you meet a race that clearly cannot form our sounds, particularly in a nontech hex, and it still sounds exactly right, watch out. That means the translator isn't translating, it's interpolating."

The Gekir chief was off the high mount almost as the huge creature stopped near the pool and snaked its long, hairy trunk into the water. The Gekir's motion was fluid, very feline, as if she hadn't a bone in her body. The forward pair of big, thick, short-fingered hands were used in this instance as if they were forelegs. But once on the ground, the Gekir chief supported herself on her four rear legs and raised her short torso and long neck in something of a centauroid fashion, although even ripples of skin under the fur gave an impression not of Dillian rigidity but almost of liquidity. The hindquarters, however, were smooth, with no hint of a tail.

The other Gekirs dismounted in similar fashion but made no effort to draw weapons or approach. Instead they simply gathered by the large animals and allowed their chief to handle the business at hand.

Although quite low to the ground, the Gekir projected a

sense of bigness and strength. Certainly the creatures were large, and their hands, with the retractable claws, looked both powerful enough and sufficiently dangerous to rip one of the big mammothlike mounts to shreds. The chief came right over to them, showing no fear at all, and first the Erdomese, then the Dillians, and finally Mavra were inspected with large catlike eyes and an enormous twitching black nose. She looked at Mavra the closest, dwarfing the small woman. Mavra was close enough to touch the protruding fangs, and the creature's breath was intense enough almost to cause her to pass out.

Finally the Gekir said to Mavra, "You be like a *zumbaga*. Where do ye say ye was from?"

"Glathriel, Excellency. Type 41."

"Never heard of them."

"Might I ask what a *zumbaga* is?"

"Tiny bipedal apes. Horrid little pests they be. Be a tribe of 'em here somewheres. Can't be touched because they be royal property—protected, y' know."

She nodded. "We've seen them and noted the resemblance. They didn't look like they fit in here."

The Gekir gave a rumbling roar that the translator indicated was amusement. "They don't! They be brought here long ago in ancient times, and the ruler of the time, whose soul should be ever cursed for it, took a likin' to 'em and bred 'em. A royal pain in the arse, they be, but we keeps their numbers managed and limited to religious sites."

"I thought this might be a temple. That is why we did not enter it. We had no wish for anything but water before going to the coast."

"Indeed? And why be ye in Gekir at all, then, when there be all the stuff ye might like or need fifty leagues north in Bug Heaven?"

"We had no intention of coming here. Our business is far to the north and west of this whole area, and Gekir is out of our way." Briefly she explained how their train had gone the wrong way without really giving her suspicions as to why.

The chief was neither stupid nor ignorant. Both Mavra and Lori couldn't help noticing that she took the translator for granted and never once asked how it was they could be understood. "We hates all them things. They robs the soul from ye and make it impossible after a whiles t' tell the people from their machines. But the Bug machines don't go wrong, least not that we hear, and I can see the injury to that one's hand, there."

Mavra nodded, deciding to tell what she could without violating the whole detour's purpose. "Someone has been following us. We don't know who or why, but they have influence and money. They tried to kill me once, but now they seem satisfied to just keep me from going anywhere. We jumped off the train when we realized we were diverted and made for Gekir through the jungle. We spent the night on the rocks out there and hoped today to reach the coast and perhaps pay our way onto a coastal vessel or fishing boat and throw our pursuers off our scent."

The chief nodded. "Aye, we smelled yer camp and tracked you here. Been curious to see what ye might look like. Where ye be headin' to at the end of this business, and why?"

Mavra felt suddenly uncomfortable. "I—I'm sorry, your Excellency, but I cannot tell you that. The knowledge is of no great use to you, but if I told you, even in strict confidence, and you were later ordered by your government to report us or tell what we said and did, it would be your duty to do so. With all due respect, I cannot in good conscience place you in that position."

The big cat froze for a moment and glared fixedly at her, looking for all the world like an enraged lion about to pounce on a crippled antelope. But instead she said. "That big, is it?"

"Upon my honor it is."

Suddenly the chief gave an unmistakable grin, and again there was that growl of amusement. "Well, I think ye be full of shit, but I likes any little one with the gall to tell me to mind me own business and make it sound like they was doin' me some favor! Come on! We'll take ye all to a village on the seashore that might get ye out of me fur!"

The rest of the Gekirs, who'd watched all this not quite sure how their chief was going to react, now showed amusement and relaxed. The ice was broken.

Once the visitors were accepted, the Gekirs proved as pleasant and hospitable as their vague reputation to the north had them. Mavra, in fact, had a tougher time relaxing with the Dillians than she did with the Gekirs. To Tony and Anne Marie, it had been like listening to only one side of a phone call, with the Gekir growling and spitting and making, in Anne Marie's term, "*horrid* little noises." She, for one, liked her cats to be *much* smaller.

The patrol was clearly out on business unrelated to them but also unrelated to the temple and watering hole. There was a certain tit for tat, though, in that Shestah volunteered neither why they *were* out there or particularly why someone whose position equated to provincial governor would be with them. Even so, the old girl was quite talkative about her opinions, and she had one on almost everything.

"It be too damned *civilized*," she told Mavra. "Ain't been a war, so much as a revolution, in so many lifetimes, the young 'uns know about it only from stories. Game's all managed, been peace with the neighbors since forever. Only thing what saves us from slow death by boredom be the no-technology laws. Keeps families together, keeps the good values, makes ye *earn* yer keep. That's why we still got huntin' parties and all the rights and ranks. Afore ye gets rights here, ye got to come out t' *here* or someplace like it, bare of all stuff, make yer own kill, and live the old style. Rest of it's mock battles against the neighbor guv's kids. Just last month a team of me girls got right into old Skisist's office and poured glue on the High Seat." Again the chuckle, but this time with pride. "Took 'em three days to unstick the old witch, and she'll be 'arf a year growin' back the fur it cost 'er!"

She had a lot of stories, and it was clear that she loved telling them to someone, *anyone*, who hadn't heard them so often they were known by heart. Still, it was time to move out if they were to reach the coast in any reasonable time.

Lori looked up at the chief's elephantine mount and then back at Mavra. "You're *really* going to ride up there with her?"

"Sure. It'd insult her if I didn't, and she'll get to tell me dozens more tales before we're there. I know, I know, but it's a small price to pay when you think of it. I'd sure rather have to listen to her than fight her."

Lori nodded. "Amen to that. But—maybe, if you get the chance, you can find out what's really puzzling me."

"Yeah?"

"There are no males. None. They aren't even mentioned."

"Yeah, I *did* notice that," Mavra admitted. "They might well be unisexual. Many races are. Or maybe here the men are home doing the dishes and minding the kids." She shrugged. "We're going to a village, anyway. We'll know soon enough. I just want you to make sure that Alowi and the Dillians behave themselves and aren't scared or panicked by anything they might see. This chief's smart and sophisticated. A full report on us will be on its way to higher-ups as soon as she gets the chance. My only hope is that whoever's screwing us up didn't anticipate this move and enlist the locals here just in case. If not, then that report will be quickly headed southeast to the capital and from there to Zone. By then we should be long gone." *I hope,* she added to herself.

Lori still didn't like Mavra's way of thinking. "What if she *is* in on it?"

Mavra shrugged. "Then we're really no worse off than we were, are we?"

The top of the woolly creature was a *long* way up, and it took Tony's aid from below and the chief grabbing from above to get Mavra up. Once she was there, however, it proved a very wide and relatively secure platform, and the blanket spread out and secured on top was thick enough to kept the beast's backbone from being much of a problem, particularly in the crease between the first and second pairs of the three sets of legs.

The Gekir chief looked down at Lori and grinned. "Ye be all better goin' *aside* us 'stead of in the rear. Not unless ye want t' be steppin' in a huge load of the world's greatest fertilizer!"

It was a good point, one the essentially city-bred and civilized foursome who would walk or run along with the party would not have thought of until it became very obvious.

"We should have one of each of us on both sides of the chief's mount," a still suspicious Tony suggested. "That way we'd have maximum speed and position if anything went wrong."

"Yes, with Chang up there and trapped between us," Lori noted. "No, it's all right. It's still her show, and she is not only unconcerned, she is in her glory right about now. She's having a *lot* of fun. Can't you tell?"

"Yes, the woman's ego is unmatched," Tony agreed, "but you will note that while so far we have been more trouble and expense than aid to her, she wants us along. Why do you think that is? Company? She is an easy one to talk to, but beyond the surface there is someone tough, nasty, and possibly ruthless inside there we aren't permitted to see. If even a tenth of what she claims about herself is close to the truth, then inside her is one of the most dangerous people any of us have ever met. Did you see how confident she was in turning down that chief, for whom being refused is obviously a new experience? Could *you* have done it? Or me? And more important, could you have gotten away with it?"

"Well, I—" he stammered. "I hadn't really thought of it that way. So why *do* you think she's taking us along, then?"

"To remove obstacles for her if need be," Tony replied. "Big obstacles she can't talk her way or think her way out of. It might be an idea to remember that she thinks herself immortal, and, true or not, she believes it. We are here to keep her from being captured or badly injured, nothing more, but *we* are not immortal. She said an attempt was made on her life by two assassins before any of us were here. She never said what happened to the two assassins or who she might have been with then. We are . . . what is the term?"

"I believe the word you want is 'expendable,' dear," Anne Marie put in cheerfully. "What Tony is saying is to worry only about yourself and your wife in the end. *That* woman can take care of herself."

Lori looked back up at Mavra Chang thoughtfully. If that was true, and it certainly rang true, why didn't she just hire tough natives rather than transformed Westerners? A Gekir, for example, would make a formidable bodyguard and would probably love the job just for its potential danger.

Anne Marie read his thoughts. "She's short of funds, dear, and we're *much* cheaper."

Alowi was concerned about Lori running. "Are you certain that your leg is not going to go out again? That it is not too soon?"

"The leg is fine," he assured her. "Running on it will actually help me get back into shape. What about you? You were weak as could be this morning."

"I am fine now. I simply needed replenishment. I will not be a burden."

He hugged her. "You are *never* a burden to me! Don't think that!"

"I look up at *her* and I feel a wrongness. I cannot say if the wrongness is me or her, but it is one of us. She rides the monster beast as if she has ridden one her whole life, and she treats the orange and black creatures as if they are old friends, yet she is weak and tiny and could be destroyed by one strike of those hands."

"I know. I knew the first time I met her that she was different from anyone I ever knew, but I did not know how very different she was. Your concern is me. I will deal with Mavra Chang."

"My lone concern is you," she said sincerely, leaving no

doubt that Mavra Chang's interests were of absolutely no importance to her at all.

He wished he felt as confident as he sounded. Damn it! What *had* happened to the two assassins?

The village turned out to be of considerable size, spreading out on all sides of a spectacularly beautiful bay and climbing the sides of low rolling hills to the east and south.

The buildings were basically of stone or brick with thick thatched roofs for the individual one-story houses and red slate for the larger or taller structures. The market and business district was surprisingly well developed, with buildings up to a block square and rising up to six stories high. The port was on the northern side of the bay, set off a bit by itself, including docks, piers, and warehouses. It was about as modern-looking as a nontech civilization was capable of managing. But that wasn't the startling part of the view eastward out toward the ocean; there was something else that commanded attention even more: a shimmering, odd effect, like a thin plastic wall, that seemed to go from north to south and intersected the two far points of land on either side of the bay.

"A sea hex boundary!" Lori exclaimed. "Right up to the town!"

"That be Ogadon," one of the Gekirs called down. "Ogadon takes in part of Muca Bay. The town be Port Saar."

Mavra, too, hadn't expected quite this elaborate a town or this good a port. "Ships *do* stop here, then!"

The chief nodded. "Not like up north in Itus, but that be far away from here, that port. Easier for us to have this and get what services we need direct than to wait weeks to get anything from the big port down at the Point. The wormies, who don't have much of a decent harbor down south, use it sometimes as well. That be why yer train thing be comin' so far south. See, that point of land just outside the border at the edge of the port is really in Ogadon, so they don't need no sail to come in, neither."

"No ships in now, though."

"Don't look it. We'll check the schedules when we gets down there. Don't expect ye'll want no big ships nohow, since they'd be goin' on from here to the wormies most like or south. Ye might be better makin' some deal with some smaller craft for crossin' the Great Bay to Parmiter or Awbri."

She nodded, not knowing if the gesture meant much here. "Do many smaller vessels actually come in here?"

The chief pointed. "Be a few of 'em down there now. The Ogadon, they be proper flesh eaters, so's they don't allow no fishin' as such, but they grows and maybe mines some real strange things down there that some folk of some nations take a real likin' to. Some of it's medicinal to some races, some is used as spices by others, and some's the kind of stuff what some folks like but other folks says is evil, if you take my meanin'. Don't know which races like what, though."

Mavra knew exactly what she meant. Somewhere, deep under the seemingly placid Ogadonian surface, was an entire underwater civilization probably as well developed as this one, and what they ate was some sort of fish or marine animal that was the equivalent of the Gekir's jackalopes or the variety of edible animals on Earth. But deep down somebody had discovered long ago that many of the sea bottom plants and growths produced substances or were themselves substances that affected other races. Southern hemisphere races, after all, had the common bonds of carbon-based life on the whole. As with other Well races, the Ogadon had turned this knowledge to profitable trade, selling the minerals that others might want or need as well as the plant material and chemicals that might be of use elsewhere. Minerals, spices, and medicines, perhaps, but among the variety in such a landscape was bound to be at least one substance that translated to a pleasure drug to one or perhaps many races on the surface. All this would be traded for such things a semitech, undersea race might well find of use but could not make itself.

"Does the government of Ogadon officially approve, disapprove, or ignore the stuff some call evil?" she asked carefully.

"Oh, they *got* to go after it to save their legal trade," the chief responded. "They even got agreements with some of the shippin' hexes to allow surface policin' of the smugglers. It be kinda hard, though, to put a real stop to it. We don't need none of it, so we just keeps out of it all."

I'll bet, Mavra thought, a sour smile on her face. This bay was tailor-made for this kind of trade. If the Gekir, and particularly the local authorities, didn't have any use for the products, smugglers would still have a great use for this area. In fact, it explained the apparent prosperity better than anything else. This was a safe haven for such ships and one that served as a convenient place to repack illegal cargo, swap it between vessels, and transfer it ashore so that it could go by Itun train all the way to the Sea of Turigen and from there to other markets. It was a place where trade deals could be consummated with little fear of fancy eavesdropping and where strangers would always stand out.

Such a ship would be absolutely perfect for them—with one hitch. There probably wouldn't be much of a problem talking one of the captains into taking them aboard, but there might well be a problem in convincing captain and crew to maintain their silence and thus getting back off again.

Isle of Mahguul, Dlubine

NATHAN BRAZIL AWOKE FROM THE DEEPEST SLEEP HE COULD ever remember in his very long life feeling energized, exceptionally well, and alert. He sat up and opened his eyes and was instantly wide-awake, and he realized that it was daylight.

He sat up, got immediately to his feet, and looked around until it dawned on him how totally stupid that was. "Gus?" he called, then, getting no answer, he yelled *"Gus!"* at the top of his lungs so that the sound went around and around the volcanic bowl the ship was anchored inside.

There was no response.

There was too little sky for him to see the sun unless it was almost directly overhead, and considering that the anchorage was on the north side of the island, that was highly unlikely.

Save for the sound of water within the little inlet lapping gently against the sides of the ship and against the rock walls around and the rush of a small waterfall pouring from a rock fissure high above to the waters of the cove below, there was only silence in return.

He half expected Gus to suddenly pop up at his elbow any second, but when, after a minute or two, that didn't happen, he had to accept the fact that the Dahir had not yet returned. That was bad news; he should have had more than enough time to get around to the harbor, get inside, steal what he could, and get back to the boat.

In other circumstances Brazil thought he'd like this place, particularly this secluded cove, but for now he saw it less as a haven than as a trap.

In daylight the passage in seemed even more narrow than it had coming through it in the darkness, so narrow in fact that it would be nearly impossible for ships of even this size to pass each other once in it and even easier for a smaller ship to block the exit. Nonetheless, he felt as if he had to wait—all day if need be, if he was patient enough to manage it.

But before nightfall he'd have to move out, and he couldn't afford to go looking for the former Earthman. He'd cut him what breaks he could, but his own fate was quite literally more important than Gus's, and if Gus could stay alive, he could do more for the fellow once inside the Well than he could in some naval prison.

It was only after he'd run through all the possible options and decided which ones were valuable that he had time to reflect on himself.

He felt—odd. "Tingly" was the best word he could come up with.

Last night, with the girl, tired and tense as he was, he'd let himself go completely. He remembered it, even felt a shiver of pleasure at the thought, but the bottom line was that all his own defenses had been down.

In a sense he was relieved to be still thinking like himself and able to shout Gus's name. Hell, he'd been wide open last night. He tried to remember, but it was harder to remember emotion and sensation than, say, a conversation or a fight. Still, as he reconstructed it as best he could in his mind, he realized that something *had* happened. Whatever was inside her had taken the opening, had rushed to consume him at the very climax of passion—and for some reason hadn't been able to do the job completely.

In a sense that reassured him, but he was also aware that

his body was subject to much of what all mortal flesh was heir to.

He suddenly realized that he hadn't once wondered where *she* was. He hadn't wondered because although she was forward and out of his sight, he *knew* where she was, knew exactly what she was doing, what she was feeling . . .

Knew exactly what she was seeing!

It wasn't telepathy, not exactly. If she thought conventionally, it did not come through. He knew, though, that he could contact her, summon her, send a whole range of basic concepts her way if need be. She knew he was inside her head at the same time he was still himself, and he knew beyond a doubt that she had the same experience with him. He could see, hear, feel, taste what she did, even feel the wind in her hair as if it were his own hair.

Man, this is really weird! he thought.

It was as if he suddenly had two bodies, one his old male self, the other hers, yet most peculiar of all, there was no confusion in his mind over which was which. *I almost feel like I can explain the Trinity to a Christian,* he thought with characteristic humor.

But while he now shared every single real-time experience with her, he had no direct control of that other self. As she lifted some of the little water that remained in one of the water traps to her lips, he felt the water—felt it on her lips, felt it go down—but he could not control any of her actions, only experience them. Taken together with the preexisting empathic link, they were totally, absolutely connected as if parts of the same organism, yet at the same time still their individual selves.

It fascinated him like nothing else he could ever remember, and it troubled him only in one way.

He could not make her body do anything at all, but she had made a sailor of a totally alien race put a pistol to itself and then, when he'd yelled and made his shock clear, made that sailor jump overboard just as if he'd been some kind of puppet.

Could she now, through this linkage, manipulate *his* body?

He very much wanted to know that, but he was afraid at this moment to find out. He *knew*, without having to think any further, that she would never harm him or cause him to come to harm, but that wasn't the point.

He tried not to think of that for now and instead concentrated on other things that were only now becoming apparent to him.

Whatever she had tried to take from him, or alter, involuntarily or not, she had clearly failed to do, but she had certainly given as well.

It was hot here, almost intolerably hot. He could see evaporation even in the secluded cove, and the very air shimmered and twisted. If it had been in the high thirties Celsius well into the night, what must it be now? High forties at the very least, he knew. Certain things were constants. It *looked* that hot, and everything he could check indicated it really *was* that hot, but although stark naked, he felt comfortably warm, quite pleasant, really, as if the air were perhaps just a shade under body temperature.

That enviable protection that she'd had against all extremes of weather had finally been extended to him as well. He had a strong feeling, though, that the ability, and possibly other as yet unknown powers, did not come without some price, and he was well aware that whatever was doing it was coming from her. Something, some power or energy field, now tied them together as absolutely as if it were a great rope tied between them. He realized, *knew*, that the bonds were so tightly knit that there was no chance of one leaving the other any more than his arms could go one place and his legs somewhere else entirely. It gave a whole new meaning to the word "inseparable," he thought.

The question was, Who was binding whom?

Of course *she* had done it, whether by design, nature, or command he didn't know, but the question was one of both motive and control. She was certainly an individual, but an individual who had been reprogrammed to a remarkable degree. The fact that he knew that her total concern for him was not only benign but a matter of genuine affection was meaningless; whatever rules now governed her thinking might have quite a different interpretation of what was in his best interest than he himself might.

He wondered how the insulation worked. It had to be extremely thin and entirely energy-based. Somehow it maintained an internal fixed environment for the two of them almost like an extra layer of skin. Things felt normal to him; the wooden deck was firm and solid and appeared fully capable of giving him a splinter if he wasn't careful. He wondered if something that was boiling hot would feel that way to him or if his tongue would still freeze to a pump handle at forty below. Probably not, considering how well she'd gotten along in the snow, but he wondered what the criteria were and whether a people living in a tropical swamp next to a subtropical region had thought of everything. It would not be wise to take things for granted.

Terry was delighted by the new contact; he felt that as well and also felt that she was somewhat surprised by it. But as joined as they were, they still did not have an effective means of communication. To Brazil's astonishment, it was Terry, not he, who attempted a real start in that direction.

She walked back over to the water collector, almost dry and smelling less than wonderful, and just looked at it. Then she turned and looked back at the entire ship, then over again to the small waterfall on the other side. It wasn't until she repeated the pattern twice more that he realized she was "talking" to him. The message was clear and so obvious that he wondered why he hadn't thought of it himself. If that waterfall resulted from the rain at the top of the volcano coming down through cracks rather than from some internal and probably foul source, just putting the ship under it would allow them to totally refill the containers below with fresh water. But it would be tricky in such tight quarters to weigh anchor and use the little bit of circular current inside the cove to bring the ship around to where that would be practical.

Now, how much of me got transferred as well? he wondered. It was time to find out. He walked forward until he had the anchor winch in sight, then made a turning motion with his hand, then looked back at the wheel, still in view from where he was.

She went over to the winch and stared at it but shook her head. He knew she had understood his suggestion; the problem was that she could not, or would not, compromise her hunter-gatherer principles even to that degree. He was back at the wheel, staring forward, more in her head than in his own but feeling frustrated.

Suddenly she stared down at the deck almost aimlessly and began breathing heavily, and he felt her go into what could only be described as some sort of trance. Her vision blurred; all outside sensations suddenly ceased. Curious, he leaned against the wheel and waited. There seemed to be no hurry.

He felt a sudden tremendous, powerful rush, very much like a gust of wind, only it went into him and through him. He felt sudden vertigo, and then something seemed to be pulling him, pulling him forward, even though he was not physically moving at all. Rather, it was as if his consciousness, his very inner self, were being sucked out of his body and it rushed forward, *through* the top of the cabin, *through* the mainmast, and deposited him forward, where the feelings of the body returned to him, yet the force that had reached for and grabbed him had not dissipated but rather was felt now as tension, as if he were stretched on the end of a taut rubber band. He had felt—*something*—pass him in the opposite direction during the pull and knew that it had been the girl, moving back to his own body even as he moved forward toward hers.

He was Terry.

He was in Terry's body, and it felt strange to him yet natural. When he breathed in and out, the body breathed, the head moved, the arms and legs functioned. Shocked, even dazed, he saw the winch in front of him, turned it, quickly raising the anchor about halfway, and then threw the lock switch. The moment he did it and stood away, the tension broke, and he was pulled out of her body and back into his own body still leaning on the wheel aft. Again he felt himself passing her as she was pulled back into her own body forward.

Sensation and the absence of that force or tension brought him to immediate control in his own body, and he had to make a quick turn and spin the wheel hard as the stern drifted a bit toward the rocks. Old reflexes took hold, and he coaxed the small ship bit by bit out, catching the tiny, subtle spin of the water caused by both the inrush of ocean water and the action of the waterfall, and managed to get it pointed directly for the falls. Now, moving slowly, he locked the wheel and went forward to the winch, the very same winch he'd used before without having left the wheel, unhooked a long grappling hook from its holder on the rail, and waited. As the bow went under the falls, he felt the water wash over him and then lashed out from the rail with the hook, deflecting the bow from going head on into the rock cliff. He almost slipped on the suddenly wet deck as he leaned against the hook, and he let go with perfect timing so that the bow only glanced against the rock and started moving back out, the waterfall now just behind him.

Thank heaven it was just a very small waterfall. A big one would have swamped them for sure. Even this one might.

It was warm water, but it seemed to be good water; he stood under, let it shower him, and he reached out, let his cupped hands fill, and drank it. It went down very well indeed.

Except he wasn't doing that. He was standing there with the hook, ready to try a push-off lest the waterfall flood the deck when the containers below were full and the collectors were backed up to topside. If a lot of water got below, inside the cabin, hold, and other parts of the hull, they could wind up sinking the ship. *He* wasn't enjoying the shower, but *she* was.

He couldn't hear much over the sound of the small falls, but he turned and watched, worried. The girl got the idea and moved out of the immediate stream of the falls, staring at the collector.

There was a sudden gurgle, and the collector filled and began overflowing right onto the deck like a bathtub with no drain. Frantically he pushed off as best he could, but it was the stern that started moving in a semicircle; the bow was getting lower in the water.

Anxiously, he ran back, trying not to slip on the wet deck. He got to the wheel, unlocked it, and tried to steer the ship out of the trap he'd put them in. *Now* he realized why he hadn't considered it. The ship moved a little but not enough.

The girl seemed to sense the problem, too, and now she stepped out of the falls and stared intently at the rock cliff. There was a sudden release of the same sort of energy he'd felt in the switch of bodies, only this time directed straight at the cliff. The ship shuddered and Brazil was knocked off his feet, but the shuddering was the action of the ship moving back slowly out of the stream, away from the cliffside. The falls hit the rail, then actually began supplementing the backward movement.

In a moment they were free of it. He grabbed the wheel, straightened it out, and let momentum take him several meters beyond the splash zone of the falls. He locked the wheel and moved forward to drop the anchor. He would remain in the center of the cove if he could this time.

He did an immediate visual check to see how badly they'd been flooded. The only pumps below were hand pumps, and they weren't the sort one handled one at a time but only in pairs.

It didn't seem all that bad, so he went forward to the cabin and went below. There was maybe 150 millimeters of water below, but it didn't look bad and certainly not enough to use pumps on. It had been a close thing, though; a few minutes more under that stream and there would have been a couple of *meters* in there, and that would have made it very difficult indeed.

Relieved, he went back topside, then aft to the wheel. He sank down on the deck and gasped for air, shaking himself as the tension inside him was released. It was several minutes before he recovered enough to think about all that had just happened.

My God! Did she really draw me out of my body and into hers? How was that possible?

He knew somehow that it indeed had happened, though, and it was another example of power that scared him. She had the power, with no training and no background, to do at least as much as if not more than the greatest of those Oriental mystics he'd told Gus about. If all Glathrielians had this kind of power . . .

Worse, she'd made a decision and split hairs like a theologian. Rather than compromise and operate that winch, she'd worked nothing short of a miracle so that he, not she, could use her body to raise that anchor for him.

And then, having gotten him to go along with her idea before he'd had a chance to think it out, she'd used some of that same power to push a ship that had to weigh more than a stegosaurus back away from the falls and all the way to the center of the channel. The total consequence of what she'd done was that she now felt a little dizzy and lightheaded.

Where did that energy come from? How was it stored? It wasn't from the Well, or anything to do with the Well, that was for sure. Somehow it came from inside her and was stored . . . *as body fat?* It seemed ridiculous, but it was the only explanation that made sense.

It sure beat the hell out of any diet plan he could think of, and it made diets anathema for all that.

She *was* paying a price, perhaps for using two such blasts so close together, possibly because they hadn't eaten very much in several days; she lay down on the wet deck forward and just passed out.

This is really weird, he thought once more. *For the first time I almost think I have a crack at making it before Mavra. I've never had this kind of power on my side before, not until I was inside.*

But *she* controlled the power, he didn't.

Or did she?

He lay down, suddenly struck by an idea. If he was now

connected to her so tightly, this energy must be the bond. There had to be some sort of energy field, automatically emanating from her to him, or the bond would be broken at times like this. Surely such abilities, in many ways like what the Gedemondans had been after, at least the last time he'd been there, had to be learned, suffered for, studied, and experimented with for countless years, perhaps countless generations, depriving those who sought such power of almost everything that might provide as the slightest distraction.

At least they hadn't also taken on celibacy, although that would hardly be practical in a grand experiment involving an entire population over thousands of generations.

Maybe that was where the lamas had gone wrong back in the Himalayas. They had brought themselves to the limits of individual higher mental attainments, but the emphasis had still always been on *individual* attainment, and although their belief in reincarnation gave them ample time in their own minds, in reality death had cut them off short. Even without that limitation Brazil had eventually abandoned that life when he'd suddenly realized that the attainment of the absolute, the joining with the That Which Is Behind All That, was oblivion. It was too much like being at the end of the line with the Markovians but not having had any fun getting there. It was, however, a god-awful amount of work, whether it was that traditional system of Earth's or the Glathrielian grand project.

The fact that the Glathrielians had given her the end results of this work, much as one would stick a bunch of programs on a computer mass storage device for easy access, didn't really matter. Everything he'd seen of Glathrielians indicated a total rejection of the physical ways of the world. The most they did was pick some fruit off trees. Even when doing that, he'd observed how their actions were almost hivelike, almost as if they were a collective organism even though on the surface they seemed like individuals. They condescended to the body only in the sense of its need to eat, drink, sleep, and reproduce.

They had given Terry those powers and imposed that overculture as a kind of control program, but she'd not been born into it or brought up with it. It wasn't a natural state to her. Like him or Gus, she had more in common in her background with the Ambrezans than with the Gedemondan mystics, but she had no way of really understanding it. She had been surprised to get any sort of a linkage with him after being together so long. That was the group mind part, the impulse to co-opt those of one's own kind into the greater consciousness. But she was still too much the individual inside, and when she'd absolutely had to, she had compromised the Glathrielian programming in a way that the group mind part of the Gedemondan whole would never have even considered.

Faced with Terry's very appearance, they had done the one thing with her that such a community, insular as it was, wasn't all that used to doing.

They had improvised.

He thought he had them now, although not by any means all their powers and strengths. He doubted that *she* knew what she could do, except it was inside her, like individual programs on disks, waiting to be accessed if demanded by circumstance. A Glathrielian would know. A true Glathrielian *child* would know, would probably have fun switching bodies and moving stones and doing who knew what else. They had the experience of the group mind and were raised and trained to know. But they'd had Terry for only the shortest time. Days or weeks, perhaps.

A television professional would think of things first in visual terms. They must have seized on that as something *simpático* with their own way of thinking. Whole chunks that made a picture, an object rather than a linear assemblage of cross-referenced information. The holographic mind with no intermediate steps, no aids, not even a linear language to slow down the process. Need? *Bang!* Entire solution. Just like that.

He could see them now, considering *him* before they had her. He'd been living very close to them for a while. They sensed his difference, sensed, perhaps, his connection to the Well. They couldn't tap or access that connection, but they understood it on their level, and they understood the potential. But what to do? Problem, even opportunity, but no solution.

Then, suddenly, Terry walks in. She's in shock, she's scared, and she's Earth-human, or close enough to Glathrielian that they recognize her as one of their own. Possibly their communal field was strong enough and she was still shocked enough from her arrival that she sensed and was perhaps even guided by the permeating group mind. They had taken her in, and they had made her one of them, or so it seemed. Compromise was necessary. In them, everything was to a purpose; in her, it had to run on automatic.

Then they sent her back with an absolute command to remain with him at all costs. Sooner or later he might let his guard down. When it happened, she was to copy everything from her mind to his. Make him Glathrielian. Then, when he entered the Well, he would be one of them. The whole of Glathriel could then be connected to the Well itself.

That was how they differed from the Gedemondans. The Gedemondans were seeking a third way, as the founding race had intended, a new way to attain power and an even greater godhood on their own.

The Glathrielians wanted to take over the damned controls!

Well, they couldn't do it, but how would they know that? It was certainly worth a shot. Worth risking one strange girl.

So last night she had made the link, made the attempt, automatically. Not even the whole of Glathriel could do it even with his cooperation, but she'd made the attempt. She'd transferred the programs and linked the two of them so that the energy that was her only tool was shared. His Earth-human body and physical brain and nervous system were still human enough for that. What they could not do, could never do, was get down to the core of his being, his "soul" for want of any better concept, and reprogram at that level. They could control every aspect of his body but not his core ego.

But the programs were still there. Perhaps not in his mind, because of their ultimate failure, but accessible from *hers* over the energy linkage. That linkage had to be physiological to some degree; she'd tapped into something inside him, perhaps inside all Earth-human brains, and activated it. Whether necessary for their plans or not, he would have to accept and accommodate the control program requirements as much as possible, but some of it could be bypassed either by force of will, as when she'd compromised for expediency, or because it was designed to filter *her* input/output, not his. He might not be able to run the whole suite of programs concurrently because of this, but maybe, just maybe, because they'd been designed to be run by someone who didn't have the owner's manual, he might run them one at a time.

He was wide-awake, even a little excited, but he remembered his own long lessons in mental discipline from long ago and relaxed, closing his eyes, clearing his mind, breathing deeply, rhythmically, letting his consciousness roam, but not without a sense of purpose. He felt her, felt everything about her, matched her own deep breathing, thought only of the secondhand but very real existence of her own body, not his own.

This time it was very gentle, very slow. There was no rushing force, no fast-forward pull, not even disorientation. He moved toward her, into her and gently displaced her, sending her, still in a deep, deep sleep, back along the path and inserting himself fully into her body.

He opened his eyes—*her* eyes, knowing that his own body still reclined aft, now sound asleep. Carefully he sat up, then discovered that he was partly sitting on long hair and pulled it free.

He felt the body's fatigue, and there were a few aches and pains where muscles and joints pleaded for more rest, but he wasn't going to do this for very long. He got up on her feet, feeling a bit dizzy, even a little sick, but nothing he couldn't manage. A smile played across her lips.

The old adage holds true again, as always, he thought with some glee. *Never try to con a con man. He'll pick your pockets while letting you believe you're stealing him blind.*

He began to walk forward, keeping one hand on something to steady her body, and considered that it wasn't quite as similar as he'd imagined. The center of gravity was different and took a little getting used to; he was more aware of the large breasts and equally aware of the lack of male genitalia than he'd considered. Still, it was basically the same: two legs, two arms, eyes, and ears. Things *did* look a bit different, and he wondered for a moment if that was something new he was tapping. After all, he was also using her brain, even if his memories and personality were being scrolled off his own sleeping form. Then he realized that it was just that there were subtle shifts in the colors. So it was true—for purely physical reasons no two people probably saw colors exactly the same. But they weren't all *that* different—green still looked green, red looked red. They were just slightly different, often in brightness or degree, although he thought he saw more gradations of each color than he'd been aware of before. There also seemed to be a vastly wider array of smells, both good and bad, indicating that the biochemists had been right in saying that women really *could* smell a greater variety of scents than men. That explained why there were so many varieties of perfume even though most men, himself included, could barely tell the difference.

He tried to speak. "Hello, I am not Terry," he croaked. Her voice was raspy and it was almost painful to awaken those throat muscles so long silent, but it sounded like a decent voice, a nice voice, although he knew it would sound different to her, or to him as her, than it would to him as himself.

This was already more than enough for now, but he couldn't resist making his way slowly and carefully aft, then climbing the stairs and looking down at his own sleeping body.

Good lord! I really am *an ugly SOB,* he thought. As many times as he'd seen himself in a mirror, it was different to look upon his body through another's eyes.

Still, he'd proved his point and gotten something of a charge out of it at that. Hell, he vaguely remembered being an animal once, for some reason, the details of which totally escaped him. But he'd never been a woman.

In the distance he heard the sound of a steam whistle. Something was leaving the harbor, something with power, and that meant the naval corvette unless somebody new had shown up. Instantly he felt a pang of fear at the thought that they might have caught Gus and were now going hunting.

He had to get back in his own body and quickly. Not only would this be embarrassing, her body was too worn out to be of any real use in a fight right now, even if he could get used to it fast enough to do the quick, automatic moves that might be required.

He suddenly panicked at the thought that he might well be stuck in her body; he had not, after all, quite done it her way even if he'd used her inner knowledge and power to do it. And with thoughts suddenly coming to him about the possible implications of that steam whistle, how could he clear his mind enough to do it, anyway?

He had to, he decided. He just had to. There was no other choice.

Carefully, he lay down alongside his body, stretched out, and closed his eyes, resisting the body's impulse to lapse back into deep slumber. *Not yet,* he thought, and tried to re-create the conditions he'd established when he had started the stunt, putting all sounds, all worries, out of the way, concentrating only on doing the one thing.

Although he'd done it more gently, there still was a tiny bit of that tension there, and he was able to use it. He naturally belonged over there, and she naturally belonged here. There was a better fit, for want of a more appropriate term, when each was in the body he or she had been born to. It wasn't like what the Well did, not a bit.

A hand slid over a little and touched his, and he felt himself flow back into his body and her back into her own without any real effort or direction.

He opened his eyes, sat up, and shook his head as if to clear it, then looked down and actually felt around himself just to make sure he was in the form he wanted to be in.

He could hear the sound of engines now, coming closer, coming their way. *Thank God they didn't let go that whistle when I was trying to get back inside,* he thought, quickly running through his options.

There wasn't any real wind; the heat and the high rock walls had created a nearly dead calm inside the cove. His mind raced through all possible combinations of sail, anything that might get him moving if he had to, but he finally realized that it wouldn't matter if he had an atomic engine.

If that cutter came in the passage, its cannon and small arms would be on him no matter what he tried, and it would be like shooting fish in a barrel.

There was only one possible way to escape, and he didn't like it a bit. They'd have to go over the side opposite where the cutter would come in and swim for it to the rock formations beyond. Most of the cliff was sheer, but there was a small break in the outer rocks that might provide a way out through an eroded, irregular crack in the wall. If they could make it through there, they might be able to get up a bit and inland enough so that the cutter wouldn't be able to find them.

They'd be stuck on a speck of volcanic rock with the navy searching for them, but it would be a chance. At least, with the protection he now had from her energy shell, it wouldn't be immediately life-threatening and would give him a chance to figure out something.

The cutter was coming very close now, *very* close. It would be at the mouth of the narrow passage in perhaps a minute or two.

Terry was suddenly up, and he felt her momentary confusion at waking up somewhere far removed from where she'd thought she'd gone to sleep, but she dismissed it immediately. She had slept through all his clever tricks, but she'd come instantly awake when she'd felt his sense of peril.

Using sign language, he pointed in the direction of the passage, then at the water, and made swimming motions, pointing to the far end of the cove where the crack was. He had no idea if that crack was big enough for either of them, having only noted it in passing, but it was better than nothing.

She nodded, and he felt her draw on some reserve of strength and become suddenly energized in the physical sense, tense and ready to jump into the water.

The engine sounds echoed down the passage and into the cove itself; Brazil was certain that the ship would be coming down the passage, was perhaps coming down even now, and that they should wait no longer.

Still, something stopped him. Something subtle, a very slight diminution of the sound, perhaps, that rapidly grew more noticeable. He looked up over the jagged rock wall and saw a plume of white smoke proceed in an orderly fashion down the misshapen spires at the top.

The damned thing wasn't coming in! It had passed them by!

He laughed out loud in relief, grabbed Terry, and kissed her. She was somewhat startled by the action but felt his joy and relief and knew what it meant.

For a moment at least they were safe once again, and, he reflected, it was the perfect end to the business he'd been playing at. Being able to tap all that power, to do all these new things, hadn't changed the fact that he was a fugitive hiding out from the closest thing to a government this world had, stuck inside a bunch of barren and smoky rocks on a fly speck of an island in the middle of an indifferent ocean.

He signed to the girl to go back to sleep. She needed the rest almost as much as they both needed food. At least he was no longer overanxious to get under way; he wanted the navy to be well on its way to wherever it was going and well over the horizon before he ventured out. But more than ever he was determined to leave and to weather whatever the nights in this hotbox hex might bring.

There was no more game playing. While Terry slept, he pored over the charts, seeking some sort of alternative source for food. There were other islands, certainly; this was the start of a crescent-shaped chain of island volcanoes, many quite a bit larger above the surface than this little dot. The question was what, if anything, the Well would allow to take root in the rich soil. Whatever it would be would have to be consistent with the fixed ecology of the hex and not injurious to it or vegetation that would be expected to evolve on the actual planet this place represented.

He examined the topographic information, sparse as it was, on the various charts and guessed by knowing something of volcanic islands and checking elevations that one larger island about forty-five kilometers northwest was the most likely. It was kind of peanut-shaped, two volcanoes that had risen large and whose flows had merged into each other at the center, creating a single unit that appeared to be a lowland plain. He wondered for a moment why the service company hadn't put an anchorage there, but a reference to the island on the chart legend showed that flows were irregular, were not far below the surface all along both sides, and tapered off at an extremely shallow slope for a fair distance. There simply was no decent sheltered harbor available, and the only anchorage spots were marked at four or five hundred meters out even for a ship with this draft. From that distance one would be expected to come ashore in a small boat or raft. It was marked EMERGENCY PROVISIONS ONLY, and the only indication that there was anything there was the note of the locations along both coasts of the flat region—the sort of place one made for if one was shipwrecked or at least too damaged to get anywhere else. There were no habitation markers, but its position and the stations indicated that it would probably be checked on a regular basis by the company, the navy, or both.

It also would take them even closer to the Mowry border

instead of toward the northern coast, but without food it would be touch and go.

Unless Gus came back, and with enough to eat, they had no choice but to try it.

The next problem was how the hell to get out of this cul-de-sac. There was a very slight gravitational tide, but without a clock or a means of recording it he couldn't even use *that*, meager as it was, nor did he know if it would be enough. He looked up at the rock cliff and the forbidding terrain beyond. He had used a slight wind to get in, essentially a land breeze or one created by the nearby storms. It would be enough to get out if it was an every-evening thing. He'd just have to wait and see. He couldn't count on the girl to move the ship again, and they sure as hell couldn't push or pull it.

If there was a breeze, anything at all he could use, he'd have to take it, whether Gus was back or not. He realized that now. Whether it came in two minutes or ten hours, that was the way it was.

For the time being there was nothing to do but lie down, stretch out, and rest. After a while he looked over at the girl and studied her features. For all the extra weight, whose purpose he now knew, she had a good body and a very pretty face. It was hard to imagine her as a hard-driving career newswoman.

That was the problem, of course, and he knew it. He didn't really want her to be any different—he wanted what they had now on the gut level to continue on and on. If he got to the Well before Mavra, or even if Mavra got there first but left his own connection intact, he would have to undo much of what had been done to her. Her future had to be her own choice, not his. He owed her that much.

But if she were restored, even with the memory of all this, what would that *other* woman, Terry, whom he'd never known, think of him? And what sort of reaction might she have seeing him not this way but as something of a monster?

As usual, he was racing to the inevitable ending of a situation that had filled him, for all that, with a sense of participation, care, even . . . love. He was more happy and content with her than he'd been or felt in his long memory, and the only thing he and fate as personified by the authorities and the Well could do was shove him toward ending it.

He wanted the situation, and her, to remain as it was now. The only woman around with no interest in a wardrobe, jewels, makeup, or perfumes and one who never nagged or complained about anything—the perfect mate, he thought sardonically, using his usual defensive humor to mask his inner pain.

Maybe he was just being a sucker again, he thought, unable to dispel his dark mood. He didn't *want* to get to the Well, which represented only a return to that endless existence he so hated. Why not just find one of these tropical islands with abundant food and water to support two people, sink the damned ship, and retire, just the two of them? *Let* Mavra fix whatever was broken and go back through. If she disconnected him, then he'd just grow old with Terry and finally die—and find the peace in that he'd never known.

It was terribly appealing, but he knew he'd never do it. It was this damnable sense of *obligation* he had.

Damn it! There were a million reasons why Mavra might have vanished in that long-ago time and place. But why had she never tried to find him in the two and a half thousand years or so since? If only to let him know, even if not to get together. Even allowing for all that, if only Gus hadn't painted a picture of a man-hating mental case . . . !

Gus had a colored view of her, of course. He might be all wrong, and Mavra might be just fine and fully capable of handling things.

She *might* be, but deep down he wasn't sure he believed it. At least, he wasn't sure enough of her to trust the fate of all those races, all those people out there, scattered, seeded among the stars. He hadn't had to take the obligation or the responsibility for them, and perhaps, knowing what he did now, he would not do so again. But he *had* accepted it, and even if he'd occasionally run from the responsibility, he couldn't really hide. It wasn't just hiding from the Well that was the problem; it was that he could never hide from himself.

Eventually he dozed off in spite of himself.

He awoke in the waning part of the day, feeling very good, very refreshed, but thirsty. But when he got up to go get a drink of water, he discovered that he was in her body, not his own. Her body, yes, but this time it felt natural, neither odd nor different, nor did the sights and sounds and smells seem out of place. Still, he went and got the drink and returned aft, only to see his own body at the wheel and other controls, dropping sail, bringing the little craft about in the wind.

"What are you doing?" he called out in her voice. "You don't know how to sail a ship! I wouldn't even think you'd want to!"

His body's face looked surprised and two dark eyes stared at the figure just below. "You can speak!" he heard his own voice say. "You've got speech back! That's wonderful!"

"What do you mean? It's you who have changed! We've swapped bodies, that's all, probably in our sleep. We'd best swap back so I can take her out. You'll wreck her!"

"Are you mad?" his other self asked. "I'm Nathan Brazil! I was captaining craft bigger and smaller than this before your world was formed! What's this nonsense about body switching? You're Terry, and you've been through a lot of shocks. Let me just get us under way and we'll have some time once we get to open sea! I want out while there's still some light!"

"But—but—you're not Nathan Brazil, I'm Nathan Brazil!"

The other laughed. "This sharing of sensation has restored your speech but given you delusions! Look! What's the name of that sail? Where's the jib? The boom? When should you run with a spinnaker?"

"Uh—I—I—" she stammered, suddenly realizing that she had no answers to those questions. But Nathan Brazil would know, of course, and obviously did know from the way he was operating things up there. She sat down on the

hatch cover and tried to think. What did she know? What did she remember? It was all fleeing, rushing out of her head even as she tried to grab on to the memories, the thoughts, the knowledge they represented.

It was all gone in a flash, leaving only the question of whether it had ever really been there. What did she know? She remembered coming into the vast chamber, reaching the place with the giant furry creatures, having met and joined with others like herself in some kind of swampy jungle, then of seeing Brazil and finding him very attractive and going with him . . . .

There was no shock, only an intense if incredibly odd feeling of relief, of a massive weight lifted off the shoulders. Why, then, it must be true, she thought. I don't have any responsibilities beyond being with him, helping him, and being happy! I'm not Nathan Brazil, I'm just Terry! I must have gotten enough from him to feel his burden and his pain, and I just wanted to take that away from him. She felt sorry for him, knowing what a burden he carried inside, and she resolved to try to make it as easy on him as she could. She loved him so much, she'd wanted to take that burden off him and carry it herself, but the load was so overwhelming . . .

"Wake up, Cap," said Gus, shaking him.

Nathan Brazil opened his eyes and for a moment still thought he was Terry, but he wasn't. No matter his dreams, he couldn't be let off the hook that easily . . .

"What the hell took you so long, Gus?" he snapped, more irritated to be awakened than glad to see the Dahir.

"Well, they got wanted posters out on you, for one thing. Probably took 'em off a blowup of the recording when you come in. Right now all it says is that you're wanted for theft of a private vessel, and they give a pretty good description of this scow, too. Good thing you decided not to go in the harbor, Cap. You'd never have stood 'em all off."

That was bad. "But what about you?"

"Well, all sorts of stuff. Best-laid plans and all that, I guess. Nobody noticed me, as usual, but when I was through pickin' up information and supplies, I found something for my own belly as well, and after I eat I get groggy and sleepy for a little, and, well, I guess I just dozed off. I still feel like a stuffed turkey, but it was well into daylight when I woke up. I decided to fight off any idea of getting some more snoozin' and get back here. Fact was, I was worried that you'd cut out. Then I heard the boat whistle. All the crew of that cop ship got back aboard pretty fast, and they got up steam and pulled out. I got real nervous that they'd made you and were takin' off after you."

"Yeah, that gave us a turn as well. Went right on by, though."

"Well, I figured that, since word was that one of the small ships that come in sometime today had seen some other ship on their wanted list a ways off to the east. Some kind of big-time smuggler craft—the way they talked, sounded like drugs or somethin' to me. Whoever it is, they want 'em as bad as they want us, and the cop captain pulled everybody out and took off as fast as he could get up steam. Seems these crooks pull the shell game at sea so you can never be sure which boat's got the goods, and they figured this one was steamin' for a pickup."

"Interesting. Well, at least it gets them off our backs for the moment, but don't think there aren't more of them around—and if the posters have hit even a little spot in the middle of nowhere like this, you can bet we're marked. Did you remember to bring the sack with the food?"

"Oh, yeah. Did better'n that, really. Come over here and look over the side. I'll need some help with it gettin' it all aboard."

Brazil was astonished to find not the meter-square aid kit container but a full-blown plastic dinghy filled with cartons. "Good lord! They let you get away with all *this*?"

"Well, they didn't stop me, anyway. Truth is, there was a lot of furry types and all in the cop crew, and this was one of the supply shipments due to go out to their boat. They left it there at the dock in their rush to pull out, so I just kinda slipped into the water and took it instead."

"Great. You're sure it's not ammo and two thousand copies of my wanted poster, though?"

"It's food, Cap. Maybe not all of it's useful, but a lot is. Nothin' looks exactly like it did back home, but fruit and veggies have a habit of lookin' pretty close, and there's flour and some kinda meal like cornmeal and other stuff like that. I checked after I got out of the harbor but before I got too far away to go back. I figured I better let them cops get some distance, I didn't want 'em suddenly rememberin' that they forgot this and comin' back for it. They might not see *me* in the water, but they'd sure as hell see this raft and figure it got loose and floated away."

"Good work, Gus! And quick thinking! This is a real break in a number of ways. If they needed this enough to come back for it, they'd have turned around by now. The company people won't miss it because they'll assume it was taken aboard the cutter, and the cutter might not come back this way for weeks or even remember it if and when it does. Now, if we can only get this aboard and get enough wind to get out of this cove, we're good for the distance."

"How's that? You mean you can't get *out* of this place?"

"Not without some help from nature, or what passes for nature on the Well World. Come on—let's get started getting this aboard so if and when something comes up we don't have to dump it or get stuck until somebody finds us."

"You're ridin' a bit low in the water, ain't you? It looked kinda different."

"Yeah, we, ah, took on a little water, but I don't think it's serious. We might have to get on the pumps later if it proves a real problem, but I'm not worried about it now."

Gus slid back over the side and positioned himself on one side of the raft. "Cap, my arms can't lift their shadows, but I figure I can get under it and get it balanced, I can lift it up on my head. You'll have to grab it and pull it aboard, though. Anything that falls in, I'll try and get afterward."

"Good enough. I hope *I* can do it. I'm strong for my weight, but I'm only sixty-one kilos or so."

"Huh? What's that in pounds?"

"Old English measure? Jeez, I barely recall. About 135, I think."

"Well, you're not a ninety-eight-pound weakling, so you'll have to do. I'll help if I can. With this flat tail and a head as hard as my mother always said it was, I should be able to give it a little oomph."

The first two tries didn't make it, but they lost only one carton to the water and it floated nearby. On the third try he was aware that Terry was now awake and watching them. When Gus came up again, Nathan grabbed the rope affixed to the raft and pulled up and back with all his might. After almost getting it, he felt it start to slip away again, his arm muscles aching, but suddenly the raft and all its contents came up onto the deck almost as if they were weightless, causing him to fall over backward.

He got up, rubbing his bottom and reflecting that there certainly was no energy protection against friction burns, but he knew what had happened. Terry had seen the problem and had added a bit of power to the equation through him. The whole raft was now securely on deck.

Gus retrieved the lost box in his gaping mouth and brought it aboard, then deposited it with the others. There were two very large puncture marks in the carton, and some white stuff was coming out of one of them.

"Whooo!" Gus gasped. "That's more heavy work than I've done since I got here! You wanna do inventory on it or what?"

"Might as well, as long as we're still becalmed," Brazil responded. "Besides, if there's anything here ready to eat, I can stand something, and so can she."

This was where the Well's data helped him, although he was barely aware of it. Among the cartons were a number of suspect items, but he instinctively seemed to know which ones to keep and which ones to discard. Gus had been right—most of it was more than useful.

"We're going to have to get this below fairly quickly," Brazil said at last. "Most of it, anyway. We'll leave these three on deck. It's a bit damp below, but I think we can keep these high enough to keep 'em out of the wet. I think I can handle individual boxes. I'd best get to it. Leave this one with the fruit open and this one with the vegetables, too, so Terry can start eating. Watch her, though. She has a tendency to eat absolutely everything, and I need something!"

Individually, the cartons weren't all that heavy, and he quickly transferred the nine remaining ones below to the unused crew sleeping quarters, securing them with netting. The one leaking the powder from the fang marks he could do little about, but the marks were high enough that even if they leaked a fair amount of the sweet-tasting meal, there would still be enough.

The water was still ankle deep, but that reassured rather than bothered him. Nothing more was coming in, and the new load wasn't so heavy that the whole balance of the ship would be adversely affected.

When he came back on deck, Gus commented, "I gotta say, Cap, you were sure right about her appetite. She's just tearin' through that stuff like there's no tomorrow. Better get some while you can."

He nodded, opened the other carton, and found some premade and wrapped loaves of what appeared to be a kind of French bread. Inside, it had a yellowish look and contained small bits of exceptionally sweet cornlike kernels, but it tasted just fine. He was just reaching to rescue a large purplish applelike fruit the size of a small melon from the ravenous Terry when he suddenly noticed something.

"A breeze! I feel a breeze!" he almost shouted. Forgetting his hunger, he ran to the wheel. "Gus! Go forward and raise the anchor. Use the winch! Yeah, there!"

At last! he thought. *Food, water, and even a little daylight left, and along comes a breeze! We're getting out of this hole!*

Out, yes, a little corner of him responded. *Out and away, toward harsh reality, outward to smash yet another good dream . . .*

Ogadon

THERE WAS NO GOOD PLACE TO HOUSE THE DILLIANS IN THE Gekir coastal town of Port Saar, and since Erdomese, too, were basically unsuited for the network of steps and ladders which the catlike natives found no trouble at all, they set up a camp on the edge of town, along the road between the town proper and the port up at the Ogadon border.

The chief, in the tradition of her people, invited them all to the royal guest quarters and to a banquet, but Mavra explained some of the problems the others might have in attending. The governor seemed to understand and instead issued them something of far more value: a provincial conscription note, which was basically an account with local merchants that guaranteed that they would be paid by the local treasury.

As was common in many smaller port towns everywhere, businesses closed promptly at sunset, so they all took advantage of the conscription note in the couple of hours of sunlight remaining.

Port Saar was not the same sort of town as the big seaports they'd seen. Rather, it seemed more like the small rural market towns of much of Central and South America, minus electricity and modern conveniences.

Like their underwater neighbors, the Ogadon, Gekirs were basically carnivores, but nonetheless they spent a good deal of time on small- and medium-sized farms growing fresh fruits and vegetables for export to the railhead just inside Itus or by coastal ships to other nearby hexes. It was, one merchant noted, actually very practical; in the farming business the pickers and other help never ate the profits.

Although adding to and freshening their provisions was the main idea, Lori, with Mavra Chang's permission, used some of the credit on Alowi, as Julian now insisted on being called. In fact, the few times Lori had slipped and said "Julian," she hadn't even responded, convincing him that wherever she was stuffing her past had absorbed even the memory of that name. In fact, it was becoming next to impossible not to think of her as a native-born Erdomese female.

He bought her a necklace she seemed to fancy, some sweet-smelling perfumes, and a set of combs that while clearly not designed for Erdomese, worked rather well on the hair and tail and in cleaning the short fur. There were also some nice-looking and modestly priced clips that were the right size for tail clips; Lori didn't know and didn't really want to know for whom or what they were actually intended.

At Mavra's suggestion, they also looked at heavy coats, since they would be going into unknown climates and might well need them. There weren't too many available for non-Gekir types and none that were really great fits, but a sufficient number of races were to one degree or another humanoid that even the Erdomese found rough fits. The Dillians, it appeared, had brought their own along, and Anne Marie insisted that she could alter the new coats to some degree to make them fit better.

They also finally met a Gekir male.

He was pretty easy to spot; thin, gaunt-looking, and smaller than a female, he was a sort of faded gray color all over except for his outsized lionlike snow white mane. He had a medium-length tail that ended in an explosive puff of white fur, further contrasting him with the tailless females. He also wore matching bracelets and anklets of a golden color with ornate designs in them and a large golden oval nose ring and appeared to be perfumed.

The people had overall been quite friendly, and so Lori couldn't resist trying to strike up a conversation with him in the street.

"Your pardon, sir, but you are the first man we have seen since coming to Gekir, and I was just curious. I mean, it began to look like there were no men at all here."

The Gekir seemed amused. "Oh, yes, there be a lot of us, only not nearly in the same numbers as women. The average be about fifteen women to one man. It be different where you come from, I suppose."

"In some ways, yes, in others, no. In Erdom there are ten females for every male, but as you can see from my wife here, the men are larger, and because of the hand development and upper muscle strength, men run the affairs while the women run the household and bear and raise the children."

"Huh! Think of that! Dunno if I'd like *that* or not! Got enough trouble just doin' me male duties."

It turned out that the males, smaller, far weaker, and fewer in number, ran nothing at all. They also tended to be uneducated and limited in what they could do. What they *could* do was have sex, apparently in nearly unlimited amounts, and they tended to do that essentially as a profession, often doing a "circuit of me regulars" and spending their time at those "regulars' " homes. They also performed services from shopping for busy women to baby-sitting and took little interest in much outside this life. If the male they met was as typical as he said he was, they liked it that way.

"See, all the time they likes us around, and once a month they needs us, so they keeps us pretty happy," the Gekir male told him. The general feeling among the women, he explained in a low voice, was that men were stupid and incompetent except at the one thing they were needed for, and the men had a vested interest in maintaining those attitudes. "They even cook for us," he told Lori. "Think we don't know how."

The male begged off further talk, since he had a "real important appointment just after sunset," but he'd revealed enough.

In Gekir, the women ruled and the men were small and weak, considered inferior, and used entirely as sex objects. It was even more extreme than Erdom by a great deal, and it disturbed Lori almost as much as the reverse would have. It answered one of those nagging questions in a way he hadn't wanted it answered.

The parallel seemed to be with many Earth insects. The black widow was obvious, but many male spiders existed only for one purpose and then died, not to mention male bees and many other examples. A lot of women he'd known back on Earth would have loved this kind of arrangement, but he wasn't so sure. Was his distaste, though, just because he was now a man himself, or was it because the same offenses committed in reverse felt no more moral?

It was a question he pondered as they went back to the camp and set up to cook dinner as the sun went down. After determining that there were quite a number of things both Erdomese and Dillians could eat in common, Lori did not object to Alowi and Anne Marie preparing the meal, with him translating as needed. It did not in fact come out bad at all.

Mavra had remained in town, she said to talk to some people before her official dinner later that night. She told them that they should not wait for her and that they should get some sleep.

Alowi did the cleanup, then insisted on using her new combs and brushes to get the last vestiges of grime from Lori's fur and tail, and he even allowed a little perfume to be used to cover the mild but remaining swamp odor.

The Dillians excused themselves and went off into the shorter, greener grass nearby and eventually seemed to lock themselves for sleep.

With his hand still bandaged and saying by occasional aches and sharp pains that it should remain so for a while longer, there wasn't much for the Erdomese to do but try to sleep themselves. Alowi cuddled up close to him and was soon out cold; after the previous night with so little sleep she had to be exhausted. Still, Lori would have liked to have discussed the oddly different sexual balance of Gekir and perhaps talked about the old days, as they always had, but he couldn't. Those conversations had been with Julian, and Julian, it appeared, no longer existed for all practical purposes.

He felt doubly guilty for that somehow. He'd treated her as less than a partner, all along driving home the division that must have raged within her no matter how much she suppressed it, and it had been his own stupid injuries that had caused the final break.

Nobody else had gotten even a scratch. Not even Jul—Alowi. Mister Macho had to leap before he looked, jump too fast, not notice an embankment. *He* had to be out first, since *he* was going to look out for the others. The poor, defenseless others. *The girls.*

Yeah, right.

Damn it! he thought, furious with himself. *When the hell did I turn into every guy I ever loathed in high school?*

It was not exactly the kind of grand commercial vessel that both the Dillians and the Erdomese had used to reach Itus. It was in fact small, low but with big masts, and had a central funnel so that it could be used under steam where possible. It was built for silence and speed, not for comfort and convenience, and for its ability to run with a minimal crew.

It was also painted a dull black, and even the sails and ropes had been dyed to a very dark gray hue. The bridge was actually exposed as in the ancient sailing ships of Earth, but there was a small secondary cabin between the main wheel and the funnel with a duplicate wheel that could be engaged and that had some very exotic-looking, if now totally turned off, electronic gear.

The captain was from Stulz, far off to the south and west across the great Ocean of Shadows, farther from his own hex than the travelers were from theirs. He was in many ways a fearsome sight, with a dark gray foxlike face filled with sharp little teeth. His beady, reddish brown eyes seemed to dart this way and that without ever settling on any one thing or person, and he had great furry wings that formed almost a cape and a hairy pair of arms terminating in fingers with very long, sharp claws. His bowlegs terminated in prehensile feet that essentially duplicated the hands, while from his back came a long whiplike leathery tail that seemed to be always under total control.

The trouble with Captain Hjlarza, Mavra decided, was that he looked exactly like a drug-running scoundrel in this part of the world should look.

The first mate was from Zhonzhorp and resembled nothing so much as a bipedal crocodile with long, thin arms and rubbery four-fingered hands that terminated in what appeared to be suckers or suction cups. The fact that he wore britches, a sash, a vest, and a tricorner hat with a feather in it did nothing to make him look less fearsome.

The five other crew members did little to reassure by their appearance. Two were giant hairy spiderlike creatures that seemed to be able to use any combination of their eight legs almost as tentacles. Two more were short and squat but looked as if they were humanoid caricatures carved out of very ugly rocks. The fifth was a purple and red creature with a somewhat humanoid face and torso, forelegs resembling a goat's, and a main body that the two legs dragged around, much like a sea lion.

Only the captain and mate had translators, so for most of the passengers it was going to be a pretty nervous trip.

Alowi was horrified at the menacing menagerie, and Tony and Anne Marie hardly looked thrilled, but Lori was concerned only when she sensed that even Mavra Chang was nervous.

The Zhonzhorpian, "Just call me Zitz," was the one who was to get them squared away.

"Could be a rough trip," he warned them.

"Are you expecting trouble?" Mavra asked nervously.

"Oh, no, not *that* kind. The captain knows what he's

doing, and we've been at this a long time. Your Dillians, though, will have to sleep up top on the afterdeck, since they just won't fit below, and if we get into a bit of bad weather, it can be pretty nerve-wracking up here, not to mention cold and wet."

"I've briefed them as much as I could about such things," she assured the mate. "I think we'll lash them down if we get into rough seas." She looked aft. "The way you're rigged, we might also be able to set up some kind of tent or at least a shelter if you have some sailcloth to spare. They can rig it themselves if they have the materials and a few tools. If we stretch it between the afterdeck and the main deck, it will have extra support while being out of the way of the mainmast."

Zitz was impressed by her knowledge. "All right. I think we can manage that. You've sailed before, I think, and not as a mere passenger."

She nodded. "A very long time ago, though. If you need an extra hand in weather, let me know. I'm not that good at hauling sails, but I know the basics and I can handle whatever's needed if it doesn't take a lot of strength."

"Very good! I may take you up on that. Weather's been less than great of late, particularly in the northern ocean. We tend to use sail whenever possible regardless of the hex properties and save the steam for weather when we can use it or if the wind's too much against us."

"You're going with cargo full?"

"Not quite, but heavy enough. We'll top it off with a stop at sea. The only nonweather problems we might encounter are in Kzuco, which we can't really bypass. Otherwise we'll be staying on the northern side, which means all nontech and semitech hexes."

She nodded. "That's all right with us. The less attention we get, the better for our own purposes. We have no interest in your cargo or activities so long as this is yet another trip when you have no problems. In fact, I'd prefer not to meet any authorities at all."

The Erdomese and Marva followed Zitz down into the

ship. It stank and had that "lived in too long by pigs" look and feel about it. The few cabins were small and narrow, but they would do. Two small cabins that might have been used for storage had been cleared out and were essentially bare; the bedrolls would have to serve both for the Erdomese in one room and for Mavra across the corridor. When Zitz left to go topside, Mavra came over to the Erdomese.

"Not exactly first class," she commented a bit apologetically, "but it will do. It'll have to."

"I wouldn't feel comfortable with this crew if they were carrying Bibles," Lori said nervously. "How long will we be cooped up on this tub?"

"With a decent wind they can make twenty knots, I'd say. Under steam, probably half that. Assuming some foul wind and allowing for the usual lousy conditions for at least some part of the trip, that probably means an average of a day and a half to two days to cross a hex depending if we're going along a single edge or across the center. That's four, maybe five days to Agon, but since they're headed past there to Lilblod or even Clopta, it might well be a week if we don't get off at some place along the way. Call it a week."

"A week! I'll never stand it! And the others . . ."

"We'll do what we have to do. If we can bypass Agon and land in Lilblod near the Clopta border, we'll not only save several days' walking, we might be able to bypass the high-tech hexes and their communications systems almost entirely."

"What about the crew? Can we trust them?"

Mavra grinned. "Not one bit. Not that I'd trust a crew looking like angels, singing like a choir, and carrying that load of Bibles you mentioned, either. In fact, watch out for the Bible carriers more than anybody. Every slave ship that ever sailed back when I knew them carried Bibles on the outbound trip; the crew all had prayer meetings and thought themselves holy and got blessed by the priests, some of whom came along. Give me a good crew of honest crooks any day. You're never surprised, and they're usually honorable if you're not worth the trouble, and the profits these guys turn in one trip make us not worth the trouble."

"Yeah? Then how did you get them to take us at all? We're really in the way."

"Well, if they're stopped, the fact they have multiracial passengers will make them seem legit, since the kind of cops who go after these types know that they wouldn't jeopardize an illegal, high-profit cargo by having innocents aboard. Also, we're not known in the region and so are unlikely to be crooks. That's one reason. The other reason is that they've been highly paid, but in order to keep that payment, they have to deliver us."

"Huh? What are you talking about? And where did you get anything valuable enough to make them consider us as precious as their cargo?"

Mavra chuckled. "It was nice to see how it all came back to me. My original profession and one I always loved. It's paid off quite a bit over the years when I needed it. Of course, I felt bad about doing that to the chief when she was so nice, but not being able to return to Gekir for a few generations is a small price to pay."

"What in the *world* are you talking about?" Lori wanted to know.

"My original profession and first love, learned out of necessity and refined to a fine art before I ever left the planet where I grew up, let alone heard of the Well World. I was the best damned jewel and art thief in the whole galaxy, I'll have you know!"

Lori laughed, finding it hard to believe. "You? A professional thief?"

She nodded, grinning with pride. "That's the third reason. These kind of folks can *sense* when they're dealing with one of their own."

"But—what did you steal?"

"Basically, some of the lesser state jewels kept in the governor's vaults. Not a big deal, but the few I picked were whoppers. They won't discover it for another month or two, though, when their big religious festival comes up and they need to take the things out. By then this business will be done."

"But you said they had to make sure they delivered us! If they've got the jewels . . ."

Mavra nodded. "I know, but they are also aware that I sent a sealed and secured packet with a courier into the Gekir capital and from there to Zone. The package is to be held for my pickup by the Glathrielian delegation, and if I don't pick it up in six months, it'll be opened and *these* boys will be fingered to the Gekir as the thieves. Simple, really."

"Um, yeah, except I thought that the Glathrielians didn't—"

Mavra put her hand up to his mouth, then put a finger to her lips. "*Shhhh!* What they don't know won't hurt us."

Lori decided to let it drop, but he wasn't at all thrilled with the news. If something went wrong and the Gekir somehow discovered the theft before they were out of the country, then nothing could save them.

"I see now why you were a little nervous coming aboard," he said.

She shook her head from side to side. "Uh uh. No problem with that. It's just that I've never had good luck on ships, and even worse on the Well World, so I'm always a little spooked when I'm on them, that's all." She turned to leave. "I'm going topside and help the Dillians. Come on up when you want to."

"Um—Mavra?"

"Yes, Lori?"

"Just out of curiosity—you said you'd been in the Brazilian jungles something like three hundred years or more. How did you get there way back then?"

"I was sold to a Portuguese ship's captain in Macao for a beat-up old musket. The captain took a fancy to me when I was loaned out to him for some hospitality. He wanted something to relieve the tedium of a Pacific crossing. When he grew bored with me, he gave me to the mate. I went down in rank rapidly. I think if he'd been a couple of years older, I would have been with the cabin boy by the time we rounded the Horn and reached Brazil."

"How *horrible!*"

"Yeah, I thought he was going to Africa. Pretty hard to escape when you're in the middle of the Pacific. By the time we reached Brazil, I was so flipped out, I couldn't even think. They painted me up, stripped me naked, claimed I was an Indian, and sold me to a sugar plantation for a couple of bottles of private-stock rum, I think. I wasn't in any shape to pay much attention. For the next several years I cut cane and planted and harvested rice along with hundreds of black and Indian slaves. Slowly I absorbed the local languages, and some of it came back to me. It was okay, but the ownership changed and the new people were pretty vicious; they decided we should be whipped and worked into the ground until we dropped dead. There was a revolt—I don't know the details because the men didn't exactly take us women into their confidence—but somehow I wound up in the middle of it. I got picked up, and they decided to have some fun with me. I flipped out—it was as if the ship's crew had suddenly reappeared. *This* time I fought, but it was hopeless. When they were done with me, they had revenge for my fighting and threats. They cut out my tongue, cut off my hands, and threw me in a swamp to die slowly."

"My God!" he said.

"Instead, of course, I survived, made my way into the jungle, and managed on my own somehow, with no voice and just stumps for hands, until I was discovered by some hunters from a local Indian tribe. They took pity on me and took me in even though I was nothing but a burden on them; by their traditions they should have left me to die. It really wasn't bad, and I was getting to like them, when, of course, I began regenerating, slowly, until it became apparent that I was growing new hands and a new tongue. It frightened the hell out of them. They decided I was some evil spirit and came to kill me, but I escaped back into the jungle, which by that time I knew very well."

She paused for a moment, and Lori said, "You don't have to say any more if you don't want to. I understand."

"No, that's all right. You're one of the few people who has a right to hear this out. Anyway, I lost all track of time, so I can't say how long I lived alone in that jungle, but eventually I came across two Indian girls fleeing from another tribe who'd captured them in an intertribal squabble. We never asked each other questions and just sort of banded together to survive. Those two were the start of my own little tribe. They never asked who I was or *what* I was or anything, even later. Of course, as they continued to age and I did not, and particularly after I lost another limb out of carelessness to a crocodile and *it* grew back, they decided I wasn't human but some kind of goddess. I spent some time long ago in Athens at its peak and in Sparta, and I remembered the legend of the Amazons, and it just seemed fitting. After that we searched out girls who'd been cast out. Centuries later we were still doing it. Frankly, you're the first sentient male I've had any sort of conversation with, let alone friendship, in all that time."

Lori sighed. "I see. You certainly make immortality sound positively repugnant."

"Oh, it has its moments. I think I did some good in that jungle or I wouldn't have stayed, but how long do you think I would have survived there without my special situation? Why did a tribe that threw out its deformed and maimed suddenly take pity on me and take me in? And there were some brief decent periods. Greece was pretty good, and Rome was really even better than its reputation. Sheba was pretty nice, too, and some of the early Hindu Kush tribal groups were okay. It wasn't *all* bad, but I tell you, if you have to live through the history of Earth, make sure that you're a man. It won't guarantee a pleasant trip, but it's a damned sight more fun than being a woman." She paused, then said, "I think I better get up on deck. It feels like they're getting under way, and I want the Dillians settled."

She went off, and Lori looked at Alowi. "You heard and understood all that?"

"Yes, my husband."

"What do you think of it?"

"I heard, but I could not completely understand it. The nearest I could follow was that she has lived a very long time, and many of our lifetimes ago she left her husband and went out on her own in the world. She was thus without status or protection, and bad things happened to her for still more lifetimes. Then she took up with some other wild females, living with them in a wild place, and she blames all men for her misfortune."

He shrugged. "I suppose that summarizes it. But he wasn't her husband. As far as I can tell, she never had one. I'm not sure what the relationship with this man was, but he, too, is here, and they are no longer friends but enemies. Still, you seem to be blaming her for leaving him when we don't know the reason. We don't even know if she left him or some accident separated them and they never again found one another."

"All I can see is that she wants to be a man and cannot accept the idea that she is not. She has the same kind of demon that made my life so horrible, and she will stay miserable, unstable, perhaps dangerous, until she accepts what she is as I did and casts that demon out."

"She doesn't want to be a man," Lori responded. "If she did, she might well have become one, if the powers of that Well are what she claims, and she didn't. She simply wants to be self-sufficient and have the same degree of independence, the same choices and respect, that the man had."

"Perhaps."

He was irritated. "Remember, she came from a civilization we would think of as far advanced, a civilization with ships that sailed between the stars and one that did not have the same attitudes that we have. She was unprepared for the primitive early history of Earth." He paused. Did Alowi even *remember* Earth?

She didn't seem to, but she answered. "I know only that their race is much like ours. There are males and females. They have different bodies and lives and each can do things the other cannot, but they need each other to do those things. I can cure your ills and bear and raise your children. You cannot do these things, but you protect me from the evil that is everywhere and you provide for my own needs. When each does what he or she does best, there is contentment. When each tries to do the other's role, there is no contentment, and no one can really perform another's role. You did not make yourself, your role, or this way of life. Neither did I mine, nor do we truly have the choices we might like. But to pretend that you are what you cannot be leads to madness. This I believe."

Lori started to continue the argument, then realized it was useless to do so. Even Julian might have thought along those lines, although perhaps a bit more sophisticatedly. He'd never been an Earth-human woman.

Still, Alowi had made a practical point he'd been wrestling with all along. Here at least, as an Erdomese, on this world, did he really have that many choices in how to act, how to live, and what he could do? The priests, the whole culture, wanted stasis. Everyone and everything in its proper place. Biology was stacked against the Erdomese, too, almost forcing on them the ancient traditional roles. What was it Tony had told him? She could adjust to being a woman, but she could never become what Anne Marie wanted. She couldn't still be Tony, the gentleman pilot from Brazil; to avoid madness, she had to accept and become what she now was. Hell, Lori Ann had never wanted to be a man. Never. And yet, now that she was a he, there were more basic differences than Lori Ann would have thought, yet few practical differences in day-to-day terms. When one became a different species of animal, the sexual differences seemed even more trivial, anyway.

The *practical* differences, the ones that crossed from the old species *Homo sapiens* to the new, were in social terms: the ability to walk freely down strange streets without more than pragmatic caution, for example. A whole level of *fear* was removed from the simplest social interactions, as well as the constant uncertainty of whether the strangers one met were seeing one as another person or as an object. That far outweighed the physiological differences, and it mattered. He was quickly becoming accustomed to the physiological change, as was Tony, but it was the sociological change that had made him feel somehow free. There was much about being a man he didn't like; in its own way it was as confining and restrictive a role as the female's. Yet he wouldn't want to trade this absence of a massive layer of tension for anything.

Maybe that was it, he thought. Compromise. Fully accept what one now was and the role and situation one was now locked into but never forget the values and achievements of who one once had been. Tony still had those skills and that knowledge from the past and maybe could appreciate things more because she'd been on both sides of the coin. She could retain her kind heart, too, and the love of Anne Marie's spirit and inner strength that she masked with that little old lady act. Tony wasn't his old self, and she wasn't Anne Marie, either, no matter how identical they were; she was compromising, no, *synthesizing* into a whole new person. Maybe Lori had to finally do that, too. Accept, become Lori of Alkhaz, an Erdomese male and husband, keeping what was valuable and universal but not letting Lori Ann torture him every time he did something that she might disapprove of. Julian couldn't synthesize, and so she broke instead, retaining only the pragmatic part.

Might that, in the end, be the problem of the two immortals? To go so long, through so many lifetimes and cultures, not only unchanging but unable to change. Somehow he suspected that if somehow ancient folk long dead could be resurrected and taken to either this Brazil or Chang, they would instantly recognize them and find them much the same. Even growing up a person changed, often radically—from helpless infant to dependent child, through rebellious teen years and hopeful twenties and thirties, into middle age, when life's course had been set and for the first time death became a reality as the years passed subjectively at a faster and faster clip, and finally into the combined wisdom and resignation of old age. Just as pictures in the photo album showing the same person at all those stages somehow also showed completely different people, life was a constant series of radical changes.

But not for these immortals. They hadn't changed in so long, they could remember being no other way. Endless, unchanging life—probably passing at breakneck speed to them but never getting them anywhere—had made even the chance of new experiences slim. They could fight against the system as Chang had and suffer, or they could roll with it and drift as this Solomon, or Brazil, apparently did. Eventually, even Mavra Chang had stopped fighting and had withdrawn to the most basic of all human existences. Now she was racing the fellow with an idea to making the next time different.

But would it be?

Just the little he'd seen of the Well World—and his understanding of it as a laboratory for founding new races and seeding the vast numbers of worlds in the universe—had convinced him that those Ancient Ones had probably thought of just about all the themes and variations that could be imagined. In Gekir, women ruled and the men were bimbos. He hadn't yet seen one, but he'd heard that there were asexual and unisexual races here, and other races with more than two sexes. Dillian society sounded as if it was like the better places on Earth, but Tony could never be regarded as "one of the boys" and there would always be a social-sexual separation no matter how equal the opportunities and how safe the roads.

There were 1,560 races here, from the radically different to the fairly similar, and who knew how many had been developed before this final batch was left at the end? And after all this time, had any of them developed the true utopia? If so, he hadn't heard of it.

Mavra might well be able to radically change the race of Earth. But if she did it too much, would it still be human or just another experiment? And if but little, would it make a difference? One might well be able to program all sorts of physiological stuff, but who was smart enough to program social development, attitudes, and cultures over the life span of a race of people? Maybe even this Brazil still believed deep down that there must be a better way but knew he wasn't omnipotent enough to create and maintain it. Greece, Rome, but also the Mongol hordes and the Vandals and Visigoths. Jesus and Buddha and Mohammed, but also Attila the Hun, Napoleon, Stalin, and Hitler.

One might well get something different, but how would one ensure that it was superior when even a race that was close to godhood as evolution could produce couldn't figure that out?

Could it be that the dark side of the human soul was just as essential to the evolutionary development and growth of a race as the beautiful side? Depressing thought, but otherwise why did the Ancient Ones leave it in?

And if *he* could think of this, why hadn't Mavra Chang? Perhaps confusing immortality with wisdom wasn't a smart thing to do. He began to get the eerie feeling that he was better qualified to play god than she was, and *he* had no real desire to take on that awesome and impossible responsibility. He knew he just wasn't smart enough to do it. Nobody was.

Maybe this Brazil knew that, which was why he always remade things the same. The fact that Mavra Chang apparently *didn't* see this trap was unsettling. She wasn't really out to correct humanity; she was out to avenge herself against the forces that had hurt her.

And *that* was the most uncomfortable feeling of all. When push came to shove, as it inevitably would if they got to this Well, on which side of this strange race should his sword fall?

He looked at Alowi. "I think I'd like to go on deck. I can hear all sorts of noises up there, and I'd like to see what's going on. Do you want to go or stay here?"

"I will do as you wish."

"No, this is not one of those kind of decisions. Do *you* want to go up there or remain here?"

"I do not like those creatures above," she admitted, "but if it is my choice, I will go where you go."

"For the record, I don't like them much, either, but come on. We're going to have to live with them for a while, it seems."

Darkness had fallen, and the lights of the city market area were still very close, but they had definitely pulled away from the small private dock and were in the process of turning the ship toward the channel. The two spiderlike beings were up in the twin masts, and the rest of the small crew were tending ropes on the starboard side of the ship.

Lori stayed as far from the action as possible and peered over the side. There, in the darkness, two huge longboats filled with very large Gekirs pulling on oars were guiding the ship like tugs in a big harbor. The captain, barely visible in the darkness, was on top of the wheelhouse getting a view of the entire area. Clearly the creature was basically nocturnal by nature and saw well in just the starlight and the reflected glow from the city. The crocodilelike mate was at the wheel, looking at some basic instruments and taking cryptic cues from the captain and the crew on the lines.

"Away all lines!" the captain shouted. "Clear ship!"

The commands were repeated even louder by the crew on the lines, and the ropes, expertly tied, were loosened and thrown into the water to be reeled in by the longboats.

"Engage rudder! All hands to embarkation stations!"

Now the mate turned and began winding hard and fast on a wooden wheel, which went around and around for a while and then held firm. The mate checked something, pulled up a large lever, then turned back to the main wheel, which had been essentially free but which now seemed to have a mind of its own. The rest of the crew scurried to positions on either side of the sails. Only one small sail was dropped, but the wind caught it and the ship slowly began moving out of the harbor at a crawl, following what appeared to be small oil-fed lamps floating in the water. Just ahead, on spits of land on either side, twin lighthouses gave off amazingly bright beams, easily marking the limits of the entrance to the bay.

The port area was going by on the right-hand side, the buildings suddenly changing in character from dark, closed shops to a small harbor filled with activity just ahead. At the moment where there seemed to be nothing on the shore, between the dark buildings and the lighted dock or warehouse beyond, Lori felt a sudden tingling sensation and started. It felt as if something incredibly thin had brushed against his full body. It was gone in a moment, but suddenly the wind shifted direction and picked up considerably, and the temperature dropped from a tropical twenty-six degrees Celsius to perhaps no more than ten or twelve. Summer had turned to spring in an instant, and the wind did not help the feeling at all.

He looked at Alowi, who was clearly uncomfortable. "Do you wish to go below or perhaps get one of the jackets?" he asked her.

"I am all right," she told him, but she didn't look it.

Mavra came over to them, still dressed only in the thin black clothing and boots she favored and appearing not at all uncomfortable.

"It's pretty impressive when you think about it," the Earth woman commented. "The Well World has no moon and so very little in the way of a tide. That's hell for a sailing ship and cuts off a lot of harbors as too shallow. Magnetic compasses are useless, too, since there's no magnetic pole. The instruments they were using to get out of there are incredibly clever but unique to these conditions. *Now*, however, they've got full instrumentation. That's a computerized compass that always points to true north in the wheelhouse, and they've got something similar to, but much better than, mere radar. It may look like just water, but it's high-tech water now."

"I'll have to take your word for it," Lori responded. "Still, all that fancy navigation equipment only helps in a third of the hexes they sail."

"True, but a good sailor has a hundred means of setting course and position and only needs those instruments in familiar waters to confirm things. You'll note they're going in steps to full sail, even though they could use the main engines. When you have this kind of wind and it's in your favor, you take it." She looked up as the crew made a series of by-the-numbers calls, and there were sudden loud, deep crackling and rippling sounds. "Yep. There come the mainsails.

The ship was clearly at sea now, the water choppy and causing significant spray forward, some of it reaching the deck. There was a pitching motion now as well, often in more directions than one, and Lori found he had to hold on tight to the railing with both hands.

Mavra grinned. "Yeah, I'm having to get used to sea legs as well. It's been a *long* time. You'll find the motion a lot more pronounced aboard this small ship than on that giant you came up to Itus on." She turned and gestured. "See those ropes? They're well secured with steel clips, and they run all around the deck. Use them to keep yourself steady in rough seas." She grinned. "Don't worry. You'll get used to it. Promise."

Lori wasn't so sure. "That's a lot easier to say, built like you are, but hooves designed for sand and rough ground don't do all that well on slick hardwood decks. I think for now we'll be better off below."

Mavra nodded. "Suit yourselves. The Dillians have things fairly well set up back there, but they're also going to have to get used to balance."

"Yeah, well, they've got four feet! I think if I had four, I might at least be able to stay upright." And with that he gestured to a very relieved Alowi, and hand over hand, using the ropes, they made their way below.

For Mavra Chang, however, it was something else, something quite different. Looking aft at the rapidly receding lights, feeling the lurch of the ship, the smell of salt air, the rustling canvas above, and the strong breeze pushing them on, two sets of opposing thoughts and emotions rose within her.

In a positive way she felt *home* somehow, alive once more. The only thing that would have made it better would be if this were *her* ship and *she* was in the wheelhouse charting courses and giving commands. In some ways, perhaps, she would prefer that even to commanding the bridge of a starship, where one was in command of a vast but lonely structure in which the crew was wholly automated and the silence and stillness were ever-present.

But there were darker memories as well, of other ocean voyages where she had been not in charge or even a passenger but *cargo*, and disposable cargo at that, where the days were full of pain and the nights full of horror.

They would never do that to her again. She would see to that.

Dlubine, Moving Toward the Fahomma Border

THERE WAS A DRAMATIC SCENE ANYWHERE ONE LOOKED AFTER dark in Dlubine. All around, at different very specific locations, one could see lightning illuminate large cloud masses or occasionally but spectacularly snake down to the sea and play along it, often for several seconds, looking like some mad scientist's laboratory experiment. Yet overhead there would be frequent breaks in the clouds, giving windows into the magnificent and colorful night sky of the Well World, while below varicolored lights crisscrossed and weaved intricate patterns, sometimes exploding into huge complex patterns for a while, although nothing on the scale of what they'd seen the first night. And now and then the winds would bring whiffs of sulfur or the rotten-egg smell of hydrogen sulfide. At least once they'd sailed past an island perhaps two or three kilometers distant that, while invisible in the darkness, betrayed itself by showing streams of red running tendrillike down dark self-made mountains to the sea and ending in great plumes of steam. Where hot lava met the sea, the combination created its own very local thunderstorms.

"You could make a million bucks selling cruises through here," Gus noted, just staring out at the amazing sights.

"Well, I suppose the inhabitants would have something to say about that," Brazil responded, taking advantage of the conflicting winds from the surrounding turbulence and making reasonably good time. "Still, what would you do with the money, Gus? What's the top of the real estate market in Dahir?"

Gus laughed. "Not that great. Oh, it's comfortable enough, but, well, this might sound funny, but they're just too much like the small town in northern Minnesota that I got out of."

"Like *what*?" Brazil chuckled. "*This* I got to hear."

"Well, the place is pretty damned dull, frankly, just like home. Nothin' much happens, and what little that does isn't important but it becomes the biggest thing around 'cause it's *something*. Everybody's into everybody else's business 'cause they don't have much else to do, the life's routine, and the pleasure for them is simple. On top of it all it's dominated by a straitlaced church that's gonna make sure you behave and go to heaven, or wherever they think Dahirs go. No imagination, no curiosity. Even the weather's borin'. And I mean, think about this kinda invisibility thing. Even that's a drag there. I mean, so you decide to rough it and hunt your own food down 'cause it's fun, right? Only nothin' can see you comin', so where's the sport? Even back home the deer could see you and make a break for it or hide out, and even the fish had a *little* bit of a chance. Nothing's even really wild in Dahir. It's all carefully managed. I couldn't stand it no longer than I did."

"Um, I see what you mean. You couldn't just find an attractive female and go off and buy your own swamp or something?"

"Not likely. Hell, it's the *women* who run the damn place. They're the bigger ones, they got the muscles, and they're all kinda muddy brown. It's us guys who have all the color and are supposed to attract a female. They lay the eggs, but the guys hatch 'em. I know I'm supposed to have been made comfortable with bein' a Dahir and all that, but that's just the physical part. I mean, the swimmin', the eatin' the way I eat and what I eat, stuff like that, no problem, but in my head I'm still the same guy. I been him too long to be somebody else. And that arrangement just don't seem *natural* to me."

"I know some women who'd like that arrangement just fine." Brazil laughed. "It's not as uncommon among either animals or sentient species as you think, but I can see your point. Some people handle the cultural differences fine, but others find things just too topsy-turvy to adjust in that department. Tell me, what *would* you do if you had your pick? You've seen a bit of this world and its denizens. Would you be something else? Or would you go back if you could?"

Gus thought about it. "I dunno. I guess I ain't seen enough of this place to really decide if there's somethin' neat to be. I sure wouldn't be no Earth-human type, not if it meant havin' done to me what was done to Terry. Go back? Yeah, maybe. I loved the job, no question. That's what I miss most. But I also had started thinkin' that I was gettin' older too fast and slowin' down and the odds were gonna catch up to me sooner or later. You know the worst thing, though? The one thing I dreaded, really hated? And it wasn't bein' shot at or bombed or nothin' like that."

"I couldn't guess."

"Comin' home. Thing was, I didn't really have one. My folks are dead; the rest of my family's as happy not to see me as I am not to see them. Got one sister who married a career navy guy and she's got a couple of neat kids, but I always felt like a stranger when I visited, like I didn't really belong there no matter how much she said she liked me visitin' her. I dunno. You get to a point in life, you don't want to stop what you love doin', but you also want something else, something more . . . permanent, I guess. And I just wouldn't feel right keepin' on doin' what I'm doin' if I had a wife and kids, particularly kids. Be worse than bein' a navy wife. Sort of like bein' a cop's wife, wonderin' if I was gettin' my ass blown off someplace and only coming home between revolutions and massacres. There's some that do it, but I couldn't, and takin' a job runnin' around to the latest drug bust or bank heist or whatever isn't the same thing."

"Permanence but with a lot of action and variety—that's a pretty tall order," Brazil commented.

"Yeah, I know. I guess I'll never find what I'm lookin' for. Kinda like the sign I once saw in a shop. 'Quality! Service! Price!' it read. Then underneath it added, 'Pick any two.' Still, I'd love to go back if I could keep this invisibility or whatever it is. You could still get caught by a random bullet and nobody'd notice you sinkin' in the quicksand, but you could walk right into the rebel camp and film away. Speaking of which, how come you ain't been spooked once since I got back? I really didn't think about it until just now, but you've had no problems seein' me, have you?"

"No," Brazil admitted. He hadn't told Gus about all that had transpired, and he wanted to keep most of it that way. What Gus didn't know he couldn't reveal if he really got captured later on. Besides, who knew how he'd feel about Brazil having that kind of bond with Terry? But a few things had to be addressed.

"I picked up her second sight, sort of," he told the Dahir. "I don't know how, but somehow she gave it to me. At least, when I woke up, I had no more problems seeing you or her just like I'd expect to."

"Yeah? You also got the power to blank out other folks?"

"I haven't the slightest idea," Brazil replied honestly. "Unfortunately, at some point in this trip I'm almost sure to find out. I wouldn't be surprised, though. After all this time I tend not to be surprised at very amazing things happening when I need them."

"You sure got the luck, all right," Gus noted. "I mean, bad as it is for Terry, she's been a real plus for you this trip, right? Then I'm here as a Dahir with this crazy, built-in disappearin' act, and she figures it out and then gives it to you when they got your picture splattered all over creation. What are the odds of *that*?"

"Very low, Gus, but that's my point. It's not luck. It's the

Well—the master computer. I'm just a glorified serviceman, like I said, but I have to be able to be there at the very infrequent times it needs me. So it kind of watches over me, like a guardian angel. It can manipulate probability, make a chain of events happen that serve its interests, although it doesn't do that for much of anything or anybody except me—and Mavra Chang. That doesn't mean that bad things don't happen to me. Sometimes nasty things happen in spades. I got sloppy this time around, didn't remember everything, and wound up spending a year and a half in Auschwitz for my trouble during World War II. It just means that nothing permanent happens. I suffered, I starved, I was treated lower than an animal there, but I survived. Barely, but I survived. That's what it does, Gus. It makes sure I survive."

"Jeez! I keep forgettin' you don't age. But what did you mean by gettin' sloppy 'this time around'? You talk like you lived through the Nazis before."

"I did—but in Ireland last time, I think. That's the scary part of it all, Gus. Inside there, inside the Well, among other routine things, is something I can't really explain but which is, for all intents and purposes, a reset button. It's a last gasp thing, something only I, not the Well, can decide to push. What it does is—complicated. Now *there's* an understatement for you! But anyway, it resets. Not completely, of course. The universe still continues to expand, the *basics* don't change, but all life out there is essentially canceled out. All people, all history, everything pretty much. Time and space become objects of manipulation. In some cases it can use the same planet and solar system again; in other times it has to find material from somewhere else that pretty well matches what existed before and re-create from scratch. Each of the worlds goes through the whole process of development, of evolution, you name it. From the vantage point of the Well World, it happens in the wink of an eye, but it can be a few billion years or more out there. Don't ask me how that's possible. I'm just the guy who has to push the button sometimes, not the ones who built or designed it or the computer capable of such godlike things."

"Jesus! And you've actually *done* this?"

"Twice. The memory of doing *that* is something that's always stored somewhere inside me. I might forget it for a while, but when I get here, I remember. Hitler, Stalin, all the mass murderers of Earth history are pikers compared to me, Gus. I've killed *trillions* with one decision, and worse, I erased all signs of their existence. All their history, culture, everything. Gone. But then I brought them back, in real time. The Well is a master of matching probabilities. Everything repeats as closely as possible. Maybe not an absolute one hundred percent, but it repeats so eerily that you wind up seeing the same people, the same empires, the same dreams, the same wars, the same nations and ideologies."

"Jeez! You mean you killed *me* at some time in the past? Or another me? And another Terry, and all the rest?"

"Well, no. You two were long dead by the time I did it the last time. The time before—I only remember that I did it, that's all. But I was still a captain both times, I'm pretty sure of that. Not of some ship like this, though, or even the big supertanker I was skippering back on Earth. Spaceships, Gus. Mavra, too. She had her own ship. She wasn't even *born* on Earth and might not even have heard of it until she fell in with me here. We moved a lot of cargo and occasional passengers between stars over a third of the Milky Way galaxy. God! How I loved that job! That's my equivalent of your photojournalism, Gus."

"Spaceships. Wow, that's neat!"

"Yeah, only the Well never inserts me at a point where I can do my job. This last time it inserted us, oh, I think maybe 50,000 B.C. or so. Since that time Mavra and I have both been, well, surviving, waiting until Earth once again headed for the stars. This time we didn't make it."

"Holy smoke! You mean you got to reset that thing again? *That's* what this is all about?"

"Maybe. I hope not. I don't know if I can do it again. I

can't imagine why I'm here, but I've been here in between for other things. Somebody once was actually smart enough to figure out the mechanics of the Well and some Markovian mathematics. The Well was alarmed, not because he could do anything major but because he had the potential to do some damage right here. Events got manipulated so I fell through a Well Gate shortly after, and it was up to me to solve the problem. No damage done in the end, and I just went back to doing what I'd been doing. The Well doesn't let you stick around to get the universe into real trouble when it doesn't need you anymore. I *can* tell you that something's off kilter and may need adjustment. Something happened, maybe recently, maybe back as far as the last reset, but the tiny differences have accumulated to the point where, over thousands of years, they made a big change or a series of big changes. I noticed that when the Soviet Union collapsed so suddenly. I knew the consequences were terrible for later history that it did, but I kind of hoped it was just the result of a local aberration, just Earth, in other words. There're a lot more worlds and races than that out there."

"Hey! Hold it! That was *great* news, not bad news!"

"Was it? Yeah, I suppose, from your local point of view. From *my* point of view it was awful. Without the tension, the pressure, the competition, discoveries that would eventually spread humanity to the stars were set back by centuries at the very least, maybe even forever unless another such power arose."

"Huh? What? We was sendin' up space shuttles all the time!"

Nathan Brazil sighed. "Gus, you come from the most bizarre nation on Earth. It looks and feels like a European culture or cultures, but its root culture is more alien to the rest of the world than the Chinese or anybody else Westerners think are inscrutable. You invented violent anticolonialist revolution and sponsored it for decades, then you turned around and acted like an imperial power and couldn't figure out why everybody else didn't do the same. A bunch of your people, half of them devoted slaveholders and at least half virulent racists, wrote the world's greatest statement on individual liberty and protecting minority rights. You continue to create and dream up most of the vital inventions and scientific principles of the industrial revolution, and then you let everybody else put them into practice better than you do, so that the only thing you wind up being absolute masters of is varying ways to destroy all life on Earth. One of your people invented the principles of rocketry and couldn't *give* it away, so the Germans copied his patents and used it to bomb London. Then you import the same Germans to make rockets for you, but you don't care even about them until the Russians use *their* captured Germans and create the first satellite. *Then* you decide you got to go to the moon before them to show them up, and you do. But they don't go, and you lose interest, and thirty years later, nobody's close to going back."

"Jeez! You're sure not givin' us credit for much, are you?"

"Well, I credit you with an awful lot, Gus, but you Americans were only masters of one specialty, and that was war. The rest you let go, and when you let the rest go, like space, you become a hollow nation without ideals, a bunch of folks doing research and development for other nations, and you lose that restless creativity that made all those advancements possible. You were rotting, Gus. Drugs, crime, poverty, and an economy mostly based on exporting raw materials and importing finished goods—right back where you started from before the revolution. A service economy isn't an energetic, growing one, it's a nation doing each other's cooking and dry cleaning."

"And the *Russians* stayin' whole would have changed that?"

"Well, it did the last time. Your people need an enemy they think is an equal, Gus. They see the world as a sports contest. Not much fun playing soccer when you're the only team on the field. The Soviets were going to assemble a big, grand space station, Gus. One *hell* of a platform up there, under the control of the Red Army. You know what would happen in your country if that became real. And then they were going to the moon and eventually Mars. Things would turn around. The game would be on again. Instead, their totalitarian regime collapsed, they fragmented, discovered the rest of us weren't so bad and that they really lived at a Third World level, and all the grandiose dreams fell apart as the money and resources got diverted to doing things like producing toilet paper and decent indoor plumbing. Fine for them, but it keeps humanity pretty much stuck on its ball with the only question being whether it'll run out of resources, choke to death on pollution, destroy its atmosphere, or just fall apart in food riots and general anarchy. Don't blame me. It was *your* people who couldn't do a thing without an archenemy. And don't look so downcast. We came from a great era for bang-bang on-the-spot news, didn't we?"

"If you think I'm gonna argue about how shitty the situation on Earth is, you're nuts," Gus responded. "You said it—you remember what I did for a livin'. But you know, I bet you saw worse, experienced worse, during all that time. Kids dyin' of no reason but ignorance or maybe sacrificed to some sun god someplace. You said you was in that concentration camp, saw the worst people can do to each other. Did you ever look up the survivors? Did you ever cry for the ones that went into the ovens? Or did you just sit there, like you was in purgatory, endurin' the hunger and the punishment and the pain and maybe feelin' sorry and disgusted that you got yourself into that fix, but unlike all them other people, them millions, you *knew* you was gonna walk out. You *knew* the Nazis would lose. Hell, you knew that even if they whipped you, even if they pulled out your toenails, cut your fingers off, tore out your tongue, you'd not only pull through, somehow, but all that would grow back. In the end it'd be just one more bad experience and the nightmares would stop and you'd do okay. Not like all them others. You like to pretend that you care, and maybe you do for one person or another right here and now, but you don't really. Not deep down. And the only thing you're *really* pissed off about is the wrong people got a good break and even though it might be better for everybody else, it slowed down what *you* wanted. *Slowed it down!* What the hell's a hundred years to you, anyway? Don't lecture me about my people and my world, good, bad, or whatever. You push a button and we all go away, but while we're here, we're *alive*. You didn't need to see a Dahir's invisible tricks. You ain't noticed the whole course of human civilization except when one comes up and shouts in your face!"

Brazil didn't respond immediately. He felt bad about what he'd said about Gus's native country and history; really, in the long course of things, it was far better than most. But Gus's accusations had hit a bit too close to him at his drifting best to remain totally unchallenged.

"You're right, Gus," he said at last. "About some of it, anyway. The cause, though, is one you should understand as well as anybody. How many people have you seen die? How many corpses have you counted on bloody streets and in killing fields? How many starving kids in some revolution or drought-stricken land have you walked past? A lot, I'd guess, in your short life."

"Yeah? So?"

"What was your reaction the *first* time you saw kids you liked getting blown away or lying in agony? The *first* time you saw a whole village die of starvation, a living death? I think you cried, Gus. If not outside, then inside. I think after you saw a village of kids who looked like walking skeletons and could barely raise their heads, you got so upset, so sick to your stomach, you puked your guts out someplace and maybe cried again. But you had a job to do. Without your pictures, nobody else would know. Nobody who could help would know where to help. A few newsreels of Auschwitz and it would have ceased to exist. The whole rest of the world would have fought like demons. Nobody made it into those camps and back out with those pictures then. That's your job, Gus, and that's part of why you do it. Part of it is a thrill ride, living on the edge, but nobody walks through the starvation in east Africa, say, because they want to see the world."

"I still don't see your point."

"The point's simple. After a while you still believe in the job, but you don't puke anymore. The ten-thousandth kid dying before your eyes of starvation isn't like the first one or even the first ten. The hundredth soldier you capture on film falling in battle isn't like the first one, either. Ask any soldier. Ask any survivor of those camps. You never like it, but you get hardened, you get immunized to a degree, because you have to survive and live with yourself. Pretty soon *you* don't have nightmares about it, either. You just get—detached. Not only to save your sanity but also because you accept that you can't feed those starving people yourself, you can't save the kid looking up at you, you can't call back that bullet to that young soldier's heart. You know it happened to you; otherwise you couldn't still do it. Some people can't. They go nuts or they quit and do something else. You can and you did. I think they call that being 'tough,' or maybe just being a 'professional.' Terry was a tough professional. You admired that a lot in her."

"Well . . ."

"So why condemn me for being the same way? When the ice sheets came down and killed off the crops and moved the people in great migrations southward, I was there. When the first temples were built to long-forgotten gods, I was in the crowd that watched the sacrifice of the children to them. When the Persians and Medes and Babylonians and Greeks marched and leveled whole cities and sowed their enemies' lands with salt, I was there. When Roman emperors threw people to the lions to the cheers of the crowd in the coliseums of the world, I was selling tickets and souvenirs or picking the spectators' purses. When they crucified thousands every few meters of the Appian Way as examples, I ran the dice game for their effects. When the Vandals vandalized and the Goths and Visigoths crushed the Romans, I sold them street maps. Then the Celts, then the Germans, then the Slavs, then the Moslem hordes, as they were called by the Christians. The Children's Crusade—*that* was a good one! All those kids, some not even in their teens, slaughtered as they made their way to the Holy Land singing hymns only to be finished off facing a professional army also convinced that God was on their side. The Inquisition—they actually felt *horrible* after they tortured you to death in the name of God. Wept for your lost soul. Want me to go on?"

"I get your point. But you *knew* better. Couldn't you have done *something* more than be an audience?"

"What? One guy? You can't buck the worst in humanity because sometimes you throw out the best, too. See, you have an advantage I don't have. I could at least hide out from the worst of that, I suppose, but I *can't* quit. I can't go home. I can't even go permanently nuts. I can't even *die* with them. After a while you just get too frustrated. After a while you just stop fighting the tide of history and just survive as best you can."

"Yeah, I guess I see, sorta. I still ain't sure how we got on this track. Maybe boredom or tiredness or somethin'. Can you answer me one thing, though?"

"If I can."

"What were you in the last go-round? I mean, maybe this machine god won't let you play really funny stuff, but you got some choice over you, don't you?"

The question actually surprised him. "I—well, yeah, I do. I have a good deal of *local* power over what happens here, on the Well World, while I'm in there, even if I can't mess with the Earth's program. I never really did much with myself, though. Every time I'm in there, I say at least I'm gonna make myself 185 centimeters tall with a face and body to die for, and I never do. It's not a Well prohibition, it's just, well, I'm generally so preoccupied with other folks and other things when I'm there, I never really think of myself. Maybe I'm just so used to being me now, I can't think of myself any other way."

"Jeez! So you're kinda the master of this world of all these races and forms and stuff and you *never* wind up anything or anybody else? You got all them other planets out there and you stick with relivin' Earth history over and over? You're right about not bein' able to go nuts. You *are* nuts!"

This new point struck him even harder than the earlier argument had because there really *was* no defense. He'd always been Nathan Brazil since—well, since this job had begun, anyway. At least he hadn't the slightest, vaguest memory of *not* being just this way. He alone knew why he'd stuck with Earth, or at least Earth humans, but even there he didn't really *have* to. It made no difference in the end to damned near anything.

Sure, he'd been—memory somewhere vaguely said a deer at one time in the past and a Pegasus for a brief time—but those had been *here* and for emergency purposes. He'd become himself again as quickly as he could.

He'd always loved the Dillians, also for good reason, but he'd never considered becoming one of them, living as one of them through *their* history, which was something of a mystery to him. They were fighters, too, and even with far more limited resources they'd managed, as he knew, to attain space consistently ahead of Earth. There were others, too, equally attractive and advanced, yet he'd ignored them all. It seemed stupid on the face of it. No rerun of history and events, new experiences, new people and capabilities . . . Even Mavra, with her own personal traveling version of the Markovian computer, had gone to many other worlds and become many other creatures, he remembered now.

"I've got no answer or explanation, Gus," he told the Dahir. "The only thing I can think of, and I'm not at all sure if it's the real reason or not, is that maybe I needed something that was absolutely fixed, unchanging, always comfortable and familiar, that couldn't be taken away from me."

Gus stared back out at the colorful scenes in the darkness and tried to imagine what it would be like to be Nathan

Brazil. Maybe he'd be just as loopy after all this time, he thought, but he wouldn't mind giving it a try.

They were passing another area of active volcanic activity in the distance, and it was a sight he found impossible to tire of. Suddenly his two huge eyes focused on a single spot in the distance, off to the left of the lava flow. At first he thought they were just reflections of some of the lights from under the sea or perhaps lights or markers on the islands, but now, as he stared fixedly at the spot, he saw what had drawn his attention to the spot.

"Cap! Off here, just left of the lava. Those lights *moved*!"

"Could be just an illusion with all the heat and distance," Brazil responded, not terribly concerned. "Or it might well be another ship. There's a lot out here, you know."

"Yeah, well, I been lookin' at it, and those lights are sure not illusions and they're on somethin' pretty big movin' our way."

Brazil looked over at where Gus was already staring, and after a minute or so he saw them, too. "Yeah, Gus. They're running lights for sure. Something pretty big, I'd say. I can't make out much in the dark, though. There's a storm moving almost parallel over there. If it kicks up some lightning, you might be able to tell what it is."

"You want me to douse our running lights?" Gus asked him worriedly. "You never know."

"Maybe. Hold on a minute and try to make sure it's heading for us and not just coming out and going somewhere else. The sea-lanes we're on here run mostly southeast to northwest. If he's legitimate and coming from that direction, he should turn parallel to us in a little bit and head off in the opposite direction. I don't like it, though. What's a ship doing that close to those islands? They're marked as too active and dangerous for landings on the charts."

"He's comin' on toward us! *Whoops!* There was a big flash. Couldn't make out much, though, but it sure looked like a big bunch of smoke. Man! He's comin' on fast and steady! He *can't* be a sailboat and move like *that*, can he? I mean, the wind's against him, right? Yeah! There's another flash. Still can't make out the ship, but that's a steamer all right!"

"Douse the running lights, Gus, quick as you can! I think we're in trouble!"

The sudden rise in Brazil's adrenaline roused Terry, who got up, watched Gus put out the lights so that the ship fell into total darkness, and immediately looked around for the danger she was already directly sensing.

She went through a whole series of spectrum shifts until she spotted the oncoming vessel, and inside of it she sensed danger in numbers beyond theirs by quite a bit. There were a lot of creatures on that ship, and all seemed to be of one mind, to catch and board *this* ship and take them.

A whole range of actions came into her mind, but none of them were useful. She could make it very hard for them to see, or notice, both her mate and herself, but they would still take the ship and sooner or later they would certainly have a means of detecting them. And there were so *many* of them.

There was a sound like thunder off toward the oncoming lights, and suddenly the sea seemed to explode just forward and off to the left of the tiny sailing ship.

Brazil spun the wheel and then began taking down sail, using the levers and pulleys nearby.

"What the hell you doin', Cap! You're headin' right for 'em!" Gus cried.

"We won't be for long, but they had our course and speed damned good there, and I needed to throw them off in the dark. They've got no radar here."

"Yeah, well, they don't *need* radar at this distance! I mean, we must be blockin' off the undersea light show just like they are to us by now!"

Brazil cursed under his breath. He hadn't thought of that! And those guys were surely using just that technique on them. They were used to these waters; he was not.

He took a deep breath, then shouted, "Okay, then, we're

gonna have to open range and sail where they can't do that!" as he put out full sail and turned for maximum wind.

"Hey! Them dark places could be *islands*, Cap!" Gus pointed out. "And you're gonna go right into the edge of that storm, too!"

"Just what I want to do!" he yelled back as a second shot landed forward and just to the right. "Damn! Straddled us with two shots at two kilometers! Those boys are *good*!"

They were making very good speed, getting up to fifteen, maybe twenty knots, but they were no match for the steamer still closing on them, particularly considering the angle.

A third shot landed perhaps twenty meters ahead of their bow, and its message was very, very clear. They could hit them any time they felt like it.

They were past the undersea fairyland lights, though, at least, and it was still water at this point. Suddenly, with very loud *splats* like buckshot falling on the deck, the rain swept over them.

The captain of the patrol boat knew exactly what his quarry was doing, and, worse, with the storm and the darkness, he actually risked losing them now that he had them cold. He couldn't wait and take that chance; there were too many reefs and shallows in there for him to follow closely with his craft. "If you can still get it, fire to hit!" he commanded, and the gun crew, also very experienced, made mental calculations, slightly adjusted the forward cannon, waited for a possible last sighting with a lightning flash, and fired a blast.

The shot struck the little sailing ship almost in the stern, and all three aboard were thrown to the deck as their world lurched and shook. One of the smaller masts came loose and dangled, caught in its own rigging.

"Everybody okay?" Brazil shouted in the fury of the wind and rain and thunder.

"Yeah! Terry almost fell on top of me!" Gus called back. "You?"

Brazil got back up, grabbed the madly spinning wheel,

and found that it was spinning freely. "Damn! They took out my rudder!" He looked up at the sails and saw the dangling mast hanging precariously, fouling lines, heard the slow rip of canvas, and knew instantly that there was no hope of steering by sail alone.

He made his way to the other two. "I hear breakers not far off, *that* way!" he pointed, a position perhaps half a kilometer away in the darkness from their current position and what looked to be a good three or more kilometers from where the lava flow should be. "We're gonna have to abandon ship and swim for it! The quicker the better, too! We could go down like a shot in this sea if enough water gets in the hole in the stern or we hit a reef!"

"Okay! I'll make it! How about if we split up, we rendezvous this side of the lava near the beach?" Gus suggested. "Hey! You want to throw over the raft?"

At that point the ship seemed to almost stop, and Brazil could feel the bow coming up.

"No time! Just go! *Now!* If she goes down when any of us are close, she could take us with her!"

Gus hesitated, then leapt into the dark waves. Brazil, knowing at least that he and Terry would not be separated but nonetheless concerned for her life, had no choice but to follow. Terry did not hesitate.

Terry had been a fair swimmer in swimming pools and such, but she had never had to swim in seas like this and for a very long moment she was convinced that she was going under for good and was certain to drown.

Then the discipline and control of the Glathrielian mind snapped fully in, and she calmed down, sensed Brazil and what he was doing, and made her way to the surface and toward her mate. Brazil had recovered as best he could but was acting instinctively; later there would be time to think about how much worse he'd been through and reflect on it.

He struggled against the waves to make his way to Terry and finally reached her. Now she would have to pretty well stay with him and trust him absolutely with her life. Her

Glathrielian mind understood that sort of logic and did not resist, having no better plan itself.

Using the waves, letting them carry the pair where they willed, Brazil managed to get them both relatively stabilized in the rough sea. At least it was no longer raining, although they could hardly tell, but Brazil was able to get at least a gut-level feeling of where they were headed and even got something of a look in that direction.

They appeared to be heading toward the lava flow and the huge plume of steam offshore.

He doubted if even Terry's bag of tricks could protect her from molten lava, but the Well would protect *him* from it somehow. If he could just stay close to her, linked to her, he might well be able to have her share *his* unique protection for a change. He *felt* her absolute trust in him and felt that she had accepted dependence for this period. She was not doing so well against the waves, though, and that terrified him. In a move as instinctive as his swimming actions, he reached out to her, first grasping her hand, then mind to mind, soul to soul. She did not resist, and now he was part of her and partly still within himself, as was she. They became as one mind, one organism, with Terry surrendering almost total control to him.

They managed for what seemed like a very long time, then, suddenly, there was a large wave that came along and picked them both up and almost threw them against a beach.

It was a granular black sand beach of the sort that new volcanoes built; it *hurt* when they hit it, but it didn't knock them out. Dizzy, disoriented, unable to stand, waves still crashing over them, they crawled as one on hands and knees back beyond the breakers, the black sand sticking to and covering their wet bodies. It took a tremendous force of his will to get them back far enough that there was relative safety. Then, with his inner voice telling him that he was safe at least for the moment, both bodies turned, gasped for air, then passed out cold on the beach.

* * *

The sun was high in the sky when Nathan Brazil awoke in a bizarre and yet beautiful landscape.

Terry awoke at the same time, the linkage between them as strong as or stronger than ever, and together the two of them got up on their feet and looked around. Both were battered and bruised and covered in thick black sand that seemed to be stuck everywhere. Brazil, seeing nothing on the horizon, decided that they could risk getting into the much calmer surf and wash it off, and Terry followed. In spite of the energy shell, it was almost like bathing in a Jacuzzi, but it woke them completely and cleaned off the sand.

The bruises were par for the course of what they had gone through, and muscles and joints seemed extraordinarily achy, but both were basically all right considering what they had survived, and that was enough. When you could notice the tangles in your hair and be irritated by them, you weren't in that bad shape.

There was no sign of the ship, not even wreckage, but it was impossible to say how long they'd been in the water or just where they'd gone down compared to where they'd come ashore. There were no other ships to be seen on the horizon, either; if the cutter had searched for survivors, it hadn't found them, but that didn't mean it wasn't still in the area.

Even so, that left the two of them stark naked with no tools, supplies, or anything else, standing on the beach, essentially marooned very much as in his personal fantasy. The trouble was, in a fantasy it was easy to conjure up what you needed, while in reality you had to find it, if anything was available.

The black sand beach stretched in both directions as far as the eye could see. About a hundred meters beyond where they'd come ashore there was a slight rise, and not far beyond that he could see nearly constant plumes of white smoke. While the lava flow itself was invisible to him in the daylight, the lava having hardened a bit on top and flowing downhill in its own thin self-made cocoon, it was clearly still expanding the island from beneath the waves. The muffled sounds of explosions could be heard from the direction of the steam as the molten rock continued to flow into the sea and react with the cooler waters.

Looking inland, it was a long way to anything interesting. The beach extended back for a kilometer or so, then turned into cracked and jagged rock in a fairyland of shapes formed when molten rock had cooled, solidified, and fragmented. It was easily another kilometer or more beyond that to where the older island missed by the most recent flows remained, with thick junglelike vegetation starting abruptly from where the flow stopped.

In back of it all and dominating the entire scene was the massive volcano itself, rising up like a huge lump several kilometers above the water, its top masked by a ring of clouds.

There was no getting around it; they would have to make their way back into the jungle and see whether the island contained enough to sustain them for now. Food and water were the first priorities.

He thought about Gus. He hadn't seen the Dahir since he'd gone overboard, and he wondered how well this kind of place could sustain such a creature. Large animals were unlikely in this isolated environment, fresh water would be more likely inland than anywhere along the coast, and that body wasn't really built for walking or even slithering over this kind of terrain.

Still, Gus had shouted to meet near the lava flow and on this side of it, fortunately, and he owed it to the creature to check before heading inland. He set off across the sands toward the billowing steam, Terry following.

The sight from the top of the rise was spectacular, probably even more so at night, with the lava steaming just below the surface in front of him and then the monstrous, churning, seething, bubbling region creating the steam just beyond.

There was no sign of Gus, nor had he expected any, but he'd done his duty. They could hardly stay there and wait in the expectation that the Dahir would suddenly appear; they'd need the daylight to explore the island. Brazil also didn't have anything he could leave to indicate their survival and presence, nor was there much he could use to create anything. The black sand wasn't even conducive to writing a message in English that only Gus would understand, and even if he could haul some rocks from the lava field inland and build something, a feat hardly possible considering how much he ached, anything small enough to escape the notice of pursuers would be overlooked by Gus and anything conspicuous enough to get noticed might well attract the wrong people.

It was Terry, either by chance or by design, who came up with the somewhat gross but only logical means of leaving Gus any sort of message.

She took a crap in the sand.

Hardly permanent, but a hunter species might well notice such a thing and Gus would recognize the species of origin, possibly the specific scent. Others might do the same, but they would first have to know to come to this specific area of the beach.

That taken care of, it was time to make their way inland to the jungle. If possible, they'd check back at this spot on a regular basis, if only to see if anything had either been disturbed or something else had been left to give them a sign.

I feel like Tarzan playing Robinson Crusoe, he thought. Friday was even the silent type, as always, although he suspected that the old shipwrecked sailor would have preferred *this* kind of Friday to the one he'd gotten.

Walking through the sand wasn't much of a problem, but the sand ended well short of the jungle, and it was a dangerous and slow journey through masses of rock that had flowed, cooled, and frozen, often shattering into huge lumps or collapsing into deep holes. It was a boulder field, but of black rock that was twisted into bizarre forms, some looking like taffy, others looking like frozen rippling rivers. It wouldn't take much of a misstep in that field to twist or even break an ankle, and so it was a slow process of trial and error to get through it, and it took them several precious hours to reach the edge of the jungle.

Volcanic areas were always fascinating for their contrasts. Where they had come ashore had probably been ocean only weeks earlier; now, here, where not much older flows had come, it might have been anything from beach to jungle, but the lava had burned and scoured all in its path, leaving no sign of anything. Yet the wet green jungle had resisted where it could, and just meters from where the flow ended it was as if nothing had happened at all.

There appeared to be no birds or animals, large or small, but somehow insects, or the equivalent of insects, had made their way here on air currents and were the dominant species. Some looked pretty fearsome, huge creatures that flew on multiple wings and were the size of hummingbirds and strange translucent creatures the size of a man's head that made their way up and down trees and vines shooting out long, creamy white tendrils.

To Terry, the jungle gave a sense not of real danger or strangeness but of an odd familiarity. She had spent some time in jungles like this, and while the individual plant and insect life was different, this jungle was no more bizarre than the Amazon had been. She felt almost as if she were in her own element, a cross between the swampy jungle of Glathriel and the dense yet protective Amazon rain forest. Terry the American television producer would have found the region creepy and threatening, but somehow that Terry seemed like another person, someone she barely knew. That Terry would have found the comforts of Hakazit to her liking, while the new Terry had felt only its sense of wrongness and had been relieved when they'd left it.

For all intents and purposes Theresa Perez was dead and had been for quite some time, save for some of the knowledge from her past that might be useful. She hadn't realized it and did not do so now; the Glathrielian way did not allow for reflection and introspection on that level, but that did not change the truth of it. She hadn't even been conscious of when it had happened; it had been quite late, though, when she'd made the decision to be the diversion for the others to get through the Well Gate. Even when she'd told Lori that she would remain in the Amazon until finally she could make her way to civilization, she'd known that she had no intention of doing so. She hadn't known until it was snatched away how much she really had hated her life or how much pressure she'd been under until it had been removed. It had long ago ceased to be anything more than a job, and that job had been the only thing she'd had, the only reason to wake up and exist every morning. She had no personal life, no friends outside the business, and she hadn't even had the glamour of being on camera. It had been over since that horror on the Congo, but she'd had no place else to go and her work was the only thing that she did better than almost anybody else.

She had hid it well, but the rock-hard woman Gus so admired had been terrified to walk alone to her car in an Atlanta parking lot.

Overcoming the initial fear, shock, and terror of the jungle and having been accepted into the Amazon tribe, she'd found a closeness and a sense of herself she'd never been aware of before. She had not thought twice about seducing those guards or felt guilt or recrimination. It had, rather, been the culmination of her transformation before she'd ever seen the Well World; it had been the act of someone who had found an element where life, where action, was a challenge rather than a reaction to fear. Even then, on some subconscious level, she knew she didn't want to be Terry again.

She had followed the others into the Well Gate almost on impulse but partly because she knew that the restrictions on the life of the People were not for her and that her friends, those she had felt closest to of any for a long time, had gone through the Gate. It had been Teysi's impulse, not Terry's. Nor could Terry have walked naked and alone into that alien swamp that was Glathriel, but Teysi could and did. And the Glathrielians, for whatever purpose, had given her the last required links to make the change complete.

They had given her the freedom from all dependency on *things*, leaving the focus only on what really counted—people—and with that the power to survive almost any conditions. They had given her protection against most of the forces of civilization and nature. And in a sense they had given her the ability to accept herself just the way she was, with no pretense or artifice.

So now it was Teysi's persona who was in this strange new jungle with her mate, and Teysi was far better qualified to be there than either Terry Perez or Nathan Brazil.

Brazil was content to let her take the lead, sensing her confidence. Food and water were the first priority, and somehow he was confident she could find them even though he wasn't sure how. On Earth a good although not totally infallible rule of thumb was to watch what the animals ate. Here the only animals were insects of a different evolution.

He watched her examine trees, vines, shrubs, and growths of all sorts and was not even aware that she was comparing them not to anything she knew directly but to elements in the vast Well database she could slightly access through her links to him. Finally, she picked up a thing that looked to him like a purple cabbage, peeled away the outer leaves to reveal a smooth oval inside skin, and bit into it. The deep red pulpy interior was kind of messy, but she kept eating rather than falling down in fits. He shrugged, picked up another—they must be falling from some of the higher trees, he decided—and did the same.

The stuff was disappointingly tasteless, with just a hint of a grapelike flavor, and the inside proved to have the consistency more of mashed potatoes than of oranges or grapefruit, but it went down easy, was filling, and had a high water content to boot.

He hoped they'd find something better and tastier, but unless they both came down with galloping stomachaches later, it was proof that they wouldn't starve here. They could at least survive.

Farther in they found a number of shallow streams that provided welcome fresh water. It tasted strongly of minerals with just a hint of sulfur, but it would do.

They did find a few more palatable things to eat as well, including something that resembled a pink tennis-ball size grape, both in looks and taste, and a thick green vine that tasted a lot like celery with a slight onionlike tang, before the light began to fail. By that time the aches and pains had gotten a bit too much for him, anyway, and she found an area near a huge tree carpeted with a light brown, spongy moss and lay down on it. It would soon be dark as pitch in the volcanic jungle, anyway; not the sort of conditions for exploring.

He lay down next to her on the soft natural matting and found it surprisingly comfortable. Still, as the last light faded and the world was enveloped in total darkness, he couldn't help but feel every ache and pain and consider the absurdity of the situation. There was no way around the fact that they were now shipwrecked on a small island in the middle of nowhere, alone, cut off from continental land by 190 kilometers or more of open sea they had no way to cross, with no means to get off and little hope of rescue by anyone save perhaps their enemies and the final objective, the equatorial barrier and its gateway into the Well of Souls, more unobtainable than ever.

She felt his pain, both physical and mental, and all she wanted to do was help him as he had helped her in the surf. To Terry, the current situation was not bad at all but almost her own concept of how life should be. All that they needed was here, and there seemed little that could threaten them in any way. It seemed as if all the fates had conspired to bring them here, and she could not conceive of it being more ideal. It was his old ways, old life thinking that kept him unhappy, forever searching for what he did not know. He had helped her when she had needed help; now it was her duty to do it for him.

She began by easing his physical pain, both by damping down the pain centers and by applying healing energies to those parts that were badly bruised. She began by massaging him, and as he felt the effects, he did not protest but rather relaxed and enjoyed it. With his pain substantially eased or gone, the massage turned slowly into far more than that, and as passion took control, she offered a unique new experience, a sharing of bodily pleasures that subtly became a sharing of minds and souls as well, in which her own will became dominant. Now, in rhythm with the passion, waves of conceptual objects of her will washed through them, through him, and as they had no words, their significance and purpose could not be divined by him, yet they were unresistingly accepted and understood by his mind as seductive, hypnotic commands in a way quite similar to what the Glathrielians had done to her, but in this case entirely of her own origin and out of her own desires.

Forget the past ... Wall it off ... The past does not exist ... There is no past, there is no future, there is only now ...

Enter my mind, my body ... Within is all that you require, all that you will ever need ... Take from my body, my mind all that you need ... Leave all else behind ... See, know, that there is only good inside me, take it as your own, renounce all else ...

He reached out for what was promised and found within her a shining kernel of something overwhelming, something beyond anything he had ever experienced before. Pure, undiluted, unconditional love; total, absolute, unconditional trust. There, inside her, was what he had never been able to witness or feel, that which he'd been incapable of believing even *existed* anywhere, at any time, on any plane.

Let it in, let it in ... Let it displace all the darkness ...

A moment he knew at some deep level would never come again had arrived, and he could not turn it away. His resistance melted; he let it flood into him, not displacing that which could not be displaced but pushing it away, sealing it off from consciousness, not permitting it to interfere . . .

The waves washed through him, overwhelming, sealing off all those things that could intrude or interfere, and once that was done, he returned them until what remained active in his own mind matched the pattern in her mind. The yin and yang merged, the puzzle pieces, shorn of all that was not relevant, fit perfectly and without flaw . . .

They awoke before dawn, the jungle no longer dark to them but seething with the varying colors and patterns of life. They took care of bodily functions, washed in a nearby stream, then started through the jungle, not with any real purpose but because it was so pretty and so alive and was to be enjoyed. Along the way to nowhere in particular they found some of the fruits and vegetables that were good to eat and they ate, feeding themselves and each other and giggling like two young people in the dawn of first love.

After a while they started off again, going deeper, following the trails of some of the larger insects just to see what made them and where they were going. They were hardly aware of the fact that they were also moving uphill, nor did they care, all places and destinations being the same to them. They were Adam and Eve in the Garden before the Fall, and they were more than that. They did not speak because such an act was totally unnecessary. Each felt what the other felt, each knew what the other knew, both thought the same thoughts at the same moment because they were as one. Each existed solely for the other and for the moment.

When they broke clear of the jungle, they were amazed and thrilled at the great sight that was before them. Still relatively far down on the great mountainside, they could still look out from its slope and see the vast colorful seascape beyond, even more beautiful when blended as it was with all the colors of life below.

Then they watched the sun come up and dramatically change the view, not to one of ugliness but to one almost completely different from the night scene. They stayed there for some time, until the sun was well up in the sky, then made their way back down into the jungle for some more to eat and drink.

He found a vine filled with pretty multicolored flowers that had become broken, possibly in the wind or by insects, and picked it up and made a flower garland out of it for her hair. She wanted to see it and so saw it through his eyes, then decided to take the flowers and place them on him, and he looked at himself through her eyes. And when they were done, they put the flowers back where they'd been found and went off in search of more wonders.

And when the thunderstorms came after dark, they did not seek cover but rather stood in the rain and the mud and watched, as if the sound and light show were being put on just for them. Everything was a wonder of a game, and everything was eternally new.

He remembered nothing of his past, his origins, or his unique nature, but he neither wondered about such things nor let them enter his mind. There was only here, and now, and *her*, and that was more than enough. She felt exactly the same, experiencing only the here and now and *him*. Neither remembered or bothered to consider that this had come about only the previous night. There was no concept of time, only the now and the other. So closely linked were they that he was not even certain that he was the *he* and she was the *she*; either could effortlessly become the other, and so such a question was without meaning and thus not even asked.

The food and water were ample for the two of them for an indefinite time. The ship had gone down without a trace, and there was no real sign that they had ever made this or any other island. All their defenses were permanently on; any searchers or landing parties would not even notice their existence, and since they built nothing, created nothing outside of themselves, there were no signs of their existence for anyone to find.

It had not been the intention of the Glathrielian elders, but Nathan Brazil, for all appearances, had been taken out of the game. Terry had allowed for all external factors, it seemed.

All but one, and she could not know about that, even though it was everywhere, not many kilometers beneath their feet.

Kzuco

THREE DAYS OUT FROM GEKIR, WHILE STILL INSIDE OGADON
waters, the small ship its passengers discovered was called
the *Star Runner* met up with its transfer ship.

Whatever illegal cargoes were involved in this mysterious underworld, they were both valuable and dangerous,
and it was nearly impossible for those paid to find out
about such shipments that were in fact taking place. Even
deep beneath the ocean waters in Ogadon, where this particular trade originated, there were civilization, law, and effective agencies trying to stay on top of things. The one
thing the authorities could not do was fully determine the
when and the where across a hex that was, after all, almost
four hundred kilometers wide, such activity took place, but
it was always a battle of wits.

Even though it would be sheer luck to locate and stop a
transfer in progress, once it had been passed off to a surface
vessel, the fact became known. The *Star Runner*'s job
wasn't to pick up the cargo but rather to meet the pickup
boat, which was a relatively local one well known as legitimate to the authorities, and then take aboard the contraband at sea. Ships like the *Runner* were built to all the
latest specifications but were particularly intended for
speed, speed, speed. As a vessel legally registered to handle
charter and consignment jobs, it always had some specific

legal mission of its own, although nobody was particularly fooled about its true purpose.

The smugglers' defense was a variation on the shell game; several ships like the *Runner* would take off from various ports on seemingly legitimate missions at roughly the same time. Each would head for a different place, but only one or possibly two would actually pick up transfer loads of contraband. Consistently stopping and boarding the wrong ones could prove embarrassing for the interhex authorities, who were in many ways privateers not much different from the crooks they chased except that they'd chosen a lesser return in exchange for doing things the legal way.

Several large waterproof containers had been taken aboard by the *Runner* from what appeared to be a small and seedy trawler, although it was hard to say just what the other ship really looked like in the nearly total darkness in which it was done. It was now the *Runner*'s job to get those containers to another ordinary and familiar coastal vessel that would take a detour at some secluded part of the coast and transfer them once more to small boats to go into shore and from there to a distribution point.

Mavra Chang was fascinated by the process. Once they were under way under full steam, she went over to Zitz, the friendly mate who'd always liked to chat, and commented, "I don't see how you manage it."

"Eh? What?"

"Linking up with a specific small boat in open ocean, in either direction. I don't see how you can find her unless she sits there like a sitting duck waiting for you, and I'm sure she doesn't."

"You're right," the Zhonzhorpian admitted. "It's actually quite simple. No state secret except for the specifics of every operation. Before we set out, we get a very fine customized grid of the entire hex. Thousands of tiny little squares. The rendezvous ship is a scheduled carrier; we know its route in advance, and we know in which of a range of squares along its route the pickup will be made.

She doesn't stop, not even, you'll notice, for the transfer. We just find her and match her course—and speed."

"It was impressive—and quick," Mavra admitted.

"Then we proceed to our destination hex, which has another hex map, another customized grid, and another series of scheduled local carriers. We plot them at all times. Once I'm there, I determine where the best one is located, head for it, and reverse the process. Unlike the pickup, I will always have a choice of two or three ships, and even they won't know which one of them will receive the goods from us, so there can't be any leaks ahead of time. Similarly, there were several ships similar to this one, any one of which might have picked up the cargo from the first vessel. They didn't know it would be us, and it might not have been. If anything went wrong, if someone else got there ahead of us, or if they were being shadowed, they would alter their course slightly from the grid and we wouldn't have seen her."

"I see," she commented. "Very slick."

"There are so many spies and agencies out there that it's impossible to keep them from infiltrating one ship or another on the two ends," Zitz told her. "What *is* possible is, since not even the captain knows if he's the one until he passes the pickup point, we control access to the goods. They pick *up*; they transfer to one of a number of similar vessels. What does the spy report when he, she, or it finally makes port? And most of the next ports are nontech hexes, too, by design. *My* crew stays with me, so I know them all. Our rendezvous ship even now does not know it will be the one, so there's no rumors or leaks from its crew. When we do the transfer, same rules applying, they will take it on and proceed immediately to a point offshore in a nontech or semitech hex and transfer it again, being met by crews who pick the position themselves, then proceed into port on schedule. By the time anyone aboard can get the word out, the cargo and pickup people are long gone. As soon as I make the transfer, I destroy the grid maps. My counterparts will eventually intersect the pickup freighter back there, by the way, see that there is no coded sign that anything is to be picked up, and proceed on as if they had picked up something anyway."

"So this is your point of maximum vulnerability," she noted. "You have the cargo and maps aboard."

"True, but for all of that we have ways of dropping the cargo even under pursuit. The captain only needs to remember one grid position and the code number of the grid map no matter where along the route we might be forced to drop it. *We* would not then bring it in, but once he transferred the grid location and grid code upon making port, someone else eventually would."

"Sounds almost foolproof."

"It's very good," he admitted. "I think it might not be improved upon. It is, however, still a risky business, particularly in high-tech water hexes like Kzuco. We try and stay out of them as much as possible, but it's not possible on this run. That makes the money much better, but the risks are far greater. That's why we're running the short side of Kzuco along the Awbri coast. Awbri's nontech, not the best vantage point, and once we're across the border into Dlubine, we're back in semitech and safer. From that point we can remain in non- and semitech water hexes. I *do* worry about Dlubine, but not as much as here."

"Dlubine has local conditions that create problems?"

"Several. For one thing, it's crawling with patrols, sandwiched between a high-tech land and a high-tech water hex and with a lot of islands with small harbors and hidden coves. Also, in Dlubine it's easier to run by day than by night. You'll see what I mean the first night we're there. The water's lit up like a high-tech city, making it easy to spot you. Easier by day, yes, but murder on us."

"Huh?"

"You can almost make soup with the water, it's that warm, and the air temperature in the middle of the day is close to lethal for many life-forms. It averages more than half the point to boiling. Even the islands seem like water kettles. Still, it is a lot of sea to find us in, and we do it all the time. Each hex has its problems, so I don't want to minimize any dangers, but we are used to them. You are not."

She nodded. "We'll stay out of your way. If it comes to a flight, though, you well know I have no stake in being arrested and returned to Gekir."

"Yes. You understand, though, that none of you can be allowed to leave this vessel until after the transfer has taken place and we are well away."

"We understand," she assured him. She did not press him on the nature of the cargo; in truth, she already knew what at least some of it was just from overheard conversations among the crew. It was a drug, an extremely addictive drug, that worked on a large variety of warm-blooded creatures. Called by many names in many hexes, it was apparently some kind of deep underwater fungal growth. Alive, one could actually eat it without harm, although it supposedly had a terrible taste. Out of the water, though, it died in minutes and dried out quickly, causing its natural internal fluids to undergo a chemical change, crystallize, and become a very sweet and addicting drug that could be eaten, injected, or who knew what else? Tolerances varied, but apparently for some races one ingestion could be enough to hook a user.

Lori had come up to get some night air, finding it difficult to sleep below, and had been listening to the conversation. When it was over and Mavra had moved away toward the rail to stare out at the black sea, he went over and stood beside her.

He'd found this business with the *Runner* both disgusting and unpleasantly familiar. "It's the same here as back on Earth," he growled. "It's as if there's no way and nowhere to escape drugs and the predators who sell them."

"The universe is composed of predators and prey," Mavra responded, not sounding cynical but rather as if she were reciting the obvious. "Everyone is one or the other, sometimes both in a lifetime."

Lori's realization that this was a ship in that sort of business and that all the crew were the same sort of creatures as the ones who ran and guarded Don Francisco Campos's jungle operation, which now seemed not merely a million light-years but also a million real years away. He couldn't help but wonder if Juan Campos hadn't already found his niche in this sort of operation here. It was a natural for him.

He often wondered what had become of Campos. How he'd like to meet the little weasel *now*, not rat to woman but rat to man. They said that when a sexual change was done, nine out of ten times it was to a female, to which poor Alowi and Tony, too, attested. He'd often thought how he'd love to discover that Juan Campos had become an Erdomese female. It would be real justice, but while Mavra said that the Well was sometimes perceived to have a sense of humor even though it shouldn't and theoretically couldn't, both Julian and Tony were proof that there wasn't a whole lot of justice as he would think of it built into the system. The bastard was probably nine feet tall with four arms and sharp teeth and more rotten than ever as befitted his personality.

He still wondered about Campos, and not just him. Where was poor Gus, for example? Had he even survived the transfer and transformation? He'd been such a gentle, quiet soul, it was hard to see him outside his element, his cameras and video equipment and other high-tech toys.

He also wondered about Terry quite often. What was she doing now? Still back there with the People in that rain forest? He *knew* when she'd decided to be the diversion that she would get the worst of it. Such a bright, educated career woman, highly competent, courageous ... There were few superlatives for Terry that he didn't think she deserved. To be shut off for good in the jungle would be *intolerable* to her, he was convinced. But to emerge, tattooed all over, with bone jewelry threaded through her ears and nose ... She'd be a freak. A news story herself for a while, then just a freak. There was no way she could ever lead a normal life like that, and the amount of removal and the cosmetic surgery on her beautiful brown skin would give her a choice between being a painted freak or looking like a burn victim. What kind of a life could she have like *that*?

In the end, she'd probably stay in the jungle, perhaps leaving the People and joining a true tribe but remaining anonymous otherwise, or she'd find a convent, become a nun, and remain cloistered for life. Damn it, it wasn't fair! Terry would have *loved* this place no matter *what* she wound up as!

He finally talked it out with Mavra. "I know it's a hell of a thing she did for us. I owe her, that's for sure. When we get into the Well, I'll see what, if anything, can be done about her. There's got to be *some* way to influence it, even though the only direct controls available that I know of from last time are on people here. Funny, though. You jogged a memory. When I got information on Brazil and his party from Zone, there was mention of someone coming in alone who appeared from the pictures to be of our race—or so they said; I never saw them. Somebody who came in after us, snuck by them all, and went through the hex gate before they even knew anyone was there. They said the other one resembled us."

Lori was excited at the idea. "You think maybe she—?"

"Don't get your hopes up. She was diverting the guards, and I know just how they planned to do that. The Well Gate would have closed and self-destructed after I—we—came through because Nathan and the other two had arrived long before. I don't think there'd be time. No, what I've wondered is whether one of the other women, one of the perimeter guards, might have watched us go through and decided to follow her goddess. It would be just like Utra or maybe Rhama to do just that. Poor darlings! What if one of *them* wound up in a high-tech hex? It'd be bad enough for them to turn into *anything* else, but a nontech hex they might handle with a lot of work. Still, there was no word of anybody else being reported, so it's hard to say anything for sure. I *do* think that if Teysi had come through, she'd have gotten word to us somehow." She sighed. "No, I'm sure she's still back on Earth, and I'm *pretty* sure she's still in the jungle. Unlike you, she found something in the jungle that she loved. I think she didn't want to come because she'd already found her version of the Well World. I think she really *wanted* to stay just as she was."

"You didn't know her. She'd go nuts living in there like that forever."

Mavra smiled. "Maybe *you* didn't know her. I looked at you over a period of a week or two, and I saw somebody willing to play jungle Amazon and go along because that was better than death, but you were always playing at it. Once you got over your fear and your natural feeling that rescue was at hand, you got into it, but it was always a game with you. You didn't ever belong there. I looked at her, though, and I saw somebody hiding one hell of a lot of inner pain. I don't know what it came from, but it was there. And once she got over the same two hurdles you did, she didn't accept things like you did, she embraced them. I've seen the same thing in countless girls who came to us over the years. Like some kind of horrible burden had been lifted, removed from inside them. You fell into a trap; she escaped one. I wouldn't be surprised if she went totally, completely native."

"We saw totally different people," Lori said, shaking his head. "I wonder which one of us saw the right one."

Mavra sighed. "Well, you've seen it happen with Alowi, and I would have bet you that Julian Beard would never have flipped out like that. We'll probably never know for sure about her. At least I'll try to find out once I'm inside. If I can, and she's still alive, where and what she is back there will kind of settle it and what I do for her—if I can do much. That jungle was already disappearing at a horrendous rate. I wish I knew how long any of those tribes can continue to exist as they want to exist. It's a real shame, but it's the way that whole planet went. Right from ancient times they called it 'progress.' I guess it is—if you're doing the chopping and not being chopped."

That brought Lori back to his original train of thought. "What about this drug trade right here? It makes me feel sleazy. Worse than that, it depresses me. Here, all this time, all this civilization, and they wind up like we were going in *my* old corner of civilization. The whole damned *world* seemed to be falling into the hands of the Camposes and their ilk."

"Well, having used drugs of a sort in the jungle, and earlier in other places, and having done a little smuggling in my time, I can't be too judgmental about these people. In a sense, they're the kind of people I was born and raised with. And I can't really say I'm surprised that this exists here; rather, I'm surprised that it didn't seem to exist when I was here last. At least not in anything that wasn't species-specific and too localized to notice. The biggest problem you have if you're born and raised on the Well World is that you have to face the fact that it's meaningless. I mean, what can you hope to do? These are the descendants of the leftovers, the last races tested out here. They're managed from on high—or, rather, from on low—and on the whole, things don't change very much. That's why they don't keep a lot of the kind of history here that we do, on the whole. Even the Erdomese, on their own planet, *might* discover electricity, *might* discover radio and video and research biology, and *might* even figure out a way to get to the stars. They just have less to work with, and it might take them longer. They might not, but it's possible. Not here."

"Well, yeah, but it's not *that* bad, I don't think."

"No? You were a scientist. I'll bet you know enough to create a small renaissance in scientific knowledge in most hexes here, including Erdom. But it's all useless knowledge, isn't it? Useless because nothing except muscle and some water and wind power works there, and even then, if you generate a current, it'll die before it reaches anything that might use it. That was Julian's problem. Just about every bit of the knowledge she has and the talents she possesses are useless in Erdom. Permanently. She can't even swagger around and be Señor or Señora Macha. Everything in Julian Beard's life was denied him as an Erdomese by itself and by being an Erdomese woman in particular. Build things? Paint? With rock-hard mittens for hands? In a land and culture where anything she *might* do intellectually is considered deviant behavior and women are virtual property—forget it. On top of that he had a ton of guilt over being less than a wonderful human being by his own lights. And his mind-set was so much Mister Macho that he was finally faced with the ultimate problem and it tore him to bits."

"You mean he just couldn't handle being a woman?"

"No, he couldn't handle falling in love with a *man*, you idiot! Even if it was with a man who used to be a woman and still has, I think, a woman's soul."

"Julian? In *love* with me? I mean, *really* in love?"

"Sure. Plain as day. But Julian couldn't be in love with a guy, just couldn't handle it, and Julian wasn't useful in any meaningful way from this point on. So Julian goes, Alowi enters. Call it a split personality if you want, but one of them won. The one who could be in love with you and be of use to you and not go bonkers because of what she could no longer be or do."

Lori sighed. "Well, ain't that a kick in the head. Mavra, I swear to you, even though I never thought it for real until just now, I really *did* fall in love myself! But with Julian, not Alowi. Not that I'm not still, but, well, it's not the same."

Mavra shrugged. "Well, you have a problem maybe unique in romance, don't you? I seem to attract the unique in that department. The thing is, though, you've got the Julian problem kind of the way *he* had it."

"What? Now you've lost me again."

"The Well World changes *bodies* around. That's not unique, you know. It's technology. The same principle as the matter transmitter. I once knew somebody who's a distant ghost to me now who discovered the same principle on his own. An Earth-human type. It's not magic. It's physics and mathematics, and enough of an energy source to do it and enough of a computer to manage all that information. It also does some physiological adjustment so you don't fall over trying to walk on those legs of yours or upchuck when you wake up as a creature that eats live prey or the like. But the process doesn't really change the mind, the personality, the soul, as it were. You can't keep the memories and such and wipe out the rest. You lived too long as Lori Sutton. Somewhere here Juan Campos is still a slimy son of a bitch. Julian completed her own transformation. She became a woman to the soul. Tony—well, that's a different personality. I think he was a tough guy but very gentle underneath. With all he'd gone through and his double suicide plans for himself and Anne Marie, I think he considered himself dead, anyway. He got an easier break in a better culture to be a woman, even though that one, too, has its sexual divisions and problems. Still, in spite of cultural hang-ups, I think he was one of those rare guys who really liked and respected women. At least he doesn't see it as a negative. I think he feels he lived a full and decent life as a man and now he's got a chance to live a second life as a woman. That's the attitude to take. Like the Hindu belief that we're reincarnated alternately male and female. To her it's a whole new life. I'm afraid Anne Marie's more a problem than a continuing love story for him."

"Makes sense." Lori nodded. "But what about me? You said I still had a woman's soul. I sure haven't felt much like it; even my thoughts sometimes would have made the old me *very* mad."

"Oh, you're obvious. You—just like in the jungle—never got to that point. You're having a lot of guilty fun *playing* at being a man. But you're not. Physically, yes, but not deep down. It's always easier for women to adjust to other roles and accept them than it is for men."

He thought about it. "Well, it's true that when you see two guys kissing, you have a whole set of reactions, maybe depending on your own feelings about sexuality, but *everybody* has reactions because it's not done. Women kiss each other all the time, and nobody thinks anything of it. And I *know* women dress more for each other than for men. I can't remember a boyfriend I ever had who ever noticed that I had had my hair redone, and most of them didn't notice new clothes or perfume or whatever until I pointed it out to them."

"But *you* still notice. Even in Erdom."

"Yeah, I guess I do. But a lot of that is how they're brought up, too, isn't it? I mean, competitive sports, competitive grades, competitive businesses, everything's competition. Even in Erdom that's true." He thought of the sword fighting and other such activities. "I wasn't brought up like that. What competition I did was on a different level. All appearances and comparing possessions. Men fight or they get the crap beat out of them. Women try to reach a consensus, and a fight between two girls, when it happens, is real scandal or real news. Yeah, I see what you mean, I guess. I stopped seriously competing real early. I was always the consolation prize, if I ever got invited to the dance in the first place, and the kind of life a business career offered never appealed to me. I just wanted to be a scientist. I wanted to find out how things worked and *why* they worked. I was good at math, and girls weren't supposed to be good at math. I loved computers, and girls were supposed to hate them. I guess I figured that so long as I was already a social geek, I might as well be a total one. I just decided to do what I loved doing. I'd love to do it here, too."

Mavra nodded. "Yeah, I understand that. That's another problem with coming through the Well. The high-tech types already know what you know, and more. The others either don't or can't use it. Coming from the tech level you do and the occupation you do, you not only would have to learn from scratch, you'd have to unlearn half of what you learned as gospel. The very fact that you stand here as an Erdomese man says that better than I could. The same went double for Julian. Pilots of any sort, and particularly jet and space pilots—well, they're useless here, aren't they? So it decided you were useless and dumped you in low-tech. You'd have had a better shot at high-tech if you hadn't been as smart, frankly. Doesn't take brains to learn how to push buttons. Same goes for Tony—airline pilot. I think somewhere there was a theory built into the Well that said that if your skills were useless, you should be put in a spot where they couldn't be used so that you might adjust and use that brain power where it would do some good. Just a hunch—no inside information there. But it kinda holds, doesn't it?"

"Could be. But in Erdom the knowledge that might be useful is held by that damned priesthood and the price is *much* too high, and the guilds leave me out of most of the other trades that might be of any interest. It seemed like the best I could be would be some kind of glorified night watchman or street sweeper or something else menial. I mean, like much of the population there, even though I know seven languages and have a universal translator implanted, I'm still a total illiterate in Erdom, and having looked at that language, I probably will remain so. I think that's why I jumped at your note even though I was under that hypnotic drug's spell at the time. Cut off or not, I knew when I had an opportunity for something better rather than facing my alternatives there."

"Well, I never figured on the hypnotic drugs, but I kind of hoped that either curiosity or ambition or both would bring you. Just a few days more and we'll be ashore in uncharted realms for both of us. I need you. Do the job for me and I'll make sure you have a future you'll like. If we lose this race, you'll have seen something of the world and won't be any worse off. Fair enough?"

"Fair enough. But thinking about those priests' drugs brings me back to what kicked off this talk. I still feel uncomfortable with all this. Did you *really* do this yourself once?"

"Sure. Okay, that shocks you, but as I said, this is a place with 1,560 tiny worldlets with no future and no past, more or less. They're kinda stuck here. They know there's a possibility that their kids might be worse off than they are but won't be better off. Mostly it'll be hard to tell one stagnant age from another. Deep down most know that or at least feel or sense it. It's why life can be cheap here, and it's little wonder some turn to chemical escapes. You mean you *never* tried some drugs out of curiosity or boredom or depression or whatever?"

"Me? Not much. Some marijuana now and then—I did it heavy in college, I admit, but less once I got a job—and some alcohol but nothing hard. I tried cocaine once at a party and darn near choked. Never touched it or anything else again. Why?"

"And these were all legal substances?"

"No. Alcoholic drinks, yes, but not marijuana or cocaine. Not in *my* lifetime, anyway. But it's not the same."

"It *is* the same. Even legal, it's used for the same purposes. Illegal just feeds the whole business. The same ones who got your illegal drugs in also brought in the rest, of which you disapproved. Your money went to help them finance the ships and men like this one. I've not only been with them on this level, I've fought the ugly side of the business, too, against the thoroughly rotten people at the top. You might say that far back in the distant past I saw the future of this as well, and nothing you see here can compare to the depravity of what lies ahead."

"But it's a matter of degree. Some is harmful, some not."

Mavra Chang sighed. "I remember a people once in east Africa. Two tribes, same ancestry, all that, but one of them lived by a great river and tilled the land and mined gold and such from the nearby mountains that served as a barrier separating them from the others. Those others, they lived on the other side, a lot of the same geography and possibilities, but their home was in a virtual cannabis forest. They were a far happier tribe and more content, but for generations they remained no more advanced than the People of the upper Amazon. I don't judge. The tribe that remained in the forest was probably happier than the other one that built a great city, but the happy ones were stagnant, stuck, just like the Well World."

"You're one to talk!"

Mavra shrugged. "We used some drugs from the native

forest, you know, and not always as a practical thing. What can I say? After being kicked around for a few thousand years I called a halt. I didn't *like* Earth much, Lori. I didn't like it much at all. It was uglier and more primitive than I could have imagined in ways I never dreamed it could be. I'm sorry, but that is my perspective. I left it. I escaped where it wasn't so ugly, and I remained there rather than come out to face more ugliness. One day things would be different. There would be what *I* considered real progress and advancement, and they would discover interstellar travel. By that time the rain forest would be cut down, and I'd be able to get *off* that miserable planet. I do know that I'm not going back there. Or if the Well somehow forces me back there, I am not going back as Mavra Chang or anything remotely like her. If I can, I'm going to be something else."

"Yes? What, if I may ask?"

"I don't know. If what I believe is true, I won't have to face that problem. If not—I don't know, but I'll think of something."

Since Mavra was in a talkative mood, there being little else to do aboard the ship, Lori was about to go into just what Mavra thought of men—at least, men who hadn't been changed into women and vice versa. It seemed to him as if she hated them in general, on a gut emotional level, even if accepting them intellectually. That Portuguese ship and crew must have been a holy horror, but had it, after so much experience elsewhere and even before, in some former lifetime, driven her over an edge she hadn't been over before? Or had she *never* liked men? Why had she separated from this Brazil guy so long ago, and why did she seem to both hate and fear him now? According to Tony and Anne Marie, this Nathan Brazil sounded like a pretty nice guy. He'd saved two lives out of clear compassion; Mavra had put lives in jeopardy, ruined one or two maybe, and waxed nostalgic for the days when she'd been a drug runner.

He never got the chance. *"Ship! Port, fifty-one degrees,*

distance nine kilometers and closing at flank speed!" came a sharp shout from the bridge, where, in this high-tech hex, all the technological gear was active.

The captain was in the wheelhouse in moments, looking at the scope. "I don't like this. It's got the size and speed to be a privateer. How far is it to the Dlubine border?"

"Twenty kilometers, sir!"

"Damn! So close and yet so far! Any attempt at communications?"

"None yet, sir. Instructions?"

Captain Hjlarza thought for a brief moment. "Zitz! Hail them, then. Ask them who they are and why they are bearing down on us. Warn them that we are an armed ship and that we deal mercilessly with pirates."

The Zhonzhorpian was on the radio immediately, barking a challenge and sounding doubly mean. With that crocodilelike throat and mouth, he could make it sound very menacing indeed.

"No reply, sir!"

"They're stalling! Okay, we've given them a legitimate reason for us to turn and run! Kill all lights! Starboard thirty degrees! All ahead full! Zitz! Man the weapons board! Others to arms stations! If they get in range, give 'em all you got! If they call us now, you know the routine!"

"Aye, sir!"

Lori looked alarmed. "I think we better clear out and give them some room," he said nervously.

Mavra returned a wry smile. "Just don't get in their way. These are pros."

The captain kept looking at his scopes. "They're closing a little, but they're only a hair faster than we are. At this heading and speed, we should still have a good two kilometers on them when we cross the border. As soon as we cross it, I'm going to give a sharp turn to starboard and full speed into whatever's there. We'll still be out of visual and off their instruments. When I do, I want everybody at their sailing positions. Engines, I want full until I tell you, then

I want a dead stop. We will put on sail the moment after I order an engine stop. Understand?"

There was a chorus of "Ayes," and the crew went to station.

"They're calling us now, sir!" Zitz reported.

The captain gave a low chuckle. "They've just figured out they won't catch us this side of the border. You know what to say."

Zitz, however, was already saying it. "If you were truly legal authorities, you would have responded to our first call with an identification signal," he told the pursuing ship sharply. "We've been suckered by pirate ploys before. No, sir, we would be derelict in our duties if we yielded to you now."

They could hear only one side of the conversation, but it was clear that the gunboat had issued an ultimatum and a threat.

"Well, sir, if you can catch us, then do so. If you are a legitimate naval vessel, we will lodge charges against your captain for failure to respond to a legitimate identification check. If you are not, we will have to fight. If we are fired upon, however, we will take that as confirmation that you are pirates and will respond accordingly and without hesitation."

The captain was just looking at his scopes, throttle wide open. Suddenly he snapped, "Engines, we've just had two guided torpedoes launched against us. I will probably have to turn if they don't both buy the decoy. Be ready." He leaned out the open window. "Torpedoes! Let go aft decoys!"

One of the spider creatures hit some levers, and there were loud splashes behind them in the water. A minute or so later, well in back of their wake, there was a tremendous bright flash and the sound of an explosion.

"One of 'em bought it; the other's still coming," the captain reported. "Launch antitorpedo from aft tube and reload as quick as you can!"

There was the sound like that of a torpedo being fired,

and then the spider creature opened a hatch and went half-way down into it, clearly doing something with its forelegs out of sight of the deck. Before it was finished, there was another bright flash and explosion behind them, much, much closer to them than the first one had been.

"Got it!" the captain called with satisfaction. "Zitz, give 'em two rockets! I don't care if you hit them or not, but it'll keep 'em back and make 'em think twice about us!"

Lori's sense of boredom had vanished, but it was replaced with a little bit of fear and concern. Still, all of it seemed somehow unreal, distant. *I feel like I'm in the middle of a cheap thriller,* he thought wonderingly.

The two rockets went away with a twin *thump! thump!* sound, and they saw them quickly rise on small jets of flame and disappear into the darkness behind them.

"I hope the folks who live in the water here aren't the kind to get too pissed off at people blowing up things," Mavra commented dryly.

"One minute!" the captain shouted. "Everybody brace yourselves and be ready to alter course!" He paused, watching the scopes carefully as the stack billowed black smoke and the wind seemed even chillier.

Lori looked forward and thought he could see some lights off in the distance, but everything looked hazy and distorted. Almost as they reached it, he realized that he'd been looking through a hex barrier at night.

They could feel the tingle of the hex barrier as they crossed it, and suddenly all the electronic gear on the bridge failed as if someone had pulled the plug, and the heated air of the new hex hit them like a solid, hot wet carpet, causing some momentary disorientation. The ship, however, continued at full steam.

Without further warning, the captain brought the *Runner* around hard right, so hard that loose things on deck shifted left and Lori felt himself being thrown against the rail, then pitched back, falling to the deck.

It seemed as if the ship would never stop its turn, that it would go on forever, but after a while the vessel, which had itself been leaning to the right, steadied itself and came back to a straight-on course. The captain was counting quietly, estimating the speed of the pursuit and the amount of time it had taken them to make the dramatic turn.

Suddenly he shouted, "Sail crew aloft!"

Expertly, the two great spiders scuttled up the masts virtually to the top, and long tentaclelike legs adjusted the holding straps, while Zitz left his dead command console aft, where the two centauresses were watching the show with a mixture of awe and concern, and moved forward to the sail control position.

There was another long pause, then the captain shouted, "All engines dead stop! Boilers to standby! Disengage engines from drive shaft! Lower center board and deploy mainsails!"

There was a sudden, almost deathly quiet save for the noise of the sails being squeakily lowered and fixed into position.

"Rig full, no jibs," the captain commanded, and first the topsails and then various subordinate sails sprouted, making the transformation to quiet sailing vessel almost complete. The boilers were not out, but since they had been disengaged from the drive shafts, there was a sudden cessation of the steady rhythmic vibration that the engines had sent through the ship.

Mavra went over to Lori and offered a hand. "You okay?"

"Yeah, I think so. Probably gonna have a hell of a bruise on my hip, but it's no big deal. The hardest part is getting back on my feet." He made it with her help but needed to lurch forward and hold on to something. "Great body for running, particularly in sand or gravel, but it's just not good with the casual stuff." He was calming down now and took stock of the surroundings. "Wow! Feels like home, only worse! This is *really* hot!"

"It's at least as hot as Erdom," Mavra agreed, "but with an ocean's humidity. Will you be all right here? I want to check on the girls in the back."

"Yeah, sure, I'll be okay. I'm just trying to get steady

enough to go down and check on Alowi." He gave a long, relieved exhale. "At least we made it!"

"Don't feel so confident yet," Mavra warned him. "They're still back there, and they're close. If we don't lose them, we'll have to fight, and we'll be well within their gun range here. This is semitech, remember, not nontech. Cannons do their usual nasty job here."

He stared after Mavra as she went aft to check on the Dillians, then said aloud, under his breath, "Yeah, thanks for telling me that cheery set of facts."

The air felt wet and sticky, and there seemed to be a light rain or mist falling that did nothing to cool things off. He looked to the right of the ship and thought he saw some kind of shimmering, a distortion even of the night fog and mist.

The captain was running directly down the hex barrier, just inside the Dlubine side.

He shook his head and decided ne'd better put his trust in the ones who knew what they were doing and tend to his own business, which was going below.

It was a mess there; the turn had spilled more down there than up on deck, but Alowi seemed all right and relieved to see him.

"I—I was afraid something happened to you up there," she told him.

"I fell. Hip's gonna feel like hell later, but I'm all right. What about you?"

"I rolled over, but once things straightened out, I was all right. Everything was flying or rolling around . . . I just did not know what was happening. Come—let me heal your pain."

"I'm all right for now."

"*Please!* Now is the best time. The last time you almost died from a bad bruise. Let me give you what you need to keep it from happening again!"

It suddenly struck him. The key to the entire Erdomese way and why things were more dangerous for him than he'd realized.

The male Erdomese's weakness, its Achilles' heel, was that he and all the rest of them had a kind of hemophilia. The females, in that second set of breasts, carried more than spare water; they carried a clotting factor. The women's nearly total dependence on the men for most things was counterbalanced by the men's absolute need to have that which only the women could make readily available. They hadn't told him or warned him about it. Why would they? Between their customs and their beliefs, and with such a huge proportion of females to males, they took it for granted. No *wonder* the men traveled with as many wives as they could afford to support!

For the first time he realized just how vulnerable he actually was to things that others took for granted. Even without cultural codes or his feelings for her, he would have to protect Alowi with every ounce of his strength and life. If anything happened to her, if they were even separated, out here, so many miles from Erdom, he was dead meat.

"My, that was positively *thrilling*," Anne Marie gushed. "Almost like one of those James Bond thrillers."

"I could do with a little less of that, particularly out here," Tony responded. Although Dillians had a natural ability to swim, it took a lot of muscle power to do so, and they wouldn't have much of a chance out here in the middle of the ocean, any more than a common horse might have. Sufficient to keep them from drowning in a river or enabling them to make a quick swim to shore or a raft, but considering their forward center of gravity, out here they'd be dead ducks.

"Well, I'm glad to see that you two are all right," Mavra told them. "They're slick, these guys. We're outside any capability the gunboat might have to spot us electronically and out of range of any of his fancy weapons, too. Hugging this hex boundary, we're in the natural mist and fog that's usually at such a border, and under sail, there's little noise."

Tony didn't feel as confident. "Wouldn't *they* know that,

too? And couldn't they really bear down on us if it were steam against sail in this little wind?"

"They do, and yeah, they could overtake us, but they have 180 degrees of possibility. They'll overshoot coming in and have to turn when they see they lost us, and they'll do it gently. It takes time. Then they have to decide which way to turn. They'll have to cut their engines and run silently to see if they can hear us, and when they don't, they'll know we're under sail. From that point they'll be farther behind and have a fifty-fifty chance of tracking us or missing us entirely. If they don't fire up their boilers, they'll be slower than we are in this slight wind, since they're a heavier boat, and if they do, we'll hear them and have a straight free shot at their bow from the stern gun. I don't think they'll risk that. They'll pick a direction and run slowly along it until dawn, which is still many hours away. By that time the captain will have slipped away."

The captain in fact was waiting until they ran into the edge of one of the local storms, and when the first one was spotted, not too far from the border position, he took a chance and eased out of the cover of the boundary mist and, when nothing was obviously in sight, headed for it.

It made for a rough introduction to Dlubine, but they were alive, the ship was in good shape, and they were free of pursuit by dawn and able to engage the boilers once more and proceed in the heat regardless of the wind.

By midday there was some debate among both passengers and crew as to whether it was worse up top or below. Most chose to be on deck and relaxed under whatever cover they could rig up. Ultimately, it became too hot for anyone to even handle the boilers, and they went to sail and more or less just drifted along, taking four-hour shifts at the wheel.

All five of the passengers remained under the makeshift canvas shelter of the centauresses on the afterdeck. All had removed whatever clothing they'd had on; it was too hot to be wearing *anything* if one didn't have to.

It was a particular shock for the two Erdomese, who were used to extreme heat, but theirs had been basically a desert environment and their bodies were designed to retain and recycle moisture. Both were as miserable as could be.

"I got a reading from the wheelhouse thermometer when I went forward for some water," Lori managed. "Doing a rough conversion, assuming that the top of the mark with the big line is boiling and the black line on the bottom is freezing, I'd say well over 50 degrees Celsius—somewhere over 120 Fahrenheit, Anne Marie."

"Goodness! How do people *survive* here?" she responded. Dillians at least could perspire over most of their huge bodies, but they required a lot of water.

"Because the *people* are a mile or so straight down," Mavra reminded her. "Down there it's probably a nice, comfortable day, although from what I can tell they're nocturnals, like the captain."

"I wish I was," Lori groaned.

There wasn't much more conversation after that. It was too hot to do just about anything.

Still, there *was* a moderate breeze, which helped slightly, taking them almost due west. Again, it was the short leg about twenty kilometers off the Agon coast, a bit too close to avoid the risk of more intercostal patrols but comfortably far enough out not to be seen or detected from shore. The only hope was to make full speed once night fell and be out of this boiling hotbox by sunup the next day. For all any of them cared at this point, Fahomma would be welcome even if it had icebergs and blowing snows.

Several times in the distance one ship or another would be sighted, but none of them ever closed with them, and such traffic was to be expected in this region. Some were even under steam, demonstrating clearly that whatever was stoking their fires might possibly have Satan as a relative but definitely bore little genetic kinship with anybody on the *Star Runner*.

Who was doing what became moot after a while as all of them drifted into varying degrees of uncomfortable sleep.

Nightfall wasn't exactly cool, but it definitely had a psychological effect on everyone. The captain took the wheel, and the weird creature who usually took care of everything below decided it was cool enough to fire up the engines. The job wasn't physically taxing—whatever fuel they used appeared to be a syrupy liquid stored in large tanks deep in the hull and moved to the engines by some sort of vacuum system—but the boilers got hot, and steam was always dangerous and needed constant monitoring and occasional release and regulation.

Captain Hjlarza wasn't very friendly or communicative, but Mavra had managed to establish at least a working relationship with the vicious-looking Stulz, who reminded her of nothing more than a gigantic fruit bat although she doubted he could ever fly no matter what the leathery wing material might do otherwise.

"How long to the border?" she asked him.

"Dawn. Perhaps a bit longer if nothing happens to delay us. There are always patrols about in these waters, and a full day is long enough for word to have been passed along a pretty good chain, I'd suspect. Still, I expected if we were going to be chased it would have been during the day, when we'd have no chance of running, boilers down, and everyone at their worst. No, I'd say at this point our most probable roadblock would be a series of storms. It *always* rains at night here. All that ocean went up during the day and has to come back down."

"What's this Fahomma like, then?"

"Oh, not too bad. Nontech, which really helps us. Under sail there's nothing that can catch us that might be able to hurt us. Warm, but cooler and more comfortable than this, but it tends to rain steadily for weeks at a time over parts of it. We will transfer our cargo there if all goes well and thus be free of patrol worries."

"Off Agon? They're smuggling into a high-tech hex?"

"Who knows? It goes to another freighter, and it's off here. Where it goes from there is not my concern."

"Well, it can't be soon enough for us, either. I think everybody except me is ready for dry land at this point."

Everyone, from Mavra to Lori, Alowi, and the Dillians,

was entranced by the colorful underwater lights that became quickly clear as darkness fell.

"Those can't be electric- or nuclear-powered, can they?" Lori asked, as always as curious about how things worked as about how pretty they looked.

"Not likely," Tony responded. "I rather think they are chemical. Still, the layout, like a vast city-state deep under the water, makes you wonder what kind of creatures they are and what their lives must be like, does it not? I have tended to just regard the ocean as ocean very much like back on Earth. I suspect most of us have. But it takes something like this to remind us that there is an entire alternative set of people, species, and cultures down there. How sad that much of the contact between us up here and those down there involves drugs and crooked elements."

"Well, we know there are centaurs here, don't we, dear? One must wonder if there are also, somewhere, mermaids."

The night was still hot but bearable to a degree, although nobody felt all that energetic. At least there were some very pretty things to look at and a few impressive if less than welcome thunderstorms as well. Still, both captain and crew seemed well satisfied with the progress and also with the fact that the only thing that really was approaching them was dawn.

It was heating up pretty quickly when they reached the Fahomma border, and the captain ordered all steam shut down and shifted entirely to sail. The area ahead, through the hex barrier, looked somewhat forbidding, dark and gray, in sharp contrast to the brightness of Dlubine. As they passed through, the temperature dropped but the humidity got even worse—it was raining steadily, although not the hard driving rain and high winds of a Dlubinian storm.

Late that night, while under full sail, they passed a small trawler that gave the correct recognition sign. Captain Hjlarza was both puzzled and alarmed at this break with procedure and somewhat suspicious of it, but he turned and paralleled the trawler's course. From the deck of the other ship, something big and barely seen in the rain and darkness threw a spear attached to a long rope to the deck of the *Runner*. Zitz ran to it, removed the small attached tube, and then pried the spear from the deck and tossed it overboard so that the other ship could retrieve it. The mate then brought the tube to the captain, who frowned and opened it, pulled out a sheet of paper, read it, then put it with his grids and had Zitz toss the tube, both ends open, into the sea, where it would fill with water and sink.

"Trouble, Captain?" Zitz asked a bit nervously.

"New orders. Don't like 'em. Not at all happy about 'em, but orders are orders. They will owe us all for this, though, Zitz. They will owe us a *lot*. Cost us a damned fortune, this will. Take a look at it when you get the chance and then very quietly pass it on to the crew. I'll need you all tomorrow night, but if anybody spills the beans, they're dead meat."

When Zitz did get the opportunity to look at it, he saw just what the captain meant and liked it even less. It was a new, local grid, a very specific and specialized one, for a new job. Still, there was no question of not doing it. They followed the grids only for a rendezvous, yet the trawler had shown no problems at all finding them in this weather in a nontech hex. Even the authorities had failed to do that except by chance. You didn't mess with the kind of people who could pull off *that* trick if you wanted to keep on living.

The next day, the ocean was relatively smooth, although it continued to rain. The steady, light rain didn't cause any real problems for a sailing ship, and there was always something of a wind but rarely more than you wanted. The air temperature felt almost chilly, although in fact it was twenty-six degrees Celsius or better. The contrast, however, with the neighboring hotbox was dramatic.

Mavra sensed a little difference, perhaps a bit more coldness from the crew, but it wasn't much and could have been put down to a number of things. She knew they'd gotten a message the previous night, and clearly the message had given them some nerves, but they didn't really want to discuss what was in it.

About two hours after nightfall Captain Hjlarza swung in more toward the coast, almost without anyone noticing until they were too close to ignore it. They were still off Agon, a high-tech hex, and there were automated lights and electrically illuminated small settlements within view. Sensing that something wasn't all that right, considering the officers' aversion to getting in close to high-tech coastlines, Tony walked forward and alerted Mavra and the Erdomese, who were below staying dry. Mavra immediately came up on deck and saw that Tony was quite correct. She went to the captain.

"What's this all about? I thought we weren't stopping until Lilblod."

"Change in orders. Special drop just up here," the captain responded. "Stick around. You may find this interesting."

They came in close, perhaps a hundred meters from shore, no more—close enough to see the hex barrier and the illuminated buoy that was just inside Agon. It was a relatively desolate part of the coast; there were a couple of individual lights atop what might have been high cliffs but nothing approaching a pier or settlement.

Two fairly good-sized black launches came out of the darkness just at the hex barrier, then turned so that the *Star Runner* could come alongside. Zitz and one of the spiders threw down ropes that tied the launches to the larger ship, then lowered rope ladders. Soon four heavily armed creatures climbed slowly up and onto the deck. All four resembled nothing so much as human-sized turtles without shells, wearing black outfits, and they carried what looked like a stylized futuristic automatic rifles over their shoulders and nasty-looking crossbows of equally advanced design in their hands.

Two of them walked over toward the bridge and spotted Mavra. The nasty-looking crossbows lowered and pointed straight at her.

"What *is* this?" she asked the captain, suddenly realizing that *she* was the drop.

"Sorry. Orders. Call the Erdomese man up on deck, very naturally. Try anything funny and I'll kill his wife and the two Dillians. Be nice, no tricks, and I swear that I'll deliver them to safety."

"You swore you'd deliver *me* to safety," she noted acidly.

"Quickly now. Just the man. And I didn't give my word on that to you. I was paid to do it."

"Yeah, and you'll lose that fortune, too."

"I hate the idea like the plague, but I'm ordered to give all the stuff back and report that we disposed of the thieves. A fortune's no use at all to a dead man. Now—call him! Very pleasantly, since there's nowhere he can go down there and all you can do by pulling anything is get your people killed. Don't expect the Dillians to the rescue. Zitz and the other Agonese have them covered."

She sighed. There wasn't anything to do, and she didn't doubt for an instant that he'd kill the others with hardly a thought even if she managed an escape. She'd gotten them into this; she couldn't very well lead them to such an unnecessary doom. But why Lori?

She opened the door. "Lori? Can you come on deck for a minute? Got a problem here I think you can help with."

"Yeah, sure," the Erdomese replied from below. She heard him come out of the cabin and come slowly up the stairs, and it wasn't until he'd squeezed out onto the main deck that he saw the situation and froze. "What the hell is this?" He paused and had that sinking feeling. "They caught us."

"Yeah, but I don't think these guys have anything at all to do with any government on this planet."

"Move out into the open, hands up," one of the Agonite gunmen hissed. "You! Big man! Bend over against the rail! Yes, that's it!"

Mavra started forward, but large, extremely powerful hands seized her from behind and put a foul-smelling mask over her face. *Gas!* She barely had time to struggle and just saw two of them doing the same to Lori before she blacked out.

Dlubine

EVER SINCE GUS HAD SLID INTO THE WATER, HE'D HAD NO CON-tact with anyone for several days. He had looked on some of the islands for Brazil and Terry but hadn't found any sign of them and wondered if, in fact, those were the same islands they'd wrecked on or if he'd been carried along far-ther in the chain before managing to make shore.

At any rate, he'd been unable to find the one with the lava coming down the side in that pattern, and that sug-gested that he was in the wrong place or at the very best on the wrong side.

It didn't take him long to discover as well that the is-lands bore no sign of anything a Dahir could eat. Some of the insects were large enough, but they not only didn't smell right, they smelled very much all wrong, and since being out on his own in this world he'd learned to trust his nose beyond all else. In any event, someone of his size couldn't expect to sustain himself on those things for very long.

That meant getting off, and the nearest mainland was at least fifty, maybe a hundred kilometers away—there was no way of telling for sure, but even if he set off in the right direction, he'd be dead of exhaustion long before he ar-rived. He was already all in.

He was not, however, the only one who'd lost Brazil and Terry, as he discovered the second day on the island while weighing what few options he had. He heard it first, then saw it—a patrol boat, a big steamer with metal plates on its hull not unlike the one back at the island harbor. Maybe—no, *probably*—the one that had caught and sunk them!

He was angry at them, but clearly they hadn't found anybody, either, or they wouldn't be poking around like that. In any event, with this black volcanic sand not taking much in the way of footprints or other signs, they had the same sort of problem he did and had to send a few of the crew over in small rowboats to look around and check for any signs of anything.

It was a pretty clear way out. If they continued searching and found them, he'd be there to help them out. If they failed, at least they'd head for some place to resupply, and that was the kind of place that might well have decent Dahir eating and he could figure out what to do next.

Besides, the idea of sitting right on the deck of a police launch and having nobody notice him was irresistible.

He worked his way up the island just beyond the beach, then out across some fresh lava rock that extended right down almost to the water, and slid in, swimming to the launch before the men were back. He waited there until the shore party did return so that they'd discount any extra weight or water when he came aboard on the same side.

They went from island to island, beach to beach, looking for any signs of wreckage or of anyone coming ashore, but found nothing. One time they did in fact come right around to a daylight version of what Gus *thought* he'd seen at night, only there wasn't any lava visible. It was only when he realized that the stuff was in fact coming down and dumping into the ocean and that this was what was causing the massive steam eruption over to one side that he understood his mistake. The lava hadn't been out in the open but had formed lava tubes, the rock hitting the air getting solid and forming a kind of roof for the rest. At night it looked like red-hot streams of the stuff, but by day it was a lot less obvious.

And that presented a real problem. If they *had* gotten on the beach and *were* on that island, what help would he be? No food, and instead of two of them being stuck, all three of them would be stuck. If it was the same as the island he'd been on, and he had no reason to think it wasn't, they could eat some of the fruit even if he could not, and there'd been water on the other island, which was much smaller, so there was likely to be water here. The way he'd seen Terry's powers in action, too, he knew they could hold out there a damned long time.

He would do more good to try to find the location somewhere and then come back for them when he could. It wasn't what his heart told him to do, but him dead and them alive and stranded didn't equal all three alive in any reasonable book. He just wished he'd realized his mistake on the volcano, when there had been time to get ashore, look by himself, and still catch the boat.

That night, after the last methodical search, near dusk, the launch gave up and headed out toward open sea. Gus just relaxed and snoozed on the bow and hoped that they were headed some place useful.

Within a few hours they were approaching land, and from the darkness Gus saw that wherever it was was definitely more civilized than he'd like. It looked like the coastline of Oregon or northern California, densely populated and brightly and artificially lit.

After they had slipped into an official naval dock facility and tied up, he waited until all but the watch and maintenance personnel were off and then just walked ashore.

Beyond the buildings, piers, and guards, though, was a kind of lunatic's seaside resort, at least to his mind. All the houses, hell, all the buildings, big and small, seemed like they'd been poured by a five-year-old out of some play-dough set. They looked, well, kind of weird, not at all symmetrical or standard but solid, colorful, and well built out of some synthetic material.

And by bright streetlights he found himself in what he thought of as the Land of the Ninja Turtles.

Well, not exactly, but they *did* sort of remind him of the cartoon characters. No shells, though, and no Ninja gear. And some of them had beards, of all things, and some of them wore what looked like Scotch plaid kilts, but most of them wore ugly, serviceable form-fitting plastic-type clothing.

There were big bipedal turtles and little ones and in-between ones, and except for the occasional oddball in kilts or other nonstandard clothing and the few with little goatees, they all looked just exactly alike to him.

Well, they seemed warm-blooded by their actions, in spite of looking like reptiles, and that made them somewhat akin to him, however different they really were. Maybe, just maybe, what they ate *he* could eat.

For a while he feared they were all herbivores, but then he discovered the refrigerated warehouses and lots and lots of meat. It was all dead, of course, and some of it might take a while to thaw out, although he wondered how long it would take *anything* to thaw in the waters just beyond the breakwater in superhot Dlubine. Rather than be piggy, he picked a half dozen smaller cuts, a mere six or seven pounds of meat of some kind, went down to the shore just beyond the town and waded, then floated out until he was in the warmest water he'd ever known.

The answer was about an hour a pound.

It didn't taste the same, not without the warm blood and all the nice mushy insides and skin and all, but it wasn't the time to be a gourmet or look gift horses in the mouth. He'd eaten a lot worse on this trip, and natural taste and instinct didn't fill an empty gullet. All in all, it was a quite satisfactory beach picnic, even if the company didn't show up.

The next day he tried to find out a little information about where the hell he was and what he might be able to do next.

This, it appeared, was a seaside resort in Agon, so even if the other two had failed to make the northern continent, he had, and he was the only one who didn't give a damn if he ever saw the place or not.

He knew he didn't like the place. It wasn't the locals, or the climate, or even the food so much as it was the fact that it was a high-tech hex. He'd had to bypass several security systems the previous night, and even so, he knew they knew somebody had broken in. In fact, a whole damned busload of uniformed turtle cops had shown up by dawn and were busily going over the place. He decided that they must have found something, because one of the cops lit out for the naval station on a crazy kind of vehicle that seemed to float just off the ground on nothing in particular but had handlebars and a hand accelerator and a hand brake kind of like a motorbike's. He decided to follow, mostly to see if there was any suspicion of a Dahir being involved.

The little fellow on the flying surfboard beat him there by a bit, of course, but he was there with several navy types of various races spouting off a storm. Gus moved closer to overhear.

". . . definitely no race on our local registry. It *has* to be something from one of your crews! You had a patrol come in just last night!"

One of the crew, who looked like a five-foot-tall version of Rocky the Flying Squirrel sans goggles to Gus, who was, after all, a television person, responded, "Now, calm down. What did you say was stolen again?"

"*Zlabruk!* Eight prime filets! Highest quality, too!"

"I assure you we feed our men well," responded another, who looked like a giant frog in full uniform. "And they earn more than enough to not go off after a very hot and difficult mission, break into a place, and steal a bunch of— *steaks.*"

"*Zlabruk!* That's imported, you know! Expensive!"

"Well, I don't think—" began the squirrel, then stopped and thought a moment. "Steaks . . . Who in the world would break in and steal slabs of meat? I wonder . . . Wait here a moment. I want you to speak to someone else."

The giant walking squirrel vanished into a nearby building and was gone for two or three minutes while the others fiddled around and the Agonite cop kept muttering about imported filets. Finally the big gray lump of fur emerged, but he was not alone. Following him was a much more amorphous creature, a creature Gus had seen before, and when it spoke through an orifice it formed within itself, it was unmistakably the *same* one as well.

"I am Colonel Lunderman," said the Leeming. "Now, what's this about someone coming in and stealing a bunch of steaks?"

Gus wasn't at all sure whether to be relieved or fearful at the colonel's appearance on this side of the ocean. As much as he needed an ally, he felt he could trust this character about as far as he could throw him.

Just great! he thought to himself. *So* now *what the hell do I do?*

Agon

THEY AWOKE, CHAINED TO A WALL BY EFFICIENT SHACKLES, unable to move any of their limbs more than a very short way.

It was a surprisingly modern room with a glowing ultra-modern ceiling providing more than enough light and vents feeding in air-conditioning at a reasonable level of comfort. Lori hung to the right of the entrance, Mavra to his left. Along the other walls were built-in work tables and fancy computer screens, and in the center were a number of benches with all sorts of science equipment on them, giving the place the look of a college chemistry lab.

Mavra groaned and looked around. "Lori? Are you all right?"

"I—well, if you call this all right, I guess so," Lori groaned, then looked around and tested the chains. "Now what happens?"

"Nothing good," Mavra responded. "You remember that I said you'd never really come face-to-face with what future technology could and would do for criminals? Well, welcome to the future. I'm just *devastated* to see this kind of setup here."

"Yeah, but I thought the equivalent of the UN or something wanted you. This sure isn't them—and why us, too?"

"Well, why don't you just hang around and find out?" Mavra snapped with heavy irony.

Lori sighed, "I guess it doesn't really matter much, for me, anyway. Without Alowi I'm a dead man, anyway."

They did not have long to wait, but the creature who walked through the door was beyond anything they expected.

My god! Lori thought. *It's Daisy Duck with tits!*

In fact, the body appeared more humanoid than ducklike, although it was completely covered by tiny white feathers wherever it was exposed, and the legs, slightly bowed, were of a tough-looking ribbed yellow-orange texture, and while the feet could not be seen, it was not beyond the bounds of imagination to think of two thick webbed feet somehow crammed into a pair of vastly oversized black pumps.

The arms seemed extremely thin, extending a bit out from the shoulders, with a ball-like elbow joint in the middle and ending in two huge mittlike hands, each with three nearly equal-sized webbed fingers and an opposing thumb, without any sign of nails, claws, or whatever. Extending from the underside of the impossibly thin arms was a row of feathers that might have been what remained of vestigial wings but that were now nothing more than decoration. The entire body, which stood perhaps 165 centimeters discounting the heels, was curvaceous and sported two rather ample mammallike breasts that were easily seen thanks to the rather slinky black dress the creature wore.

The head sat atop what appeared to be a very thin, short neck; it was large enough to match the body and began with long, straight black hair parted in the middle and going down to the shoulders on either side; the eyes were huge and oval-shaped, with the longest points vertical rather than horizontal as on Earth-human eyes, and contained large, round jet black pupils. These sat atop a long, curved ducklike orange-colored bill that extended a good twenty centimeters out from the head and was wide enough to be hinged on the sides of the lower face. Two small black slits atop the bill served as the nostrils; no ears were obvious.

Not Daisy Duck, Lori decided. More like Donald's wet dream. Even so, the effect was comical enough that somehow the figure did not seem threatening.

The bill proved amazingly malleable, almost like a human mouth at its front, and helped the creature shape its words. These words, however, came after it stood there for a very long time and just stared at each of them in turn, but particularly at Mavra, to whom the huge black eyes kept coming back.

Finally it said in a deep, throaty feminine voice that seemed to come from somewhere far back in the head, "This is a surprise I hoped for but one that I did not really expect to catch. In fact, I was actually not expecting to catch up with you at all. The net was basically out for Brazil and still is, but you will do nicely. *Very* nicely." That last was said with just enough menace to chill them.

"Who are you?" Mavra asked in as confident a voice as she could muster. "What is this place, and what do you want with us?"

One of the oversized fingers came up and gently stroked under the beak. "Who am I? I am hurt at the question, but I will answer it in due course. *What* I am is a Cloptan. It is not far. Right now you are in an underground laboratory on the border with Lilblod. *It* is in Agon, but above there is something more—ordinary. To get in and out one must go through a tunnel into Lilblod. It solves not only the technical but the *jurisdictional* problems rather nicely. You might have guessed that what is processed and packaged here is not exactly popular among most of the world's governments."

"Drugs," Lori sniffed.

"Yes, drugs. Specifically, two types. One is of little interest to you, but the other is the one you knew was in those containers aboard the ship that brought you to us. It has many names, but in the form we process it here we call it 'rhapsody.' It has different effects on different species. In fact, for a number it is lethal. for others it causes brain and nervous system damage, while to yet others it is simply a tasty spice. When processed into slightly different forms, however, for those races that are similar enough in brain chemistry and share some common enzymes in the cells, it is a drug. A *wonderful* drug, in fact. You take it, and all of your pain goes away. All of your physical pain, if any, and much of your *mental* pain as well. All the bad, negative things, the psychological scars of a lifetime, they all have little effect on you. It's all there, but it can't hurt you. I am told that the initial effects are like nothing else imaginable, but as your body gets used to it, you just sort of settle down into a situation where life is—simpler. The effects last for varying periods, the average being eight to ten hours before it gets down to where you'll need some more—but slowly, very slowly."

"I'm sure you'll spell it out in excruciating detail for us," Mavra commented dryly.

The Cloptan ignored the comment. "First the little aches and pains start returning, then full physical awareness, and looming on the horizon is every single horrible thing in your mind, all your worst fears and nightmares. You can feel them, almost see them coming. Fear turns to desperation, desperation to terror. There is nothing at all you can do. The only way is, of course, to take more rhapsody. Eventually, of course, your system gets used to it, and you level out, becoming more normal on a regular basis and with only one big overriding fear—that the supply will stop and you will face the horrors of your own mind."

"How horrible," Lori muttered. The bitch was enjoying this!

"Even the strongest minds cannot withstand it forever. Some can fight it off for hours, a few for days, but they tell me no one succeeds in breaking it completely. The depression becomes so absolute, you will kill yourself first. It keeps the business—profitable." She walked over and stood right in front of Mavra.

"They say you are possibly immortal, that you cannot be killed. I am not certain I believe that *anyone* can't be killed, but I think it will not make much difference. It *would* be a nice experiment, though, to see just how long you could go without it. If you could not even kill yourself, would your mind crack? What form would the insanity take? I wonder . . . It *is* tempting, but I think I have other plans in the end. Oh, yes, the blood tests say that one form of it will work *quite* nicely on you. Sutton, on the other hand, is sufficiently different from you to require a different formulation, but the science folks say that it will work on him as well."

"For God's sake!" Lori cried. "What do you *want*? What are you *doing* this to us for? We're thousands of miles from home and surely can't be of any use to you here!"

"I should think it would be obvious to you by now," the Cloptan replied. "Because of *this*," she said, gesturing down her body with her hands. "*She* made me like this!" she snapped, pointing to Mavra. "And *you*—you went along, Doctor Lori Sutton. And *you*—*you* became the man! The big macho hunter with his little devoted four-titted bitch! I do this for *revenge*! Venganza! Revenge for daring to drag into hell Juan Alfonso Campos de la Montoya!"

"Oh, God!" Lori sighed, feeling all hope vanish.

"So that's why they wanted only the two of us," Mavra said.

"The Dillians are nothing to me and too large to have handled in any case. What are they going to do? It will take them days just to find their way out of Lilblod. Then what? Report to the authorities? They are already looking for you and would find you now if they could. As for Sutton's crazy little bitch, she, too, was nothing to me and just so much excess baggage. Do not worry, *Doctor* Sutton. The computers here are excellent. We know of the deficiency in your system, and we have the means to fix it. If I had wanted you dead, I would have just had them kill you."

Lori shook his head in wonder, unable to understand this kind of thinking. "What is it with you? I didn't pick this body any more than you picked that one. I'd trade you if I could. There are times I would have *killed* for a shape like that. But look at you! Is it so *awful* being a woman? You're young, probably very pretty by the standards of your race, and in an incredibly short time you've managed to get this far up in the drug trade. Some new start, but I guess it's what you know. I'm broke and helpless in a backward medieval desert, for god's sake!"

"Being a woman is bad enough," Campos responded angrily. "It is *hell* to me! And yes, I am *very* beautiful by Cloptan standards. Do you know how hard it was to adjust to that? To have every lecherous Cloptan man *pawing* you? Do you know what I had to *lower* myself to do to get to this? I do not own this lab, nor do I control it. Finding the Cloptan underworld was not difficult, and they were interested in me because I came from the same business but on a different world. No, getting inside was not difficult, but once there I was just another girl, just another piece of *furniture* to them! *Me!* The son of the greatest patriot of modern Peru, the man who could strike and corrupt and bring down the most evil and powerful oppressor of all Latin peoples with a weapon as simple and impossible to fight as common coca! I had to *defile* myself! To swallow all pride and self-respect and put myself in the *gutter*! I am *nothing* in this organization except a powerful man's current favorite toy! But now, now, it is all worthwhile. Here you are. If I can get the others, too, it will be complete. Brazil and that other bitch. Even if fortune does not smile, however, it has smiled enough. For a while yet we will play games so that I may have the satisfaction to repay my humiliation! Then, when the time is right, *you*, 'goddess of the trees,' will willingly and cheerfully *beg* to let me let you put things right. It may take weeks or months yet, I hope not years, but one day you will put things right for me and repay all the suffering that you have caused! Once you are under the drug's spell, you will willingly tell me anything and everything. If you *are* what some say you are, then one day we will take a trip, just us girls, and you will go inside this world and *put me right!*"

So that was it, Mavra thought. One more horror to endure, one more long torment, but the direction that damned

Machiavellian Well was taking was now clear. It was sad that Lori yet again had been dragged into this. Mavra had mostly wanted to help them. Well, if he stayed alive, maybe someday she still could. There was certainly nothing to be done now. She just wished she'd listened to them and left Juan Campos back on Earth or finished him off. *Damn* her sense of fair play! One could totally change such as him, but he remained as evil as ever. He had already changed more than he knew or wanted to recognize, judging from what he'd done as a female and even how she now spoke and moved. But the Well did nothing to change that inner self, and Juan Campos had been an insane, evil, power-mad egomaniac in his former life, and the new persona had done nothing to change that but had reinforced it.

Sooner or later, though, no matter what was to come, she'd be taken to the Well. There was no question that such a sophisticated operation could get the truth out of her. It could only be hoped that Campos was so insane she believed that inside the Well, in a Markovian body, she could still dictate to Mavra Chang.

Campos stood back and looked at both of them with satisfaction. "Do the shackles hurt? Well, soon you will be free of them, I promise. And the medical teams here, freed of such stupidities as government oversight and ethical colleagues, can do absolute *wonders.* Even though you are one of the most wanted people on this planet, these people specialize in making wanted fugitives unrecognizable, although in most cases they do not have the level of freedom they have in *your* case. You, Sutton, might be quite useful as a courier once we give you some motivation for making appointments on time. But not *you,* 'goddess.' You are *mine.* From you they will carve a work of art. *Then,* as my *dear* boyfriend Giquazo, who I will definitely kill someday, promised, you will go home with me. You will be my pet, my toy. Oh, we will have a *fun* time, I promise you!"

Mavra's heart sank as one of her bitterest Well World memories surfaced: living all those years with those donkeylike legs, always looking down . . .

But she had survived that and worse, and she would survive this for as long as it took, until opportunity knocked. And if Nathan was having the same kind of luck, she might yet be first to the Well.

"Some technicians will be in shortly to inaugurate you both into our widening family," Campos told them. "I go first to speak with those who will see you next, and then I will see you once more before leaving. But do not worry, my little goddess. I shall be back for you." With that, the Cloptan turned and left the room.

"I think I *would* rather die than go through this," Lori told Mavra.

"Don't! *Never* give up! She's too insane to have them mutilate me so much that I won't be able to speak to her and she to me. To that type, life is all about power. Everything else—drugs, money, you name it—is to gain power. That's what she really hates about being female now. She's lost power, and I'm the only way for her to get it back. There are only two more hexes after Clopta to the equator and an avenue in. So long as Brazil isn't also caught and trapped, he's as much a threat to Campos as to me. If I can just convince her, no matter what I look like, to get me to the Well before Brazil, we win. Stay alive. Even now, hope's not gone."

Lori very much wanted to believe that.

Juan Campos, or Wahna as her name was pronounced by the Cloptan tongue, made her way through the labyrinthine underground complex to the medical section. There she met with Nuoak, a giant creature resembling a huge brown-furred slug with countless long, tiny tendrils that in combination could perform the most delicate operations, and Drinh, an Agonite resembling a human-sized shell-less turtle with long powerful hands and fingers.

"They are yours any time you want them," she told the medics. "Now that you have their scans, have you decided what you will do?"

"Well, the Erdomite is not difficult," Drinh commented.

"He must be castrated!" *Like I was* . . . "But he must not die! I wish him to work for us, becoming what he most fears and helping, even promoting our own interest which he hates so much! And the rest of what I asked as well, so he will always be reminded of me."

"We have not had either of these species before, but they seem to represent no serious challenges. We believe that we can adapt your Erdomite to become a courier for us over possibly difficult terrain. We have noted the lack of proper clotting factor in his blood, but the gland that aids in its production is merely immature, not missing, and so that problem is easily dealt with. Do not worry. He shall be fit to do only what is useful to us, and all that you request be done to him will be a part of it."

"Perfect! Do it! But what about the other? *That* one requires *very* special treatment."

"There's not as much to work with," the master surgeon noted. "Still, the small size and lack of major features and your own requirements make it obvious that the best way to ensure that no one who ever knew her or saw her picture recognizes her is to create from her an animal. It can be a unique animal, since with the countless varieties of the Well World there is nobody who knows them all or will question a convincing appearance. *This* is what we came up with after much study." He pushed a few buttons on a console, and a hologram of a figure appeared.

Campos laughed in delight. "Oh, that is *wonderful!* Perfect! But—can you *do* such a radical thing?"

"It's not as radical as it looks. Mostly a matter of adding a lot of fatty body mass, moving the knees, implanting the natural feathers, that sort of thing. Then reinforcing it with a *pictin*—an artificial virus tailor-made to her and her alone. It will methodically go from cell to cell and manipulate the stock DNA chains that will make the change permanent. Internally there's not much changed, so she'll still have to eat what she normally would and such, you understand."

"That is all right. Appearance is everything. *Delicious!*

And her speaking? She must be able to speak to me, and I to her, but with limits."

"Much simpler. We will simply remove her translator and replace it with a synthetic one. As you may or may not know, we've never successfully created a translator crystal, but we do have ones that are very limited. We can tune this one not only to one language but to the specific harmonics of your translator. When she speaks, it will be instantly translated into a preset, encoded binary sequence which can be received and decoded only by your translator. To anyone else it will sound like meaningless squawks and screeches. Similarly, since that code will be fed to your translator alone, she will understand you as if you were speaking normally no matter what language you use, while all other speech will be picked up by her translator, which will overload trying to decode what isn't there and produce meaningless random sounds. No one but you will even think that she is a sentient being. Is that satisfactory, madame?"

"*Perfect.*" Juan Campos sighed. "How long will it be before I can bring her home?"

"Not long. Two, three weeks tops."

"*Do* it, then. Do it as quickly as you can, but do it *right.*"

The Erdomese constitution handled the drug a bit differently but just as effectively from the point of view of the dealers. There was not any massive high but rather a continuous feeling of being just a bit isolated from reality, a "slight buzz" as Lori thought of it. It was when it was withdrawn that its full power and potency revealed' itself; the pain, the horrors, the hallucinations were beyond anyone's endurance. He knew he could not exist without the drug but was not so insulated that he did not hate them for doing it to him. That, and the way they treated him, half the time as some sort of interesting lab specimen and the other half as no better than a slave, he thought, the worst possible existence imaginable.

But that was before he met the duo he began thinking of

as Mengele Turtle and Frankenstein's Slug. He knew by
their detached and clinical discussions that they were going
to do something more to him, something awful, but he had
no way of knowing what.

Then, shortly afterward, the keepers came for him and
gave him an injection, and he remembered no more.

The first realization that he was waking up from a sus-
tained anesthetic-induced sleep was an awareness that he
was on all fours. *That* was odd; Erdomese men were *never*
on all fours. He opened his eyes, but they refused to focus
very well, as if still mostly asleep, but he reached out and
tried to stand—and found that he could not.

His first thought was that they'd taken his fingers, and
then he managed to put his head down close to his arms
and saw hooves.

Not even the kind of hooves Alowi had—real hooves,
like on his feet.

But his feet, too, were on the floor. How could that be
without him being at an angle or on his knees? It was as
if his legs had been shortened and his hips turned so that
he was now a four-legged, four-hoofed beast a mere three
and a half feet off the ground!

With a sinking feeling he realized that it was exactly
what they had done. He still had his tail, but it was down
and dragged on the floor, trailing between his—hind legs.

And with less shock than he might have thought, he realized that the tail was the *only* thing between those legs. In
far too short a time he had gone from female to male to—
nothing. There weren't even any internal muscles there to
feel or flex.

You didn't have to go to med school to figure out Campos, did you?

Still, even with blurry vision, he could see that there was
something in back of his—well, forelegs. He not only could
see the shapes in a somewhat blurry way, he could *feel* the
dead weight hanging down.

Breasts? Four breasts on a eunuch? What on earth for?
Particularly such a large and heavy set, which cleared the

floor only by several inches. Sensing something else, a wrongness, he flexed his back a bit so that they did touch the floor, then straightened again. If they had nipples, there was no sensation in them.

He wondered why he hadn't bled to death during their butchery and then realized what the breasts really were. Not just more Campos humor—they had placed in him, or activated by hormones, the internal engine of the female, the healing factors. No nipples, because whatever function they served they did so for his benefit, and he was one of a kind.

The neck was very long and supple. He could look forward or down, although his vision seemed to be limited to about two feet clearly, three before almost everything was lost. Still, he could see very close, and it almost looked to him as if he had some sort of muzzle on, as if he could see part of his nose and jaw.

Then the door opened, and he smelled Mengele Turtle enter. The doctor—if that was what he could be called—began making a lot of very stupid silly noises at him, until finally he heard, "One . . . two . . . three. Ah! I see you can hear me now! Very good! We, of course, removed your translator, among, ah, other things. It has been replaced with an artificial device that interpolates speech both in and out. You can speak, but to be understood you will have to be heard by someone with the same sort of device set to the same frequency. Similarly, you must hear something through the same conditions to understand it. Otherwise, even your native tongue will sound like nothing more than a noise pattern. It is quite useful for couriers such as you will be trained to become. It can't be removed or bypassed without causing permanent damage to the speech centers of the brain, and it can be reset to any frequency we choose or even reprogrammed with a whole new code by remote control. You see how handy that is. You can convey the most sensitive message, but only one who has both the device and your code and frequency can retrieve it. You, on the other hand, sound like an animal making random noises. If anyone attempts to play random sequences and hits it but does not give the code header, it erases, cutting you off completely. Absolutely secure."

"Very clever," he admitted sourly. "But what sort of courier would *this* body make? And what makes you so sure that I'll transfer the right information?"

"Well, you will be trained, of course, both in the uses of the body and in courier technique. You will be used locally, basically between Agon and Clopta through Lilblod. The system itself is simple. There is a specific version of the drug you are on. To survive, you will have to make your assignations, for only they will have it. If any of them find out later that you gave false or incorrect or even incomplete information, they will notify someone and they might well forget your dose. As for finding your way, it will take practice, but you will find that your senses of smell and hearing are incredibly acute. You will learn to follow days-old scents and interpret a vast number of sounds. As most of your route will be through dense forest at night, sight is of little use anyway. The drug will motivate you and ease your pain and exhaustion. Your digestive system can handle most of the ground-level plants of Lilblod. Save for an insignificant amount of the drug you need, you are, shall we say, cost-free and maintenance-free labor."

"Yeah, well these breasts are going to cause no end of trouble in the woods."

"They are tough, and you will get used to them. In addition to supplying your absent clotting factor, they can carry enough food in the form of fat and water to allow you, if need be, to exist for a week or more eating and drinking nothing, so if something happens and you fall behind, you can skip food and water to make up time. You also have a small pouch of which I'm quite proud. It will hold small microencoded materials and even carry the receiving code and frequency for you. It will, however, dissolve such material in gastric juices if you are very late getting your dosage. Withdrawal, in other words, triggers it, so even if you are captured, nothing will be learned."

"You must have studied hard to think up things like this."

The doctor ignored the comment. "Food and drink will be necessities, but they consist of raw leaves and grasses and water—only water will really do—and they'll taste pretty much like what they are. Anything else will make you sick. You won't have much in the way of conversations or companionship, obviously, and you are as asexual as a machine. We were able to locate and neutralize the actual sexual center in your brain. You can't have sex, do not and will not want it, won't even fantasize about it; indeed, if we've done it properly, you won't even be able to figure out why you or anyone else liked it in the first place. It boils down to this: The only thing, the absolute *only* thing that can and will stimulate your pleasure center is our little cube. Over time, as brain and body adjust, it will become your sole reason for existence and our sole expense. Perfect, are you not?"

"Yeah. Perfect." *Drug or not, I'll kill myself at the first opportunity rather than live like that.*

He seemed to anticipate the thought, "If you think of suicide, be sure you do it, because otherwise we'll give you no cube at all for one full cycle . . ."

That was too much. He knew he'd never go through with it, *couldn't* kill himself with *that* kind of threat.

They had won. All this way and the bad guys had won!

For the other captive it was possibly even worse.

At one time or another Mavra Chang had been put on or tried an enormous number of drugs, but nothing like rhapsody. Within minutes it seemed as if every pleasure center in her brain and body exploded in continuous delight while all else, *everything* else, faded into total insignificance. She knew she was still chained to the wall, but it just didn't seem important, nor did it when they released her and she dropped to the floor. Everything, every touch, every move, was a new delight.

She was aware of others, of being asked questions and

answering them, but it was of so little consequence, she didn't even remember the specifics of the conversations. Darkness, light, colors, sounds, creatures moving around, all had their wonders and delights. She was being poked and probed and moved here and there, but none of it really *mattered* to her.

It was hard to say how long this lasted, but the coming down was very, very slow. Awareness outside of herself returned in dribs and drabs, shapes and creatures took on more realistic appearances, and things began to seem more logical. Even so, she remained high and knew she was, able to function but still somewhat bathed in a nice, soft, comfortable cocoon. Things being done seemed peculiar or even hilarious but caused no alarm.

By the time real rationality had returned and there was just a glow and slight lack of coordination, they had put her in a small padded cell. Her feet were free, but her hands were cuffed behind her back. Overcome at that point with a seemingly insatiable hunger and thirst, she found a pot of some cold liquid and three very large varicolored loaves of different things, what she couldn't guess. The urge to eat and drink was just irresistible, even if she had to do it on her knees or prone, biting into the loaves as best she could and manipulating the container of liquid with only her mouth and neck. It tasted sweet and heavy with a kind of creamy aftertaste, something like buttermilk, and she managed to drink most of it while spilling only about a quarter, and that she found herself lapping up with her tongue. She had left nothing when she was done.

She now felt sleepy but tried to shake it off and think. That rhapsody was the most dangerous drug she'd seen since sponge. In fact, it might be an ancestor of just that for all she knew. She *did* know that she would be mentally incapable of turning it down if it were offered again, and that brought forth the first and primary fear. They *had* to give more to her! Nothing, absolutely nothing was of more importance to her than that. She'd kill her own friends and betray any trust to get it.

She knew she was hooked, on the line completely, but as much as she hated the thought and those who'd done it to her, she knew they'd accomplished what they had set out to do.

Why keep me locked up and shackled like this? There is no way I can leave this place. Not now.

But she was a new species for them, she realized, and they couldn't be sure of her compliance or even positive that they'd gotten the dosage right. And they were probably scared of her, scared of the rumors about her possible powers. They would make very sure.

Within a few more hours she was in tears, hysterically banging her head against the padded door and begging, pleading, promising anything if they would just give her more and stop the torment. She hated them, hated their cold, callous way of treating her in this, hated Campos for what she'd done to her, hated herself for being so damned vulnerable, but it was horrible, awful . . . Far worse than heroin, which she'd managed to kick more than once. But the withdrawal pains hadn't been nearly at this level. The waking nightmares, the hallucinations of every horror she'd ever lived through, the onrush of all the fear and pain she had ever endured . . .

She was descending into madness with the speed of a spaceliner when they'd finally come and given her some more. Within a minute, maybe two, it was all receding, all going away, things were wonderful once more . . .

After several cycles, as her system became accustomed to having the drug in it, they were ready for the next phase.

She was put under for the bulk of it. She had almost no memories of it or who did it or where or how long it took or how the hell they did it at all. Nor was there any real sense of how much time had passed, only that it had. By the time she was able once again to awaken and move about on her own, it was done.

She felt—odd—beyond the high and knew that Campos had accomplished her total threat. They had done something to her. Something major. It was only a question of what.

She had no feeling at all in her arms. They'd never let her use her arms or hands, not since the beginning, and so it wasn't totally surprising, but it bothered her. She was walking oddly, too, as if she couldn't bend her legs. *Nothing* felt right.

She was in a small but ordinary room furnished only with a thick pillow, but one wall seemed extra polished and she made her way laboriously over to it. Then, seeing the ghostly reflection, she looked down at herself to confirm the worst.

She was almost completely covered in feathers. Tiny little feathers that made a second skin, feathers of bright colors: gold and emerald and crimson and deep, rich blue, making intricate random designs. She couldn't feel her arms because she no longer had arms, or shoulders, for that matter. Somehow they'd managed to transplant some of the muscle tissue, though, because she still had breasts, fattier and larger than before and also feathered right down to the nipples.

But for those she was shaped pretty much like a turnip. She had a large, rotund, feathered stomach and rear end, and they'd widened her hips. That had been done as much for balance as for design, since they'd taken her knee joints and placed them just below those widened hips, as if the upper calves and thighs had been turned upside down, and these terminated in a pair of very wide leathery feet that were more like pads with a flat extension both forward and rear. She did not walk so much as slowly *waddle*. It would take some practice, and she wasn't sure how she'd get up again if she fell over.

She had to get very close to the reflection to see her face. They'd done something to the skin to make it look very dark brown and leathery, extending her nose until it was virtually a hawk-nosed bill of the same consistency as the face. They'd brought in the mouth to almost a pucker and replaced the lips with a short curved birdlike bill. Only the eyes seemed familiar, but even there they'd done something, or maybe it was the drug. She saw quite well but only to maybe one and a half, two meters. After that everything was a blur, even in the small room.

They've made me into a human owl, she thought, more in shock than in disgust. In fact, while the overall effect was somewhat comical in the same way a penguin was comical, the combination of colors and the fluidity of the design were quite attractive. It was also true that she could appear like this in public and no one, not Lori, not the Dillians, not even Brazil, would recognize her.

It was also true that she was now more helpless and more dependent than a captive songbird with clipped wings. She could waddle, first one side forward, then the other, like a penguin, but not very far or very fast. Climbing or getting her own food was out of the question. She might manage a little something with her head and mouth—beak—but not a lot. She was totally defenseless. She couldn't run, fly, or grab or use a weapon or tool, and even her bright colors were a problem, making concealment difficult. That was if the enemy came within two meters so she could see it.

Even her hearing seemed off. True, they'd recessed the ears into the head and covered them with feathers so it appeared she had none, but even so, she thought it odd that all she heard from the corridor outside were what sounded like snorts, clicks, and silly noises.

She suddenly felt foolish. That drug *did* make one stupider, she thought. Of *course* they would have removed the translator. Did they do more? She opened her mouth and called "Hey, out there! Shut up!" but the only thing that came out was a series of awful-sounding squawks. They'd altered her vocal chords or replaced them. And she couldn't even form words with her lips. Not with this rigid beak.

Helpless, dependent, no ability to talk or understand, no way to form words silently or use sign language . . . they'd really cut her off. To literally everyone else, even those she knew and who knew her—save only the ones who had done this with masterful skill and a technology far beyond expectation, and Campos, of course—she'd be seen as—she *was*—the world's first exotic animal junkie.

Well, she'd kept Campos around, a captive, drugged and hauled about through the jungle, and had wound up making him into the world's sexiest duck creature. Now Campos had in her own twisted mind attained the perfect revenge.

What was odd was how she was taking it. She herself noticed this, but only as a curiosity, not because it really bothered her. She just *accepted* it fatalistically as something that was. She knew it was the drug, placing a soft, pleasant haze between herself and reality, but she did not want that haze to disappear. So long as it was there, she could accept almost anything. It was her only friend, her only protector.

Still, there was the practical, pragmatic need to get used to it. She waddled over in the direction of the door, blurry though it was, and the usual food cakes and drink were there. Although a little nervous about it, she discovered that they'd set the balance and center of gravity exactly right. These doctors were geniuses with the souls of monsters. She could bend completely forward on those knee joints, and the bill, serrated a bit, was perfect to break into the loaves and get pieces she could mush and break up inside her mouth proper and swallow without difficulty by raising her head a bit while keeping bent over. Drinking was harder to master and amounted to using the tongue or a back part of her mouth to get some suction through the tiny bill if it was immersed, but it, too, was manageable.

The only real problem was with the breasts, which amounted to dead weight tumbling down when she bent over and which, with no arms and true shoulder muscles to stabilize them, went every which way, pulling on her neck and throwing her slightly off balance. She'd never had large breasts as a human, and they could well have dispensed with them as they did with other parts of her, but instead they'd enlarged them and created a problem. More of

Campos's revenge, she understood. She would learn to live with them with practice, she decided.

A technician or guard or whatever who looked like an underdressed turtle gave her the drug regularly, in the form of a solid soft cube. It was far slower to take effect when eaten, but the creature was never late with it. Campos, she worried, might not be so punctual.

And finally the Cloptan came for her. Campos seemed absolutely enthralled by the redesign, and Mavra was again taken aback to discover that thanks to the legs, she was now even shorter, no more than a meter or so tall. She had always been small and mostly looked up to see other faces, but this meant craning her neck.

"Oh, but this is *so* excellent!" Campos gushed. "Revenge is seldom so perfect! Can you understand me?"

To her surprise, Mavra *could*. "Yes, I can."

"Wonderful! You see, the little device inside you is tuned *only* to me. It even blocks out other people's translators from your mind. And what it transmits, only *I* have been given the ability to translate and understand. And all I have to do is *think* about it and I can turn it off, or on, at will. So you will communicate, and understand, only to me and when I wish. What you send is a computer code that sounds to all others like the noise of a bird. You will truly be my pet, and you will *act* like it. You will guard me and protect me at all costs if you can, and the rest of the time you will be a nice little trained birdie and do *everything* I say, because *I* and I alone have those nice little red cubes. You will exist to please me and never to displease me, now, won't you?"

"Yes," she replied resignedly.

"Oh, no! We begin right here. It will from now on be 'Yes, *master.*' Not even 'mistress,' not 'madame.' *Master.* Understand?"

"Yes—master."

"And you can spend your time thinking of ways to sing my praises. How beautiful I am, how intelligent, how simply *wonderful* I am. You will spend your time thinking of new ways to praise, flatter, *worship* me as your one and only god, and you will do it with *conviction,* with *enthusiasm*; you will *convince* me that you believe it. And in the same breaths you will do the opposite to yourself. Remind me and yourself how low you are, how dependent, how miserable and undeserving a creature you are and how lucky you are to be my property, and you will say *those* things, too, with the same fervor. And any time I find either part unconvincing, I might just forget your little cube for a while. Maybe a very *long* while, until you are totally believable. *Understand?*"

One pang of true abject fear pierced the insulating haze. "*Yes,* my most wonderful master, from whose great kindness all blessings flow. Please forgive this most miserable of helpless wretches who is nothing without you!"

Campos smiled. "It is a start. We shall have many, many long conversations together, and all of them, even the ones that matter, will be partially tests. Practice it in your mind. You will come to believe that what you say is true so that it becomes second nature to use it. Now, come. I have a travel cage for you, and we must catch the return steamer for Buckgrud, the city where I live in Clopta. There, in my flat, I have a nice little place provided for you."

"As you command, most powerful and magnificent master."

The worst part of it was, the words weren't even sticking in her throat.

Still, now would begin the trial, until one day Campos would decide for whatever reason that she'd had enough or wanted more. Then Mavra would be the only means by which Campos could have her revenge on just about everything and everybody she hated, and that was almost the entire universe now. The Cloptan had already thought ahead on this; that was why they could still speak to one another, and she was conditioning her "pet" to think like an obedient slave to ensure complete control. Otherwise, when Juan Campos had the burning desire to get her hands on the Well World controls, how could she make Mavra let her do it?

The worst part was, as she was, Mavra didn't even care.

Lilblod

"You separated me from my husband! I will *kill* you for that!"

"Now, calm down, I tell you," Zitz soothed. "There was nothing I could do. They'd have killed you anyway if you made a fuss."

"They might as well have killed us both!" Alowi cried. "My husband cannot *survive* without me!"

"Nothing to do with love, I'm afraid," Tony explained. "She produces something inside her that heals his injuries. We've seen it in action."

"Well, it's done, and that's that. I can't even give you a clue as to where they took 'em. I don't know nothin' about the land part of this, and I don't wanna know. I'll tell you, though, that either we did what they said or they'd have took 'em anyways and blown *all* of us out of the water the moment we dropped the load. Blown all three of you away as it was. Think we liked it? We're gonna lose a *fortune* because we gotta give back them stolen jewels! And it'd have been easier for us to just knock all three of you off and dump you in the ocean. We're droppin' you here instead. That over there's Lilblod. It's not a real nice place, but you take care and keep to the trails and keep your nose out of where it don't belong and you'll make it. About fifty kilometers north is Clopta, a high-tech coastal hex where you can get a ride into a Zone Gate and a quick pass back home. South maybe sixty, seventy kilometers is Agon, same deal. Don't think you can go down there and stir up stuff and find them. They probably never made shore there. Got picked up by some other ship and are maybe anywhere or heading anywheres else by now. Go home. It's over."

"Come, come dear!" Anne Marie said sympathetically. "Let's get off this terrible ship first and be on our own. *Then* we can decide what to do next."

With neither the Dillians nor Alowi having a translator, it was up to Zitz to interject.

There was no purpose now to further protests, and Alowi nodded and tried to calm down. "All right," *But I will feed the name of this accursed ship and all of its crew to my people back in Erdom. Such an assault on our honor cannot go unavenged.*

"This *is* going to be a problem, though," Tony commented. "We really can't speak to or understand her, nor she us."

"Sister, if she's nuts enough to go off tramping in that crazy forest by herself, let her," Zitz responded. "You won't find much with a translator in *there*, but it's easy in either Clopta or Agon. Just get everybody out, huh?" He turned to Alowi.

"Okay, lady, here's the way it is. They're gonna head for one or another of these places where you can get home and they'll take you. Maybe you can't talk to each other, but you'll make do. You ain't cut out to be an avenger. You just ain't built for it. Relax. Take it easy. Tell the authorities if you want to once you get there. It's no big deal to us. But one way or another you're gettin' off this ship as soon as we get in a little more. Either you *get* off with all your gear or we shoot you and shove you off and keep it. Your choice."

"We'll go, curse your black heart," Anne Marie responded acidly.

"Oh, yeah, one more thing," the Zhonzhorpian said. "You *can* report this and this ship, but remember that all three of you are wanted in Gekir for jewel theft. And even though they'll still check it out, we'll show that this ship, under an alternative name and registry, was thousands of kilometers away at the time. You're out of your league here. Forget it. You won't find them—hell, the authorities couldn't anyway, could they, or you wouldn'ta been aboard in the first place. All you'll do by stirring up trouble is to make sure you all get sent back to Gekir, where you'll be blinded and sent out for life to work in the salt mines until you die. *Nobody* wins on this one. Sometimes it happens."

It wasn't much of an answer, but it was a collection of hard truths that was impossible to ignore.

The *Star Runner* came close enough to the shore to scrape bottom, and that was as far as it dared. Anne Marie picked up the sobbing Alowi and put her on Tony's back, where she clung as hard as she could, and Anne Marie hefted the saddlebags and packs, and they jumped the short distance from the rails down into the water and quickly struck mud. It was a little tough to get some footing, but finally both of them managed to force their way up and onto the shore, Alowi still clinging to Tony's back, looking wet and disheveled but otherwise none the worse for the wear.

It was very dark and very quiet on the shore; there were no lights to be seen anywhere.

"*Now* what?" Anne Marie asked, trying to see something other than forbidding swampy forest in the thick gloom of the night.

"We camp as soon as we can find a dry place, of course," Tony responded. "We still have some matches in a waterproof container, and we might try a fire, if only to scare away anything unwelcome. When we get some light, we'll see about finding a road."

"Which way?"

"It really doesn't matter, does it? I should think, though, if we have any real chance of tracing them, it should be south. At least they'll have communications, possibly enough to get word to the embassy in Zone. Then we might be able to arrange to get this poor girl home and maybe be out of this and home ourselves. I've had quite enough of discomfort and double crosses. We did our duty as best we could. Now we deserve a chance to live our own lives."

"Duty! *Bah!*" Anne Marie almost spit. "This poor dear won't go home willingly. She'll try to find her husband, even if that's impossible, because it's *her* duty and because she's in love. You heard what they said about that dreadful culture. She'd be married off to some old bum she didn't know and die of a broken heart!"

"Anne Marie, this is not a romance novel."

"Tony Guzman! What in the *world* has gotten into you? It's not like we are innocent bystanders in all this! Nor entirely without some responsibility, too, simply because we weren't all that honest with them, either."

"We didn't *ask* to go along on this adventure!" Tony argued. "We were *drafted!*"

"Nonsense! That nice young man from the Zone embassy came along and *asked* us to do it. To go and link up with this Mavra Chang and find out as much as we could. And we found out a great deal, I think! We were also to get off a report to the ambassador if they lost track of the party. Thank *goodness* we didn't have to do *that*. I would have felt just *dreadful* about it!"

"But it's *over*, Anne Marie! *We're* the party now. The only satisfaction we might have is rubbing it in that smug drug runner's face after he discovers we were not fugitives but shadows."

"Spies, you mean. Spies for our government."

Tony sighed. "Anne Marie, spies are professionals. Espionage is a highly regarded art. We were rank amateurs dropped into a situation where we might have been hurt or killed by a government that wouldn't have really cared, and now we got out with our lives and whole skins. I don't *want* to be blinded or crippled. Not again. Now we have a second chance. I want to go home before something *does* happen. We were very nearly killed back there, you know. Anne Marie, we're sixteen years old again, only this time we're sexy blond bombshells that had the men of Dillia already making fools of themselves around us. I've *been* on that side. I want to find out if it's any more fun on *this* side."

"Well, then, you go home," she told the other centauress. "I suppose I should have seen it coming long before this, but I didn't want to. You've *had* a good life. You were handsome, from a well-to-do and well-connected family, skilled, educated, a pilot and world traveler. I never did *any* of those things. I couldn't. I was homely and plain and stuck mostly in a broken body. I made the best of it, but it wasn't fun, let me tell you! Your coming along, your love, was the one truly wonderful thing that happened to me. I shall always cherish it, and I shall always love that inner part of you, but surely you must have known from the moment we woke up like *this* that it could never be again. In a sense, this is our afterlife, mortal though we remain, goodness knows. I faced it more and more as we went on this trip. I shall always love that memory of you, and I shall continue to love you, but as a sister. This is after the 'death do us part' as surely as if we'd done away with ourselves, and you know it if you'd just face it."

Tony laughed.

"What's so amusing? I'm deadly serious."

"Anne Marie, I've rehearsed almost that identical speech a thousand times in my mind, and up to now I never had the nerve to give it. I was afraid of *hurting* you. And I thought we shared one another's thoughts to a degree!"

Anne Marie laughed in return, then finally said, "I guess not. I suppose it's what we thought we would think if the situations were reversed or some such. Or, since we actually *were* thinking the same, maybe it's true. Maybe we just didn't believe we were." She sighed. "Well, then, I guess this is what we'd call a divorce by mutual consent. Who would have *dreamed* we two would ever say those words?"

"We'll always be closer than any other two women of our race," Tony noted, taking her hand and squeezing it. "But no matter that we see each other in a living mirror, we are two different people who will lead at least slightly different lives."

"Agreed. And if you want to go back and have all those silly fools swoon over you, be my guest. I suppose, if all else comes out in the end, I'll wind up doing it, too, but I'm not so eager to start as you."

"Anne Marie! What can you *do*? It is like the man said—it is *over* for us!"

"For you. Go on, I understand completely. But I know how skin-deep those lusting fools are, and they certainly weren't there when I needed them, going off chasing some—some dumb blond like you. I'm having *fun*, dear! For the first time in my life I'm *living* it instead of watching life go by! I very much *hope* that I'll come through in one piece, but, in the end it really doesn't matter to me. Perhaps it was because I was so devoted, to charities, to the unfortunate, to you. Perhaps it's just divine grace. But God gave me, at the end of my half life, a chance to live a *full* one, at least for a little bit. I shall probably give up in disgust and go home after a few days, but if there is *anything* perhaps I can do, if there's just one little thing I can add, I'll stick it out." She looked around at Alowi. "Oh my! The poor dear's cried herself to sleep!"

"Exhausted, probably. She's been throwing a tantrum for three days now."

"We should stop chattering and build that fire, then."

The next day proved tough going through the thick and ancient trees of Lilblod, but with no sign of who or what was the dominant race there or why they were feared.

Still, before midday they reached a road that, while direct, seemed very well traveled by the depth of the wheel grooves and the marks of all sorts of feet in the clay.

"Runs pretty much straight, northwest to southeast," Tony noted. "I guess this is the main highway to civilization. He said that place—Clopta or some such—was closest, which would mean we might well make it at a trot before dark."

Anne Marie raised an eyebrow. "But Agon is where they took the pair of them. If nothing ate us last night except the bugs—goodness! I itch all over!—then I doubt if anything will eat me if I spend one more night by this road. Give me the poor little darling and we'll head south."

Tony stared at her. "So this is it? Already?"

"I suppose so. It had to come sometime. It might jolly well be now." She gestured with her arms to Alowi to get off Tony and climb up somewhere on her back.

After a few moments' confusion Alowi figured it out enough to act, slid off, and managed, with a little help from Anne Marie, to get up on the other twin.

"Good-bye, Tony," said Anne Marie. "I'll see you in a few weeks, I suppose, unless we have a lot more luck than we have had in this matter so far." And without another word she started off southwest, toward Agon, at a brisk trot.

Tony stood there and watched her go until she was almost out of sight, then muttered, "Oh, hell," and trotted off southwest after them.

Just Off the Crab Nebula

THE KRAANG WAS NOT AT ALL PLEASED. WHAT HAD LOOKED from the start to be a fairly straightforward affair had now turned into a series of Gordian knots that threatened all its plans.

Nathan Brazil, happily and stupidly diverted making flower garlands for his girlfriend on a desert island well removed from the action, was nicely out of the game, although the Kraang understood the Well sufficiently to know that this would not, could not be allowed to become a permanent condition. Still, thanks to a race playing with powers it was not capable of handling or comprehending, the first job had been accomplished.

The Watcher had been diverted from the Well.

That should have provided more than enough time for the other to reach it first, but instead that mad, sick interloper had captured her and placed her in a situation where she, too, was no longer in control of events but which, instead of representing the Kraang's interests, now threatened to do horrible, irrecoverable harm.

Not that the Kraang didn't have a grudging admiration for Campos. If the vengeful cutthroat succeeded in destroying Mavra Chang's last vestiges of ego and will, she would open the entrance for him but be unable or unwilling to interface with the master control center. That would leave Campos free to roam those vast corridors unhindered, and after realizing that he could not comprehend, much less activate anything inside, he might well do terrible harm in his inevitable rage. Once he was inside its bowels, the Well would be helpless to control events concerning its own welfare.

And because she could still draw on the Well database to the limits of that primitive ape brain, she might even be able to tell him how to do some simple things that even so limited a creature could manage.

Probability was too complex to allow that. As a tiny stone in a pond made great ripples, even a very minute alteration of the basic matrix might, just might, create a series of alternatives that would take the whole universe into uncharted and unpredictable realms. Without one capable of handling and manipulating such power, like the Kraang itself, the results could be disastrous.

Even the Watcher, whom the Well would undoubtedly summon with great urgency if such a thing occurred, might not be able to fully straighten things out.

And yet without Mavra Chang to open the way, the Kraang could not reach those controls itself.

Why hadn't they simply hibernated, as the Kraang had, until they were needed? What could possibly be gained by a Watcher, or even two, living out meaningless lives on some distant dirt ball until rather crudely summoned in time of need?

Perhaps, it reflected, the judgment of eons had been wrong, after all. It had always thought of the Others as wrongheaded and foolish, but until now their competency had not been called into question.

Something would have to be done, and quickly. It was not used to thinking in such terms, but this was clearly not the time to ponder but to act.

But how?

Accessing Chang or even Brazil was out. It had managed a brief access while she was in transition, but once on the Well World, access to either her or Brazil was blocked. As for the rest, so far they were accessible only as viewers, strictly one-way communication. They were neither mentally strong enough to be used nor tied into the Well matrix.

There had to be *some* way, somehow, to break this apart, to create a flood from the logjam. Options had to be weighed, possibilities explored if they existed, and risks taken, even if it used up precious energy it could ill afford to squander if things didn't go just exactly right.

It was a question of divine intervention in a situation where there was no god.

More than ever, though, it was convinced that it was right, that it had been right all along.

This universe required a god and was instead stuck with two incompetent repair technicians.

There *had* to be a way. There had to be *something* that could be done.

But after four billion years of meaningless existence driving to and fro among the stars, finding even vast blocks of time meaningless, it wasn't used to thinking that time, any time, was quickly running out.

Coming to bookstores everywhere in October 1994, the stunning conclusion to the Watchers at the Well trilogy:

GODS
OF THE WELL
OF SOULS
by Jack L. Chalker

In the dramatic conclusion, readers will finally learn the truth about Nathan Brazil—and Nathan Brazil will discover a truth that has eluded him for millennia . . .

Read on for the exciting opening pages of
GODS OF THE WELL OF SOULS . . .

Published in trade paperback
by Del Rey Books.

Between Galaxies, Heading Toward Andromeda

THE KRAANG HAD BEEN WONDERING MUCH THE SAME THING. The limitations placed on it still prevented it from direct contact with beings on the Well World unless, thanks to the happy accident that allowed it net access, someone was in the transitional stage, totally energy within the net in midtransmission. Otherwise it was strictly read only, and that was proving less amusing now than frustrating.

Monitoring the lives and thoughts of these beings had reawakened in the Kraang a feeling it had thought long dead, a taste of what it was to be *alive* again. It wanted that now more than anything; the lust for it was cracking its heretofore absolute self-control, bringing back longings that it had believed it had long outgrown.

The Well perceived no threat to itself or its master program; it only desired that what it considered an anomaly—the relinking, however tenuous, of the Kraang to the net—be rectified. A simple matter, really, for anyone capable of plugging into the net; not even seconds to find, comprehend, and repair, cutting the Kraang off once more from the system. Brazil was the threat—he'd been there many times, been changed into the master form, and would hardly even think twice about it. He'd do whatever the damned Well said and be done with it, and he would understand the threat sufficiently to be impervious to the Kraang's entreaties and offers. There was nothing Brazil really wanted except, perhaps, oblivion, and the Kraang wasn't so certain that the captain would really take it if it were offered in any event. Brazil was so damned . . . *responsible*. Duty above all.

No, if the Kraang were to effect a return, it would be Mavra Chang. Human, inexperienced, self-involved, and unencumbered by any sense of duty or mission. Mavra Chang would listen before she acted and believe what she wanted to believe. She was certainly tough, no pushover, but she was far too—*human*—to blindly obey the dictates of an ancient race she neither knew nor understood. According to the data, she'd been close to being a goddess before, going from world to world, taking many forms, playing both explorer and missionary to the misbegotten.

The Kraang could deal very comfortably with an activist.

Brazil was at the moment romping in mindless joy with that silly girl on that speck of land in the ocean, but the Well would never leave him there. If Mavra Chang's progress to the Well had been stopped, then Brazil would again get the nomination and be forced to accept. The longer there was no movement or probability of movement by Chang, who was by far closer to the Well gate than Brazil, the more likely the Well would be forced to make the switch. The others would never find her, and it would be all the worse if they somehow did track down Campos but never recognized Chang in her current form.

Campos was the key. Such a *limited* mind! Not stupid, not by the likes of the races there, but sadly warped. Campos was so enjoying her revenge and was comfortable enough in an environment not all that different from the one back on the home planet that had bred and shaped her, that she was in danger of losing sight of the ultimate game. The Kraang had not counted on her adjusting, though, and that was the real problem. Since Campos had been a male from a background that had little value for women, the Kraang had been certain that she would be driven to the Well to reclaim her manhood.

It wasn't happening.

If Campos had gotten hold of Mavra Chang earlier, it would have, but the Well had its own ways of subtly adjusting a subject to a form. The brain chemistry, the hormonal balances, and being completely immersed in a new culture eventually took hold. A transformation that seemed horrible when first discovered began to seem normal; prior life and existence were distanced in the mind as it adjusted, becoming more and more remote. If one were to go mad from the process, it tended to happen rather quickly; otherwise that barrier the mind erected became progressively insubstantial until it either shattered, as in the case of Lori and Julian, or, as in Campos's case, just slowly evaporated to nothingness.

Without even realizing it, or perhaps admitting it to herself, Juan Campos no longer thought it odd, or even wrong, to be female, let alone a Cloptan female. She had managed in a relatively short time to gain a fair amount of power and influence, in part because she was attractive to male Cloptans who already had that power and influence, and she was actually enjoying it. Experience counted. The Well might have played a joke on Campos by making her female, but it also had dropped her into a totally familiar milieu. Being the tough girlfriend of a drug lord wasn't much different from being the son of one, and the knowledge and ruthlessness actually made her a valuable asset to the organization. After that first month she hadn't even experienced much of the fear and insecurity that being a woman in such a society inevitably produced; everybody dangerous knew how suicidal it would be to mess with the boss's girl and how vicious that girl could be if she perceived one as a threat.

Not that Campos didn't want to get at all the power the Well represented; it was just that she was smart enough to know that before she let Mavra Chang near the Well, her control had to be ironclad. And until Juan Campos figured out how to do that or was forced by circumstance to gamble, she'd keep things pretty much the way they were.

It was frustrating to the Kraang. If only Campos would

go through a Zone Gate. *Then* some contact, some influence, could be attempted. But Campos wanted no part of those Gates if she could avoid them. She remained where she could ensure protection.

Somehow there just *had* to be a way to kick Campos in the ass. There just *had* to be!

But until and unless it found a way to make contact, the Kraang knew it had to depend on forces beyond its control. The psychotic former Julian Beard—now turned into a complaisant wife for that female astronomer turned male swordsman who was now gelded and trapped as a courier for the Cloptan drug ring—was showing some promise, after all. Aided by the Dillians, who were somewhat in the pay of the Zone Council, she might well disrupt things sufficiently to cause a major move. When one no longer cared if one lived or died unless one attained one's objective, it made for a spicy and dangerous time for all those in one's way. The threat there was the Dillians. If they *did* come upon Mavra Chang by some miracle, helpless though she was, would the Dillians' first loyalty be to their former Earth comrades or to their new leaders and lives? Unknown to any of them, forces were moving in on the region and the situation was getting very, very dicey as the council and the various hexes weighed their own options. If they captured Chang, no matter what her form, while the surprisingly resourceful Gus liberated Brazil, everything could go wrong. Of course, there was always the colonel . . .

Possibilities! Far too many! This was getting much more difficult than the Kraang had originally thought. And there were far too many ways for things to go wrong . . .

Buckgrud,
Capital of Clopta

LATELY, IT WAS ALWAYS PRETTY MUCH THE SAME DREAM.

A dense, living forest filled with strange, twisting plants shimmered in a nearly constant but gentle breeze. Not familiar in any waking sense, yet familiar somehow to her in her dream. Comforting, safe, secure.

She would awaken into this living darkness in the Nesting Place, along with many others of her kind, and then proceed out from the hollow tree and onto the forest floor. Most of the night would be spent in the hunt, sometimes searching out and sometimes lying in wait as still as one of the bushes that were all around, waiting for prey to venture forth. Tiny animals, large insects, it didn't matter, so long as it was alive and small enough to be swallowed whole. There was always plenty of prey, for they bred all the time, or so it seemed, but much needed to be eaten to satisfy, and it was a task that consumed much of the night. There was no particular fear on her own part, though; there were no natural enemies in this forest for such as they, and the Big Ones who lived among the treetops ate no flesh and seemed appreciative of the service she and her kind did in keeping the crawling things in check so that they could not become so numerous as to threaten survival. She knew each by the scent and by the sounds it made.

The scent from a small mound nearby told her that there were delicacies inside; she moved to it, and her powerful

347

claws dug into it, and she bent down so that her long, sticky tongue could go inside and sift through and find and draw the little insects into her beak . . .

It was near dusk when Mavra Chang awoke. She slept more than she was awake now, it was true, but that was blessed relief in more than one way. It not only meant escape from the sadism and torments of Juan Campos, when, of course, the Cloptan was awake and not busy with other things, it also was relief from the strange and unpleasant sensations that seemed unending.

There were feverish flushes, dizziness, unexpected pains of varying degrees in various places, and, above all else, a nearly universal itch that was driving her crazier than Campos ever could.

At first she thought that the sadistic surgeons employed by the drug cartel had been butchers as well, but over the passing weeks she had come to realize that it wasn't that, either. Something—strange—was happening to her, something even someone with her vast life and long experience in what evil could do had never undergone before. Still, that life allowed her to understand to a degree *what* was happening, if not exactly why.

She had been surgically altered, mutilated, disguised, but that was only the start of it. She had become other creatures before, but always the way the Well did it: quickly, without pain or sensation. She was becoming another creature again for the first time since she had last been on this world, but by a different method, and slowly by the standards of the Well but with astonishing speed by any other means.

She knew that now for several reasons, not the least of which was that what the surgeons had removed, such as her arms, had not even begun to grow back. She recalled that sensation well. Her body was changing. Grafted feathers were being replaced by real ones just as colorful and even more dense. Her center of gravity had moved down, and her midsection had thickened, while her head seemed to be enlarged and set flush on the shoulders, but with a neck that could pivot the head amazingly far. All this had been at the cost of an already shortened height; she was now a bit under a meter tall, but somehow she knew she would grow no shorter.

Her backbone had become increasingly limber, to the point where she could bend backward and almost touch the floor with the top of her head while still standing or lean forward so effortlessly and with such good balance that she could touch the floor with her beak.

From that vantage point she could see that her stubby, mutilated legs were rapidly changing into huge, thick drumsticks; the rather stupid feet they had fashioned for her now were solid, enlarged, and black and were gaining almost the prehensility of long, thick fingers, with sharp needlelike nails developing at the tips. Even the large, curved beak they had fashioned over her mouth was no longer the crude but effective graft; her tongue, now thin and greatly elongated, told her that beyond the beak was the gullet. Bright light blinded her, and even normal daylight was pale, washed out, and difficult to see in, yet the darkness glowed with sharpness and detail. Through the beak, countless strange odors came to her, each somehow separate even when mixed, and it was a bit of a game to try and identify and classify them. It was something to do.

The same went for sounds, although she could understand nothing of speech. She could understand only Campos, and then only when Campos directed something specifically at her; only Campos's translator could accept the eerie clicks and moans, some from deep in Mavra's chest, that passed for her speech. *That* little gift of a dedicated translator remained, but she was glad of it somehow in spite of her hatred of Campos. She knew that the sounds she could make were really bird sounds, animal sounds, not any sort of intelligible language to any race.

The animal urges disturbed her more. She could no longer physically tolerate any vegetable matter. Campos had been feeding her raw, bloody meat strips, it being a bit too civilized in the city to go pick up a carton of worms or grubs, even if Campos would have entertained the idea of

349

live creepy crawlies in her nice apartment. Although Cloptans resembled giant humanoid ducks, they were omnivores and even had tiny rows of teeth inside those remarkably elastic, oversize bills of theirs.

Campos had hardly failed to notice the metamorphosis; it was happening at a rate that could not be seen by the naked eye but fast enough that something new would be evident between the time she left in early evening and the time she returned to sleep.

Now she came in the door and turned on the light, washing out Mavra's vision. The door slammed, and the Cloptan kicked off her shoes and threw a purse on the chair.

Campos looked over at the corner where Mavra stood, held there by a strong chain fastened to an anklet and to a welded-on socket in the wall, allowing perhaps a meter's movement one way or the other.

"Ah, my pet! And how are *you* this evening?"

"Food, master! Please! Food! Birdy begs you!" The worst part was, she no longer even felt humiliated by begging. It said something about Campos's mind-set, though, that she had insisted on being called "master," not "mistress."

"In a minute, my sweet. I need to freshen up and get a drink. It is going to be a long evening, I fear."

"Please, master! Feed Birdy!"

"Shut up! No more, you miserable little shit or I *might* just forget to feed you at all!"

It was not a threat to be taken lightly. The craving for food after sunset was overwhelming, more even than the craving for the exotic Well World drug that Mavra's made-over body no longer needed or even noticed. Mavra had not, however, volunteered that fact.

Campos went into the bathroom, and after an agonizing wait there was the sound of a toilet flush and then water running. Finally the Cloptan emerged, now naked.

Although it was nothing unusual now, the first sight Mavra had had of Campos naked had been something of an odd feeling. The shape was very human to a point, but even

350

the breasts were covered with countless tiny white feathers except at the very tips. The shoulders were unnaturally squared off, it seemed, the arms and thinly webbed hands oversized for the body. The neck was quite long and thin to be supporting that oversized head. Below the waist it became more birdlike, with a definite rounding, almost turnip-shaped, with the turnip top angled back and slightly up, becoming short but large tail feathers. The legs extended straight down, a golden yellow color, and ended in two wide, thickly webbed feet that could still be consciously rolled up and fit into shoes.

She shared the huge apartment with two Cloptan females who were apparently attached to other drug cartel kingpins, but they stayed away from the big bird's area and Campos rarely referred to them or appeared to interact much with them. They ignored their roommate's "pet" and gave it a wide berth and seemed otherwise to be fairly typical of their type.

There had been more than a few naked males in as well. If they were representative of the race, they tended to be larger, chunkier, with almost wrestler builds, bent a bit forward on the hips in a slightly more birdlike fashion but without much in the way of tail feathers at all. Male genitalia weren't visible at all; they were apparently hidden by a thick clump of feathers growing forward between the widely spaced legs, which explained why they all seemed to be bowlegged.

Campos went to the cold storage compartment and took out a box of something, then popped it in a fast defroster that might have been operated by microwaves or some other means.

"Ah! I should tell you that I got word today from those nice doctors who made you so very pretty for me," the Cloptan said as the defroster whirred in the background. "They said you were genetically reprogrammed using the *actual* genetic code of a *real* bird in a hex very, very far away. I forget the name, but what does it matter? They said not to worry, that you would still be able to think and re-

351

member but that you'd also have all of the bird's instincts. They even said that by three months or so you would be so physically like this bird that you would even be *fertile!*" She laughed. "Just think! The zoo here doesn't have any of your birdie kind, but you're on their wish list, and the other girls here still seem a bit frightened of you and keep trying to talk me into getting rid of you."

Mavra said nothing. Anything she could say would only cause trouble.

"Just think of it!" Campos went on, enjoying herself. "The nice zoo people say that if they had you, they could secure at least the loan of a male of the species. That might be quite the answer here. I won't have to worry about your care or suffer your presence here, but you'll be secure and in a happy little nest I can visit any time. That would be *very* amusing, seeing you sitting there hatching eggs, knowing that all your children would be birdbrains. Would you like that?"

"Whatever master wishes Birdy will do," Mavra responded as if by rote, eyes on the defroster.

"You bet your sparkly feathered ass you will!"

It was far from hopeless, but how the hell she would get this stupid asshole to head for the Well was something Mavra Chang was far from figuring out yet. The zoo wasn't a very appetizing new destination, but maybe it would provide some way out. Zoos didn't usually plan on animals being as smart as humans.

Somehow, some way, she had to get to the Well. She was building up too long a list of people to get even with to fail.

JACK L. CHALKER

Published by Del Rey Books.
Available in your local bookstore.

Call toll free 1-800-733-3000 to order by phone and use your major credit card.
Or use this coupon to order by mail.

The Dancing Gods:

___THE RIVER OF THE DANCING GODS	345-34501-0	$4.95
___DEMONS OF THE DANCING GODS	345-30893-X	$4.95
___VENGEANCE OF THE DANCING GODS	345-31549-9	$4.95
___SONGS OF THE DANCING GODS	345-34799-4	$4.95

The Four Lords of the Diamond:

___LILITH: A SNAKE IN THE GRASS	345-34420-0	$4.99
___CERBERUS: A WOLF IN THE FOLD	345-35247-5	$4.99
___CHARON: A DRAGON AT THE GATE	345-29370-3	$3.95
___MEDUSA: A TIGER BY THE TAIL	345-29372-X	$4.95

The Rings of the Master:

___LORDS OF THE MIDDLE DARK	345-32560-5	$4.99
___PIRATES OF THE THUNDER	345-32561-3	$4.95
___WARRIORS OF THE STORM	345-32562-1	$4.95
___MASKS OF THE MARTYRS	345-34309-3	$4.95

The Saga of the Well World:

___MIDNIGHT AT THE WELL OF SOULS	345-32445-5	$4.95
___EXILES AT THE WELL OF SOULS	345-32437-4	$4.95
___QUEST FOR THE WELL OF SOULS	345-32450-1	$4.95
___THE RETURN OF NATHAN BRAZIL	345-34105-8	$4.95
___TWILIGHT AT THE WELL OF SOULS	345-34408-1	$4.95

The Watchers at the Well:

___ECHOES OF THE WELL OF SOULS	345-38686-8	$5.99
___ECHOES OF THE WELL OF SOULS (trade)	345-36201-2	$10.00
___SHADOW OF THE WELL OF SOULS (trade)	345-36202-0	$10.00

Name _____

Address_____

City_____ State_____ Zip _____

Please send me the DEL REY BOOKS I have checked above.

I am enclosing	$_____
plus	
Postage & handling*	$_____
Sales tax (where applicable)	$_____
Total amount enclosed	$_____

*Add $2 for the first book and 50¢ for each additional book.

Send check or money order (no cash or CODs) to:
Del Rey Mall Sales, 400 Hahn Road, Westminster, MD 21157.

Prices and numbers subject to change without notice.
Valid in the U.S. only.
All orders subject to availability.   CHALKER4